Marc Watson's

CATCHING HELL

Part 1:
Journey

FLUKY FICTION

Newport, ME

Catching Hell Part 1: Journey

Print Edition ISBN: 978-0-9987173-9-5

Published by Fluky Fiction

Copyright © 2021 by Marc Watson

www.flukyfiction.com

For Hayden. You are the start of the only journey worth taking.

CHAPTER 1

A "Man" Walks into a Bar...

In all the years he'd tended bar in this dump-water town, Ollie was sure he'd seen bigger men. Those who had come from the northern mines were strong and rugged. The people of the west, where the dark-skinned warriors seemed to be bred to be intimidating, were also a sight. But Ollie was sure he'd never seen one more, for lack of a better word, powerful.

He stood much taller than the portly Ollie, and it likely would take two of the old barman to make the scales equal in weight. If an ounce of fat was anywhere on him, it was well hidden beneath the mountains of muscle clearly visible even under the black, heavy armor he wore. Darker than night and as clean as a polished mirror. If this was a normal man, born of woman, Ollie was a dead dog's maggot. Whoever this was, they had surely embraced the forbidden ways. For that reason alone he was more trouble than an old drink-slinger wanted. His hair flowed like fire down his neck and over his shoulders (which were almost as wide as Ollie was tall). Even his eyebrows had that ethereal red shimmer, which stood out against his

1

ghostly skin.

The mountain of muscle took in the now-silent patrons and proceeded to walk to the bar and the sweating man behind it.

The armor clinked and clanked as he moved, and the sword on his hip, clearly a well-maintained and valuable weapon of a style Ollie had never seen before, swung with its own rhythm like a pendulum you wanted no part of. It was large, but looked proportional next to the man's trunk-like thigh.

Despite his visions of being manhandled by this demon for whatever purpose he desired (Ollie guessed information or a really stiff drink, which are the only true uses of a bartender), he was quite shocked and relieved when the beast sat at one of the bar stools (which had surely seen bigger men, but still seemed about to collapse), and smiled at Ollie.

Ollie was shocked to feel the uneasiness slip from his mind (not entirely, but certainly a little).

His smile was so well-suited to him, yet so out of place. There were even dimples at the corners of his mouth like a child. Despite his astoundingly inhuman features otherwise, this man had a smile that could make a baby sleep.

Ollie approached the man slowly and asked him what he would like. He was disturbed again to see his eyes. Where others would have white, theirs were black like his armor. Instead of regular color, there was the same uneasy flicker of deep red and orange tones as seen in his hair. There were no iris visible. Just a red sun on a black field. They were the eyes of the devil, given flesh.

The beastly man reached into some unseen pocket of his breastplate, produced several coins, and placed them on the bar. Most were of common enough origin to the man who'd seen many a currency in his time, but others were strange, with odd writings and pictures of men he'd never seen on them. Their metal, however, was

2

plain as day.

Gold and silver, enough to send an old warhorse like Ollie on a long vacation from the rabble and the drunks. The two's eyes met.

"A glass of your stoutest beer and a little bit of your time," the man-beast said in an accent that was simply alien to an ear who'd heard it all. It sounded like "Ah glahs ove yer shtoutest beer and ah lit'l bih ove yer' time." It was understandable, but no less mysterious.

The tender half-turned to his rows of kegs, all old and well-used for a few generations of guzzlers. Each was tapped with a spigot with a bright LED light on it, so out of place in this low-tech society it was almost offensive. Most were green, some pulsed yellow, and two flashed red like a warning beacon. Green equaled a full keg, yellow for half or less, red for a keg that needed to be changed soon. Some avoided Land'O'North Tavern for this reason alone. Even in small amounts like this, the tools of the ancient ones were sure to only bring suffering. To Ollie, the ancient ones were nothing but ghosts, and he never once had to lift a keg to check the draught levels. That was more than enough reason to dance with the devils of the dust. Despite his constant complaints and frequent post-fight blood clean-ups, he loved his life and job very much and welcomed any tool that would help him carry on a little longer.

He kept watch on the black-eyed man as he picked the required keg and passed an old glass beneath it. A soft click as the spigot's magic eye saw the glass and began pouring the stout as perfectly and with as much velocity as the beverage required. When it neared the top of the glass, the same click was heard, and the drink stopped flowing. Only a beer thick as molasses with a head like a crown of white remained.

He delivered the glass to the stranger and allowed him to view his perfectly poured glass with a smirk. "I dare say a finer pint has ne'er crossed my eyes," said the man in that strange, lilting drawl.

"Ah, it's nothin'," said Ollie, not really knowing what a pint was but knowing a compliment when he heard one. "The tap does all the work. I'm just the eye candy."

The man's smirk intensified. "Indeed."

He took a sip of the bitters and smiled as he swallowed. Dropping the glass, he revealed the telltale mustache of a man who enjoys his drink. As he wiped the foam away, he let out a deep breath, as if he'd ran many miles just for that one sip of stout. Ollie got a whiff of the smell as he did so. The first thing he noticed was how hot it was. The odor was one of beer and sulfur, like the kind of smell that wafted down the mountains above the many hot springs that littered the land around here.

The barman felt his uneasiness creep back into him. All at once he was reminded that this was no ordinary man.

"Excellent!" said the man, still smiling while raising the glass again. "Ya' know, there are some tha'd call it 'eresy t' use such devices." He indicated the digital spigots.

Ollie raised his eyebrow in mock surprise. "Really? Well, let them lift a half-full keg six times a day and see how long they cling to their half-assed notions of God."

The man put the glass down on the bar a little harder than Ollie would have liked and looked at him with those dark, flaming eyes. Ollie wondered if his witty banter had hit a nerve he had every intention of avoiding, but his face held the conviction he felt, even if his knees did not.

"Well put, sir." The glass returned to his lips. "Half-assed notions indeed."

Ollie didn't know how to react to this comment. Staying on caution's side, he looked toward the coins on the bar for a change of topic.

"You wanted a bit of my time, stranger?" he asked, not at all sure he knew what was wanted of him.

The peaceful smile was out now in full force, and the man nodded as he put down the empty glass. "Yes, yes, o'course."

He placed his hands on the bar to aid him up. Even the hair on the back of his hands seemed to have that burning shimmer.

Once upright, the man reached to his side and grasped the handle of his sword, slowly though, so as not to arouse suspicion. He pulled it out of the sheath with a soft whisper and held it sideways inches from Ollie's face.

Ollie saw a few of the patrons, who had been watching the scene unfold with the same curiosity as Ollie himself, reach for hidden weapons and defenses in case of an emergency. He knew it had nothing to do with saving the bartender as much as themselves if things went a little hairy. Ollie had few friends and fewer enemies, like a bartender should.

Truth be told, there was a veritable arsenal of weapons behind this bar. From knives to assorted guns and carefully arranged projectiles. An old rifle was just under the spot the man had chosen to sit, but going back to his first thought upon seeing this newcomer, he was sure that even his highest caliber firearm could not stop this power that sat before him.

"I'd like ya' t' take a good look at this sword," he said, "and I want ye' t' focus not on 'ow it looks, but 'ow it makes ya' feel. Does it conjure any thoughts, or create any deep emotions?"

Ollie was so confused by the words he looked away from the man and his sword and gazed around the room at the men (and occasional woman of the working variety). Many of them looked away, not wanting to get involved in this incident before it started. Others shrugged at him, as if to say they didn't know what he wanted either.

At the back, in a dark corner sitting alone, an old man simply stared. Ollie looked back, not at the sword, but at the man.

"Look, mister, I don't know what you're asking, really, but I..."

"Please, sir. Just a moment and nothin' more. I'd just like ye' t' look and see wha' I mean. I promise, no 'arm is intended, I'm only lookin' fer' information."

Ollie relented, letting his eyes follow the blade from tip to tip. The handle was not much to speak of as far as detail and was wrapped in what looked to be some kind of reptile skin which Ollie had never seen before: dark and bumpy. The hilt and guard were unlike the standard style preferred by Riders and other military from the area. It was straight and slightly curved up at each end. It didn't wrap around but only jutted out at two sides, like a cross instead of a dome or full circle. The blade was very wide and flat with no bend. Ollie was sure he'd have a problem lifting it with two hands, but this man wielded it like a twig with one.

Near the base of the blade were etchings in a language so abstract it was almost like pictographs, but since none of the images were at all familiar, Ollie didn't waste time with them.

Once he took the whole image of the sword in, it came to him.

"*POWER,*" he thought instantly. "*HISTORY,*" "*BLOODSHED,*" "*PEACE.*" The images and feelings came quickly to his head, like a collage of infinite beauty, and just as equal ugliness.

"*GREATNESS,*" "*RESTLESSNESS,*" "*PAIN,*" "*BALANCE,*" "*LOVE*"

"*HORROR*"

"*HORROR*"

"*HORROR*"

"*DEATH*"

Ollie ripped his eyes from it as the final feelings and images continued to repeat over and over. He felt sick to his stomach.

"Mister, I don't know what your definition of 'no harm' is, but I've never felt so violated in my life! How on earth did you get into my head like that?"

The smile slipped away and he became very serious.

"Have ya' seen anything else like this?" he asked, voice lowering, his eyes reading every nuance in Ollie's face. Tracking his eyes, watching his mouth, reading every twitch and quiver like a book.

"In all my life, not only have I never seen anything even close to that, if I ever did again I'd likely kill myself."

"Rest assured, sir, if ye' e'er saw something like this again, you'd be dead before ye' 'ad the chance."

He swung the blade around and slid it back into the sheath with that same silent whisper. The man turned to the rabble and took them all in with one glance. "How 'bout any of ya'? I can see by the looks on yer' faces tha' most of ya' saw the same thin' he did. 'Ave ya' e'er seen somethin' like this before? Anywhere or anytime in yer' life?"

He walked slowly around the tables, taking in all the people, reading them all like he read Ollie. A loud man came in, laughing uproariously with a working girl on his arm. He turned to the scene of a man, huge and demonic, walking around a stunned and silent bar with all eyes on him in a mix of fear and amazement. He quickly shut up, gripped his evening's entertainment around her waist, and quickly led her back out the door. The motion would be quite comical in later retellings.

The room was fixated on this man, but no one seemed to be able to help him. Shamed faces and looks of uneasiness were everywhere he looked.

"I have seen what you seek," said a grizzled voice from a dark corner.

Ollie knew without looking that it was the old man he'd locked eyes with before. The large guest turned to the source of the voice and walked briskly to his table.

"If ye'd tell the tale, old man, I'd love t' hear it." Once the way out

7

was clear, the bar emptied quickly, with everyone racing for the door pushing each other and scampering like dogs to dinner.

Ollie had to see this play out, so he held his spot behind the bar while resting his hand on the well-used rifle nonetheless.

"If I tell you my tale, I want your word you and your damn sin-stick will get the hell out of my sight and not ever come back. I've seen your kind before and no good ever came out of it. Not here, not anywhere."

Ollie was dumbfounded that this old man had the gall to talk like that to someone so much bigger than him. He sat frozen, hand on the rifle, prepared for any motion toward the drunken old-timer.

No hostile motion came though. Just a "Humph" from the man and a steely glare from the senior.

"And wha' kind of person am I?" the man asked. The geezer seemed to have his attention.

A cold smirk came to a toothless mouth and the old man hissed, "A slave of the forbidden ways. A minion of the Power. Mark my words, fire-man; no good ever came out of embracing what you play with."

The man seemed to relax and settled into a chair across the table. "I've not the time to tell ye' wha' I am and how I conduct my business. And I certainly can't get into the inaccuracies of yer' thoughts about the powers ya' speak of, but I give my word tha' if ya' give me somethin' worthwhile, I will ne'er trouble yer' ol' eyes again."

The old man spat in his hand, although not much moisture came out. He extended his arm straight, like a branch from a young tree. "We shake on that, and should I ever see you again, I'll get the delightful chance to run you through myself."

Ollie nearly fainted as the man sat there looking at the extended hand, seeming to hesitate a moment. Could it be that this old man threw this stranger off his guard? From where Ollie stood, it sure looked that way.

The man began to speak but was cut short by the older man shushing him and thrusting his hand into his face. "Don't burden me again until you make my deal!"

Ollie wasn't sure it was meant to sound so forceful, but it didn't seem to faze either one of them. Ollie was glad he didn't leave.

Without saying anything else, the man spit into his hand, which gave the bartender the shivers as he saw sparks fly like fireflies from his mouth as he did so, followed by what he guessed was steam or smoke rising from his palm.

He wanted to stop the old man as this was clearly a deal with the Devil Himself, and then thought better of it. This was not his situation to deal with, and if he was a devil, it was better not to stop a deal in progress. Stay silent and live to tell the tale.

The old man seemed not to care, if indeed it was hot at all, as they shook hands with force and purpose.

"I won't trouble ya again, and I'm a man o' my word. Now let us talk."

The old man looked up to Ollie and quickly asked for another drink. The man turned and requested a refill of his. Ollie brought them over, sure to be as efficient as possible, and quickly faded away back to the bar.

"Leave us, Ollie, and lock the door, please. I promise we won't be long. The less I have to be around this godless devil, the better."

Ollie never questioned the order and went over to latch the door, not caring in the slightest about the lost income. Thanks to the coins the man had given him he had more than enough to cover the evening take. Ollie left into the kitchen, thankful to be away, though he was quite sorry he didn't get to hear the tale.

CHAPTER 2

Melancholy Mountain

The clean mountain air filled the lungs of a young man high above the scene in the bar. Where. despite his promises. the old man was taking a very long time to tell the demon-thing what he wanted to hear.

That scene had nothing to do with this young man (who was an old boy not too long ago). The man was familiar with the Land'O'North Tavern, having his first drink of spirits there less than a day ago, but he doubted the old bartender would know him if he was to walk in again. His kind passed through this way all the time, as part of the ritual.

His traveling companion was working their way up to his position, sure to be envious of his find. It wasn't often you found an item of this quality and style in such a remote place. After all the hardships of the last year, a final piece of luck was warm and welcoming.

"You'd better not be much higher!" said a voice from below. He didn't answer, needing a moment alone to gather his thoughts.

He lifted his find into the air, amazed at its lightness and grace. He'd never seen one like this before. The ones he'd see were generally wider, broader, or curved. This one was thin and straight, and so much lighter than one would think just to see it.

"Why are you up here?" he asked himself aloud. "What was my purpose in finding you?"

Naturally, there was no answer to this. Man only finds things by chance. Rare is the item that wants to be found, and this one was no different.

It was lodged in the rock face, clearly buried for some time. Only the base showed any passage of time, and that may have been that way for a good deal longer than it looked like it had.

He placed it on the ground behind him, sure to reveal it to his friend when he wanted to and not before. He saw a tuft of black hair and a tall backpack before he saw the face of his best friend climbing higher to where he sat and waited.

"There you are," his friend said, gaining good footing and walking toward him. "Just couldn't wait, could you. And what's with that shit-eating grin?" He was always full of such colorful expressions, which he'd inherited from the grandfather who had raised him. "Don't get me wrong," he puffed, "I appreciate the fact that you keep both feet on the ground for the sake of your poor, non-gifted friend, but please remember that it's because of your damn gift I have to carry this stupid pack just to make you look normal."

The sitting man smiled half-heartedly. "I never told you to fill it, did I?"

"Yeah, well you never told me *not* to either."

At the time, knowing they had a year of hard footwork ahead of them, it seemed a great idea to take everything they could ever need, and although time had made them stronger and more immune to the weight of the packs, they were no less a burden on a steep climb up a rocky mountain face.

Their packs were now actually quite empty save for a few basic, well-used supplies and some remembrances of the past year. These men were not far from their home, a village to the south of where they were now. They had set out exactly one year ago on their traditional pilgrimage to the depths of these mountains.

They had traveled north from their home, full of ideas and that indubitable youthful sense of adventure only found in a person at a certain age. The age occurred when the desire to see what's beyond their doorstep outweighed the need to remain inside.

They trekked deep into the mountains, found their manhood in some individual way, and traveled south again. They emerged from the mountains three days prior. Then, as horribly stereotypical as it is (and as awful as it is to say, most stereotypes are little more than glamorized versions of the truth, twisted by those with reasons to create negativity), they found the closest town, dropped their gear at an inn, and went straight to the bar. The same bar that was currently being filled with an informative story between a really big guy and a very old man.

With their fill of drink and success, they received their directions to their home and went on their way.

They traveled to the mountain for one last night of rest and story before they were to head back. A pretty young girl in town had directed them to a good mountain meadow she claimed to know that would provide the perfect, picturesque spot before the nasty slog to their hometown. Men of their kinds types were quite prone to flights of melodrama and were easily swayed by a pretty face.

"We've been going straight up for hours, and I don't think I've even seen a sprout or scrub!"

"Well, how were we supposed to know that there wasn't a good place to eat up here? I thought it was fairly basic logic: mountains equal meadows, right?"

The sitting boy smiled. It made sense to him. "Well, this is as flat a spot as any, so let's not waste time going any higher."

His friend sighed in agreement. "Man, isn't that the way. I hate it when a pretty face lies." Although clearly dejected, he took a look around. The mountains here came to an abrupt end and became flat land all the way to the sea in the south. Their current location was like standing on a podium addressing the world.

He dropped his pack with an audible grunt and it kicked up the loose dust that surrounded them. They were both young, freshly-minted men, with shades of youth still in their faces. As time had passed and the world had changed, age was only used by strange people in strange lands with the means to measure such things. These two were simple people, and it wasn't age that mattered but how they looked and felt. When the boys of this land had the maturity and wisdom enough to survive on their own, they were given the option of staying at home in their village, living well but likely living to serve, or going out into the north, finding their own path and returning after a year with stories and sights. The women, although given the option of leaving, mostly chose to stay, knowing that they were bound for something grander than a life of service. The women bear the children, run the village, and govern the land. As such, they had the right to do whatever they wished.

After unpacking their small meals, the men sat together on a rock looking out at the view of the brief expanse of foothills beyond, and past them, the flat nothing of a world they had not seen in a year.

They ate mostly in silence, only making short remarks about nothing really worth talking about. Only their familiar refrain of "For Tan Torna Qu-ay!" when they raised their drinks to each other seemed to break the silence noticeably. Though their love for their home was sometimes in question, it was still their home. They'd started many adventures and meals with those same words.

The return to Tan Torna Qu-ay was only a few days away and they each had a million thoughts to organize before they returned. The secret find remained hidden.

"Any bets on who else left on their quest while we were gone?"

"I'll bet Esgona and his little tag-along did. He was so upset that we left first," the secretive man replied.

A nod in agreement. Esgona and his best friend-nay-bootlick Hogope were almost certain to be away. Esgona was the son of the First Lady of the Council. A fact he was keen on repeating to all who would listen. Nimble and strong, his ego was almost as big as his worldview was small. These two in particular had suffered his wrath since infancy, and the fact that his mother was so powerful in their world created a firestorm of pomp and bravado.

And as every leader needs a lackey, Hogope was as dutiful a friend as he was a blindly loyal manservant. He was quick to align with someone whose aspirations of power were more in line with his own: fast, unyielding, and plenty of it. Unfortunately, he didn't realize what his real role was in the relationship: sidekick.

Soon their ridicule would be unwarranted as they returned home. Johan Otan'co was a man of both wit and misfortune. He was an outsider from the day he was born and treated as an inferior form of life. He developed a keen mind to accompany his life-hardened physical prowess. His father, in his early years, had left for his journey into manhood only to return after two seasons. His arm was broken badly and eventually needed to be amputated, and he was severely dehydrated. He begged to be readmitted to the village, knowing that doing so would mark him for life as a frail and embarrassing quitter. His shame would be passed down to each of his progeny until one had completed the quest. Johan was adamant about making it a very short list of successors to attempt it. Soon both his and his father's names would be cleared, although his father had died ten years prior to his leaving, as did his mother a short time later. His maternal grandparents had raised him from then on, shamed by their burden of a disgraced and dishonored grandchild.

How sweet it would be. So many seasons of ridicule and shame were about to end. He was bigger, stronger, and far tougher of mind and body than the lanky, wavy-haired, dark-skinned child that had left Tan Torna Qu-ay a year ago. He had seen life, death, and all points between in that time. Now he looked forward to smashing the cold truth of his triumph straight into the faces of all those who had spurned him. Esgona and Hogope were high on that list to be sure.

His secretive companion, Aryu O'Lung'Singh, was by far the worse off. Even without his curse, he would have been an outsider. His family came to Tan Torna Qu-ay when he was a baby, seeking to escape his assured death at the hands of others.

He looked different, with pale skin and light brown hair, eyes as green as grass, and a face and body far too thin and gaunt to be a local. Long arms and a hard, wiry frame made him stand a full head above anyone else in the village, and he was thin enough to look malnourished despite how much he ate. As shameful as it is to say, children (and sadly, parents as well) were always quick to pounce on one so unlike themselves. His parents knew this place and its customs. No matter how different one was from another, every child had a chance to prove their worth, either as a servant or successor to the quest. It was long ago discovered here that on paper appearance does not denote heart, since heart is a rare commodity in this barren world.

Children can be so cruel. Over the past year, in many discussions on the topic, it was agreed that even returning successfully would likely do little to change everyone's minds about Aryu. They would be much quieter and more polite about it, but someone so different would need more to appease the masses. Tradition is grand, but rarely does it change minds overnight. Indeed, tradition is generally what put their minds in that state in the first place. Tradition and stereotypes go hand-in-hand.

Setting aside the obvious differences, the one that was the most glaring was the one he kept hidden. The curse in the backpack is one no man could overcome. Indeed, his parents had told him that in the east where they came from, over the ocean in a world far enough away to be practically alien, Aryu was certain to be killed for his deformity.

Aryu was smart, charming, friendly, helpful, brave, and loyal. Even boyishly handsome despite being so different from the locals. Still, it was not enough.

Aryu had wings.

Large ones by this time, too. Large and strong, yet extremely flexible and pliable. This was how they fit so neatly into his large pack. It was custom made by his mother, with the back cut out to fit these jokes from an inhuman God (though it must be pointed out that despite feelings otherwise, God was once very much human, and as such, would know enough not to play such a terrible joke on someone). Mutations of this kind were quite common all around the world, but rare and scary were ones so perfect and purposeful. Green skin, third eyes, scales, extra legs, horns, faces with no mouths, mouths with no faces. All were well-documented, and all were quite useless. Wings are concise of purpose, and useful to the umpteenth level. Wings allow you to fly not by machine or by the power of the mind. They were something far more than patches of dense hair or an extra limp, boneless finger.

Wings were not an accident of mutated evolution. Wings have a purpose and Aryu mastered that purpose the second he realized he could. His back where they connected just between his shoulder blades was unlike any other human's. It was thick with muscle and bone structure only he possessed, and his chest was larger around to accommodate a heart that was large enough to pump blood through them and the rest of his body. They were no accident. They were a part of him. Almost overnight the rumors of the demon-boy of Tan Torna Qu-ay were born.

But now they would be the stories of the demon-MAN. After all, the last year was not experienced for nothing.

▶◀▶◀▶◀▶◀▶◀▶◀▶◀▶◀▶◀▶◀▶◀▶◀

Aryu and Johan rested. Farther up the slope was a small trickle of fresh water, and this clearing they had found was large enough to fit both of them plus their gear. Aryu took his treasure and had it hidden before prying eyes could glimpse it. It was still not time.

Sadly, there was no meadow on this mountain or any near it, which would have been perfectly obvious to anyone not blinded by melodramatic tendencies. These mountains were nearly barren from top to bottom on all of these southern-facing slopes. Feeling cheated, but much too tired to care, they made their camp as the sun went down. For the youth who set forth on this quest from Tan Torna Qu-ay and the other villages of the land, it was an unofficial tradition on the last night out before the true stretch for home, they would sit around a fire and lay out the spoils of the adventure. No meadow meant that there was nothing to burn, so there would be no fire.

Aryu had very little, his pack being mostly full of wings this whole time. His wings were now free from their woven prison and were stretched out behind him, draping away from his shoulders like a deep greenish-brown cloak. These were not feathered and beautiful like glistening gossamer. They were thin and tough, like a lizard or bat. Veined and sinuous, with a full expanse that was twice as wide

17

as Aryu was tall.

Johan had his items out. He was particularly fond of a long, ornate dagger he'd acquired during a stay they'd had in a mountain village far north. The people of this northern village were living in a constant threat of attack by a very aggressive Hooded Stalker: a reptilian beast with a long tail and frilled head and neck. Hooded Stalkers, like most of the Stalker family, were particularly nasty because of their tenaciousness. Their hides were scaled and nothing but the finest blades was able to penetrate them. Unfortunately, just getting close was a challenge unto itself. Stalkers were white-hot to the touch, their blood a blend of chemicals that could be mixed at its will to searing levels. If you didn't catch one off-guard, you didn't catch one at all.

In the case of this village, they were ill-prepared for the creature, not having encountered one that far south in recorded history.

Stalkers are amazingly intelligent. It's not uncommon in lands far enough away from this one to encounter Stalkers the size of elephants with the ability to talk.

The two brave travelers came to them. After helping build rock and mortar walls around the mountain village, they realized the futility of their efforts one night as the Stalker smashed a section of wall, destroyed several lodges, and devoured half a herd of alpine goats.

Needing another plan, it was Johan who suggested the classic enemy-repelling solution of the moat. Being a history buff, mostly in the areas of weapons, armies, attack, and defense, etc., he was well-versed in classic moat techniques. Using the existing irrigation system, the villagers redirected an irrigation canal around the most exposed sides of town. Stalkers, although strong and very fast, do not jump well, and any cold water was a very strong deterrent to something that could be so incendiary. The moat took days to build, but Johan was pleased with the results.

The Stalker returned, surveyed its new dilemma, howled in rage, and carried off back into the high country. No sign came thereafter, and once the villagers were satisfied, Johan was heralded as a hero.

The village got together and offered the dagger to him as a token of appreciation. It was a gift from a popular hermit that lived nearby and wandered into town on occasion to trade, drink and talk to anyone and everyone. Johan accepted gladly, seeing full-well the quality and craftsmanship. Had there been a fire on the mountain that night, its deep onyx blade would have gleamed with pearl rainbows in the light.

Aryu had little to show, in part because he couldn't fit much more into his already full pack, and also because he simply had never been a man who dwelled on the past. Before him were trinkets and knick-knacks, but the truth was, these few items were here out of luck and whim. If you were a man with the ability to fly (or glide, as was more the case), what use was imagination? If not for his parents, he'd have taken to wing the moment he could. He didn't have any foolish thoughts about sticking around Tan Torna Qu-ay any longer than necessary. His quest near-complete, all that was left was to go before the Council, regale them with harrowing tales of adventures deep in the high mountains, and accept their blessings on becoming a man. Then, off he'd go to see the world.

He had told his parents his plan, and although they were saddened to hear it, they would respect his choice. "Just promise not to go back to our old lands, Aryu," his mother had said. "Flying can't save you there." He never argued. He loved his parents and respected what they did for him and the risks they had taken.

His past was generally agreed to be heartbreakingly poor, so he focused on the future and little else. All he had was these useless trinkets, his unmentioned find, and a piece of paper with a simple note:

"More poetry by moonlight, perhaps?" was what it said.

It was elegantly written and still smelled faintly of mountain wildflowers, though that may have been his imagination.

She was a young server at a roadside town in the Komoky Valley, a vast and sprawling plain that ran between the Great Range to the south and the higher Hymleah Crest, which was the start of the huge and impassable mountains to the north. So towering they were said to scrape the stars themselves, so massive they had put the spin of the planet on a slight tilt and so dangerous that even the great Ruskan Stalkers were no match for their peril. None of those statements were true, but myth becomes fact in only a few generations. Lack of information quickly breeds mythology.

She and Aryu joined in deep conversation for the better part of a day, with him retelling the quest to that point (his pack seated FIRMLY on his back) as well as reciting some poetic bits he'd heard and taken a liking to while away, and she listened with genuine interest and amazement. Few on their quest ever came so far into these peaks, and that fact gave way to her belief that other from there shared his strange appearance. As was said, in the right light he was rather boyishly handsome. She was smitten after his first ten words.

Aryu was as oblivious as any man would be in that situation, regardless of age. That was unfortunately something that had not been bred out of them by this stage in the evolution of the species. The natural charisma he had developed to compensate for his oddity had unknowingly turned him into an elegant and almost poetic speaker. His detailed descriptions of peoples and places had taken her to far off vistas and introduced her to amazing characters, none of which was she ever likely to see.

He did find her attractive, with her soft skin, deep brown eyes, and dark hair in ringlets that surrounded the smooth curves of her face. During his formative years, any girl he'd desired knew of his deformity. As such, he had never developed the trust needed to pursue this passing affection.

"Perhaps one day I'll leave this place and journey out to see your home," she had said, being sure to be both sincere and flirtatious in her delivery. Truth be told, she was very happy with her life and home, but she didn't hate the idea of such a venture taken with the exotic stranger.

"I'm afraid that, even if you should, I wouldn't be there to greet you," Aryu replied, obliviously melting her with every word. "I've seen enough to know I want to see more, and I don't plan to remain home much longer than I have to. I've come too far to stop now. But still, I hope this won't be our last meeting." A truer word was never spoken. Aryu clicked into her advances. He liked her and she him until, he believed, the pack would come off. Until that time, he was quite content to live this fantasy for a few hours longer.

With her time at work ending and her duties at her home calling, they said their sweet goodbyes and agreed that another meeting between them would not be something they would be averse to. She had given him the note he held now on the mountainside as she kissed his cheek and almost floated away down the street.

Aryu and Johan left the town soon after, that second fateful meeting never coming. His fear, at last, overcame him despite his best efforts. He had convinced himself that she was already too perfect for him, that this one moment was enough.

Unknown to him, she wouldn't have cared about the wings. Love, even so early blooming, sees only challenges, never barriers. Perhaps had he stayed, both of their lives would have been different. She, saddened by his failure to appear that night, cast herself into a pit of her own malaise and foolishness, which, thanks to her kind nature, she would overcome in less than a day.

Aryu, on the other hand, may have never had to deal with the strife and hardships that shortly awaited him. It is best to know this now that these things were close at hand and terrible in nature.

All due to fear of truth, love, and acceptance ingrained in him by classmates since his youth.

"More poetry by moonlight?" he read again and again.

Children can be so cruel.

CHAPTER 3

Homeward and Duty Bound

The two awoke the next morning to the sunrise barely visible to the east. Cloud cover had moved in overnight and it seemed that rain may fall for at least the early part of the day. The foothills below were beginning to go from mist to low-lying cloud and it looked to them as if Heaven had swallowed the world below.

The prior evening's reminiscence was short-lived. Each man agreed that a good night's sleep should win out over an unofficial tradition. This marked a key moment in their lives: the first of many times reason of manhood outweighed the fancifulness of youth.

They packed up their belongings and trekked back down the mountainside. With their bearings confirmed they set off on the road that would take them home.

Even this early in the morning they were passed by many people and transports on this well-used road to the southern ocean. Some horse-drawn, others large and mechanically powered, generally by some rudimentary fuel engine that refused to die. The more advanced and cleaner methods of travel such as lithium, ionic, and cold nuclear were still very evil, or at the very least, unspoken of and taboo. The fuel engines were far more efficient than some in mankind's past, but compared to the now-shunned alternatives, they were starkly primitive.

Aryu had still not revealed his mountainside find to Johan. Something in his heart had told him not to yet. It wasn't selfishness as much as it was a sense that something like this needed to be finessed into a moment, not forced. During the walking done that day, he'd come to think that should such a moment never arise, Johan might never even know he had it. A quiet secret he may just have to carry with him to wherever his post-Tan Torna Qu-ay life took him.

Aryu couldn't say what made him feel this way. Being a guarded person was nothing new to him, despite his often talkative outward nature. All he knew was it was the truth. There was a meaning to finding it, but he'd need time to decide what that meaning was.

Johan was keeping a brisk pace ahead of him, making sure to check back every now and again to see that Aryu was still there. Johan had known he was lost in thought ever since yesterday afternoon on the mountain. He had noticed the crumpled note in his hands last night. He loved his friend like a brother and thought him a fool for passing up that chance with the pretty mountain girl, but they rarely spoke of it.

Johan gravitated to Aryu at an early age, attracted to the prospect of having a friend even more shunned than he was. He didn't care about the wings or the stigma that came with them. All he saw was a nice kid with a big heart, sad eyes, and common interests. If he could carry Johan to some far-off place for a day's adventure a little quicker than others, all the better. The topic of his wings was barely mentioned. By the time the two of them became close, Aryu had perfected the art of hiding them in backpacks and loose clothing, before they'd grown too large.

The two grew up studying things they both were attracted to. Johan had an interest in the more primal of man's tendencies. Weapons and wars, battle tactics and historic military actions. The attraction of the classic tales of one versus many. And to a point, the past technologies (and mistakes that came with them) of the world they lived in.

Aryu joined Johan often in his research (the histories of which were very well-documented in books and pictures, dating back many thousands of years). Each child of the village was generally challenged to discover their passions early in life, so they may grow into a field as opposed to having one forced on them. If there were an inordinate number of children who wanted to become bakers or weapon makers, it was common for a town or village to keep one or two of the more gifted ones and "trade" other places for people whose passions would lead them down the path of a profession Tan Torna Qu-ay was lacking. It was a beautiful symmetry that kept the people moving and the villages and towns well-connected in a place where long-distance communication was nearly impossible.

It wasn't a surprise to Aryu that Johan had a passion that would surely lead him to the west, where the military of the areas was active and often clamoring for new blood. Just like Aryu, Johan wasn't so ready to forgive those who had done him wrong. Soon his name would be clear, but a lifetime of abuse does not disappear overnight, and rightly so.

Clear to Aryu for some time was that Johan wasn't just passionate about these things; he was extremely talented in them as well, the moat incident standing most clearly in his mind. A moat. Unbelievable. A word-of-mouth hold-over from another age of man. Yet he thought of it as a viable option after only a moment. That was Johan. Strategist, warrior, and man hell-bent on fighting his own war.

It was while pondering these incidences and lamenting the fact

that very soon their two paths would likely cause them to separate
that they were passed by the first cart of casualties.

They thought little of the approaching caravan. They'd been passed
by more than one already. Large caravans powered either by an
animal team or engines were the main source of transportation of
goods in this part of the world.

They first spotted it on their horizon. Taxing beast and engine
(they had both) to their limits, they moved quickly. Even on the well-
packed and moistened road, they kicked up a fury of dirt and rock.

"There's a group heading somewhere in a hurry," Johan noted,
drawing Aryu out of his self-imposed mental stupor.

They watched the band approach and began to understand its
size and speed. Traveling caravans in this area could easily grow to
such sizes, but never went anywhere in a hurry. Sale and trade were
their bread and butter, and no one would dare risk passing by a
potential customer as they traveled the same roads.

Two men on horseback crested the ridge closest to the travelers.
They weren't dressed as merchants, nor were their mounts of the
questionable lineage and poor stock. They were clearly pure-bred
horses: armored and imposing. Hybrids had long ago begun to
dominate the stock lines as people, cut off from other societies, bred
for their own needs. In this area, horse/camel crossbreeds called
folmes were the preferred beast of burden. They were strong, fast,
and exceedingly adept at the long, hot, dry trips the people of this
land endured. They were at times ungainly and most certainly
smelled terrible, but they always did the job.

These two wore the red suits and the dense plates of Inja Riders.
Indeed, if this land had to be qualified with any kind of name, Inja
was it. It was not a name generally accepted this far east of the
borders. People this far away from everything but themselves often

refused such qualifications. Names made countries, and countries made wars.

The head Rider could be seen pointing directly at the two as they stood aside. Riders were an important member of their respective brigades, and it was almost a given that they'd have room to pass, even here. The other nodded and began to slow. Soon, the lead rider was upon them, thundering past like lightning on land, his horse nothing more than a black and silver blur, its nostrils flaring madly.

The men were nearly dumbfounded at the sight, and more than a little curious as to why Riders were so far east and why they needed to speak to them.

As the first beast blazed past and was off again the way they had come, they turned to the second Rider now slowing to approach them. He waved with the standard military style, right arm snapped straight to his ear, elbow out and locked, then with a quick motion brought his arm around in a semi-circle, ending with his hand palm-up before them. "I listen, I offer" was its meaning.

The two men nodded back, tense at his arrival but knowing him as what he was: a friend to them and all of this land.

"Hello and good day!" he called down to them as he stopped some ten paces from the two bewildered faces. He was young, not much older than them. His light hair beneath his rounded helmet was cut very short, and his face was clean-shaven. Eyes bright and sunken, like those of a man with little recent sleep to his credit. The men nodded back, collectively mumbling back their responses.

The Rider apprised each of them and the pack they carried. "I'm assuming you are from this land, off on your blood-quests?" (An uncommon but still apt term.)

Johan stepped forward, nodding. "We are on our way home. Our year is over."

The Rider noticeably firmed himself and nodded back in

recognition. "My congratulations. It's difficult to separate the men from the boys on these roads close to so many homes." They said nothing, simply looking at him as if expecting him to continue, each silently pleased at this new level of respect they seemed to command.

"I am Rider Stroan, cadet for the Inja Army and its people. I have been asked to inquire about your destination. Where are you from?"

"Tan Torna Qu-ay." Johan wasted no time in his response. Such a direct question from any serving man of the army required no less. "Southeast of here, in the Valley of Smoke." It was so named for the vast clouds of mist that once carried through it. Now, however, no mist would be found, its river little more than a stream and its lands hot and dry.

Stroan seemed to regress into himself, emerging with a curious expression. "You may be the most fortunate bunch I've met so far. I don't believe they've trekked that far east yet. Still, it's likely best not to waste time getting there. Who knows how far they've come since last I saw them."

Confusion on each face, Johan was the first to put his thoughts together and ask the obvious.

"How did the Tiet Westlanders ever make it so deep into our territory?"

Aryu got the feeling the answer wasn't as easy and obvious as the question. His gut told him it wasn't anyone from Tiet before Stroan had spoken a word.

"Westlande…" he began, reading each of their faces, piecing together the puzzle he suddenly found himself in. "Of course, you've been in the deep mountains up until now, haven't you." His face revealed nothing of what he was thinking. A man clearly locked into the task of giving nothing away.

"Let's let the caravan pass. Its noise would likely only drown out what I'm saying. Then I can tell you what has happened." With that, the road train crested the last ridge, still traveling at full tilt, and much larger than the two had originally assumed.

The first to pass them was a series of engine-powered wagons, each taxing their top speeds as they went, and the storage beds behind them full of what were clearly not merchant goods. Each one was full of people. Sitting, standing, even some barely clinging to the backs and sides; some with only a bag of personals, others with nothing at all. Following them were more engine-driven vehicles, mostly small farming tractors pulling trailers of more people, hardly anyone making so much as a glimpse at the two young men and Rider who were now off the road.

Engines whined, and folmes and other mixed breeds snorted past as they were strapped together in teams, pulling yet more trailers and carts at full gallop.

Aryu wondered what could get this many people moving so fast and so far from home. They were local villagers; he recognized their clothes and styles as such. Lightweight tops, wrapped skirts, and light pants marked them as people from inland, not even as far south as the ocean. People very much like those of Tan Torna Qu-ay. He looked as far down the line as he could, searching for an end to the madness. He was sure by this point that the Rider Stroan had something very important to tell them.

A cart full of women and small children, many of whom were crying loud enough to be heard even over the racket of hooves and whining engines, passed them by. The mothers seemed not to notice the shouting and tears, almost as if they'd given up trying to console their little ones long before they reached this point. Some of the calmer kids looked at them, pointing, fear in their eyes as they held their mothers. Exhaustion and fear were set deep into every face they saw. More than one person had their eyes glued to what lay behind them, something beyond the scores of trailing carts and tired faces.

Johan was shouting at Aryu, trying to pry his eyes off the scene, waving him over as he did so. "Any thoughts?" he shouted to him, confusion just as prevalent on his face as Aryu assumed it was on his own.

"It looks like they were chased away. They're just staring off behind them, looking for something." Johan watched some carts pass, noting Aryu's words as true. His eyes tried to follow theirs, but all he could see was chaos in a straight line. "What could bring the Inja Army so far east and force this many people to run so far?" Aryu hoped Johan of all people would have an answer.

"Nothing, my friend. Not one thing. The Westlanders and the Inja Army are far too entrenched to have it move this far, and there's only water to the south. Whatever it is, it isn't Westlanders."

Fate has a fantastic sense of timing, as shortly thereafter, four large carts pulled by giant elephants roared past, each teeming with large, dark-skinned people. They stood in shock, never having seen such beasts before, and the people they carried and pulled were equally strange: Westlanders. It wasn't uncommon to see some from time to time, but never so many.

The end came into sight and the men pulled closer to Rider Stroan, eyes full of impatient expectation. Stroan only regarded them with a frown. Whatever he had to say was weighing heavily on his mind.

The last few carts went past. An old woman screamed hysterically on the back of one, legs dangling like a small child as she shouted, "There is no peace here! Save your souls! Your lives are already lost!" She looked right at the three as she shouted. "Lost! Lost to the hell that brought them!"

Her ragged voice died away, but her words echoed in the din thereafter.

The men looked to Stroan, and Stroan knew it was time. He

30

dismounted and approached them. It wasn't going to be easy for them to hear. He had his orders, given to him by his captain. He was to break off from the caravan shortly anyway to spread word to more villages along the mountains. He may as well start here with these two. As proven men, they deserved no less. The cadet took a deep breath before beginning.

"Two weeks ago a fleet of ships appeared on the ocean horizon, spread out farther than eyes could see. Large ships, of a style and seaworthiness we didn't recognize.

"We were locked in battle on Tiet borders. We were in the southernmost regions of Inja, directly on the ocean. Without warning the Tiet army we were fighting was obliterated with one massive explosion. It was much more powerful than any weapon we possessed, and there didn't seem to be anything they had that would malfunction. Destruction simply rained on them from the heavens.

"In surveying the damage, our troops were shocked and sickened by the complete annihilation of the Westlanders in one step, yet still had no answer for it. Then explosions hit the entire coastline, indiscriminate of target. Both Tiet and Inja armies were targeted without warning or remorse, and thousands died before we had any thought as to why.

The young cadet shuffled a bit in his own skin, growing more uncomfortable.

"It had been the ships out on the horizon, and they were barely visible to our eyes."

"How?" Johan asked immediately. "No bomb or other weapon can reach farther than the eye can see. Not without the powers of the Old."

Stroan looked at him, saying nothing while his eyes revealed all. Johan, though still lost in thought, urged Stroan to continue.

"Not only were they the powers of Old, these vessels brought with them the people of the Old themselves." Rider Stroan began to fidget, clearly upsetting himself by telling them this news. Something was scaring him with every word. "Explosions began lighting up the coast in each direction, forcing both armies into full retreat. They kept coming, falling deeper and deeper inland and chasing the retreating men with no thought to decorum or valor."

The two listened, trying to envision the horror and destruction. No army they knew of would dare attack the enemy in full retreat. There was no honor or glory.

"They landed in the destruction they caused three days after appearing, their assaults clearly doing nothing more than clearing a path for their arrival. We attempted skirmish after skirmish, each a greater failure than the last. After a time of doing nothing more than repelling our assaults, they began their march north, and we clearly saw what we were facing. That was when we knew that we had to run..."

Aryu could barely stand to see a trained Rider of the Inja Army falter, but that was what was happening to Stroan. Stroan had his orders, knew his responsibilities, and was duty-bound to fulfill them, but this was his first true recounting of these events, and it was becoming more than he could take.

Johan, remaining composed, asked yet again the question they all were thinking. "It's all right, Rider Stroan. We'd hear what you'd have to say if you'd tell us. We are men of the world now. We are ready." Lies and bravado, every word of it. Aryu wanted no part in the story of an enemy with the apparent powers of the Old, with the ability to send armies running like Death Himself trailed after them.

"Machines," he said, his voice beginning to trail off into a whisper. "Wave after wave of metal, robotic, heartless, evil machines. Each one of them bearing the stink of the forbidden ways that spawned them. Dear Great God of Dragons, we have lost the entire south coast of Inja to the Army of Old, and we have no way to stop it."

Despite tens of thousands of years of history and evolution, a timeframe full of glories and mistakes, mankind as a people had insisted on empowering their own self-destruction to the point of near extinction on four very well-known occasions, each one ingrained in almost every sentient mind.

The first was a rumor. A legend no one alive could substantiate. It told the story of a great flood sent by God to purge the earth of those who displeased him. Only after the concurrent destructions did the rumor earn a place in the history books as a possible example of something similar happening. It was a fable that suddenly became feasible.

The second was at the dawn of more modern times, when mankind was evolving beyond its infancy. In a time of war, mankind chose to flex its muscle and revel in its own impossible strength. The stories of hellfire engulfing the earth in wave after wave of cleansing abomination was a tale repeated and altered very little with each subsequent generation. Retold to near-perfect accuracy by the few alive who were there so long ago.

From that time and after, most lived in a constant leeriness of anything of a mechanically advanced nature. This part of the world seemed to avoid it completely. Here, in the land some called Inja, so strong was the fear that most electronic and mechanical devices were banned, feared, and rarely spoken of. A self-imposed exile that had lasted centuries. This was where those with the greatest fear chose to live.

The only thing more feared were Embracers of the Power: which were the creators, commanders, and destroyers of God Himself. Embracer wrath and fury brought about the third Fall of Man. That was an extermination of the Divine so overwhelming in its scope that few alive could fathom it.

The fourth and most recent epic human mistake was an unmitigated and disastrous attempt by humans to grasp and control the wonders of the Old. Attempting not to harness the destructive powers of the Old but the creative and inventive aspects, the most recent near-apocalypse was during an age when man, feeling cocky in its survival of the inhuman wrath of God, traveled once again onto the path of the machine. Although an excellent story for a later time, the conclusion was the same.

It did not go well.

Mankind had escaped its own demise four times, but as two of those times were at the hands of "technological marvels," machines had by this time developed a mythically evil quality. People all around this land were now so deathly afraid of anything more complicated than a combination of gears and pistons, they had elevated technology to something akin to undiluted, pure evil in its most basic form.

And, with a harsh wind attempting to kick up their terror, two men who not long ago desired nothing more than the peace and respect that was awaiting them in a village not far away, were now told that that evil had returned, reformed, reorganized, and was marching a path of horror that leads straight to their doorsteps. To imagine how one would feel knowing that the vanguard of Hell was approaching their home and loved ones, one would be at the threshold of understanding the terror these two felt at this moment.

Stroan couldn't bring himself to continue much more beyond the basics. All the southern colonies had begun a hasty retreat, with caravans like the one that just past them, and some much larger, charging north to the safety they thought they could find in the Great Range. Mankind always had a place in life for illusions.

Stroan knew the power of the enemy, and entrusted to these men that he wasn't at all convinced the Great Range would be any kind of barrier against such an awesome level of brutality.

Johan's face expressed a painful mix of confusion and nausea. Aryu could only stand mouth agape, in cold shock.

"They couldn't be..." Johan choked out at last, breaking the silence fear had created. "It was gone from here. It was TOLD to us! We got rid of it! Destroyed and buried it centuries ago. This whole part of the world is defenseless!" Rage was beginning to add itself to his simmering pot of emotion. No one knew more than Johan about the history, the results, and the unmitigated lunacy of dealing with the power of the Old. There had never been a good result, and every victory was bathed in the blood of countless innocents.

Stroan had no answer. He simply shook his head, composing himself as he did so. "I can tell you nothing but the truth as I know it. They began a strong push to the northwest shortly after landfall, following the coast. Based on what we know, the Valley of Smoke was not in their immediate path. They were heading westerly, into the Vein Valley. But a force so large is bound to be everywhere eventually. If another Rider hasn't alerted them, you can be assured that one will soon. All towns and villages are being told the same thing. Pack up, go north, and run until you can't run anymore. It's all we can think of to do.

His words were heavy, and nearly unbelievable. Aryu and Johan shifted back and forth, praying Stroan would offer something more in terms of comfort.

"Southeast from here is your home, still three or four days away by way of the road we're on now, and then to the Traveler's Trail at the north end of the valley. I'm sure you know it?"

They did. The Travelers Trail was the main north/south road through the valley.

"And what about going straight, going day and night, non-stop?"

Johan asked.

Stroan looked confused as he puzzled it out. Aryu already smelled the beginnings of a Johan plan.

"I guess no more than two days," Stroan decided. "Hard country between here and there, though. Harsh, dry valleys would be the least of your worries. There's also the risk of hidden raiders, deadly creatures, and at least a few shifting sandpits. It'd be better to stick to the roads you know, especially in these times. The only upside is it's all downhill."

Johan barely heard Rider Stroan's opinions on the matter. He was already looking at Aryu. "Can you do it?" he asked, partly curious, partly pleading. "With water and supplies enough for the journey?"

Aryu thought about it. Although he'd embraced his freakish deformity's greater benefits years prior, his embarrassment and shame kept him from trying at a trip so long. That said, he couldn't say it was impossible, and that was enough for him.

"Yes," he said at last. "As long as we keep it light. It won't be easy going that far."

Johan nodded and dropped his pack to assist Aryu with what he needed. Stroan looked on in wonder and finally brought himself to speak. "It won't be any easier with only one of you. I dare say it'd be more dangerous that way. I wouldn't consider it if I were you two."

Johan gave Aryu dried meats and enough water for the trip. Anymore, and Aryu feared the extra weight would be nothing but a hindrance to him.

"We can't thank you enough for your information, Rider Stroan." Johan was eager to send the young man on his way. "You should go now, continue to the north and save more villages. We'll be fine from here on."

Stroan hesitated, watching as Johan handed Aryu the last of the needed supplies. His duty was to the north, though, and the foolish actions of these two were no longer his concern.

"I advise against this course of action, sirs. No good can come of it. Just stay togethe..."

Aryu had unlatched his strapping and was tearing his pack from his back. Thick, dark, leathery wings slowly unraveled themselves to their full length as a terrified Stroan looked on.

"By Gods and Devils, you have got to be kidding me," Stroan stammered.

Johan had gotten used to it by this point. "Of all the things you've seen lately, I promise you this is the least of your worries."

He supposed that was true. He had seen too much to be surprised anymore. If the Armies of the Old, long thought destroyed, were currently tromping across the land with little resistance, a man with mutant wings was just another drop in what was becoming a very odd bucket.

Aryu gave the wings a few strong test strokes, kicking up the dirt at his feet, causing the others to shield their faces.

"Wait." Johan was digging into his pack again, eventually emerging with his coveted dagger. He held it out to Aryu. "It's no defense against machines, but it's all I have to offer for protection."

Aryu at last knew it was time. The sixth sense he'd felt since its arrival told him so. He waved off the offer of his friend, instead digging into the long storage pocket on the inside of his own pack.

What emerged was a straight, sheathed sword; its square, golden hilt and wrapped handle grasped firmly in his hand. At its base were two small protrusions, not unlike latched horns.

Aryu took a spare piece of strapping and secured the hidden treasure to his back between his wings in a fashion that wouldn't interfere with them.

"You son of a bitch." Johan looked on, anger just as obvious as confusion. "Since when?"

"Last night. On the mountain, while you were still climbing." Johan looked very doubtful. Aryu waved it off. "Later. For now, keep the dagger and I'll tell you about it when we meet up again." Johan wasted no time tucking his blade back in his pack, almost ashamed with himself that he'd offered it in the first place.

By this point, Rider Stroan had returned to his horse, which had stood like chiseled stone this whole time, and mounted up. "May we meet again in this life or the next," he offered, giving them the wave of his position once again.

Johan looked to him, returning the salute, and smirked. "Preferably the former," he answered.

"Indeed, men, indeed. Good fortune to you!"

"And you, Rider Stroan," Aryu replied.

With a click of the teeth and a dig of his heels, Stroan took off at full gallop after the caravan, his own destiny off in the looming shadows of the Great Range.

"Alright," Aryu began, recapturing Johan's attention. "I expect you in no more than four days."

"I'll push hard to cut it back," Johan replied. "I can't wait that long."

Aryu began to run, but stopped. "Wait... What if it goes sideways?"

Johan didn't care for the sudden pessimism but knew where it came from. They were far too close not to think of a backup plan. "The village," Johan answered. "The one from yesterday. The bar with the electronic spouts."

Aryu nodded. He remembered how startled he'd been when he saw those lights along the kegs. Was he really about to fly into this nightmare when a beer spout had rattled him so much?

His supplies in hand and treasure on his back, Aryu gave one last wave and then began to run with his wings folded behind him. As he

38

reached a gully farther down the road, his abnormally large and powerful back muscles flexed and the wings stretched out beside him, catching the wind as he headed into it. In moments, his feet lifted off the ground. His wings began to arch and bend in long strokes like a kite picking up speed. His body began stretching out behind him, and after a moment of apparent weightlessness, he gave one huge twist with his wings, which took his whole body upwards. He bent himself forward like the demon he was rumored to be, gliding with the wind, and then dove slightly to gain speed. He couldn't 'fly' like a bird, his body was too heavy, but he had mastered controlled gliding as soon as he was strong enough. From there it was only a matter of mastering the techniques that allowed him to move forward and gain altitude if conditions permitted. His friend looked after him until he was no more than a speck in the distant sky.

Johan re-shouldered his pack and stepped back up to the road. He checked what remained of Aryu's pack, taking whatever he thought he might need.

Where in the name of The Great God of Dragons did that damn sword come from? Johan thought with jealousy. He saw in one quick glance that it was a well-made weapon, just like his knife.

He began down the road at a brisk pace, already regretting the decision to add what little Aryu had to his overloaded pack. His best friend was a man with wings. At some point, he should stop being surprised with the details of life.

CHAPTER 4

The Face of the Enemy

Nixon of the Great Fire and Ash, or just Nix to his few friends, emerged from the poorly lit bar with the excellent draft sometime after midnight. Or, at least, he assumed it was midnight. The truth was he'd been away so long that he could no longer rely on the moon and stars to aid him while seeking his whereabouts.

The old man had spoken in great detail about an item Nix was interested in, but the big man was upset early into the conversation to find out that the item the spirited old man wished to speak of was not the one he'd hoped. Still, it was as good a place as any to start.

With the conversation over, the information shared and the deal to never appear to the old man again sealed and honored, he secured the beastly sword on his back and began down the road and out of this town to where the man had said he'd find it.

"The place you seek is a small village to the southeast of here," he'd told him. "The pup who took it was out on his blood-quest, a mission to manhood favored by many in those lands. "It's all a load of fart in a wind to me. I'd say it takes more than a little hike to make a man, eh? Well, a *normal* man anyway, which you, my ridiculous demon-friend, are most certainly not."

Well, he was part right in that at least. Nixon was by no means a man, but he was most certainly not a demon either. Had the old man not been so bold and so damned likeable in Nix's eyes, it's safe to say his constant references to Nix as a demon would have seen him smash the old goat's face in. Nix was no demon, but he was also not the nicest of God's creations, and it's true that he often found violence to be a needed friend if the situation had called for it.

Nixon of the Great Fire and Ash was most definitely one of God's creations from a time when God was more than just a man. From a time when God was a *god*.

That God was long gone from this place, this world, and its peoples. Most never even knew of that deity, only of his purge, the so-called 'First Fall of Man.' They only knew of the one they had called God. Nixon knew better than any alive, even those that had beaten time and lived far longer than a person should, that their deity was just a man. A mortal too lost to go home again.

Nix had been around, in one form or another, for just as long. He might even say longer, but he'd spent so many years and so much time chasing his target that he could remember nothing that came before that, provided there was anything to remember. He assumed there was. He assumed there had to be the great Power and deadly beasts that needed his disposal before the time of the false god. There had to be, didn't there?

It sometimes upset the fire-haired man-thing to know that his existence had become nothing more than being the janitor to what he considered mankind's greatest mistake. No man born of woman was to possess the kind of power the false god did. It was too unstable, too unpredictable, and too reckless to let him continue on the way he did.

It wasn't Nixon's place to criticize. His job sadly had never been to destroy that particular worldly menace, only the useless, overtly powerful legions that followed in his wake. That damn sword they held corrupted far more than it ever empowered.

Every time someone possessed it for purposes unbecoming in nature, Nixon of the Great Fire and Ash was there, bringing about the *true* balance of things, not the balance the false god swore to uphold. That bastard was always one tiny slip from becoming another of Nixon's clean-up duties. It's just for the best, though. Had that day ever come, Nix was certain their battle would have just gone on forever. Neither could die in the traditional sense, and neither would give quarter.

Nixon had better things to do than battle a fool until the world fell apart at its seams.

But still, he was dead now, finally gone despite Death and its idiocy in delaying his final verdict. Nixon wasn't sure who was more to blame for the catastrophic disaster that little episode created. The false god should have known that Death hated following the rules. And Death should have known that 'God' would never just accept a cruel fate. Death should have known no meager mountain could hold him.

It was a mountain that was not far from where he was currently. Odd how the world always seemed to spin him back here.

Death had been a fool, and the two fools together made for a terrible end. If only Nixon had been there. Stop the madness in one swoop. But by the time the false god had let the wicked evil sweep through him enough to awaken Nixon, the deed was done. The world was destroyed, the power of the ages released, and Nixon was left with the god-damned clean-up job.

He smirked at the thought of the moment the false god was allowed to die. "It should 'ave been me t' deal the killin' blow. I would 'ave enjoyed it so much more." But he knew it never could have been. The false god was too damned egotistical to allow anyone but himself to end it.

This left one rather large question in his mind: what the hell was he, Nixon of the Great Fire and Ash, doing back here? In this part of the world, the Power had been lost and the people had been cast into fear at the mere mention of it. Even those that had once followed the same path of power had abandoned it, choosing instead the life of either solitude or the always refreshingly ridiculous path of false prophecy. Years ago, a man whose life's ambition was to entertain the foolish masses had said something so apt in every age, Nixon was likely never to forget it.

There's a sucker born every minute. Amen, good sir. Amen.

Many of the people who once embraced the life of the Power were now scattered across the world. Some believed themselves seers of the Divine, but all they saw were self-indulgent lies and hubris. Some remained hidden from the eyes of the world, safe from its horrors. However, if they didn't foolishly seek out more power than they should, they'd get no trouble from Nixon Ash.

Nixon Ash. What a stupid name it was. He thought he might as well have been called Big Fire Man if he was to be named so obviously. He was, in his heart, nameless, a vessel for God's will, and as such, no name was ever required. The people of this world would have none of it. Things must be named, lest they even exist.

Magnus, his first and most trusted guide and friend, now dead longer than Nix chose to dwell on, had told him he needed a title to simply fit in, as there would be times he would have to spend months, possibly years walking the earth for his target. His appearance, although always different, would also always be strange. He had been small, big, dark, light, man and woman. He'd been old, young, and all points therein.

He had not, to the best of his memory, ever been anything like he was now. That was his first sign when he awoke that something was different. Never had a foe required such a large and powerful appearance. He was very curious to see whom it was he was chasing.

Nix passed beyond the outer border of the town and set off down the road. Although he did possess the ability to fly, his trained senses couldn't track his target when he was this close. Flying only got him great distances quickly, but once the gap was shortened, walking and investigation were the best options. Besides, for all the time he slept, it was often quite nice to stroll for a while. He had nothing but time. He'd catch up to his prey when he had to and not a moment sooner. Other than that nasty little hiccup with the foolish (and alas, cunning) Man-God, that was the way it always was. When Nixon of the Great Fire and Ash arrived before you, you had gone too far down the dark path, and now your time was up.

This time was certainly different. Although he had his great tracking skills, ones attuned to the rise of the Power as well as his sword, his constant companions were all absent. There had once been a worldwide network of people, places, and things dedicated to the old God and His Word. Now they were all gone. Where once he could jump from place to place, fly even closer and then track the Power, this time it was just his home. He had looked for the other places, the pockets outside of time that only the wisest (or craziest) of the Embracers inhabited. All but one (a place he had no desire to ever return to) were lost or closed against him.

The items that would guide him such as maps or symbols hidden in churches and places of worship were also lost. This was likely due to the amount of time that had passed since last he had arisen. He had suspected that the time would come when the land itself forgot his kind. He was very upset it had come to pass in what seemed to him to be rather short order.

Worst of all was the loss of his people. Men and women dedicated to him and others of his kind. Even after the loss of the True God, there had been thousands around the world who aided him with news, information, and advice. Magnus had been his first, there from the time of Nixon's current sentience. He had taught him all he needed to know about the world and its inhabitants, the Power and the Knowledge, Earth's two undividable yet infinitely different absolute truths. He taught him his purpose.

And when Magnus was lost, there had been others who served God. Others who heeded the righteous call and let him know the truth of the day.

Even when God was lost, there had been many who had found ways to keep him informed. A vast network of information gatherers who funneled it all back to one or two who stayed by his side for all time. He would awake, gather the information he required, jump to his destination, and let the hunt begin.

Days ago he awoke alone in the body he wore now, more beast than man in appearance. His sword, thank God, was where it always was at his side, ready for service. He would have to question it all later. If he was awake, it meant he had a purpose. Find and destroy the fool, which meant the source of the greatest power had been found. It made him weary to think about it. Always the source was found and always a fool would use it. No rest was likely ever to come to him. He supposed eventually the sun would expand and explode. Then, maybe, he could get some much-needed peace.

The road stretched ahead of him, a long line slicing through dry rolling hills. Large caravans passed him often with many people, racing off for who-knew-where at top speeds. Damn it, he wished he knew what was going on. He wasn't accustomed to being so out of the loop. Something big was in the direction he was going, but he had no idea if it was the Power or something else entirely. The old man in the bar had mentioned something about troubling times coming but refused to go into details with Nix, as it did not pertain to his promised story.

"You'll get nothing more than what you were promised from me, beast," he had said. Nixon could be very polite, amazingly charming, and patient like none other. That old bat had seen right through each tactic. He likely knew Nixon was a man out of sorts, and he certainly took great pleasure in seeing him on the ropes.

It wouldn't be easy breaking down someone's fears in this particular incarnation, but he had great patience. He'd learn it all in time. Until then, he just had to keep walking to his destination. The place the old man had mentioned. The village of Tan Torna Qu-ay.

▶◀▶◀▶◀▶◀▶◀▶◀▶◀▶◀▶◀▶◀▶◀▶◀

He had walked long into the night when he met the scout.

He chose to walk since he was so close, following the road to the Valley of Smoke. He was passed by many people, either on foot or in a caravan, but most either ignored him, running from their own demons, or spotted him only in poor light and gave a wide berth.

It was for the best, at least for the moment. Being so close, Nix was much happier focusing on the task at hand. He could have tried to talk to someone passing by for information as to why they were all so keen on leaving the place he was heading, but someone who can't die has little reason to fear anything. He wondered what made them run more out of curiosity than fear.

After the moon had been high and the night grew shorter, he'd noticed no more passers-by. Whatever they feared, it would soon be apparent.

The first of the larger explosions burst off at a good distance from him on the southwest horizon. A fireball rose into the night like a spark from a distant flame, but fire and Nixon were old friends, and he was certain wherever that had occurred it was likely to have destroyed everything. It was something serious, and also far beyond the capabilities and technology these people possessed. It wasn't just an explosion; it was a literal pillar of fire, erupting from the ground in a skyward cylinder.

He smirked to himself. No wonder they were scared. Whatever it was, it was big, foreign, and powerful enough to strike the fear of God into these common people. Nixon had served the common people his whole existence, so any threat to them was something to be watchful of. The enemy of his friend was his enemy.

Lost in the thought of the 'who's' and 'what's' of the situation, he was almost oblivious to the eyes that watched him. Only by luck did he catch a glimpse of reflection when another explosion lit up the sky ever so slightly.

He let the observation pass, keeping a good eye and keen ear to its location. As he walked, he sensed it following him. Whatever it was, it certainly didn't walk on the ground. It was far too silent for that. *No,* he thought as he moved, *this lit'l bugger can fly.*

Something in this land was advanced enough to fly like a bird yet be silent like a soft wind. Nixon's curiosity continued to grow. This was truly becoming a land of mysteries.

The object (it was certainly just an object. He could feel that it was not alive in any way he was familiar with) followed after him, making a very soft 'click' 'click' 'click click' as it moved. He kept his knowledge of his spy a secret. He would have more to learn that way.

A bit farther on the object, which had circled around him from the front to the rear and back around again, emerged from behind a small scrub, the only cover it could find.

It was round and simple, no bigger than Nixon's hand. Its shell was an onyx black and seemed to absorb light as it moved. Anyone with less attuned senses would not have seen it, and that was likely on purpose. Scout and inform. A simple device. A common one through all ages, be it plane, machine, or even bird.

Nixon stopped, making no more illusions about his awareness. With its emergence, it was clear that it was now ready to be found. Thus, he could deduce several things from this. It had either collected all it needed to know, it had malfunctioned in some way, or it was preparing to communicate in some fashion knowing it had been found out.

Discretion being the better form of valor, Nixon smiled, bending and bowing the formal greeting of his people. "Greetings t' ye', little one. T' wha' do I owe the pleasure this night?"

The clicking increased instantly, getting louder and softer in random waves. It moved higher, possibly to be beyond Nix and his none-too-hidden sword.

A blue light came from the bottom of the object, its clicking intensifying as the light grew brighter. Nixon suspected he'd either triggered something or someone else had done it for him. Either way, any fool could see it was building to something.

Nixon couldn't be sure that this item wasn't the source of the explosions. He had no idea how advanced the people who'd sent this thing were. He drew his sword, feeling the power build from his hand and up to his arm. A welcome feeling he was sure he'd never be tired of, one of confidence and familiarity.

He stepped back, searching the night for any other of this scout's kind. Confident there were none, he attempted to continue the discreet approach.

"Well now wee one, what's all this?" No response, just blue light and clicking. "Well, if we 'ave no further business, I'll continue on my way. G'day." He bowed and began to walk once more.

A blue light hit his face almost immediately, bright and blinding.

It dazed and dazzled him for a moment, causing him to step aside. Rare was the light that could affect him like that. His eyes could see in the darkest darks and the most blinding lights.

The light no longer in his face, he looked again at the object and paused to watch it as it clicked. The blue light still glowed from its base, yet did not follow him. He looked about, searching to see if it was illuminating something else. He found it: a pinprick of light in the middle of the road. A laser. He should have known. Those damned things never seemed to go away, and damned if they didn't disrupt Nixon's vision in any age.

Then the clicking stopped. The light still glowed brightly, marking its spot on the ground, but the night fell perfectly quiet. Not even a wind blew.

The object was seemingly happy with its information. Nixon watched as it flew away, and eventually it was gone, back into the night it came from. The light remained planted firmly in the road. Somewhere, getting higher above, it was still there shining it down.

Nixon had been called upon many times in his life to chase the unbalanced Power and the misfortune it brought about. He'd seen man revert from one phase of life to another. From simple and nomadic to huge and powerful. He'd seen all ages and all peoples from the eyes of an outsider with no real sense of time. He remembered all these things very well. The fortunes they'd brought and the treasures they'd destroyed.

Essentially, Nixon had been around a long time and seen much. Because of that, Nixon knew a targeting laser for what it was.

He grinned slightly, finding the coming storm very amusing. Soon, he began to laugh, getting louder and louder as he heard his fate falling faster toward him.

By the time the bomb hit, he was nearly in hysterics.

Stupid people. You can't kill a phoenix with fire.

Then the pain began, and his laughter turned to screams.

▶◀▶◀▶◀▶◀▶◀▶◀▶◀▶◀▶◀▶◀▶◀▶◀

Not much farther ahead, Johan was slogging across the intensely rough terrain when the explosion lit up the sky behind him.

His shadow stretched out before him as the pillar of light turned night into day. Terrified, Johan knew enough to brace himself, and he fell quickly to the ground. His mammoth pack tumbled down over his head as he did so.

Then the shockwave hit.

It roared over his head like dragon's breath. Fast and hot. He was far enough away that the air had cooled it greatly from the point of impact, but it was still searing and difficult to breathe in.

The wind toppled Johan's pack, tearing it from his back, straps and all. Luckily, he had long since put his prized dagger on his person.

There was no use screaming or moving. Both would have been fruitless. The noise was ear-shattering, and any attempt to shift one way or another would have meant being carried away to wherever ill wind blows. For the moment he just crouched there, head down, waiting for the end. He clutched his head, shielding his ears from the noise, eyes clenched tight against the dust and debris. Then with great difficulty, he peeked between his eyelids, trying to make sense of whatever he could see, desperately trying to gauge the distance to the epicenter of the blast.

The winds and noise died out slowly, seeming to take forever to get within manageable levels at which he could begin to move and assess the situation more thoroughly. The fireball had fizzled out by now, and the night was dark once again.

Johan rose, eager to learn what he could while he still had time.

Dirt and dust fell off him in piles, invading every inch of his body, exposed or not. His arms were red and sand-blasted but didn't hurt yet, the shock of the situation softly numbing the pain like a conversation in another room. He knew it was there, and was likely to be much louder shortly, but for now, it was more than manageable.

Smoke filled the air where the blast had been, and it allowed him an excellent chance to judge the distance. About two hours walk behind him he guessed.

He had listened to Rider Stroan's words about the country but decided the best course of action was to leave the road and break trail anyway. He was from this land, after all, and its dangers were all too familiar to him. Sand pits weren't a worry; he'd learned everything about them years ago. As for raiders and rough country? Sure, the country was rough, but the gain of time outweighed the hardships. Any raider this far off the beaten path was likely more insane than anything. Johan could manage insane.

Whatever had been blasted, it was back on the road he'd come from at the beginning of the night. He thought regretfully that the target may have been another caravan of people, like the many that had passed him after Aryu and Stroan had left.

He briefly looked for his pack. There was nothing in his that was truly irreplaceable, and in the times ahead there was nothing that could help against machines, but he figured he'd better look all the same. He found it in a dried creek bed. The pack was quite beaten, but not beyond repair. Straps could be tied and holes mended. After giving the pack a thorough search he saw nothing of value had been lost. Some clothes, some cooking instruments, nothing more.

He sat in the creek bed for a rest, the events up to then upsetting him enough to finally stop his youthful energy. The echo of the shockwave still rang in his ears.

The power, closeness, and pure *reality* of that blast had shaken him quite a bit. This was actually happening, and it was terrifying. All the books, all the stories, and all the warnings of the 'evils' of machines and technology were nothing compared to the explosion he'd just witnessed. He wanted to be home, despite his soft loathing of it. He wanted to be there with his friend and welcomed a hero. Now, he wondered if he'd ever see it again.

▶◀▶◀▶◀▶◀▶◀▶◀▶◀▶◀▶◀▶◀▶◀▶◀

It seemed that Aryu could still surprise even himself.

Barring any unforeseen difficulties, he had presumed that he would be able to fly in elongated bursts, gliding as much as possible. The evening was still cloudy after he left, followed by a typical chilly night, so there were no thermal updrafts for him to ride. Still, he could glide a great distance. His wings were strong and his body and supplies relatively light.

Once the sun was down, it was all he could do to simply pick a direction by the stars and go. There was no ground to see in this blackness. No markers or points of reference. Just an endless field of black, highlighted briefly by bits and pieces of darker or lighter gray illustrating the undulations in the ground below. Once the sun rose again, he figured he'd take to wing as high as he could and search for any visible sign of the Valley of Smoke, a rather large reference point on this landscape, and follow that to home.

Provided there was a home to arrive at.

He'd seen from his vantage point the pinpricks of light in the far west that likely marked more large explosions. They were still some days away by foot, or even cart, but they were much closer than Aryu was comfortable with. He'd spent much of his flight thinking the same as Johan had not too long before.

It's amazing the difference a day can make.

This time yesterday he was perched on the mountainside, eating a cold meal, and relaxing with Johan. He was now flying as fast and as far as he could to get to a home that may have long ago been destroyed by the Army of the Old, stomping out of history to claim his land.

Stroan had certainly not been sure as to the condition of the Valley of Smoke. Only that he *"didn't think they'd made it that far east."* Hardly a resounding reason to sleep easy. Besides, it was clear in the words he said (and didn't say) that he expected the Army of the Old to make it there soon, had they not arrived already.

Aryu was often lost in thought at the multitudes of possibilities that had presented themselves in the last day. Often as he thought, his gradual rhythmic gliding motions would slow down or stop outright and he'd drift through the vast emptiness, descending as he did so. He'd then snap awake as the ground approached, give his body a good mental ass-kick, and begin trying to climb into the night sky again.

He had surprised himself with his abilities and endurance in the last few hours. Although he had initially thought he could float like that forever, enjoying the feelings he rarely got to indulge, by the time the moon was high he was beginning to get tired. The muscles on his back were straining to keep him aloft after so much time.

He had landed to eat and rest earlier, hoping a few moments on the ground would be enough. After taking to wing again, it was obvious that he'd need something a little more sustained to keep up at this pace. He reluctantly planned to go until his body and mind could truly go no more, then rest for as brief as he could before continuing on. He'd hoped, in his mind's eye, that he would be close enough by sunup to be home sometime that day, but with no real references to go by, it was all just speculation. Aryu had to be prepared for the likely possibility that Stroan had misjudged, just to be on the safe side. It wouldn't do to have him so tired that he'd have to walk days more just to get home. Better to play it safe.

It was just after he accepted his exhaustion that the sky lit up far behind him in a plume of fire and smoke.

The change in vision and scenery was very disorientating for a moment. The explosion had been large enough to light the ground far below him. He turned back, angling himself to see what the cause was; eyes straining to make sense of most of what he saw, ground and sky becoming separated once again. He was certain it was back the way he'd come, confident (or perhaps praying to the fact) he'd not wavered from his course enough to make that large a difference. It was certainly an explosion like those in the distance, tall and powerful, reaching high into the night before dying out. He could not be certain how far it was, as he was not certain how fast he'd been going. Fear gripped his heart as he realized that Johan was back in that direction somewhere, and if he wasn't at the center of that blast, Aryu was quite confident that he would have been close.

He circled lower, mind wracked with possibilities and uninformed suggestions. Did he go back? Did he keep going? How far was it? How far were they? Damn it, if he'd only been more confident in his flying he may have been able to make a better judgment, but as it was he was too ill-prepared to make an informed decision. Yet again, the shame of the wings reared its terrible face and Aryu was just a puppet in its grip.

He began descending, hoping putting his feet on solid ground would help him focus on the tasks at hand. He had almost touched down when the shockwave rushed past him.

It had traveled much farther and lost much of its strength since it had passed over Johan. The terrible heat and storm-force winds were significantly lessened. It was still a loud, powerful, and destructive force to any and all things hovering in the air.

Aryu's wings folded back in the force of the blast, losing all aerodynamics and converting themselves to little more than leathery pennants in the wind which carried him upwards. Aryu twisted backwards awkwardly, snapping like a rope was trying to pull him away, only to slacken and release after a moment too late. He tumbled back, trying to brace himself against the approaching ground. In the blackness, he had no idea which way was up, seeing stars no matter which way he fell. The rush of wind in his ears was a constant equal, and all he could do was close his eyes and hope he didn't have much more to go.

He heard the ground rush to meet him before he felt it. Like closing your eyes and walking down a hallway, you know where the walls are and can sense which doors are open without seeing. That was the only warning he had, but it was enough for him to put his hands up and hit arms-first instead of with his head, which certainly would have killed him.

He hit hard enough to snap his arms against his head and neck, punching himself twice in the process. He tumbled back, feeling the strain on his back as the joints and muscles that connected his back and lower shoulders to the non-human joints and muscles of his wings heaved while they were wrenched up over his head and back down his face like a grotesque blanket.

Being so large and fragile, they never felt pain like the rest of his body. He'd strained them a lot when he was first learning to fly, landing badly or twisting the wrong way while trying to turn too hard, but this was an all-new feeling to him as he tossed like a circus tumbler, hitting rocks and ragged scrub as he went. The sand and thorns scraped at any exposed flesh like fishhooks.

When at last he came to rest, he was facedown, his appendages akimbo like a marionette that was dropped. His head hurt terribly, and that was only step one on his mental checklist. There was still a whole body to go. His arms were above his head, his left arm twisted around in a way no arm should be. He attempted to move it, realizing instantly that he was pinned down somehow. Neither arm would move. He couldn't account for why until he felt the soft hide texture under his right hand.

His wings, after their brief foray above his head, had become wrapped around his body like a bedroll, pinning his arms into their current, extremely uncomfortable position.

"This is going to take a little finesse," he said to himself, feeling better that neither his voice nor ears seemed to be damaged.

He moved what he could of his arms, testing each body part as he went to ensure there was no serious damage. He knew right away that his left shoulder was hurt and likely out of joint. A common ailment to a man who had wing muscles constantly pulling other upper-torso anatomy around in ways regular people aren't accustomed to.

The next stop on his mental itinerary was the back and wings. Even growing up with them, he was never comfortable with the way his wings felt, likely a holdover from the part of his mind that was normal and human, so it was tough for him to immediately discern if something was wrong.

The muscles controlling the wings were very strong, much more so than any other in his body, having been tried and trained to lift and control a full-grown man in flight. As he twisted this way and that, he could feel the wings begin to unwind piece by piece until one (he couldn't be sure which) slipped out from under his right hand. This allowed him to prop himself up that extra little bit, taking more weight off the wings.

After a few more tries, he could slip over to his side enough to free up his left arm, feeling it pop as it went back into place, sending a chill up his spine at the odd sensation.

Able to get up fully now, he got up on all fours and began folding his wings behind him, careful not to go too fast in fear of aggravating a wound he didn't yet feel or ripping the skin that covered them on a nearby rock or thorn bush. They seemed alright, not sending any immediate warnings to the rest of his body. He'd have to wait until it was light to see if there were any rips or tears. He'd had some minor ones over time, but they were almost completely nerveless, and he barely felt a thing the times he had.

He brought himself up to his knees and began to stand. Each leg screamed in protest but did little else to stop him. Whatever their issues were, they weren't bad enough to keep him from standing, and to Aryu that was good enough.

He pieced together what had hit him instantly, feeling stupid as he did so. Naturally there would be a shockwave, and he felt himself a fool for not realizing it sooner. He supposed it was because he had other things on his mind.

As to those particular "other things," he pieced together his options to decide the best one.

He hesitated to fly again, not knowing if his wings (or the rest of him) were quite up for it yet. If he felt the way he did right now in the morning, he wasn't sure he could continue anywhere. But, bridges to cross and all that.

It ate him up not knowing what had happened or where. He tried desperately to piece together the possibilities. Johan very likely was not in the blast itself, he'd concluded. Even with Rider Stroan's warnings, he still was likely to have broken off the road and crossed the open land. Where he was unsure was the aftershock, and if it had been that powerful even by this point, how deadly was it when it hit Johan? If he were close to it, would he even be able to find what was left of him? He doubted it. A shiver ran up his spine at the thought, but the reality was it could be a possibility. There was far too much ground between here and there to find him even if he knew where to start. If he was far enough away, his chances were slightly better, but not by much. Besides, if Johan was far enough away and he did find him, it would just end up being a waste of time.

No. He knew the course of action. Going back made no sense now. Even if Johan had been badly hurt, he could never find them in the dark, he could never carry him to safety, and it was still hours until morning.

He slipped back to the ground, body screaming as he did so. The only logical choice was to keep going and hope his instincts were right, that Johan had made it off the road and trekked far enough away that he survived. He had no alternative but to believe it. His mission was far too important to delay his arrival in Tan Torna Quay by another day or two of searching.

Eventually he took off again, adding a few more miles behind him before he landed and slept, wrapped once more in his wings. A part of him hated them for helping him so much in the last few hours. He assumed the days ahead would be hard and time to sleep would be rare. Of course he was right, but he didn't know that for sure. And so, he simply slept the peaceful sleep of ignorance.

CHAPTER 5

━━━━━━━━━━━━━━━━━━━━━━━━━━━━━━━━

The Village of Tan Torna Qu-ay

The pain had been unbearable. Never in all his considerable years and all his many lives had such a feeling overwhelmed him so completely. Not the pleasure of his first kill, or the invasiveness of his first rebirth. Indeed, not even the pain and guilt of losing Magnus those eons ago could compare.

He questioned if he was even still alive for a moment, finding it difficult to think clearly beyond the pain he felt.

Nixon of the Great Fire and Ash was a wreck. His mind jumbled and his body nearly obliterated, only particles and soot remained. Nothing in any time he could remember had ever so utterly defeated him, and that was proof enough to him something out there was very wrong.

He could still reform, but this was not an easy process. Even the ashes could still feel the pain, or at least the memory of it. The ground around where Nix had been standing was scorched; mixed about with the mess were the remnants of Nixon. He began pulling himself together, mentally drawing each bit to him. His body began to come together in a difficult jigsaw puzzle.

His mind began reconstructing the blast and the moments before it. At first it was all pain and confusion, his body reforming itself like death in reverse, creating his look and structure out of nothing. He remembered the drone, knew it now for exactly what it was. He remembered the impact as he began to recompile into something looking more and more human (or as close as he could get). How he had laughed at the idea he could be so easily dispatched. How he had laughed and laughed at the ignorance of the enemy. The rush of nothingness beyond him as the explosion drew out all the air in the area. The welcome feeling of the heat, his oldest and dearest companion.

But the heat grew too quickly, and before he could even react it had melted away his armor, a living piece of himself, followed by his hair and skin. Eventually it went down to the bone, each step deeper, creating a new and more intense level of pain. It went beyond his tolerance for heat in microseconds. A tolerance Nixon had no idea he had. He was certain he could live peacefully on the surface of the sun, but this was something else.

His reformation was nearly complete. His armor grew out of his skin, his hair returned to its long, ethereal shimmering length. His thoughts became more organized. He was born of the fire. He lived and breathed nothing but the fire his whole life. If it had done to him what it did, it could not be fire as he knew it. But what else then?

By God, Nixon needed someone with answers.

His form retaken, his body whole yet again, he began to sit up and regain his composure. A moment of pure terror hit him as he realized his back was devoid of his trusted sword, only to breathe a large sigh of relief to see it some distance away, but still whole. Not a mark or scorch on the sheath could be seen.

He walked over to it, getting more comfortable with his body. He returned as he was, large and foreboding, armor black as night and eyes the same. Each microscopic piece fell into place, but sadly the memory of the pain lingered like an old wound. Nixon doubted he'd ever forget it, thanks to a perfect memory.

He drew the sword from its sheath with a reassuring whisper. No nick or mark could be seen. Nixon had a good reason to be afraid. This sword was not a Divine creation like him. If by some insane miracle something could destroy it, it would be gone and it would not come back. Still, even at the center of this blast, its breaking point was a long way off yet. God be praised.

Now Nixon had a larger problem than he'd originally planned. He knew he had to make it to the village, still some days southeast of here, but now it seemed that there was a rising issue in the same direction that had some form of weapon that could not only harm him but decimate him, rendering him useless and leaving the valued blade he carried unguarded for who knew how long.

It made him pause a moment as he considered his options. He wasn't useless without this sword, but it was still his bread-and-butter weapon of choice. He'd never thought he'd be without it, and he foolishly believed it would never be without him. Although it had never been proven to be true, Nixon knew that this weapon could do some very serious and perhaps lasting damage to him. He wasn't sure it could destroy him outright, but he couldn't say it couldn't either. Then where would the world be? One person would go too far down the dark path with the Power once again, and no one would be around to stop them. The world and all within its borders would be at their mercy.

One little sword. Well, one very large sword, but small in the grand scheme of things. Even Magnus hadn't considered the possibility of Nixon losing it somehow, but Magnus had never lived long enough to see what man hath wrought.

The sword slept silently, the power within it resting until Nix had need of it. "Lord, let this chase be a short one," he whispered to himself. "Per'aps my return t' rest would see me awaken in a better place."

He surveyed his surroundings. Black, hot, and steaming. Any mortal man would be killed instantly to stand where Nixon was now, the residual heat enough to melt steel and burn rock. For Nixon, though, it was a welcome feeling in what was quickly becoming an unwelcome world. He certainly would have to keep his eyes and ears open for another of those damn black orbs, but for now, there seemed to be none around.

After only a few minutes of walking on the glazed surface which had once been a dry, scrub desert, he came to a decision that he knew was wrong but seemed to him to be his best option. He would fly the rest of the way to the village. He hated to fly being so close. Previous times he'd done so, to save time or make it somewhere faster than his legs could carry him, he'd often overshot his target; his ethereal Power alerting any with the senses to detect him, telling them of his presence and intentions. Those who carried the blade and embraced the Power knew to beware of Nixon of the Great Fire and Ash, even if it was just subconsciously, and he'd been led on chases lasting years just to catch someone who had been alerted to him too soon.

His options seemed more limited this time. He risked further discovery by the scouts if he walked, and he could not guarantee he would always know they were there. Some aerial targeting laser could light him up before he even knew he'd been found. Not a welcoming possibility. Still, flying and using his gift from God could alert the prey to his presence, leading to an extended hunt in this mysterious and obviously dangerous time. Equally unappealing.

In the end, as was often the case in many situations, Nixon decided better the Devil he knew than risk further exposure to an enemy that could strike without being seen. He knew that somewhere there was someone who could help him. Even if his legions of followers and helpers had finally faded away, some things were constant. He could think of one or two people, defiers of time and Embracers of the Power, who may still be his friends. He hoped nothing had happened to them. One person in particular was almost certainly still around, regardless of Ryu's actions in the Third Fall of Man.

Love was one thing that could stand against even madness, be it centuries old or not.

He would set off for Tan Torna Qu-ay, see what he could see, and either be done with this whole damn thing (*Please God, let it be so!*) or see if the chase was on yet again, at which point he'd attempt to track her down.

He braced himself, focused his mind, and allowed the power and the fire to emerge from within. The heat built up as he focused deeper and deeper. At last, flames surrounded him, first wild and uncontrolled but eventually gathering form and substance around him. The flames settled behind him as giant wings. Fierce and beautiful in their perfection, they glowed hot and ready like the master they served.

Nixon knew this form well, and it only required one mighty push from the wings for him to take off like a shot, sparks trailing behind him as he went, glowing embers adrift in the fading night. Nothing but scorched earth and desolation remained as the sun began to rise in the east, signaling the beginning of a new day.

▸◂▸◂▸◂▸◂▸◂▸◂▸◂▸◂▸◂▸◂▸◂▸◂

Aryu awoke with a sick feeling as the sun began to rise. An unfortunate side effect of his repeated blows to the head the night before, he wagered.

He was impressed by how well his wings had kept him comfortable. He'd not felt a nip of cold that he could recall.

He unrolled himself slowly, knowing he was likely still wounded from the fall. He found his shoulder was still tender, and his cuts and scrapes still stung, but his legs and arms seemed no worse for wear and that was as good a result as any.

He slung his treasured find to his back, spreading his wings wide and inspecting them. "Not a scratch," he said aloud, grinning like a fool as he spoke. All that tossing through rock and thorn and not a rip or wound could be found. He gave them a few powerful test flaps to make sure all the mechanics were in working order. The motion upset his stomach more, and it did no favors for his questionable left shoulder, but otherwise, he seemed fine.

He salvaged what little he could, drank the last of the water he had carried, and attached the water skin to his side. With a slow run and then a rush off a nearby depression, he was back to the air, slowly gaining what height he could in the early morning updrafts to inspect his surroundings.

It was close to home. He knew the area he was in, near the north end of the Valley of Smoke. Not only had he made it closer than he believed possible, but he had actually overshot the Valley somewhat, heading back out into the open drylands that stretched out in both directions. Either Rider Stroan was off on his directions or Aryu was even faster in the air than he had thought. No matter the answer, the most important point was that he was only a half-day from home. An excellent result.

He circled around, looking northwest again, straining his eyes to see fire or destruction. Any sign that something big was brewing again. He couldn't see a thing; the horizon a thin wavy line in the distance south, and the peaks of the Great Range north. The morning was warm and clear, with no sign of the rains from the previous day.

He hoped Johan was alive and alright.

He still questioned the choice he made the night before to go on, but his faith in his best friend seemed to help reinforce his resolve to keep going home.

Aryu never really had time for faith. Beyond the natural feelings about his cruel physical jokes (though this morning they weren't quite as much of a burden as they were at this same time yesterday) he had simply never subscribed to the grandiose notions of divinity. The truth of God's existence was not in question. Even after so many thousands of years, His mark on the world was left quite effectively. It'd likely be another few millennia before such destruction was forgotten.

Where Aryu lost his faith was in the belief that God gave one fat damn about this land, this planet, or the people that dwelled on it. Since he was certain He did not (Correctly so, it should be noted. God no longer lived here, and as such, did not care about anything anymore), he felt it was a waste to believe in anything at all. Science was gone, the Power was gone. All that was, he saw, and that's what he believed in. Tactile feelings versus useless emotions.

Mankind is a fickle thing though. Some part of him still believed. Why else would a man born with wings have this chance to rush home when a man without would be days away and unable to help? The paradox, which has shaped mankind for ages, was still alive and well. As far as faith and divinity go, always keep your options open. Now more than ever Aryu knew the master plan for him in this world was far bigger than Tan Torna Qu-ay. He just had to find it.

Off he went, warm sun shining down as he flew. No thought but to get home entered his head, and he certainly had no reason to believe a beast of fire bore down on him, closing the distance quickly, with noble yet murderous intentions on its mind.

►◄►◄►◄►◄►◄►◄►◄►◄►◄►◄►◄►◄►◄

Aryu rushed through the Valley of Smoke as quickly as wind and wings allowed him. He was nearly home now, the day barely half done. He didn't stop or even slow down since he'd left that morning, and he was quite sure he wouldn't have to before he made it to his destination.

The creek bed was still lush and green on each side, springing up trees and bulrushes in small estuaries. He and Johan had grown up playing in these pools. After being away so long, the only feeling more prevalent than how much he missed it all was how much he wanted it to stay safe.

The valley walls were high on each side of him, closing in as he approached Tortria Den, a tight part of the valley where the walls became high and close together, leading to a drop-off into the more sprawling valley below. In times past it had been a great and powerful waterfall but now was just a unique rock formation with a small creek trickling through it, cascading down onto levels, and forming pools. It was a popular picnic destination for friends and families.

It was also the last major step to pass before the valley opened and widened, creating the nestled, lush home of the village of Tan Torna Qu-ay.

As the walls tightened about him, Aryu felt a rush of exhilaration at the thought that he was almost home. He gained as much momentum as he could before the walls and floor of the valley suddenly fell away and he was thrust out above the wider expanse of the Valley of Smoke below.

The horizon returned, and the sun beat down on everything he saw. The creek and valley floor stretched out straight ahead of him, bending to the right in the distance. Beyond that small bend was his goal.

Nose pointing down, wings collapsed back, Aryu began his dive to the new valley floor, a maneuver he'd mastered when he was younger. Moments from the ground he pulled up, using the speed he'd gained to glide fast and far along the tops of the small trees by the creek, bending in and out like a small bird chasing a fly for dinner.

He followed the turn to the right, and Tan Torna Qu-ay came into view.

He had remembered it being so small because he had so thoroughly explored each nook and cranny it possessed, but it was actually a decent-sized settlement of nearly twenty-five hundred people, spread from one side of the valley to the other and deep into the north and south. At its center, which Aryu could now clearly see, was a park with a swimming pond and areas for warm outdoor lunches and trees large enough to provide good shade. A rarity in this part of the world, which was so often dry and deserted.

Once he passed over the edge of the village, Aryu knew instantly that something was wrong. Where the outlying farms and folme herds had been was now filled by more buildings and people than Aryu remembered. The village didn't just look bigger; it was bigger, and now he saw why.

The parts of the northern border that he could see were filled with caravans and make-shift shanty settlements. He could see people milling about. As he looked to the east and west, he could see the sprawl continued in both directions, straight to the valley walls. Aryu figured there to be thousands of people gathered here, and he had no idea why.

It occurred to him they may have been caravans from the south that had stopped here on their journey north. The highway passed in the opposite direction from where he believed the Army of the Old to be, so it was a possibility, but from what he could tell these people were quite hunkered down and appeared to be in no rush to be on their way. A stark contrast from the caravan they had come across yesterday.

He passed over familiar homes, businesses, schools, and churches built to honor Gods both new and old. The village's center was where the hall of the town council was located. It was there he had to go, and he began winging his way to Longhold Park at the center of town.

When he was low enough, eyes began to turn skyward, spotting him against the blue.

Instantly, all hell broke loose.

Aryu had been raised here his whole life. People here had seen him and his wings grow. They shunned him but were not afraid by this time in his life. That was not the reaction he was receiving now.

Every man, woman, and child began pointing skyward, screaming and yelling as he passed by, terror on their faces. Many began running, either into their homes or following him as best they could. Soon, a crowd was following, running at top speeds to keep up with his pace. As he got closer, it looked like all the children had disappeared. Aryu scanned the group for his parents but couldn't see them. They lived on the other side of town and likely didn't see him coming.

Aryu was shocked by this reception. Even at this time of great uncertainty, he was sure that no one returning from their quest would be greeted like this. Aryu and Johan had concluded that this success would do little to change people's minds, but this was certainly not what he had expected.

Either running after him or running away, one thing was clear; these people, many of which he'd known all his life, were absolutely terrified at the man they now saw gliding over them, and suddenly

68

Aryu became terrified as well for reasons he could not explain. Something was more than wrong, and it was entirely to do with him.

He set down near the council building next to Longhold Park, letting his feet touch softly. The crowd that had been following him, shouting one thing or another, was still approaching. They tromped across the park, coming at him from all angles. Aryu didn't know which way to look first. Each was a face he'd known forever, now twisted in fear and rage, directed at him as they ran. As the crowd approached, he began deciphering words and phrases, none of which were encouraging.

"Get him out!" one shouted over the noise. "Don't let him be seen!"

"Why are you back?" said another. "Why would you do this to us?"

"Get rid of him!"

"We must hide before he's discovered! There's no time!"

Had torches and pitchforks been readily available, they would have likely all had one or the other in hand as they came.

Aryu was dumbfounded, not knowing what to make of the scene as it unfolded all around him. Without thinking, he took another panicked look around, inadvertently spreading his wings as he moved.

That was all it took to hold the mob in its tracks as they stumbled to come to a halt, tripping over one another. All he knew was that his wings were a trigger to something.

"Stop it, boy! For the sake of everyone, are you trying to get us killed?" said a familiar voice from behind him, a voice that had no right to call him 'boy'.

He turned, finding the face he didn't want to see, that of Esgona. Or, what was left of him.

Esgona was always brash and cocky, but popular in circles

beyond the realms of outsiders such as Aryu and Johan. A smooth talker from a young age, he also fancied himself a ladies' man thanks to his clean, curly hair, dark eyes, strong build, and handsome features.

That was certainly not the boy he saw now.

His face was badly scarred down his left side, from hairline to jaw, like he'd been dragged across broken glass. His left eye barely opened, and what eye Aryu could see was opaque. His hair was cut very short, with what appeared to be another large scar across his scalp on the right side. The clear limp he approached with served as notice that the rest of his body likely hadn't fared much better. His right eye was still good, though, and it was locked on Aryu like a dagger.

"You put those damn things away before we all suffer for your stupidity!"

Aryu turned quick, sweeping his wings around like fan blades, kicking up a stiff wind that had those in the inner circle shielding their eyes. Now was not the time for his tolerance of Esgona and his arrogance.

"You will address me properly, Esgona, before I get angry enough to *make* you!"

"And how would a fool like you be addressed, BOY!" He hobbled forward, his injury clearly making his life difficult, but doing nothing to stop his running mouth.

The crowd grew angrier, shouting in agreement with Esgona's words. Had Esgona gone on his quest, he should still be away. Esgona was still around when he and Johan had gone, and there was no way one would even return a day sooner than they should. Be it a day, a week, or a month, you never came back from your quest before you were supposed to. Dishonor and ridicule followed you and all your progeny if you did, just as it had Johan.

"Before I show you just how I *will* be addressed, you had better tell me what the hell is going on and why you *dare* treat me like this!"

Each word seemed to rile up Esgona even more, almost like Aryu was spitting in his face with each syllable. Esgona stared at him incredulously before making a motion towards him again, this time his intentions of expressing himself in a more physical nature were written across his face, bad leg or not.

Aryu was a much tougher man now than a year ago. He'd had many fights in that time. Stood against many foes. Won some and lost some, but learned something each time. He knew he could take Esgona at a whim, especially in his obviously weakened state. He had no desire to do so, though. All he wanted were answers, and a fight was no way to get them.

In a clean spiral motion, he pulled his wings tight around him and spun away just as Esgona had gotten within arm's reach, the crowd cheering and encouraging Esgona with every step and hobble he made. Aryu ducked back and tried to stop him, but Esgona was clearly enraged and came at him again.

Aryu drew the sword.

He had no intention of even touching Esgona with it, but in the state of madness and confusion he currently found himself in, with unfriendly faces all around him cheering on his old bully as he tried to fight a man clearly his superior, he had no other options. His wings could glide, but he couldn't just take off. They weren't strong enough for that. If drawing this sword and using it to keep the masses at bay was what he had to do, then so be it.

The sword came about and pointed directly at Esgona as he approached again, bringing him to a swift standstill. His eyes widened instantly as he looked at the blade. Silence from the crowd followed as every eye locked on in horror at the weapon. Aryu at last had their attention.

"Now before you do something very stupid," he began, "I believe we should first start with the meaning of your disrespect. I've gone too far and seen too much to be spit on by a whelp like you, Esgona."

Esgona, still staring at the blade, stuttered as he began to look up, meeting Aryu's eyes.

"You...you've got to be kidding," he answered. "You would seriously ask me that...me?"

"Yes, you and only you, Esgona. You seem to be the one out of all this madness who wants to talk with me the most, so here's your chance. I'm just laying the ground rules and making sure you listen." He nudged the blade tip closer to emphasize his point.

No answer came before someone in the crowd shouted again, "They're coming! Over by the council building, by the Gods, people, run!"

The screaming and madness resumed as people looked over to where the voice indicated. Aryu could see nothing in the chaos, and he opted to keep the sword fixed on Esgona, making sure he had no funny ideas while the masses dispersed. Esgona, to his credit, stood his ground and made no move this way or that. He only glanced around at the spectacle, trying to see the council steps. Aryu slowly followed his gaze, intent on finally seeing what the madness was all about.

Answers are like rain. Sometimes you get what you want, sometimes not enough to satisfy, and other times you can get a flood when all you wanted was a trickle.

Esgona's mother, Sia, head of the council of the village of Tan Torna Qu-ay, was coming down the stairs, watching Aryu hold her son at bay with a very impressive sword. Aryu barely saw her.

All Aryu saw was the robotic beast in the shape of a man that was lumbering after her like a grotesque motorized puppet, walking at her side as she approached the scene. Two blue lights where a man would have eyes spun about wildly, the centers locked on Aryu.

Aryu's sword dropped to his side as Esgona shied back away from the approaching monster as he did so. Aryu's mouth went dry as they came to him, the sound of gears and pulleys grinding to a halt until the machine stopped.

"Hello, Aryu O'Lung'Singh," it said in a voice so pleasantly human it made Aryu gasp as he fell to his knees, terrified beyond words. "I've been waiting for you, sir. I am the Herald, and I believe we have some rather important things to discuss."

▶◀▶◀▶◀▶◀▶◀▶◀▶◀▶◀▶◀▶◀▶◀▶◀

Nixon hid away in the shadows of an inn on the outskirts of the mob scene. He was wracking his brain trying to understand everything he'd just been witness to. There, not more than a stone's throw away, was the bearer of the sword. He could see it on his back the moment he landed. He could watch it clearly emerge from the sheath as the bearer drew it against the other man (*Or are they just lads?* he wondered. *They've not been out of infants' clothes for long.*).

He could see the perfection, power, and history of the blade, just as he could his own. Yet the owner did not turn to meet him. Even more interesting, the owner didn't seem to know he was there at all.

Through all the hunts and all the bearers of that sword, all of them had used its powers and their own to grow more dangerous than the world could handle. That was Nixon's purpose. If the darkness and evil intentions welled up enough in someone to have them be a danger to the natural order of things, Nixon awoke from his slumber, began his hunt, and tracked his prey to the ends of the earth until, should he meet them, the moment in time that was dedicated to their battle. If the bearer saw him coming, even if he didn't know about Nixon and his charge by name, he knew a fight was looming. They

73

could sense the power of the phoenix, knew it was against the path of their own, and began the battle until one fell.

Nixon, of course, had never fallen. Not until last night.

His abilities had always been the purer. That was his edge. A bearer of the sword always had great power but would never have had it long enough to grasp the level of mental understanding required to wield it. Even the false god often questioned if he had the Power fully under his command, and he'd been alive as long as Nixon.

Now, in this place, Nixon watched a young man, who had likely not even been in possession of the blade for long judging by the inefficiency with which he was using it, ignore him completely. The young man was focused on the argument he was currently engaged in with an obviously handicapped opponent, only to collapse at the sight of an old woman and mechanical man.

Nixon needed time to ponder all these things. Eons of life had never brought about such a scenario.

Jus' wait, he told himself. *I'm not beyond understandin'. I need more time t' know wha' is goin' on.*

He drifted deeper into the shadows, a thousand new possibilities dancing through his mind. Not one of them making the slightest bit of sense.

CHAPTER 6

The Cleansing Wind

The next few moments of Aryu's life were a blur of scattered images and feelings: mostly painful, largely fearful, and entirely negative.

Aryu remained on his knees as the machine came towards him. The sword was at his side but never fell from his grasp.

He wasn't aware of any crowd noise as some stood in horror and others ran for their lives, but his mind (somewhere in the back where unimportant things were stored) recognized that the shouts of anger and fear had begun again. The words were meaningless. There was only Aryu and this thing from another time and place. A thing that, as far as Aryu was concerned, was an incarnation of the Devil Himself. A bringer of the darkness. A messenger of the apocalypse. Machines and Embracers: these things were the enemy.

He could have deduced that the thing had been here a while, seeing as how the crowd did not react the same way as he did. Sure, they were scared, but scared enough to run or at least not be paralyzed at the sight of it. He could also surmise that it even went a step beyond that. Sia was escorting the beast the whole way from inside the village council building, where one may go so far as to say it was a welcomed guest. Aryu could also likely deduce that if he and his village were doomed to destruction, it would be so already.

These were all things a rational person could have put together very easily.

At this moment, Aryu was not rational. In fact, it's a safe assumption that at this moment, he was one step up from a feral child raised by animals in the deep wilderness. One who knows only three things: hunger, fear, and survival.

The spinning, glowing blue eyes remained locked on him, whirling about the solid cores at various speeds. The thing was much taller than Aryu, but was skinny and ridged, like a steel skeleton come to life. No face. Barely a head, really. Just eyes in a round, flat metal plate.

Was he really home?

What was happening?

....How?

The thing was almost in front of him, gears and servos grinding until it had bent down to what could be called a knee, meeting the terrorized man face-to-mock-face.

"I believe, Aryu, that I understand your reaction entirely." That voice! Gods, it was clear as a bell and twice as pleasant. It was surreal, like an educated teacher trying to get across a point to a child who won't listen. It was firm but understanding.

"Indeed, this whole village reacted the same way when I arrived. It took some..." a soft clicking somewhere inside its short, odd head, "...convincing, to have them understand that we mean no harm to them or you. We've been waiting for you, Aryu. You are very important to us."

It spoke the words clearly, with proper inflections and emphasis. If you closed your eyes, there was no way to tell it apart from a regular human voice. The creepiness grew more and more.

Aryu heard these perfectly formed and well-chosen words, but they may as well have been garbled and unintelligible for the amount he understood. Confusion and fear continued their waltz through his head, neither daring to take the lead.

Aryu remained where he was, trying to grasp the words the thing was saying, head cocked slightly like a dog, confusion written all over his face.

"As I expected, it will clearly take a moment for my words to sink in. But rest assured, Aryu, I speak the truth of things." Aryu's body tensed as the thing grew closer, but he remained silent. "Huh, well, not surprising, really." It let out a sigh, just like any other living, breathing, exasperated thing. "I believe you should come with us, Aryu. Ms. Sia and I both believe further discussion is warranted, but in a place a little less public."

The first of the rational thoughts to come rose in Aryu. Aryu tore his vision away from the monster and its intrusive eyes and found Sia, now standing with her son Esgona, eyes softly staring at nothing specific. She was no longer the woman whose bravado and saber-rattling had shaken so many council meetings. This was a woman beaten to the limits of her mental strength. Aryu began to doubt she'd heard a word the thing had said. Her face said she hadn't.

"You must forgive her current state, sir." *Sir?* "She is quite exhausted from the events of the last few weeks. Believe me, though. I speak for her, and I speak very clearly. We must adjourn to a more serene environment if we wish to continue. I believe the..." the clicking began again, "rabble, as it were, may cause us unnecessary distraction."

The background drone of the crowd that hadn't run in terror became louder and louder until at last Aryu heard it for what it was: terrified people screaming for this thing to leave and take the winged man with him.

Aryu's sense of survival was as keen as ever, and his most base instincts grew with every mental step he took back into the here and now.

He slunk back, away from the machine.

"Aryu, I am afraid I must insist on this matter." It began to match his movements, inching forward as he moved away. "My purpose here is far more important than your petty fears and useless questions."

With that, it began extending its arm, four grasping digits opening to grab Aryu.

When it was inches away, Aryu's most primal urges, coupled with a newfound sense of power, didn't let it get any closer.

He pulled back quickly, rising to his feet as he did so, his right arm grasping the light, straight sword like an old pro, twisting it around his body until it came between him and the nightmare before him.

"I believe I made my stance on this issue quite clear, sir." An edge of actual impatience inched into its pleasant voice. "There is no time for stupidity."

As it rose to meet him again, grasping claws again coming closer, Aryu's mind became clear as fallen snow. With one fluid motion of his wrist, the blade came across the lunging appendage, severing it like it was freshly baked bread right above its rotor-driven elbow. The scream of fear in the crowd was almost instantly drowned out by the inhuman noise that erupted from the machine. All hints of pleasantness were completely gone.

It was unlike anything Aryu had ever heard. Like an animal attacked by wolves, screaming for help or in pain, whichever instinct was stronger, but was then passed through some electronic megaphone.

The mechanical man staggered away, black and red fluid squirting out of the appendage that had moments ago had an arm attached. Now it flapped about like a giant chicken wing.

The claw on the ground still clutched and grabbed wildly, causing the rest of the arm to shudder back and forth like a fish. Soon it stopped as the fluid within ran out.

Esgona and his mother just stood there, terrified at what Aryu had done. The machine's scream ceased instantly as it got proper footing. Its head swung wildly, looking for Aryu like a top on a stick.

Aryu was in the same state as before, tense and ready for another attack. The story of its arrival no longer mattered. His fear was being overrun by adrenalin and the rush of what he'd just done. If he had cut through it so easily, he had all the faith in the world that he could overcome another assault.

The eyes, those crazy, unreal eyes, narrowed and locked in on Aryu's own. "You are as stubborn and useless as the rest of your kind, boy!" The voice was not calm but was certainly more human than that scream had been. "You WILL come with me, or I will burn this village to the ground, with or without you in it!"

Suddenly Aryu regained focus and remembered the blast from the night before. His left shoulder seemed to ache at the sudden remembrance. This thing was not lying. It had the power. He lowered the sword, keeping it at the ready. "I'm willing to guess I could cut you down before you had the chance to give the order."

"Perhaps that is true," Aryu could almost see the smirk on the featureless face, "but what about the army that follows me, Aryu O'Lung'Singh? I doubt you could stop every one of us. You must know by now we are coming, and it is only by luck and our good graces we haven't destroyed your home like we have everything else."

"I really doubt your graces are good."

"Huh, good and bad are simply a matter of perspective, fool. All it took was this brief conversation to give the order. This town now has five minutes until it is destroyed, and that's an order that can only be deactivated by me."

Aryu started to think it was a poor choice to antagonize this thing, his original fear returning as the situation played out.

"For the sake of the Gods, you idiot." Esgona came forward, hobbling as he now did. "Haven't you done enough? Look at this place! Look at its people! Look at *me*! You! It was all because of you. We surrendered to them to keep us alive, you had damn well better do what..."

Aryu laid him out on the ground with the most forceful and emotion-fueled punch he could muster. Now was not the time to tolerate Esgona and his juvenile bickering. As an established and proven man of Tan Torna Qu-ay, this boy had said enough. Besides, telling Esgona to shut up was obviously a useless gesture.

Sia yelped as he went down, rushing to his aid as blood began pouring from his mouth and onto the ground. She held his hand while looking up at Aryu. "Please, Aryu, do as it says; we're the only place that's safe. That's why there are so many others here; they know we're safe if we have you. That's all they wanted. You and only you can stop this!"

Tears filled her eyes. Her straight black hair, which had started neatly pulled back, was falling around her face. So much seemed to have happened here, and Aryu didn't even know where to begin. He just stared at the two of them.

"Four minutes, Aryu. Make the most of them." The chipper edge was returning to the thing's voice as it regained command of the situation. It made Aryu sick.

He looked back to the thing silently, studying it, still as horrifying and grotesque as the first time he saw it, but now loathing mixed with his fears. "Why me? Why am I so important?"

"Well, I believe that would have been explained had you allowed us to do so in the first place. As it stands now, you have less than three and a half minutes to agree and come with me. I will not waste any more time on this matter. My life, as it were, is very much expendable. Yours, and those of your fellow villagers, however..."

Things just seemed to be going from bad to worse. Aryu, filling more and more with contempt as he did so, sheathed the sword and rested his wings against himself. A beaten man. "Where am I going?"

"Away, that's all that is important right now. Three minutes left."

"I need to see my parents before we go."

Clicking started again in its head, longer than previous times. "Ah, Mr. and Mrs. Toma and Riva O'Lung'Singh. No, you may not see them."

Aryu's blood boiled. "You had better give me a good reason why, or I'll have...."

"They're gone, Aryu," said a quiet voice from below him. Sia was looking at him, sadness in her eyes. "They left the day after you and Johan. They never said anything to anyone. They simply vanished."

Aryu was lost to emotion once more. There was too much to process. Pure, raw egotism emanated from the mechanical man. "The loss of your parents was unexpected, Aryu. We wanted them alive. We had many questions for them about you. But we cannot locate them. I can confirm that they are no longer in this village, and as such, you no longer have a familial connection to this place. The choice sounds simple, and the clock is ticking. Come with me and we may still find them."

Aryu heard nothing past Sia's first words. Without thinking, without feeling, without a moment's thought to anything but the faces of his loving parents: the mustached face of his father or the wavy-haired gentleness of his beautiful mother. His first instinct was that it was lying, but that only made Aryu madder. His parents had sacrificed so much for him. They would not abandon him.

Blinding, unbridled rage surrounded him like fire. He ran screaming toward the metal giant, eyes burning with tears of pain and anger. Unlike the last time, the machine was ready for his assault, side-stepping quickly to avoid him, swinging its good arm across the back of his head with a sick "thud". Aryu was unconscious before he hit the ground, blood oozing from the back of his head.

"So predictable."

The thing approached him, looking him over top to bottom. "No permanent injuries detected. We were right. An angry Aryu with nothing to lose *was* easier to apprehend. All's well that ends well."

It bent down, grasping Aryu between the wings. With one almost graceful motion, Aryu was tossed over the thing's broad shoulder as it turned to leave.

"Wait! Is the attack called off?" Sia was helping Esgona to his feet as she called after it. "You said we'd be safe as long as we delivered you Aryu."

"And so you have. A deal is a deal. You were safe, he is delivered, and the deal is concluded. Thus, the attack will go ahead as planned."

"WHAT!" She ran at it, throwing herself in its path. "Aryu is yours now! Call off your attack! Thousands will die!" Sia suddenly realized how foolish she sounded. It was right. The deal was done.

"Ms. Sia, I never had the ability to call off the attack. Your naïveté is as delightful as it is pathetic. I believe you have less than two minutes left. Make the most of it."

A rumble started at its feet as a controlled burn began to erupt from its lower legs. In an instant, it had begun hovering, readying to leave. Sia jumped at it, throwing it off and causing it to spiral away, nearly losing its grip on Aryu as he dangled lifelessly with his wings flapping about.

"Now, Ms. Sia, this will not do." A quick rotation of its lower torso spun one of its legs around, the other pointing down to maintain its balance as it hovered there. The extended leg came across Sia's face, shearing off skin and muscle before the burn of the rocket ripped through whatever was left exposed. Sia was dead long before her body hit the ground.

Esgona, still woozy from Aryu's hit, could only whimper before falling himself, the situation catching up to him as he passed out from shock and terror.

"Now then boy, away we go." The feet came together again and began lifting it skyward once more.

It was still not to be. No sooner had it began its acceleration, it detected the movement from behind. Its head swiveled about just in time to see the blade of a very large, oddly colored man begin to rip through it, the blade moving through its hardened body just as easily as Aryu's had.

"N...N...Nix...Ix...Ixon..." was all it could get out before falling back to earth in two equal pieces.

▶◀▶◀▶◀▶◀▶◀▶◀▶◀▶◀▶◀▶◀▶◀▶◀▶◀

Nixon was content to just let the scenario play out as he saw it. Clearly, the sword-bearer was at the mercy of the robot before him and would be defeated shortly. Problem solved.

Nix had exquisite hearing, learning all he could from a great distance while still concealed in the shadows. The dispersed crowd made it that much easier to see and hear everything that was going on.

It was a simple decision to make. Hearing the plans unfold, he knew another of those freakishly strong bombs was on its way here, and as a maintainer of the natural balance, so many lives wasted was

83

heartbreaking even for one such as him.

Time makes all men (and non-men) realists, though. He knew the time he had left (thanks to the machine's convenient updates), and he knew there was nothing within his considerable power that he could do to help them. A sad truth, but the truth, nonetheless. The bomb was too powerful.

He could save one, or ten, or maybe twenty before it was too late, but one stupid glitch stopped him from doing even that. Should any one of those one, ten, or twenty be a difficulty he'd not anticipated, a foot dragger if you will, he could very well be at the mercy of that bomb blast again, in a place he knew hostiles to be. A risk he simply could not take.

He would weep for these people, but he could not save them.

The upside to this destruction was that his target would be destroyed as well. He clearly could not make it out before the blast hit, and should he leave with the mechanical man, he would be an easy target to track.

Ah, but the best-laid plans and all that.

It would have gone off perfectly, Nixon ready to leave, until he heard the conversation turn to the target's parents and their subsequent abandonment.

He had seen these sob stories many times before. The tragic upbringings that led to the heartless killer who wielded the Power and the blade-like toys. It seemed almost all of them he had faced would wax nostalgic about the terrible series of events that brought them to that point and how it made them justified in their choices and right to do what they had.

Nixon never cared. His purpose was absolute, his methods unwavering. No man was above God's law, no matter how hard the road they had traveled.

What caused him to pause was that this was clearly the moment the target, an apparently winged man (he'd seen winged people before, but never so far from their home) found out this information. That alone was more than he had expected to be a part of.

Nixon had always shown up late to these parties and had never been privy to such a heartbreaking scene. He had no parents, only parental figures, and even then he could not fathom the pain this young man had just been subjected to. If that pain didn't make him summon the Power, he clearly had none of the Power to summon.

Once again, that unrelenting feeling that this was not the way it was supposed to be was upon him. He had only brief instances to think out his next course of action.

He watched as the target rushed at the machine, only for the swift and nimble mechanical intruder to dance away. The extremely skilled blow to the back of head at just the right location had just the right power to knock him out with no serious damage. Still, the Power wasn't summoned in any way Nixon could feel.

He watched the lifeless body get hoisted onto the machine's shoulders. The woman attacked suddenly, and he flinched knowing what was coming next. Sure enough, she was dead moments later. Nixon couldn't stay inactive much longer, and the weapon was getting closer.

There was no more time to delay. No matter the series of events that had brought him here, this kind of ruthless and unjustified terrorism was not going to be tolerated. Nixon had always had some levity in his missions for such causes.

He paused, for just an instant, considering the consequences of the action he was about to take.

Was he really about to save the life of the target during this act of revenge against a merciless, unfeeling machine? Was this even the target? He had not embraced the Power, had no intentions to use whatever powers he did have at his moment of ultimate suffering (this was key, as Nixon knew such self-control to the possessors of the Power was unfathomably unlikely). He was still a boy, or barely a man. Nixon had rarely been called to dispatch a mortal man or woman, and when he had, they had been ages older than this.

It all added up to more confusion inside Nixon. He was utterly lost, devoid of direction.

Then, clarity. Purpose was purpose, even if that purpose was to be determined later.

The flame-infused broadsword was unsheathed, and Nixon moved as fast as lightning to the machine and its prize that was about to escape.

One swipe was all it took. The metal man slid apart effortlessly, crashing back to the ground with a horrible racket as it did so.

The notion of success was short-lived when Nixon swore beyond God's glory in Heaven that it said his name before it permanently shut down, cold and frenzied eyes blinking out like old light bulbs.

Nixon wasted no time in his retrieval of the limp body of the target, now his burden to bear on his heavily-armored shoulder. He turned to leave, knowing that time was quickly running out, when his mind held him back.

He remembered the other.

He had seen the boy pass out after being helped by the woman, who he now could only reasonably assume was his mother. He turned to find him a few steps away, breathing very shallowly, blood still dripping from his mouth from the punch.

He hesitated again. What was the point? Why save just that one more? The answer came to him as he stood there. This one was already out cold as well. No fuss. No feet dragging. He was there; his life could be saved, and that was enough. Nixon knew anger and remorse would come with him. The inevitable 'Why save me? Why not leave me to die with all the others?' moments were practically guaranteed. Nixon was a man of goodness, though, despite the ends he'd gone to at times. He could think of no logical reason NOT to save this boy. That was enough for him.

Logic. Huh. He almost sounded like Ryu.

He walked over, deftly swung the other up onto his free shoulder, braced both bodies, and summoned the fierce power within him.

It lit like dry wood to a spark, his mighty wings taking shape instantly. With a single, only slightly labored push, he and his two new charges were off like a shot while the park below emptied.

"Even in death, God has a plan," he said in part to break the silence, in part as a prayer.

◄►◄►◄►◄►◄►◄►◄►◄►◄►◄►◄►◄►◄►

Had it lived (as it were) to see the moment of impact, the mechanical man who had been sent before Aryu's arrival for the expressed purpose of obtaining and securing the winged man for a return to his superiors, he would have had no joy in knowing that the bomb would have arrived precisely .000237 seconds after it had predicted. It would have been enough for him to request a full upgrade upon return.

Instead, its non-functioning body was simply obliterated like all the other people, places, and things of Tan Torna Qu-ay.

To any one human who may have been paying attention, the impact arrived with pinpoint precision.

Impact is a poor choice of words. From launch to target, the ordinance never had any intention of hitting the ground. Indeed, should it have, it likely would be considered a dud or failure.

A weapon such as this one can do multiple times more damage if it detonates above the blast target. The resulting explosion and concussion wave then instantly fires downward, hitting the ground like a spring, firing back up and using its cumulative force to feed the explosion that is heading outwards from the epicenter, creating a far more powerful explosion than one that had just hit the ground. It was far more efficient and destructive to have it done this way.

No one in the village had any idea what was about to happen. There was no whistle or hum as it approached. Most of the citizens had become aware of Aryu's return and feared a moment like this was about to happen anyway, so the majority of the population was seeking some form of futile refuge. They'd never seen the distant explosions, had no idea the destruction they had caused, had no way of knowing that their village was far too small for anything to escape complete incineration.

It was much better that way.

Nixon had made it well past Tortria Den and its high cliff walls by then, counting on the solid rock barrier to act as a buffer against the coming blast. Although it caused an amazing amount of turbulence and unsteadiness for a moment, his considerable power and strength were able to compensate. His flight returned to normal and he continued on his way, determined to make it much farther away before any robotic scouts or reinforcements were able to survey the damage.

The village was quiet when it hit, most inhabitants either cowering or somehow oblivious. A blast of this power and magnitude would create a shockwave so strong that force and fire would hit you long before you even knew there was a problem.

Yet again, it was better this way.

The village center, starting in Longhold Park, was heaved up into a ball of dust and fire in an ever-expanding circle, disintegrating each thing it met along the way. Things in the way did not burn. They never had the time. They were quickly and effortlessly wiped away, no trace of them ever being known. All that was left was a hole in the ground that was left shiny from the instantaneous transformation of rock to glass.

Homes were blown off their foundations milliseconds before the flames devoured them and anything inside them.

Five seconds after the blast began, a man and his young son, who had come with one of the caravans from the deep south when the ships first arrived on the horizon and were seeking the rumored solace of Tan Torna Qu-ay, were out hunting between the rise that was Tortria Den and the village outskirts. They were the only citizens of the village to recognize what they were seeing before it hit them.

The father instantly grabbed his son, hugged him close, and turned as much as he could in that time away from the blast, desperately trying to shield his child from the coming horror.

His was not the only desperate act of heroism to come from this place, but it was to be the last.

In the end, it was equally as useless a gesture as the others. They were still consumed and vaporized by the storm of Hellfire that had approached them. Neither felt pain. Death was swift and merciful.

Such was the case for all who lived and loved in the village of Tan Torna Qu-ay.

May we all be so lucky.

⋈⋈⋈⋈⋈⋈⋈⋈⋈⋈⋈⋈⋈⋈⋈⋈⋈⋈⋈⋈⋈

As promised, Nixon wept many tears for those who had died so needlessly just moments before. It was likely he was the most singularly powerful being in the world since the destruction of the false god, and even he stood no chance against this new power.

He'd seen the weapons of the old days. Their power and their weaknesses. They could perhaps put a cramp in his day, but not outright defeat him the way these could.

Now he was winging away as fast as he possibly could, carrying a man he was sworn to destroy and another whom he had no invested interest in.

Each new day brought more questions than answers. All he could do was hope he could find someone to help put it all together. That was why he knew his next step was to find Crystal, the true love of the false god, former bearer of the sword now in the possession of the unconscious person slung about his shoulder, and the one person alive who knew as much about the history of it and its holders as he did.

He had no way to know if she was still alive. So much time had passed. However, there weren't a lot of options open to him right now. He would take the sword-bearer to her, leave the other to his own devices somewhere down the line, and try to find out all he could.

It was terrible to be so alone, worse to know he was trapped there. There would be no sleep until his mission was fulfilled. Judging by his current whereabouts and predicament, it was clear that was not going to be as smooth as it had been in the past.

Nixon shed his tears and carried on.

CHAPTER 7

The Benevolent Rotations

He wasn't stupid.

He wasn't naïve or foolish.

He wasn't optimistic.

He was a man now, and men know better. Perhaps not in all things, but certainly more than when last he was at this place. This road both to and from his home that no longer existed. A home he saw destroyed before he could say 'Goodbye'.

He was not about to run in a desperate search for survivors, knowing full-well that a blast like that would leave none.

One more day. He only needed one more day. Loved or hated, his family was waiting with open arms and the honor he deserved. Welcoming and proud. He'd have died with them.

Johan found a quiet space among a small thatch of trees and sat, broken-hearted and alone. No man or woman of any age could ever be expected to hold it together in such circumstances. It's simply too much weight to put on someone's shoulders.

The strength he had built was easily defeated. The things he'd learned, forgotten.

Where once a man stood, there was now a helpless child.

See him now. See him in this moment of abandonment and unspeakable fear. Imagine your feelings upon witnessing what he witnessed. Think deeply. Feel the heat. See the flames. Recognize his moment as if it were your own.

Every loved one's face. Every park and tree. Every summer meal or winter rain. Gone. Taken away without reason or mercy.

Know now that this is not a moment documented often. The factors that lead us all to this moment are never so terrifying and blatant. They are almost always organic and prolonged. The experiences of the youth make the strengths of the adult. Rarely is it so obvious at the time. Memory makes the moment brighter and more significant.

For Johan, it will be so unlike any other.

He didn't need years to know the truth of the moment. He didn't need time to recognize the obvious.

This is his moment. Not the last day. Not the last year (although both did help greatly).

He is a child now, a boy regressed into the past, just as the last year had pulled him into the future. For every tear shed by Nixon as he carried off on a far northern breeze, Johan cried ten and then ten more. It was his home. They were his family. It is his right.

When the screams became whispers, the eyes ran dry and the unrelenting sadness became something more akin to unbridled rage; the afternoon had long passed, the moon was up again, and the evening was quiet.

There would be no scouts this night, although they were around. No clicking orbs or mechanical sentries.

Not tonight.

Something in his pain and loss transcended the space he lived in.

It caused the world to recognize his situation and tilt its axis just enough to spin whatever trouble there was nearby away and avoid him.

There was no fire. There was no need. All feelings of hot and cold were lost to him. There would be no sleep, as sleep was apt to bring about that moment of wakefulness that recalls something that has happened without focusing on what it was. Such a momentary lapse and eventual realization was too much to endure again. He wanted to remember it all. To even forget for a second was an act beyond disrespect.

He would not sleep. He would not eat. Yet the world, in its infinite mercy, would continue to tilt and bend in such ways as to spare him the exhaustion and hunger he would have felt. The new day would see him strong and ready as if he'd slept for thousands of years and ate until the world ran empty.

The morning would see him for who he would be forevermore.

Two men. Brothers in arms against all the evils Hell saw fit to release on them. Now, one was likely dead.

He would carry only what he needed. Remember only what he must. Go to where he could do the most good and inflict the most damage. But now, the night must simply carry on. He could not slow time. He wouldn't even if he could. The farther from that moment, no matter how significant it was to the great and powerful man he would be, the better.

The Army of the Old were close now. The destruction they wrought was in the palm of his hand. There would be no mercy. There would be no draw. There will be no quarter given and none received.

But first, the night must come to allow the day ahead to follow.

Sitting in the wake of his suffering, Johan had only the faintest idea that it was all true. That small, powerful idea drove him forward and forced him to endure the pain.

He would endure. He must. For Tan Torna Qu-ay.

⊢⊢⊢⊢⊢⊢⊢⊢⊢⊢⊢⊢⊢⊢⊢⊢⊢⊢⊢⊢⊢⊢⊢⊢⊢

Nixon could have very well carried on forever, winging his way to wherever it was he was able to go, but the larger one stirred. The one he was created and sworn to kill. He opted to touch down and let the inevitable flurry of useless questions and monumental arguments begin. The moment had to come eventually; it may as well be now, in the dark and stillness of the aftermath.

He went to the foothills of the Great Range before turning east and following the line the majestic rock towers created. If Crystal was still alive, it was a safe assumption that she would be in the same place as always, so that's the direction Nixon turned.

He touched down in an open patch. The ground was a mix of grass, jutting rocks, and mossy surfaces. Not the most welcoming place to talk, but the sword-bearer wasn't worthy of nice places in Nix's mind.

He placed the lucky one down first, sure to make him as comfortable as possible. Judging by his breathing, it may be a while until he came around. It appeared his brain would require a little more time to reboot itself after all that had happened.

The other was a different story. He walked across the open space and set him down against a rock, back to a closed-in space to limit his chances to escape.

Nixon hadn't understood much of what had happened to him since he'd awoken, but what he did know was that this was the sword-bearer, and young and inexperienced or not, he would not give him an inch until he had more information. Just because it appeared one way rarely made it so. Centuries of this hunt had made him far more suspicious of every situation as far as the target was concerned.

Once down, wings pinned beneath him, Nixon went the final step and removed the sword from his back. Nixon had no desire to keep it, his being just as powerful. He wanted it to give himself that much more of an advantage should things go south. He then walked back to the first boy, sat down on a small rock ledge, and waited as the other awoke.

The start of the groaning and twitching meant he would not have to wait long.

He removed his sword from the sheath softly, careful not to make any sudden movements. Held at the ready before him, Nixon took a deep breath and prepared himself for yet another situation he was completely unfamiliar with.

▸◂▸◂▸◂▸◂▸◂▸◂▸◂▸◂▸◂▸◂▸◂▸◂

Before there was anything else, there was pain. Deep pain unlike any he'd ever felt before. His ears rang, his eyes blurred, and his teeth ached. Also, he seemed to have fallen in a very uncomfortable position; twisted against a rock, pinning his wings beneath him.

Aryu felt like shit.

It was his head that hurt the most, like it was caught between the hammer and the anvil. Each heartbeat was agony, and they were plentiful.

It all rushed back to him in flashes: the arrival at Tan Torna Quay, the angry crowd, Esgona, the machine-man and Sia, the abandonment of...of...

... Of his parents...

He remembered it all now, right up to the blinding rage that consumed him as he attacked the mechanical thing.

Dear God, were they really gone? Sia seemed too defeated to lie. Even now in the murky aftermath in his head, he remembered its annoying smugness and pleasant demeanor. Just the thought made him sick.

Had he been out long? Where was he? Had the beast taken him? Was he dead? How did he make the pain go away?

He propped himself up, trying to adjust his eyes before he realized that it was dark out. He made out what he could. He was on a rocky landing. Why? Where was the village? Had the thing destroyed it as promised?

He placed a foot underneath himself and started to rise very slowly, each strain making his throbbing head that much worse. At last, he gingerly made it to his feet. It was then he saw the crumpled body of someone across from him. He couldn't be sure, but it looked like Esgona as his eyes adjusted to the light.

Then he saw it.

It could have been a man, but it was like no man he'd ever seen. Even sitting he was huge. His eyes glowed like fire and his long hair shimmered red in the dark. It looked like black emptiness filled where clothes should be, causing his head and extremities to almost float in the poor light.

In his hands held before him was the largest sword Aryu had ever seen. He quickly became aware of his treasure being missing and the defenseless position he was suddenly in.

"Easy, lad," the man-thing said softly. "I'd take a seat and relax a moment if I were you."

The stranger spoke with an accent completely foreign to him. He caught the meaning of it, though. He fumbled back and found the outcrop he'd been propped up against, coming down on it with a force that seemed like tons.

"There's a good, lad. I can only wager how much tha' noggin's hurtin' right now."

Noggin? Aryu assumed that was his head and nodded slightly.

"What happened to the village?" he croaked out. "And my parents?" He became aware of the sensation of what he could only assume was blood trickling down the back of his neck. He then remembered the blow that felled him.

"Well, I'm sorry t' say tha' yer mechanical friend was speakin' the truth about his threat."

Aryu thought it over, trying to remember the conversation. "So it's gone? They're gone?"

He saw the nod as the glowing hair moved up and down, the burning eyes never losing their grip on him.

"I over'eard about yer missin' parents as well. I'm sorry for yer family."

Who was this thing, and why did he seem to care at all?

"So it's true? About my parents?" No answer right away, as if the thing was studying him.

"I can'na say, lad. I only arrived in time t' see wha' happened t' ya"

Aryu couldn't believe what he was hearing. After a moment of confusion, he looked around, suddenly overwhelmed by a need to see for himself if it was true. "Where are we?"

"A week's walk from your 'ome tha' was. Due east."

"Dear Gods, have I been out that long?"

Aryu could hear the grin in the thing's words. "Who said we walked? No, lad. We arrived by other means."

Aryu was getting even more lost in pain and confusion. His head hung low between his hands trying to sort things out. Loss consumed him as visions of his parents flashed into his head. They were good people who only wanted the best for their son. A loving husband and wife who had risked everything to save their son. Why did they leave him and Tan Torna Qu-ay without a word? The tears began.

"I hate t' be a nuisance, but I'm afraid I mus' ask about the sword. Specifically 'ow ya came t' possess it?"

Aryu couldn't believe this. The sword? The stupid sword? After all that he'd been through, *that* was what seemed important? Who cared! Aryu just sat there, ignoring the question. His problems were so much larger than that.

The man-thing rose and closed the gap between them, his sword still in front of him pointing at Aryu as he moved, stopping inches from his head.

"I've no problem dispatching ya here and now, lad. Frankly, it would make my life tha' much easier. But I'm afraid I need more from ya before we reach tha' end, so I'm askin' ya for the last time. The sword. Where did ya' get it?"

Aryu cried on in pain and waved it off at first, but looking up into those glowing eyes he saw the truth. This thing *would* kill him. Today was not the day for any more tragedies.

"I found it," he said finally. "A few days ago, I guess." He had a hard time remembering now. He assumed it was still the same day as he thought it was; the day Tan Torna Qu-ay was destroyed. "I found it buried in rock on a mountainside. Why does it matter?"

His voice escalated and the anger caused his head to ache anew. The man seemed to be thinking over what he'd just been told. The seconds passed by with Aryu's anger growing with each one.

"Tell me, lad, do ya…"

"Listen, who or whatever you are. I just spent a year away from home proving my manhood. I've also spent the days suffering the most extreme lows a man can reach. You say my home is destroyed and my parents are gone. By this point, you had damn well better believe I'm no lad, and you had better treat me as such."

The big man seemed taken aback, almost as if the words had

struck a chord. Then he smiled, and almost instantly Aryu was relaxed. Something about that smile was so reassuring. Despite everything that had just happened in the last few days, Aryu felt a small ounce of peace again.

"Indeed, sir. Indeed. My apologies. It's safe t' say Imma' man outta' place here. I beg yer pardon. If by yer ways yer a proven man, then I shall treat ya as no less.

"Now, again, I must know, and speak no lie t' me, sir. Is wha' ya say tha whole truth? Ya simply found it?"

Aryu nodded slightly, tears still flowing freely. "Yes, that is the truth. If we are a week west by foot as you claim, then we are just over that far from the mountain. It was our final night before setting off home." Recognition dawned on the thing's face as if Aryu had confirmed a suspicion he'd had. Aryu barely noticed it.

Our. He had said *our*. The thought of Johan came to him instantly. He was likely still out there, either going home or wherever. He had to get back to him to let him know what had happened and that he was alive. Surely Johan saw the explosion, but the truth of why had to be told. Machines had come to the village, which meant that they were already coming into the central Inja. They were all in danger.

"I need to find my friend."

The man looked at him, lost in thought once more. "Friend?"

"A man like myself. We set off on our quests together. I was sent on ahead by air. I need to find him. I need to know that he's alright."

The man seemed unaffected by Aryu's plight. "Not yet. As odd as it sounds, I need ya with me right now. I believe ya hold some answers tha' I need."

Aryu was up again, head and body be damned. "Now I don't know who or what you are, but my place is with my friend, and if you don't take me there, I'll go on my own. I've told you everything I know about the sword, now please give it back and let me go on my way."

The man shook his head calmly. "I can'na do tha'. I need ye and this sword with me."

"Forget the damn sword. Keep it, I don't care." A lie. After only two days he was already irrevocably attached to it for reasons he could not explain, but he hoped his lie wasn't detected. He hoped his tear-soaked face hid it well. "I don't need it. What I do need is my friend, and you are not going to stop me."

Aryu didn't know what kind of shape he was in but knew it was as good a time as any to find out, stretching his wings out with a minimum of trouble as he began to leave, hoping to find somewhere to take off from. "I do thank you for saving me, sir, but I'm afraid I cannot do as you ask. I have my own way to go."

Before he could begin to leave, the large man rose to his feet and lifted his sword to Aryu's face. "I'm afraid I must insist. Ya got more important things t' do now."

"So you say. My way is west and to my friend." He turned to leave with a quick wave over his shoulder, telling the other this conversation was finished. He needed Johan. He needed to see if the machine was true to its word.

It was then he felt the heat and saw the light grow behind him. He turned quickly and was blinded by two very large walls of fire protruding from the other's back, almost like....

...like wings. Son of a bitch. He had wings, and not ones like his own. This man was something so much more. Dear Lords and Ladies, he was an Embracer! After all this time of peace and silence, why was Aryu suddenly inundated by a mechanical Army of the Old AND a practitioner of the forbidden ways? Eyes wide and heart racing, Aryu stepped back and slumped down onto his rock again. It was all way too much. The tears became sobs as the weight of it all pressed harder.

The man's wings died down, shrinking in brightness and intensity until they were no more.

"Ya canna' escape me, and I highly recommend ya don't try. My path is tha correct one, and I insist ya follow me on it."

"Who… who are you? Why me?"

"Well now, finally some logical questions." The big man relaxed and sat back down, sword resting in his hands. "My name is Nixon. Nixon of the Great Fire and Ash, t' be precise, but most jus' call me Nix.

"The history behind my bein' here is more stories than I care t' tell at this moment. Know this, though. I am and 'ave forever been, drawn t' the bearer of tha' sword and 'ave hunted 'em since long before ya could imagine."

"Are you an Embracer?" Aryu spat out between gasps.

A confused look on Nix's face. "Of the Power? Ha! Not in tha slightest. Those are mostly fools and tha fools who follow 'em. No, I'm somethin' more'n tha' entirely. My power is God's power, as it was He who gave it t' me."

"God's power?" The sobbing slowly crept away as the conversations steadied him. "Lord Ryu gave you Power?"

"Wrong again. Not him. Ne'er him."

"Good. Then I'd know you were lying."

Nixon looked perplexed suddenly. "And why do ya say tha', may I ask? Tha' was a very real man with very real abilities."

"With very real lies," Aryu answered while sniffling heavily and with more than a dose of cynicism in his response. "Most around here disagree, but I've never once believed in him as any more than a very powerful man. Only a man could have done something so reckless and self-centered."

"Ah, so ya know of his final days, then?"

"Yes. It's jammed down our throats from birth. He was denied his eternal rest and punished the world and those hungry for power, with no discrimination in his anger. Embracers of the Power at the time were all killed. None were spared. Such a clear overreaction could only be the work of a man, not God." Aryu hated that story, but he hated the people who worshiped the God Ryu even more. One who had not spent their life shunned, mocked, and generally hated likely would have been more receptive to the moral of the man and not the action he had taken.

Nixon's smile returned in full force. "I admit ye're a little hazy on the details, but tha bottom line is tha same. You're correct, and it truly warms m' heart t' hear ya say it. I'm glad t' know tha poison of 'is words is slowly bein' purged."

"Most people believe his to be the ultimate power, his story being one of warning and not foolishness." Aryu tried remembering more details to the story, but his head was still murky, and they didn't come quickly. "You say you are granted the power of God, yet claim it wasn't him?"

"No, sir. Not at all. I'll not bore ya with preachiness, but I serve the one true Lord, He who reigned long before tha one ya speak of, and with considerably more mercy. He is whom I serve, and will forever, despite his essence being gone from this place fer so long." Nixon seemed to sadden slightly with these words, as if they were difficult for him to say. As his smile slipped away, so did Aryu's brief respite of peace as the visions of a machine murdering his parents rushed back. The tears still came but the sobbing ceased, so he opted for a change of topic.

"You'll forgive me if my interest is elsewhere right now, but I'd like to know why that sword is so much more important than me finding my friend."

Although his eyes didn't brighten any, his soft smile did return. It seemed to Aryu that he was thankful for a change of topic as well.

"Well now, that's a very long story indeed. Suffice t' say it'd take much too long t' regale ya with it here and now."

"Listen Nixon, my eyes are red with tears and revenge, and I need to see my best friend alive again. My hatred is just enough to make me consider running and taking my chances against whatever you are. All I'd like to know is what's so important that you'd save me, just to torment me now."

Nixon seemed to agree to the logic. "Ya make a strong point, sir."

"Aryu."

Nixon faltered. "I'm… I'm sorry, wha'?"

"Aryu. Aryu O'Lung'Singh. It's my name, as opposed to 'sir'."

Nixon looked astonished, an expression Aryu could read even in the poor light. "Ye've got to be kiddin' me! Aryu? Aryu O'*lung*'Singh? Ya canna' be serious."

Aryu didn't know what to say. His parents had told him that where they came from it was a perfectly normal name, although he was the only one he'd ever know with it. "What's your issue with it?"

"Well, it all but confirms my original assumption about ya, that's all."

"And what assumption is that, Nixon?" Now *there* was an odd name.

"My assumption tha' I'm supposed t' kill ya, and do it very quickly, Aryu O'Lung'Singh."

Aryu was still alive. That was something he was certain of. But his words were so precise. So purposeful. He knew that this man-thing across from him was not lying.

Aryu was still breathing. His head was still aching. His family was still gone. "Why? Why save me only to kill me?"

"Believe me, I wish I knew." Something very large was tormenting Nixon. "I'll put this as simple as I can, and if after I tell ya, ye still feel the urge t' pester me further on it, I'll gladly do wha'

103

I'm supposed to, make no doubts about tha'."

Aryu understood. Embracer or not, he was still associated with the Power and needed a wide berth.

The large man rose and pointed to the ground partway between the two. With a 'SNAP' and a bright flash, a bolt of fire shot from his hand like a bullet from a gun. Aryu wobbled back on his rock, shielding his eyes for a moment as he did so. Looking back, he saw a crackling fire now between them, but he could see no wood or kindling. Simply a hearty fire burning on nothing more than a bed of rock. The light it gave off illuminated them both, adding to Nixon's terrifying and powerful appearance. He then took his seat again.

"I want ya t' see me and hear me true as day, Aryu. Do ya promise?"

Not a doubt in his mind. "I promise."

"Good, because I have many, many reservations about telling ya any of it and not just cutting ye down right here. Do ya believe tha'?"

"I do."

"Alright then. Listen. Cry yer tears until they run dry. Mourn. I know ya want t' see yer friend. I know ye are trapped with a man sworn to kill ya. I know how difficult this story will be t' believe and understand, but I am not a man prone t' lyin'. It is all true. Agreed?"

"Yes."

"Good, now listen and listen well. What year is this, Aryu?"

An odd question to start, but a simple one. "It's the one hundred and thirty third year of the second cycle."

Nixon looked confused. "Alright, um, poor start. 'Ow many years inna' cycle?"

Aryu was amused by the flustering of his would-be executioner. "One thousand. A thousand years is considered a full cycle of human existence."

Nixon smiled with pleasure. "Oh really now. I was unaware tha' such a thing was measurable. Tell me, then; how ever did someone arrive at such a fine number? What was year zero? Surely ya must know tha' mankind has been around much longer than tha'."

"Yes, we know, but year zero was the year Ryu purged the Power from this land and cast the remaining humans back to a state of primitives."

"Ah, well, is tha' how long it's been? Well, see, ye've already given me more than I had.

"Alright, so it's been one thousand, one 'undred, and thirty-three years since then, is tha' correct?"

"Yes, that's right."

"Alright then, lemmie do a wee bit'o math 'ere." He looked as if he was trying to put together a puzzle from Aryu's perspective. "I'm almost five times tha' age, t' give ya an idea."

"If that's so, how did you escape the wrath of the false god?"

"Well, tha's also a long story, but tha short version might be tha' I was asleep. Know this: his powers didn't completely wipe tha slate clean. Many lived. Also, as I said, I dunna' embrace the Power as ya know it. My abilities are Divine.

"My sleep lasts as long as it must, be it a day or a thousand years. My purpose, the reason for my creation, is t' balance the Power in tha world. Good and Righteous are strong, and those who follow those paths become lit'le more than hermits and prophets. Still, they cause no 'arm, 'elp all they can and believe their causes t' be more spiritual in nature.

"Evil... No, that's a poor word. Let's say malcontent Embracers of tha Power are who are n' bound by strong moral code are my business. Often, one of tha 'good' meets their end at tha 'ands of one of tha 'bad'. In a usual mortal lifespan, it 'appens all tha time. Over eternity, it 'as a lasting effect. When it gets t' outta' 'and, I awake, track tha most powerful of these 'malcontent' and dispatch 'em before they shift the balance t' far t' be repaired. They upset the balance an' I keep it. There is no good and evil. It's always strictly a matter of perspective."

Words Aryu had heard not long ago. "And the sword?"

"Well, tha's an easy one. For as long as I can remember, tha individual I've 'ad t' dispatch has 'ad it in their possession. Rare is tha bearer of tha' blade who dunna' follow tha unrighteous path."

"But there are those who do? People who've held this sword and done good things?"

"Well, first ya must remember tha' good is relative. Of all tha people who I've seen with it, only a small handful believed their cause t' be evil fer tha sake of evil. Most were just seekers of power who went t' far. Likely good people, at least on some level. It's their actions I punish, not their intentions."

"That's unfair. What if they want to change? What if they are savable? What if you've killed many who could have done greater things than the crimes they've committed?"

A thought Nixon was plagued by every waking hour. "I'm not judge or jury t' these people and their actions. I am and shall always be n' more than God's right hand in these affairs. The simple answer is this: if ya follow tha right path, I will remain asleep. If ya don't, then I will sleep only as long as it takes for ye t' go too far. I awaken, speak with my followers and search for any information t' assist me. I begin my 'unt and tha moment I finally arrive to ya is, as ordained by God who made me, tha moment ya pay for yer actions. If I e'er doubted this as the truth, I'd doubt the word of my Holy Father 'Imself. Tha' is something I will ne'er do, so I hunt, I kill. I am tha vessel of His retribution!"

Nixon was getting fired up now. The emotion with which he explained it held Aryu in awe, his mind removed, albeit briefly, from his current pain and plight. Something in the way he told it filled

Aryu with wonder.

But then, there was always the obvious question that needed asking.

"Why me? I just found the sword. I've only just become a man. I've embraced no Power, and more to the point, I'm terrified by it. I've caused no harm, and I've killed no one, though I really want to. Yet here I am with the sword, and here are you, an old god's holy executioner, sent to kill me. Why?"

"I dunna' know, sir. I truly dunna' know. This time is different. This time everything 'as changed. I have no followers t' answer my questions. I 'ave no signs t' follow or information t' collect. I woke alone, only my sword by my side. If I'm awake, the Power is outta balance and I must right it. I am in tune with the strengths all possess. I can sense its ebbs and flows. By tha', I can track it. It brought me 'ere. It brought me t' ya."

"How do you know it's me you're supposed to track?"

"Simple. Ya 'ave tha sword. Tha sword tha' 'as been buried for thousands of years. I was awake while it was buried only once, and tha' one time has been tha only exception to these rules I've ever seen."

"And when was that exception? When were you last awake?"

"I was here right after tha Third Fall O' Man. I awoke t' kill the false god, whose powers were always far beyond need o' the sword. I am limited by time and distance though, and he embraced maliciousness so quickly I could'na reach'im in time. The Power was purged and mankind brought t' its knees before I'd even sat up from my slumber. It was all I could do t' survey tha aftermath, weep for the innocents who'd fallen, confirm the loss of the false god and 'is sword and return to my sleep."

Nixon began telling this mesmerized young man minor details of his history, and each time Aryu had to agree death was the most necessary course of action to reach the ends Nixon was bound to if these tales were true. After twenty minutes, Aryu wondered more and more why this Hangman of the Lord was letting him live to hear them.

Were he to enter the head of this Heavenly Avenger, he'd see that that was the exact same thought in his head as well, with the simple exception of the one powerful, overlying fact.

This time was different. This time nothing was as it should be. The world had changed, moved beyond what was considered normal for so many years. This simple fact seemed to break every barrier Nixon had. The routine was broken, the patterns shuffled. It now went beyond a need for answers. In this conversation, Nixon had convinced himself that although he may find some, a satisfactory one would not arrive.

By the time the talking was finished (or at least, all the important parts, as full stories of all Nixon's past and targets would likely have gone on forever), Aryu was certain that despite his certainty on the matter, Nixon had all but talked himself out of killing the young man, and Aryu was not about to remind him of his pledge. Not after all those stories. Not after all he knew now.

All for the luck of finding that one little sword amidst the rubble. Nixon informed him that he could not recall a time anyone had happened upon it simply by accident, and although he wasn't about to call this the first time, he certainly couldn't dismiss the option. For all either of them could see, that was all it was. Aryu was not powerful or worldly, and beyond his obvious difference (which he was not self-conscious about at all while with this man), he was just a young man only beginning his path in life. His direction could not be determined yet. His intentions were not, as Nixon had said, worth punishing.

"So do you doubt your God's intentions now?" Aryu regretted

saying it the moment it slipped from his lips. He hadn't reminded him of his task outright, but he had just stepped into the next best thing.

Nixon lost his radiant smile. The darkness consumed them both as the baseless fire died down, seemingly tied to the emotions Nixon suddenly found himself entrenched in.

"No. Ne'er tha' far, but I do doubt His ability t' predict and command the powers tha' control me so long after his leavin' this world. Just t' say tha' may be considered blasphemy by some I knew, but I am afraid tha' while I have always considered his power beyond great, it was not so great tha' it was infinite and everlasting in his absence. He drew power and strength from the world and tha people tha' inhabited it. Even gone, His strength was eternal as long as the faith remained. When the false god purged tha power and the eternal peoples tha' possessed it, in one swoop he abolished what remained of any great belief in Him. It's a sad fact, actually, as it was the false god who cast him away, essentially destroying him in the first place. It is only bitterly fittin' tha' he cast the final blow. Thousands of years dunna' make rememberin' easy. Quite the contrary, it blooms new myths and misinformation, and 'ere we are inna place where the machine, once revered, is looked upon as evil, and tha false god is remembered fondly and worshiped while his far-more noble predecessor is dust in tha wind."

The fire was nearly dead now, fading more and more as Nixon became lost in the gloom. Aryu, desperate to return his spirits and resist returning to a world with dead parents and a destroyed home, said the only thing he could think of to perpetuate the conversation to a lighter place.

"Nixon. I'll go with you east. I'll help you find your path and do all I can to help you sleep again. For not killing me yet, and it was something you were clearly set on, I think I have to. I am clearly a link in a chain you need to piece together, and from what you've told me tonight, you are someone worthy of helping."

It sounded so cheesy coming from his mouth. Not contrived, but not far off. 'A link in the chain'? Not Aryu's usual choice of words, but he was trying to sound as sincere as he could. A few days ago, it was just as likely that he'd have pissed himself and cried after this meeting, but growth came in pouncing on someone who'd been through all he had in that time.

Nixon looked at Aryu, reading his sincerity (or perhaps just trying to cut through the schlock). The fire grew after a moment and Nixon spoke.

"You'll na'run? Not attempt t' escape until the deed is done? Ya know if ya do what my reaction will be."

"You'll find me and kill me, yes, but that's not why I'm agreeing. I will not run because I don't want to." It was true. Despite Aryu's need to confirm what the Herald had said and done, something triggered in his head. This was something he wanted, and he had good reasons for it.

Nixon gauged the answer. He was no fool, and he was not tricked easily. He believed Aryu to be telling the truth. "There's a *but* here isn't there?"

Aryu smiled. "Of course there is. It's about my friend. My friend and him." He motioned to the resting Esgona, whom he'd by now identified. While this long discussion had been going on, he had selectively chosen to ignore him. As long as he didn't wake up, Aryu didn't have to go through the painstaking process of fighting with him and explaining all that had happened in his unconsciousness.

"I'll listen, sir. Ya've earned tha' much from me." Nixon looked on, interested.

"I assume you don't want him tagging along with us?" Nixon nodded. "Help me find my friend. He can't be far now, and until I see proof otherwise, I refuse to believe he's dead. We find him, explain it all as it's been explained to me, and leave the two to do as they will, likely go north to the Great Range I'd guess. I'll accompany you until our task is finished and your answers found, but I want your promise that you will let me return to them and continue as I was before you ever showed up, never to be bothered by you and your threats of death ever again once we're done.

"You should know that I am beside myself with anger and sadness right now, Nixon. But the reality is that my friend and I can't just destroy this inhuman army. Time with you, one who's seen so much, might just help me come up with a plan on how we can."

Nixon thought it over briefly, but the answer seemed clear to anyone in his position. "It seems a fair deal, Aryu O'Lung'Singh. Agreed." He rose, walked over to where Aryu was sitting, and spat in his hand; sparks and sulfur flying forth just as they had done days earlier with the old man in the bar. His hand extended, his face determined, chiseled from solid rock.

Aryu met his huge hand, finding it hot, but not so hot to pull away. They shook hands, the fire blazing to life behind them as they did so. The deal made, the mission clear, and the moment locked forever in stone. Aryu smirked, the first hint of a smile in days.

"Wha' is it, Aryu?"

Aryu shrugged. "My home is destroyed, the weapons of the Old have returned, my best friend may be dead, my parents are lost, my greatest childhood enemy is steps away, and you, a holy hitman who may be able to help me make it right, came to me needing *my* help, so long as you don't kill me like you're supposed to."

Nixon frowned. "The Lord works in mysterious ways."

CHAPTER 8

░░░

What's in a Name?

Aryu didn't know if the deal was a good one or not. From the brief stories Nix had told him, his missions could take years to complete. Aryu was not going to wait that long. He was currently under the notion that finding a woman named Crystal, an Embracer who lived long before year Zero and seemed to have a history with Nix, would be the first, and hopefully last, step in the quest.

The notion was misguided for reasons even Aryu could see plain as day. Was she alive? Even if she was, Nixon described her as a recluse; a woman locked in a self-imposed prison to the east of here, deep into the lands that he feared.

The clarity of tragedy was his primary reason for why he had made the deal with Nix. This was a creature of power. One who had lived for years learning and gleaning information about all kinds of enemies and situations. Aryu was not a man prepared to battle an entire Army of the Old, and he doubted Johan would have any ideas so grand as to defeat them. Nixon was a creature of the ages. He had seen these kinds of things before. Perhaps he could help Aryu find a way to defeat the monsters currently ravaging his homeland.

At the very least, he had guessed he could pick up something useful by being around him. It was a helpful thought in very unhelpful times.

Nixon agreed that they could do nothing until the sun rose again, at which point they would return west to find Johan. If he had followed the plan, Aryu knew where he'd be.

The big man tended to Esgona, careful not to upset him or wake him before his mind was ready to do so. "He 'ad a 'ard day too, I'd wager. He jus' doesn't know 'ow 'ard yet."

Frankly, Aryu didn't care. He'd never been high on Esgona's personal favorite list, and the feeling was more than mutual. He couldn't say he wished Esgona hadn't been saved, but he was closer to that awful feeling than he'd like to admit. Esgona's disrespectful treatment of him after his return was as close to unthinkable as he could get. Esgona, wounded or not, had not completed his Quest. Aryu had. Aryu earned his manhood with each step. Esgona had only earned shame.

Aryu tried to explain this to Nixon after giving up trying to get some rest. Nixon didn't seem to care about such things, at one point even going so far as to call Aryu's quest an "unnecessary attempt to prove one's self in the eyes of others." He didn't understand. It was the way it had to be, if for no other reason than to shut others up about his damn wings and prove he was as much a man as any that had come before him.

"It's not the journey tha' makes the man," Nixon had said finally. "The sooner you people would realize tha' tha better I'd say. So ya learned t' start a fire, fight fools and look within yerselves fer some kind of maturity ya didn't know was there. Wha' was out there in those mountains tha' ya couldn't find right on yer own doorstep? A different view? Prettier, perhaps, but no more enlightenin'. Sorry, but

I really don't see tha point, and I never really 'ave."

Pushing it further was clearly a waste of time. Nixon was a man removed from such social obligations. He could not understand how important it was that Aryu go and finish what he felt he must.

Nixon, convinced that Esgona was still a good ways off from coming to, moved him closer to the phantom fire and let him sleep off the shock. "Look at him, Aryu. If all you say is true, think about the time this man had…"

"Boy, Nixon. He's still just a boy."

Nixon sighed heavily. "He's not my enemy, Aryu. I'll address 'im as I wish. This man is clearly crippled, weak, and most certainly pushed far 'nough to 'is limits to be lying 'ere after all he'd seen. Yet still he confronted ya like a man in 'is situation should. Scared, sure, but strong enough t' stand against ya when he deemed it necessary. And don't fool yourself, Aryu; yer little knuckle-duster 'ad nothing t' do with 'is current state other than a bruise and a 'eadache when he comes to. Now, tell me Oh Worldly One, 'ow is he any less a man than you?"

Aryu glared across the fire but said nothing. His resolve would not allow him to be dragged into this argument. His 'oh worldliness' knew a moment to agree to disagree. Esgona's treatment of him in youth would become apparent once he woke up. Another conversational sidestep was needed.

"You looked surprised when I told you my name. You even said it was further proof that I should die? Why?"

Nixon smiled, but not the reassuring smile. More a leering one that both informed Aryu he knew what he was doing, and told Aryu the answer was not one he wanted to hear. "A bad piece of luck on yer behalf, I'd say."

A moment of silence. Aryu pushed him on, urging him with his eyes, trying to wordlessly convey that he needed this conversation.

"Alright, if ya must know." Nixon met Aryu's eyes, sure to send the message that Aryu had better listen to what he was about to be told. "Through the ages, there 'ave been those tha' carried the sword fer one reason or another. Their reasons always varied but usually along the same paths as those before 'em.

"The first sword-bearer was the one ya know as the false god, but he was really a man named Tokugawa Ryu, the 'alf-breed bastard son of a ruler of an old empire now long dead. He and 'is twin brother were born t' parents of two different races, and born where they were, tha' was a 'orrible taboo. He and 'is brother were raised 'n trained in what's called Martial Arts, a varied and confusing array of self-defense and attackin' techniques, thankfully lost t' the ages because of its ridiculousness. It was durin' this intense trainin', more so devised to keep'em away from their father and 'is position than to strengthen 'em, which they learned o' tha Power or whatever name it 'ad at tha' time.

"Now, an Embracer of the Power will always 'ave an item t' assist 'em as their power grows. A talisman t' focus their thoughts 'n energy. They don't need it forever. Ryu outgrew this sword long ago. They don't need it to live or die, just help 'em embrace and, to a very, very small extent, control the Power. Control of the Power first leads t' great longevity, and eventually, if one's not careful, immortality. Immortality tha' can only be taken by someone with similar or greater power. Will, Aryu, is what determines these things. Never strength.

"Anyway, the long and truly sorted details of Ryu's life are not important. All tha' is needed is this: he was a man whose power got tha better of 'im, and 'istory has made 'im a god.

"Now, long after he discarded this sword the first time, others found it. Each would take on tha title and power it possessed. Tokugawa Ryu, after a long period o' time, lost tha' name and was simply referred to as Ryuujin, loosely translated from 'is native tongue as 'Dragon God', or per'aps 'Dragon King,' is closer. The point is, 'is reputation and 'is prowess with this sword were becomin' legendary, and when he cast it off t' grow the Power without it, many bearers thereafter would take on the name Ryuujin, even though the original man was still very much alive and well.

"The sword, for its part, as every such item of focus does, became more than itself as well. Once used so well by a master o' the Power, something Ryu certainly was despite 'is relative youth, it became an item of focus t' others. Each time its legend and power grew until all one had to do was 'old it and its purpose and 'istory were clear, but only, and this is important, if the bearer knew wha' to look for. One trained glance at it and it would tell ya its history in a single moment. Not everyone sees it, but a general rule is anyone with an aged and open mind will at least hear it whisper to 'em."

Aryu somewhat understood what he meant. When he looked at the weapon, a whisper of something otherworldly filled his mind, but not as strong as Nixon was describing.

"Some of my earliest memories came soon after it was discarded the first time. It eventually fell into the hands of a man named Adragon Sakata. He was a ruler of a small island close t' where Ryu and 'is brother were born and raised. Sakata was a man bent on gainin' more power than he truly deserved. He was not 'appy with what he thought was a meager island, and when the sword and its obvious abilities came t' his hand, he began a silent war against all above 'im, determined to undermine 'is way to tha top. When he began t' cut down powerful Embracers, 'is sword doing so with ease, soon he'd unleashed enough fury t' awaken me.

"By the time I reached 'im, 'is power was considerable and he was well entrenched in its seduction. Our battle was long and impressive. 'Is prowess with a blade even edging my own slightly with each move, and were it not fer the interjection of Tokugawa Ryu, I dare say I may 'ave not been the victor tha' day. Ryu, havin' seen the terror 'is blade created, interjected himself to appease 'is guilt fer all tha' had been felled by it. By tha' time, 'is brother was dead and 'is lover missin'. 'Is son was lost t' tha ages and 'is purpose driven by lit'le more 'an 'ope tha' he'd find a way t' die. He jus' wanted an escape from the life tha Power 'ad given 'im.

"Word o' mouth spread from one Embracer t' another of tha power tha man Adragon Sakata 'ad commanded and tha blade he'd wielded. If one was in possession of the blade and sought nothin' more than knowledge and peace, they were Ryuujin, or fully, Ryuujin of the People. If they swayed tha other way too far, even if their ends weren't as ruthless as Sakata's, and believe me most were ne'er so crazy, they became Adragon of the Rage."

Nixon's dark, haunting eyes loomed heavily over the young man across the way. "Do ya see now, Aryu, the seemingly ironic title ya possess?"

Aryu thought it over, piecing it together. "Ryu. Ryu is this old-world tongue for dragon."

Nixon nodded as he saw Aryu piece it together.

"In this old language, my name is Adragon."

Nixon nodded again. "Well, more or less. 'Lung' is dragon in yet another tongue. You've got dragons all over yerself, Aryu. I suppose t' some tha' could be open t' interpretation, but the coincidences are far too close for my liking."

Boldness filled Aryu. "Such things are rarely coincidence, Nixon. I can't say I'd have had your restraint in killing me. I am a man with a lot of terrible thoughts right now." It was a more honest answer than Aryu wanted to give, but now was not a time to hide. If Nixon wanted him dead, he'd be dead, so the truth was the better way to go.

"Tha' answer alone, sir, is more than enough reason t' keep you alive."

Nixon knew that a man who had completely succumbed to those feelings would never even know it, and they would convince his mind that the path he chose to kill and terrorize was the correct one. Indeed, they'd likely find others who agreed with him. The question was if the desire to keep Aryu alive was a passing thing, or if it would grow and fester from this point on. For once it seemed Nixon actually had a say in it how things turned out, and if things went downhill from here he'd be by Aryu's side, ready to steer him right or cut him down.

Nixon liked Aryu. He acknowledged that he was young but smart and logical. Traits Nixon knew and respected. Their acquaintance had been brief thus far, but considering everything that had befallen this young man in the last few days, Nixon saw in him a strength that many people hundreds of years older lacked. Strength no doubt built throughout his life from the torment he'd suffered.

Still, one step down the wrong path, and Nixon would end this. It was his purpose and God's will that it be so. No one was above that fact, even one so young.

So, with less reservation than he expected from the act, Nixon extended the blade known as Shi Kaze, the Four Winds, a ninjutsu sword created for revenge tens of thousands of years ago, back to the man who had found it resting in the remains of the mountainside that had held the false god Tokugawa Ryu in his rocky prison until he broke free to end his life and all the lives of the fools who followed him.

As impossible as it seemed, Aryu took it with a hint of hesitation, unheard of for many bearers of the Shi Kaze. Most wouldn't have thought twice.

Aryu had heard many stories that night, each telling him this

118

blade was more curse than salvation. Still, he knew he must have it. It was a powerful weapon. He may not have heard it whisper to him clearly, but the simple act of grasping the handle sent sparks of unspoken energy up into his body, like reattaching an arm he'd not known he'd been missing. It may not ever do for him what it had done for others, but it was still something more than he'd had only days before.

Nixon tended further to Esgona, slipping him water and little else. The fire burned brightly and kept them warm. Aryu lay there for a long time, thinking of his family and friends now gone, and all, apparently, because of him. He didn't look forward to Esgona waking up, but when he did, he had a lot to answer for. No matter what Nixon had said, it was Aryu's right by tradition to demand these things from Esgona, and he fully intended to do it.

In time, he did fall asleep, with Nixon watching over him quietly.

As dawn broke, the day was chilly and only the faintest light could be seen to the east.

Aryu arose to see the fire dead, the spot it had burned so fiercely the night before not even dark from the heat. He grabbed a quick snack of berries and edible plants Nixon had collected before he had awoken, thankful to get anything into his stomach. His mother always said to eat when you can because you may not know when you'll get to eat again. A pearl of wisdom he wondered if he'd ever hear more of. Darkness consumed him.

Nixon was ready to continue on his quest for his answers. "Good mornin', sir. May t'day be better for ya than yesterday."

Aryu smirked. It was the best possible wish he could have been given.

Daylight brought a new vision of the man who had saved him. He could see clearly now the armor he wore, black as night and fit to his form perfectly. His great broadsword was on his back, his hair falling back around its hilt and handle like fire. He had known his eyes were dark, but not as black as what he was seeing now, the red flicker inside them reminding Aryu with absolute certainty that this was no ordinary man.

"I must ask, Aryu, before I get t' tha point of tha matter. What's the story with the wings?" Nixon didn't look all that curious, as if he already knew, but he'd rather hear it from the man himself.

It occurred to Aryu that in all the previous night's conversations, the topic of his wings was never mentioned. Nixon had done most of the talking, but it seemed odd that the subject wasn't mentioned even in passing.

Not a fan of the topic at the best of times, Aryu hoped to keep the talk short and to the point. "I was born with them, a mutation I've been cursed with." Quick, easy, and a clear statement of his disdain for these things.

As expected, Nixon persisted. "Cursed? An odd feeling toward such a useful gift."

"Ha, useful? Do you have any idea how people here react to them? Fear and name-calling to start with, from children and adults. The only reason my parents came to that village was that the name-calling was the worst of it. Where I was born I was supposed to be put to death as a demon or something. That, and when I finished my quest, I was going to be recognized as a man and treated like one. Guess that won't be happening now, will it."

Aryu began to get fired up, reminded of his lost home and family coupled with the respect he would now never receive. Nixon didn't seem ready to let it go.

"Really? Just a random mutation? I don't deny the shortsighted foolishness of people on average, but I'd hardly call wings a mutational anomaly. Can ya use 'em? Can ya fly?"

"Yes." Still trying to be short, but still failing to get Nix off the topic. "Well, glide anyway."

"If you hate them, why keep them? Surely you could find a way." More antagonizing than a question.

"No one would touch me. No one had ever seen them before, so no one knew the effect it would have on me. I'd rather live with them than die needlessly. I hate them, but not enough to risk that." Saying that out loud gave instant rise to doubt about his proposed hatred. Both he and Nixon noticed it.

"Well now, there *is* some common sense in there. Tell me then, where do ya come from tha' you'd be burned at the stake for yer appearance?" It still felt like further pushing, to see what Aryu would say.

"Burned at what?"

"Sorry, I guess tha's not a common act anymore. Killed. Killed for yer 'random mutation.'"

"I don't really know. East. Over the ocean."

Nixon's eyebrow rose. "And you've never been back?"

"No. I've barely left Tan Torna Qu-ay all of my life. I did have intentions of going soon, though. I wanted to see where I was from, see the people who would cast my parents out and see me dead thanks to an act of chance."

"Well sir, tha' is a chance ya may well get, as I hope our time together is brief after I find Crystal. She lives in what has been called many things, but when I left it was called Napponia." Aryu smirked. It was still called that, the land of the Embracers. "It seems everywhere changes, even my home, given enough time."

Nixon seemed unaware of the door he'd opened. Aryu saw the chance and grabbed it. "And where are you from? A place that sees gods give rise to large men of power?"

"No gods. There is none but one. That's a point I'd like t' be very clear." Aryu nodded in relent. "When I was given life, it was in a place then known as Scotland, but o'er time it changed and became many other things. Should word of it e'er 'ave reached this far, I believe you'd call it Lion's Den."

Aryu looked amused. "Lion's Den? Wow, that is quite a journey, isn't it?"

He knew of the place, more from myth and story than fact. It was supposed to be a great distance away, farther than any man Aryu had ever met had traveled. The name instantly conjured up images of a barren and rugged landscape, devoid of life and bristling with unseen dangers. It was a common location for the bad guy in a child's story to come from. Although he knew they were just stories, Aryu had never heard of anything good coming from Lion's Den. "I suppose I shouldn't be surprised. A person like you could hardly have come from anywhere else."

He explained his history with the name and what he knew. Nixon seemed to glower at every word, but Aryu pressed on, happy to return the favor of uncomfortable conversation topics.

"Aye, ya speak true. Tha' is how it is now, perhaps even worse than ya say. It wasn't always like tha'. Once it was lush and green, full of rollin' grass hills and the liveliest people ya'd e'er be likely t' meet. Good, 'ard workin' people."

Aryu questioned the thought of pressing more, but Nixon carried on for him. "Lost, it was, long ago t' the hands of a powerful man, one with that damn sword I'd like t' add, lost t' his foolishness and greed. Tha's one thing ya learn when you see what I've seen. He was just one of so many. He wasn't unique at all. It just so happens tha' his reign of terror affected my home. There are a thousand instances of such things all over the world. It is sadly a common story in the time when fools had the Power."

"Did you kill him?"

"No. He met his end by another means and I slept in perfect ignorance while my home was destroyed."

Aryu saw then the commonality in their lives. He pressed on no more, lest he be pressing against himself as well. Both of them were helpless in the loss of their homes, and he had to agree that Nixon's reason was far more painful to take, as he clearly could have stopped it before it happened. Aryu couldn't help but question the mercy of a god that would allow that to happen. It seemed every god thus far could be deemed fallible quite easily.

"It was a sad fate, but it happened long ago and time 'as been said t' heal all wounds. Even now it's not as 'orrible as it once was. Per'aps I'll see it green once again. The reappearance of tha' sword does little t' let me believe tha' I'll be sleepin' fore'er any time soon. But, things 're different now. Maybe my bein' here with ya is tha beginnin' of an end. Why else would I be huntin' a man tha' as near as I can tell shouldna' be hunted?"

Aryu smiled passively. "Thank you. Still, I'd rest easier once we both go our own way and I'll never have to see you again. Not that I don't enjoy your company, but you should know you're not the most peaceful and reassuring person I've ever met."

"Ha, perhaps my next form would be a little less intimidatin'."

Aryu doubted that. Something told him the essence of power this man carried with him would not go away, despite what he looked like.

"Do you believe it's time for you to go soon? For real?"

"No. Not really. Sadly, I believe it t' be no more than wishful thinkin'. My job is eternal by nature. No matter if tha God I serve is gone, His vision and word live on through me, even if I'm the only one who knows wha' they mean. Now, about those wings. Are ya fast?"

"I think so." He didn't think himself a slouch, but against Nixon, he bet he'd be the slower man.

"Well, I'm ready t' see if ye are. Shall we be off?"

Aryu agreed, and Nixon lifted the still-comatose Esgona to his shoulder effortlessly.

"Nixon, before we go, I ask just one thing." Nixon looked over, sure of the question, but not the answer he should give. "What would you say I am? I hold the sword, granted just briefly. If you're here I could be Adragon, but as you said, I'm not someone worth hunting, so does that make me Ryuujin? Does the mission or the master make me what I am, if your god is so infallible?"

"Ye are a young man who found an old sword. God 'as a place in 'is 'eart fer luck too, and so do I. My purpose 'ere has not been proven t' have t' do with you. Per'aps it's the sword, or per'aps something else entirely. If I e'er get my answer, you'll be the first t' know."

Even in this place, so out of sorts and somewhat purposeless, Nixon refused to believe the God had made a mistake. Without help, Nixon would simply have a harder time finding out what his mission was this time around. Luck had never played into the finding and use of the Shi Kaze, so he continued to be buried in new situations. No matter what, he would watch Aryu closely until he was satisfied with the answer.

He reached deep down to summon the fire, letting it burst forth, startling Aryu again. The great flaming wings took shape, his unconscious charge was secure and Aryu had his small collection of belongings and his wings extended, ready to go.

With a mighty flap, Nixon took to the sky, dazzling Aryu with the feat. Aryu braced himself and found a spot to launch overlooking where the mountains ended and the fields of nothing led off to the ocean far beyond. Soon he'd taken to the sky, heading back west to find Johan before heading off to the east and with any luck (which by now was a word Nixon was not fond of at all) Crystal Kokuou, who was hopefully still alive and had more answers than he had now.

CHAPTER 9

The Enemy of My Enemy

Within moments of leaving the craggy plateau, Nixon knew that for all the acid spit from Aryu's mouth regarding his wings, he was a bold-faced liar.

His face was what betrayed him. Despite all that had happened and the obvious physical pain he was feeling at that moment, he was still smiling softly as he gained altitude and looked down on the world in a perfectly controlled glide. Nixon now began to see that although not as fast as Nixon would have liked, Aryu wasn't slow either, and once they leveled out he built up his speed to a fair clip with a minimum of effort. Finally, with his deft movements and skill in maintaining balance and rhythm, Nixon concluded that Aryu loved his wings, enjoyed using them, and only hated them for the fear they incited.

With the wind rushing past as it was, talking was out of the question. Instead, Nixon fell back and motioned to Aryu with his free hand to begin a sloping dive to increase speed. Aryu, after taking a moment to understand the gestures while also concentrating on his own flight, nodded his understanding and arched his wings back slowly, becoming more aerodynamic.

Soon Aryu was drifting down to the ground. The same move he'd used a hundred times emerging from Tortria Den over the valley below. A move he'd perfected. Further proof of his lies. Nixon, careful not to lose Esgona, followed, his wings of fire folding back and streamlining themselves like a bullet. Soon he was following Aryu perfectly, and moments later he was gaining.

Aryu didn't look back and couldn't see the approaching rocket behind him. He simply assumed Nixon would follow him, his youthful arrogance letting himself fly faster and harder than he'd done so in the past while his worry and purpose justified the act despite his body protesting. He was nearly bowled over by shock as Nixon blasted past him, close enough to touch, at a speed he was certain he would never be able to match. He could only watch as Nixon became a blur ahead of him, followed by the slipstream. When the slipstream hit it was like being kicked from behind by a horse. It carried over Aryu like a funnel cloud and forced him forward like he was being pulled. In a few seconds, he was starting to match Nixon's speed, being carried behind while trapped in a bubble of circling wind.

It was nearly impossible to control at first. He was just a ragdoll along for the ride. After the initial shock passed and he had a better grasp of what was happening, he was able to balance himself in the turbulence and ride along with it. It was no wonder he had made it so far so fast, and this was likely not even his top speed. Aryu's spirits rose as he thought about how this kind of speed was possible and how it could get them back to Johan that much faster.

Aryu felt himself press against a heavy wind below him as the slipstream moved with Nixon back upwards. Although not as fast as the dive, Nixon could still keep an incredible speed as he moved, making Aryu labor to keep up.

Eventually Nixon slowed, landing to allow Aryu a moment of rest. Aryu caught him, heavily out of breath and looking very tired.

"Ha, a good show, sir. I'd not expected one who loathes wings as ya do t' know how t' keep up with me. Well done."

A trick. A god damned trick to rub the lies into Aryu's face. Aryu didn't see them as lies. He did not say what he said about them to hide his true feelings. He did hate them and wanted them gone, and he would still trade them away in an instant if he could. But Nixon had done a very good job of showing him that he was just as likely to be lying to himself as well as others, and that realization made Aryu's tired face that much deeper a shade of red.

"Can ya keep up tha pace?" Aryu wasn't sure but nodded anyway. "Very well. We continue like tha' until I say t' stop. Esgona twitches, so we may be short on time and I'd like t' find yer friend quickly."

It was like he was reading Aryu's mind. He took a silent laugh at the thought of Esgona coming to during a dive, finding himself plummeting to earth at a shocking speed while in the arms of a fire-born demon-man. That would be truly fantastic.

They carried on like this, with Nixon falling, climbing, and repeating with Aryu at his heels riding the wave of wind. The whole time Aryu thought of reaching the village and its bar with the pleasant, fat bartender. (*What was his name? Pauly? Sully?* It was so long ago in his life that Aryu couldn't remember much before the last few days.) He daydreamed of walking in and seeing his friend sitting there. Soon, he'd know for sure if that were true.

Not yet though, as Nixon began the fall and did not pull out, allowing each of them to fall farther and farther until they were barely off the ground. Soon, from their left, leading out of the south, a dirt road came into view, and Nixon began slowing himself with clear intent to land on or near it. Aryu broke away, following him down to a grove of low grass and eye-high scrub bushes just off to the side of the road.

"Break time already? I was just getting warmed up!" A playful lie, as Aryu was so out of breath and sick with exhaustion he couldn't even stand, and he found a spot across the grove to sit down almost immediately.

Nixon smiled, which returned that peaceful feeling to Aryu. "Oh, of course, sir, my apologies for not bein' as up t' snuff as ya, but we're 'bout t' have a nice-sized problem present itself." Nixon looked back to Esgona, passing on his meaning to Aryu with a thoughtful, silent look down. Esgona was waking, and they had not made it to Johan. Aryu looked on like a Great Stalker following his prey. He had no wish to face Esgona like this, but if this meeting went anything like their last, he was damn sure he'd be coming out swinging. Aryu unsheathed the sword and held it before him, the power of the blade starting its surge through his exhausted body. Soon, it fueled his strength enough to stand again.

"You'll have no need of tha', Aryu. This man will be no threat t' ya as he is."

"I'll be the judge of that. You just do what you do, but forgive me if I stay as I am."

"Suit yourself."

Moments later, Esgona's dark eyes opened.

With Nixon doting over him as he roused, Esgona slowly came around, groaning as he did so. Nixon never left his side as the minutes ticked by as they always do.

"Do you have to hover over him like that? I'm sure you've done all you could."

"Aye, I must. Until he's well enough t' carry on his own, he is my charge. I saved 'im; I must make sure he isn't led to an even worse fate because of my actions."

"A worse fate? If he's been through all you say he has, plus the loss of our home, his fate is about as poor as one can make it."

"No, Aryu, it can get much worse. All the times I've battled the Adragons, more often than not they 'ad a story similar to 'is. The past ne'er justifies the future, but far too few realize tha'. I must try my best t' help 'im see 'is strength in comin' this far, not 'is weakness in wha' was lost along the way. A lesson you'd do well to remember, because like it or not I intend t' do the same for you."

"My course is already set, thank you. I'd just as soon finish your quest of self-discovery and be on my way."

Esgona sputtered as he began to sit up, spitting to his side once he'd rolled over. He sat there for a moment in the bright grove facing neither of them as he appeared to be sifting through the haze in his head. He sat up, instantly coming face to face with Nixon, who knelt watching carefully like he was ready to pounce if Esgona went out again. The act of it all from Nixon sickened Aryu to no end, but he owed his own life to this man and was bound to his wishes by a promise.

"Hello sir," he said softly, careful not to startle him as someone the size and power of Nixon would be very apt to do. "Don't get up. You've been out cold fer almost a full day and I'll wager you'll need a momen' t' regain yer strength."

Esgona blinked quickly, not believing his eyes. At least Esgona's first vision of him would be in broad daylight, unlike Aryu's dark meeting. Esgona shifted away sharply, wincing as he did so.

"Easy, easy. You've got more than a few nasty bumps and I fear a rather fierce knock on the head." Esgona moved gingerly, appraising the man-beast in front of him. Nixon continued. "My name is Nixon of the Great Fire and Ash. I brought ya 'ere t' escape."

You're welcome, thought Aryu.

"Where am I?" A croak more than a voice. "What happened?"

Nixon was clearly hesitant to speak, as reluctant to discuss the subject as Aryu was. "A lot, sir. A lot. Perhaps ya should lie down."

Esgona shook him off, his natural defiance returning. "Tell me." A whisper this time, as the memories continued to flood in. "What of the village? My mother?"

No hesitation from Nixon, who was eager to get it over with quickly. "Lost, Esgona. Lost t' the machines and their devices." It was all that needed to be said.

The wind kicked up, taking Nixon's eyes away for a moment to scan the south horizon for who knew what. The wind subsided and he looked back. Esgona had his head up again and was looking at Nixon with eyes of steel: dark and cold, even with one as cloudy and blind as it was. The visage of whom or what Nixon was didn't register any unease on Esgona's face.

"I knew that they were liars. I warned my mother not to believe them and leave the village. I saw what they could do. I'm proof of It, but still, she did. Gods damn her and her foolish hopes."

Aryu was instantly taken aback by the comment. It was certainly not what he'd expected from him, and the venom with which he said it was unmistakable. What had this boy been through? Was it the machines that crippled him?

Silence as Nixon thought this over, and then with a sudden sharp clap of his hands to bring himself back around, he continued. "Well, tha matter at hand, then." Nixon rose to his full height, taking in the situation anew while pushing his frustrations to the back as he set his mental course to continue with the plan. "Do either of ya know where we are? Per'aps how far from the nearest town?"

Esgona looked around for the first time, not realizing that there was anyone else around. When his eyes met Aryu's across the grove, he neither shouted nor charged in a fit of rage. He simply stared, as if seeing him for the first time. Aryu, unsure how to react, held his ground. He was still exhausted from flying but ready for a fight.

After what seemed to Aryu to be an eternity, Esgona rose to his feet effortlessly, seemingly unaffected by whatever fatigue and pain he was feeling. His eyes locked on Aryu's. With his new hobble, he made his way slowly across the grove, the wind intensifying as he did so, tossing around his curly hair.

"Say it and be done, Esgona. I have no time for this. It was my home too."

Esgona looked at him. No blinking. No movement. Two weary people in a standoff of wills. The wind began getting faster, blowing small leaves and dirt everywhere, rustling the leathery material of Aryu's wings.

"You…" began Esgona, eyes intensifying at the sound of his own voice. "You." The last word a whisper in the new silence. "You do not get the right to call Tan Torna Qu-ay home anymore." The chilling certainty with which he spoke was unquestionable. Even Aryu didn't know what to make of it. The level of emotion behind these quiet words was enough for Aryu to momentarily believe it was true, but he had no idea why.

The silence deafening, Aryu responded the first and only way he could think of. He simply turned away and let the world spin as it would. Aryu looked out beyond the grove to the waiting road. He could feel Esgona stare into him, but he let it pass.

Nixon, seeing the moment for what it was, only looked on. What had he been through, and what did it have to do with Aryu? Nixon knew of Aryu's quest, knew he'd not been home in a year. What little Aryu had told him led him to believe they had a childhood rivalry, but nothing more. Why must every new moment bring more unanswerable questions? They were starting to grate on Nixon's nerves.

He let the moment pass, admiring Aryu's strength and intelligence in not confronting Esgona. Aryu saw the situation for what it was and chose wisely to step away and not antagonize him. A lesser man would not have. Proof positive that he was more of the man he said he was than Nixon had originally believed.

"What is your plan with us, Nixon of the Great Fire and Ash?" Esgona asked, turning from Aryu and meeting Nixon's eyes.

Nixon was cautious. "Well sir, if we can find a town nearby, I'll leave ya to yer own devices. Ya should know tha' it was only by luck, should ya see it good or bad, tha' ye were saved at all. Ya were there and ya couldn't put up much of a fight." Esgona looked back over his shoulder at Aryu, finding the statement either amusing or insulting. "I saved ya because tha' is my charge and tha' is my way. Aryu and I 'ave business far from 'ere and I 'ave no intention of draggin' ya along."

"Ha. Luck." Esgona looked back to Aryu. "Anywhere you have to go with this *'man'* is certainly in for the bad kind. It seems to follow him lately."

"Look Esgona," Aryu could stay silent no longer, "I don't know what you think I'm guilty of, but I haven't been back home for more than a year. I walked into this situation just a few days ago. I didn't know about any of it until then, so don't go blaming me for your problems. I've lost just as much as you have."

He raised the sword again, waiting for the fight, but once it was at eye level, Esgona instantly turned away. "Put that thing away. I'd rather look at your face than the images in my head that thing gives off. You claim to be innocent, but you carry what looks like a very powerful weapon of the Embracers."

Both Nixon and Aryu were once again speechless. Nixon stepped forward first. "'Ow do ya know its power?"

No answer from Esgona, only blank silence. Aryu lowered the sword and Esgona relaxed. Remembering what Nixon had said about the ancient blade and its ability to bombard someone's mind with its history in images, but only if you were wise enough to see it, he wondered again what Esgona had been through in the last year.

"You two really don't know, do you?" he said at last. He looked at Nixon.

Nixon shook his head. "I'mma man out of place and time, Esgona. When it comes t' information, I am currently lackin'."

"That figures," Esgona spat with contempt at both of them.

"Listen and listen well," Nixon shot with sudden impatience and fiery eyes that began to burn into them both. "I am sorry fer both of yer losses, but right now there is a very powerful army on the way north with terrifyin' weapons in their possession, and I will not sit by anymore while you two mope about what ya canna' change. Now, t' go back to my original point, are we close to yer town, Aryu??"

Aryu looked to the far west. "Yes. Do you see that large peak?" Nixon looked; Esgona stared at nothing, not willing to listen to anything Aryu had to say.

"I do. Wha' of it?" Nixon knew that mountain very well.

"Near it, in the foothills to the south. That's where it is. A town with a bar that had forbidden machines in them to pour drinks."

Nixon knew the place right away. The bar with the old man and his story. A man he was sworn never to meet with again. "I know of it. Lights on the spouts. An ol' fat bartender named Ollie."

Ollie! That was his name. "That's the one. It can't be much farther away. Maybe a few hours if you can carry Esgona?"

No motion at the mention of his name. Esgona was as far away from these two as his mind could take him.

"Perhaps, but ya should know I canna' return t' tha' town any time soon. I made a promise to tha' end, and I canna' break it." Aryu looked at him, confused, but Nixon wasn't up for another story right now. "It's the truth. Deal with it. I canna' go there. I can get ya close, if that's alright with ya, Esgona?"

A soft shrug. No more.

"A yes it is." Nixon looked hard and intensely at Aryu. "I'll have t' leave yer company while ya go into the town, but ya know wha' will happen if ya run?"

Aryu nodded, making no mistake in his actions. "You don't have to worry about me. I'll be back as soon as possible to stop you from killing me." Levity, but seriousness as well. Nixon saw it and thought it to be the truth. "If I'm right, that would be where Johan should be by now, if he's still fine and going north like we planned."

Esgona snapped out of it, brought about by something suddenly. "Who... who did you say?"

Aryu looked exasperated. "Johan. We went together if you recall. I left him behind to make it back home faster. I agreed to go with Nixon if we could meet up with him first. I need to be sure he's alright." He left out the part about wanting to leave Esgona with Johan. One unfriendly face was enough for now.

"Johan is... is alive?"

Aryu looked at him, gauging his seriousness. Reading plenty, he answered. "Of course. We went into it together; we were supposed to come home together. He likely doesn't have a clue what's been going on. I'm sure he knows about Tan Torna Qu-ay by now, but not that I'm alive, or you."

Esgona looked honestly shocked and confused. "They said he was dead."

"Who did? Who's dead?" Aryu felt like he was talking to Nixon all over again, only hearing disjointed thoughts that offered him nothing.

"Johan. They said he had died, that you killed him."

Aryu couldn't believe what he was hearing. "I killed him? Ridiculous! I've saved his life a dozen times by now, and he mine. Why would I kill the man I call my brother?"

"That's what they said. Right after they arrived, the Herald and its companions. They said you killed him then returned to the south before disappearing into the north once more. It was why they came to us looking for you."

"Return to the south? Esgona, I've never been south in my life! We went north, the Great Range and beyond. Why would I go to them at all?"

"Because one like you leads them, Aryu. Someone with wings, and they said you worked with them."

The Shi Kaze dropped from his hand effortlessly. All the power it possessed couldn't keep it from being released in the wake of such an emotional onslaught.

"Esgona, they just destroyed my home, killed my family, were ready to take me away, knocking me out cold in the process, and you think I work *with* them?"

"That's what they said." Esgona looked lost, a common state for this trio.

The one most accustomed to this feeling interjected at last as the two young ones pondered what they've been told. "Are either of ya really surprised tha' they would use trickery and deception t' meet their ends? They lied to the villagers t' more easily obtain their goal; they lied to ya both about tha destruction of yer town. 'Ow much easier was it t' agree to 'and over Aryu upon 'is return if ya were to believe tha' he was the one who 'ad killed his friend and joined 'em?"

"It wasn't so simple, Nixon. They had proof. Moving images of him that appeared to show him holding that sword barking orders to masses of machines. It was unmistakably him."

Nixon thought about that, realizing the man had never seen a video recording in his life. He'd likely never even heard of one. This culture's avoidance of technology was apparent from the moment he arrived in this land. He described to them both how ancient races had the abilities to not only record and document images, both static and moving, but to also change and manipulate these images to show anything they wanted. The process of creating one that showed what Esgona was referring to would be relatively simple for an army with such advanced technology.

Esgona remained unwavering. "Alright then, Nixon. That's all well and good, but please explain why I saw one like him there, in the south, with my own eyes?"

Nixon and Aryu looked at him unbelievingly. He said it not with arrogance, but with something closer to embarrassment, possibly shame.

A twinge of realization hit Aryu. "Esgona, why were you in the south?" No answer. Aryu pressed on. "Esgona, we have a hard time believing you unless we have a damn good reason to."

"I was there," he said quietly. "I was there when the ships appeared on the horizon. I was there when the attacks started and the Army of the Old made landfall. I watched them march through the towns and villages, killing and burning indiscriminately. Some they captured and asked questions. If they said something they took interest in, they took them away. The others they killed."

"'Ow do ya know this?" Nixon asked, interested in the story, but aware that time was quickly wasting.

"Because I said something they were interested in. I had been away from Tan Torna Qu-ay for some time, but when the machines attacked, they collected a random selection of people and began asking them the same three questions: 'Where are you from? Do you know anyone with a mutation, and if so, what is it? Have you seen anyone with Embracer weapons?' I learned later they were looking for something like that sword. Hogope didn't answer fast enough. He was killed before he finished pissing himself in fear. Fortunately, once I was asked the first two questions while imprisoned, they were satisfied enough with my answers. They released me, giving me over to the Herald and his small entourage. That was when I saw the one like you, telling the armies where to go and what to do from a platform high above, wings and all. I promise you, I'll never forget that."

He paused, hesitant to tell the next part of his tale. Nixon coughed, urging him on. Esgona continued, pain on his face. "They took me away and then brought me back home, following my directions along the way. After we landed for a short rest I told them I needed to get my bearings. I attempted to escape, only to be shot in the leg and tortured for my insubordination as they called it. Although they healed my wounds with amazing efficiency, they were certain to maintain the scars and limp it left me with. I didn't try to escape again."

He told them of his subsequent return home and the meetings with his mother, who refused to give Aryu up. "Even after the evidence and my word of mouth about your true nature." Aryu held his tongue. Esgona was just getting fired up again. Better to just let him. "My mother was a fool. It got her killed."

"I know tha' once they 'ad Aryu they would 'ave done the same to yer home anyway. They've shown no 'istory of keepin' their side of any bargains."

Nixon was getting ready to leave for the village to the west, the other two following, when Aryu spoke only to Esgona.

"Whether you believe me or not, I can tell you for certain that I've never been south, I've never seen the army, and I am absolutely not associated with the one in charge of it. Although, for the life of me, I have no idea why I need to justify and explain myself to a coward."

Esgona turned to him with a look of rage in his good eye but was instantly subdued by the Shi Kaze, which was back in his face. "How *dare* you! What right do you have! I have seen *Hell* itself trying to save everyone. Would you have died for us all? It seems like such an easy answer when you're on the outside looking in!"

Aryu smirked, an action that infuriated Esgona even more, causing him to hobble closer, just beyond the reach of the ancient sword. "I never questioned your motives in that regard, Esgona." Esgona looked at him, full of immeasurable hate. "In that situation, I would have done the same thing. I call you a coward, boy, because that is what you are and why you were south in the first place." Esgona's fury died with astonishing suddenness, his face changing from red to white before their eyes. "Do you deny it?" Aryu asked. Esgona could only look away, growing paler by the second. Eventually, ever so slightly, he shook his head. "I thought not. Don't you dare claim sympathy for an action you had no right to be involved with in the first place."

Pressed for time, Nixon wanted to wrap this up quickly, though he was curious what was being spoken of. He expressed his need for expedience to them both but asked for an explanation anyway.

"Esgona left on his quest like Johan and me, but instead of going north as we are decreed to, I'm willing to bet he doubled back and went south instead, far enough away from Tan Torna Qu-ay that he didn't worry about a local recognizing him. While Johan and I were slogging away in the depths of the Great Range and beyond fighting bandits and Dragon Stalkers, this coward was likely lounging on a beach letting time pass by. Does that sound about right?"

No response. Answer enough for all.

"So I thought. You brought them straight to Tan Torna Qu-ay. You brought this on yourself. At least this way you'll suffer for your cowardice. It's the least you deserve."

Nixon watched the two in their moments of ill-gotten triumph and heart-crushing defeat. Aryu looked at Esgona like a man looks at a sick dog, disgusted at what he saw. Esgona could only look into the nothingness, denying none of it. Nixon wondered if either of these two young men could be saved.

CHAPTER 10

⊩⊩⊩⊩⊩⊩⊩⊩⊩⊩⊩⊩⊩⊩⊩⊩⊩⊩⊩⊩⊩⊩⊩⊩⊩⊩⊩⊩⊩⊩⊩⊩⊩⊩⊩⊩⊩⊩

Unsettling Developments

Johan stood on the edge of a town he thought he'd never see again. Off to the north he saw the tall and mighty peak the area was known for, reaching the sky with its white cap and imposing demeanor. Just to the west was the smaller peak, the one that not too long before had housed two young men for a night. A sacred night of reminiscence and reflection. A cold, miserable night now that he thought back on it; when the world was small and the quests were over.

Now he had returned, older and more miserable than that night that seemed so long ago. His home was destroyed, likely his good friend and brother Aryu as well. Their family and friends (or at least whatever they had that was close) were all lost. He was a beaten man as he began heading north again, eventually catching a ride with a small caravan back to this place. "*No one left now,*" an old carriage driver had said. "*We held on as long as we could, but when we saw the explosions get closer, we couldn't wait anymore.*" The old driver had offered to take him farther, though even he was unsure of the destination. Johan declined. If Aryu was alive, he'd be here as promised.

The town was far livelier than it was when he had left. Multitudes of caravans were in each direction, collecting supplies and preparing for the next phase of their trip. Overheard conversations led Johan to believe that no one really had an idea where to go. Many wanted to hide in the false hope of the mountains. Others wanted to go west, following the trail of the ones who had left before them. However, the army was known to be heading in a northwest direction. Time was all that stood between them and their eventual demise.

The reckless and foolhardy even said east but were soon shot down by shouts of 'madness' and 'stupidity!' Although it was known that most of the east was as peaceful and welcoming as any other, the stigma of it being full of Embracers was strong.

People filled the streets, some carrying items or children, others trying to barter and sell anything they didn't need wherever they were going. The desperate even attempted to barter children, making Johan sick. This small foothill town had become the major jumping-off point for miles around, and the sense of impending doom was palpable on everyone's face. For many, this was the last stop before the real running began.

Johan laughed to himself. The foolish idea that they could run far enough and fast enough to avoid the fate of Tan Torna Qu-ay was ridiculous. Nothing he could say would dissuade any of them, and he was content to let them continue their descent into madness.

The inns were bare as Johan looked for a place to sleep for the night. It seemed no one was content to simply rest for rest's sake these days. Many of the travelers stayed with their carts and powered trailers, ready for a quick escape if need be. The explosion on the road, with which Johan was all too familiar with, was much too close for comfort. It seemed the panicked rush to be gone had begun right after that. Even locals could be seen seeking a ride to who knew where.

An innkeeper asked for no money for his stay, making it known to him that she and her husband had no intentions of remaining much longer and the inn would be abandoned to the winds of fate the following morning. "Stay all you like," she'd told him. "Come sunrise, you're the best option I have to be the new owner!"

The thought amused him. At least he may get something out of this ordeal.

After dropping what little belongings he had in a quiet room on an empty floor, Johan set out to find the agreed-upon bar where he planned on doing two things: drinking and hoping.

From one side of the town to the other, people were bustling about trying to leave as quickly as possible. Some passed him an odd glance, clearly wondering who this young man was who seemed to be in no hurry to go anywhere. Glances were all they offered, though; their problems were of far more importance to them.

Land'O'North Tavern was the only business in the area that seemed to be thriving, with people coming and going freely and the sounds of laughter coming from inside.

The crowd was raucous, to say the least. At least two fights were happening between groups of obviously drunken men (and women), yet no one seemed to take the slightest notice or attempt to stop it. Indeed, most were watching and cheering it on like sport. Elsewhere, men and women were dancing (though no music could be heard), couples were kissing and fondling each other with a ferocity generally reserved for the bedroom, and all around the 'chink' of glasses meeting was present. Indeed, if one were to guess, one would have never suspected that an army with unmeasured power, size and ruthlessness was approaching at great speed not far away.

In a way, Johan understood it completely. The last few days had been trying for everyone here, not just him. Before the race to wherever they thought was safe, why not tie one last one on and have a bit of drunken fun? Although not quite as chipper, at least not enough to join in, he was thankful for the aura of hedonistic euphoria the crowd emitted. He pushed his way to the bar, with more drinks spilled on him as he passed than he was likely to consume, and found a busted barstool that wobbled and creaked as he sat.

Ollie was the only one behind the bar, unable to keep pace with the orders, but caring not the slightest. Money poured in as the booze poured out, despite his insistence that people were paying too much. Gratuity jars were filled, and then quickly emptied before someone got any bright ideas.

The barman was nearly tackled by one particularly loud and generous fellow. "A drink for me, a drink for him, a drink for you! We're all goin' to hell anyway, better drunk than sober! Oh shit, man, a drink for that one down there! Now *he* needs one!" He was pointing to Johan, who seemed to be the only one on the premises with a sour face. In times like these, that likely seemed to mean he was the hardest up for a drink.

Ollie poured the drink, a cloudy brown ooze that was more sludge than beverage, finishing the bottle into glasses (each save one were grabbed by the loud man, money tossed in Ollie's face as he turned to rejoin the rabble). The barman brought the remaining glass down and set it in the hands of Johan. "Courtesy of the polite gentleman over there," he motioned to the general direction of no one in particular, "somewhere…"

Johan took it with a nod and thanks, and it would have ended there had not Ollie's wife rejoined the fray, harassed by patrons who would simply shout at any man or woman foolhardy enough to be behind the bar. A reprieve for the old slinger, it seemed.

As one may recall, Ollie enjoyed his job very much, and a brief opportunity to console the seemingly inconsolable in times like this was too tempting to pass up. He took this moment of grand foolishness by his wife to focus on the youngster at his bar.

"I'd be careful lad. That's not for the timid."

Johan smiled. With a nod to the tender, he sucked the ghastly sludge back with the grace of an old pro; his lack of experience only to show a moment later when he erupted into harsh coughing and wheezing while slamming the bar with his hands.

Ollie gave a large laugh, the only kind he was capable of, and slapped him on the shoulders with large, weathered hands. "Well done, sir, well done. Most can't handle my special blend for another twenty or thirty years or so." Ollie had seen it bring larger men to their knees. This one's reaction was downright tame by some comparisons.

Johan looked at the man with red eyes, tears forming (though from sadness or the drink, Ollie couldn't say). "Another, please."

The good nature of the old man faded slightly. He had poured this beverage for the loud man and his rowdy friends to hopefully get them off his back for a moment, and this one had simply been an innocent bystander. Now, after the rank liquid had gone down to what seemed to be unanimous disapproval, the desire for a second wasn't as much shocking as it was off-putting. This one had seen some terrible things to be in this kind of mood.

Ollie went back over and popped the top on a fresh bottle of his 'special blend', a mishmash of chunky, sloppy still-leavings of various home-grown spirits and old beer. He returned, his wife cursing him, saying something clearly unladylike under her breath as he passed, and filled the glass with what seemed to be an even ranker concoction. Every bottle was a little different, and this one seemed to be very potent.

"In times like this, I'll not ask you why you seem to be intent on dying so young, but I will ask why you still seem dour despite the…festivities?"

Johan looked at him, money in one hand and drink in the other. "I'm from Tan Torna Qu-ay." He put the money down and slugged back the blend, this time with little reaction. Unfortunately, the horrid taste wasn't strong enough to force away the memory of his hometown's mentioned name.

All at once, Ollie understood. The memory of this one and one other he seemed to recall came back to him. Yes, they'd been here a few days ago, sitting in the same place. They ordered a few beers each, drank, spoke briefly to the barman about the last year (a familiar tale), and were on their way home, south of here. Although they never mentioned their home by name (at least as far as he could remember), south by foot was exactly where Tan Torna Qu-ay was. Or at least had been.

The passers-by to this little den of the drink had relayed to Ollie the possibility of safety in the picturesque village in the valley. Some said they thought about staying but continued for prudence's sake. Others were certain the people there had made a deal with the devil and were to be avoided. Either way, the result now was well-documented.

It had been the farthest north town to be destroyed. Farthest by a good margin too. If this terrible army could strike so far so fast, it was generally believed that nowhere was safe. Then the mass exodus had begun.

"I'm sorry, fella. Sorry like you wouldn't believe." Ollie felt at a loss for words, albeit only momentarily. For a bartender, that could be a lifetime. "Whatever you want, let me know. I'm sorry to say that I haven't seen anyone else from there yet. I pray you aren't the only one I meet." Johan slumped. That meant Aryu hadn't been here.

He left the bottle of brain-killing sludge behind and let him be. Others here had been through a lot, but something about this one gave him pause. As such, was entitled to a few rounds on the house. Money was no object now.

He returned to the rest of the crowd, his wife giving him an earful the whole way, and began filling orders once more. The kegs were near-dry, each evil little spigot either yellow or flashing red. It seemed that despite their technological relation to the Army of the Old, people could overcome their trepidation enough to suck them dry. Fear apparently did not know hypocrisy.

Another momentary glance revealed Johan taking another round down the gullet, and with that, Ollie returned to the task at hand.

It was obvious by the middle of the night that the party was not about to die. The old and drunk were replaced by the new and sober in a never-ending cycle.

Johan could barely see straight after so much special blend. Without saying a word to anyone, he got up and staggered out the door, his spot at the bar being promptly filled.

He really didn't have a hope in hell of finding his lodgings while in his current state, but he had a rough idea of the direction, and so he followed his sloshed senses in the way that felt the most correct. Johan found a street he swore (for the umpteenth time that night) was the one with the inn on it. Halfway down the road he passed several buildings and alleys, clearly pillaged and ransacked by anyone with the mind to do so in these times, and he was instantly shadowed by three men of ample size and nasty disposition.

By the time the men passed him, taking off down an alley of pure blackness, even in a drunken state he knew something was wrong. Part of him was afraid, but a larger part had an air of not caring, the malaise and drink mixing into a form of total apathy.

When one appeared before him, knife in hand with the other two flanking to the rear, Johan had already admitted to himself the truth of the situation and the likely outcome. He was a strong and skilled fighter, but only when sober. He also knew the likely reaction when it was revealed that he possessed not a single thing of value save for a few coins and the dagger. Indeed, the whole scenario had been played out in his head long before the lead thug first spoke, and frankly, he didn't care much by that point.

"Dangerous times to be wanderin' 'round, boy." He moved closer, face hidden.

"Yep. But here I am." Johan had no need for false bravado or posturing at this time. Their intentions were obvious, and he had no desire to bait them or run. Johan had the gift of strategy but was too far from caring to use it.

Silence for a moment. Johan had hoped his answer had tipped them off to his knowledge of their intentions. Perhaps he'd missed the mark?

"You seem out of place? Perhaps for a small fee, we could point you to your destination?"

"Perhaps." Tired of the confrontation before it had even started, he was too drunk to pretend anymore. "But perhaps I'll just keep wandering for free."

He made no motion to proceed, yet the dark man moved to stop him anyway. "Well then, that's not going to be as simpl…"

"Look, you either have a point or you don't, but this little act for your amusement is pretty fuckin' thin. I don't have money, I don't have anything you'd want, and I think that's pretty clear. If you want something else you either spit out what it is or hit me and be done."

"Oh I'll do more than hit you, son. I plan on fuckin' killin' ya."

The large man was now inches away from Johan, rot and beer on his breath. With a quick awkward motion he grabbed Johan by the scruff of his woven shirt and lifted him off the ground, other hand moving backward in what Johan only assumed was a windup to a nasty left hook.

As he followed through, Johan felt the grip on him slip just enough to pull up his arms and slip out, landing on the ground, dagger (strategically removed as he fell) in hand. The motion was so quick the large man lost his footing on the follow-through, stumbling a few steps to the side as he regained his balance.

To Johan it was still a blur, the alcohol winning over the adrenalin rush, but the speed and power were with him as he brought the blade about. His right hand sliced across the shadow of his assailant. He felt no resistance as he moved, and at first, he thought he had missed the mark, but then there was a howl of pain and the sound of something hitting the ground with a thud. Johan jumped back, and from what little light he had to work with, he saw the dark man hunched over grasping his arm.

With the next turn to the left, Johan saw he had no arm left to grasp. Now the sound of blood hitting the ground in spurts was audible as the man stumbled back in agony.

No way! thought Johan. *No way did I just do that. I didn't even hit him!*

But the proof was right there. He had hit him clean just below the elbow. He even could make out the arm on the ground, fingers and all.

"Take his fucking *head*!"

The others rushed Johan. The adrenalin began to win what battles it could over the booze and he ducked down, spinning between them like a seasoned dancer.

Screams of something unintelligible (and likely murderous) echoed behind him when he turned to run, and he knew he was in a race for his life. If only he had a way of knowing where he was. Johan was constantly afraid of running into a post or a person or something. Any idea would...

BANG!

Something very loud and very close exploded behind him. It threw him off for a second and he hit a bench on the street side, causing him to tumble. Limbs flailed and skin burned as it hit the packed dirt ground. In moments his pursuers were on him, stomping loudly as they came to a stop.

There was more light here, spilling out from local homes. In ribbons of illumination Johan saw what appeared to be a gun in one man's hand. Basic firearms were still widely used, though not often, as the ammunition was difficult to come by. This man didn't have a regular gun. This man had what illogically looked like an Ark 1 high-energy confined-beam pulse gun, a small but very powerful handheld weapon that used unbelievable amounts of power to produce a razor-thin beam of compressed energy for less than a millisecond, more than enough time to create a long and damaging stream of particles that could cut through almost anything with explosive results.

This was ridiculous. He had to be seeing things in his drunken haze because although they were once very popular, Ark 1s were long gone from these lands. They were as foreign and frightening as any mechanical beast that populated the army to the south, but here it was in the hands of an unkempt attacker in a small town, right in front of his eyes.

"An Ark 1? How the hell did you get an Ark 1?"

The gun made a low grumble as it leveled at Johan's face from a few paces back. "Shit, son, you have no time for questions after that stupid little stunt back there. You're lucky it'll be so clean."

A soft click and the grumble stopped, followed by the brightest light and the loudest bang anyone who had witnessed it had ever experienced.

▶◀▶◀▶◀▶◀▶◀▶◀▶◀▶◀▶◀▶◀▶◀▶◀

He had been afraid he'd be hard to find. Doubly so when night fell. The hustle and bustle of this lively town made it that much more difficult when he and his gimpy companion sauntered into town in the late afternoon. Asking around was quick to yield little results. Everyone was too preoccupied with leaving as soon as possible to answer him. It was incredible how much this place had changed in so little time.

Aryu's first thought was to make it to the bar. Should he be here, he'd likely follow the plan. Gods knew he needed a good drink himself.

The trip back to here had been quiet and disgustingly uncomfortable. Esgona did nothing but hang his head and hobble along, refusing outright to be carried aloft by Nixon (which was fine by Aryu. Fools walk). That had added unnecessary time to the trip; however, Aryu was pleased to see the limp didn't hold him up much. He'd clearly had the wound long enough to be comfortable with it, and even though he was so hang-dog, Aryu suspected that a large part of Esgona refused to yield any more perverse satisfaction to Aryu. Bullies never enjoy losing a battle, emotional or otherwise.

Aryu kept his mouth shut for the trip, talking to neither Esgona nor Nix unless the need was urgent. He had nothing more to say to Esgona, but Nixon seemed to be lost into himself. Something within Aryu told him that he was not free from fault in that matter. Nixon had been very quiet ever since the revelation about Esgona in the grove. Something about the whole situation between the two people from Tan Torna Qu-ay wasn't sitting right with the fire beast, and he did little to hide it.

As they approached the outer boundary of the town, Nixon left their company. He told Aryu when and where to meet him, allowing slightly less time than Aryu would have liked to get the task done, but he knew the man was in a terrible rush and was thankful he got any time away from him at all. He was honest with him, having no intentions to run away from the deal and the creature he made it with, but was still leery of Nixon's constant judging of him.

Also, the whole business of him not wanting to enter the town was just plain odd. So he'd made a deal with an old man not to return. So what? It wasn't as if Nixon had anything to fear from him, so why not come and help? Aryu doubted the logic, but he agreed to Nixon's terms and left with Esgona.

The plan of finding Johan, should he still be alive and at this destination, was revealed to Esgona as they walked. Expecting a fight again, Esgona only nodded in understanding and carried on.

The bar plan went terribly on the first try. Aryu by this point was doing nothing to hide his wings, his pack long since left behind in tatters. This fact, coupled with the edginess of the people in general, only ended up leading to shouts of "Stay out freak!" and "Don't let him in!" Entry was going to be an issue for him.

After searching the town as best they could, Esgona and Aryu ended back at the bar to give it another try late at night. The crowd was no more hospitable.

Esgona, who up to this point had just tagged along behind Aryu doing little to aid his search, suggested he be the one to enter and see for himself. Aryu was out of places to look and agreed. Esgona likely couldn't make it too far if he ran, and even if he tried, Aryu was likely to just let him go. Only the agreement with Nixon had him helping Esgona as much as he had. If Esgona made a break for it of his own accord, Aryu had never agreed to get him back.

He did come back, though, and with all the information they

needed. Esgona had spoken with Ollie the barman, learned that a young man matching his description had indeed been there and had been bellied-up to the bar for the better part of the day. He told Esgona that Johan had left only a few minutes before their arrival.

Aryu was ecstatic to find out that Johan was still alive. Although he had faith it was true, until this moment he wasn't one hundred percent. Eager to find him, Aryu had suggested he take to the air to cover more ground. Apparently, he had been pretty drunk and wasn't likely to get too far in the dark in the middle of a strange town. Esgona regressed yet again, nodding in agreement with the plan that would see him go to one of the inns they'd passed and await Aryu's return.

After climbing to the top of a nearby store and taking off over the town (an act that nearly caused a riot outside the bar), it only took a few minutes for Aryu's first lead: the scream of terrible pain from a darker corner of the town. Upon inspection, he made out the shadow of a large man who seemed to be short an arm and who had apparently lost it recently, judging by the shadow of blood at his feet and the amount of profanity spewing from his mouth.

Seconds later came a deep grumble and an ear-splitting explosion from not too far away, down an adjacent street.

With a launch off a tall inn, he took off in the direction of the calamity and drew the Shi Kaze for safety's sake. Only a few paces down the dark road he saw what he wanted to see more than anything in the world: the face of Johan, who appeared to be facing unseen assailants. He had only registered the scene in his mind, overjoyed at finding him, when he saw the closer of two men raise his arm and point what Aryu assumed was a gun at Johan's face. Aryu folded his wings and dove with all the speed he could muster. Shi Kaze taking the lead, Aryu struck the weapon cleanly as he rocketed past, a perfect hit to the middle of the gun.

Despite all the time he'd spent with Johan, Aryu had taken little interest in his talks about ancient weapons and tactics, enjoying more the stories of battle rather than the weapons that fought them. Had he ever paid close enough attention, he may have recognized the weapon he struck for what it was. An Ark 1 was a weapon famous for its accuracy, ease of use, mass availability at the peak of its popularity and, of course, the uncanny amount of energy it could store during an attack, particularly the moment it was fully charged and ready to fire.

That much energy wasted no time escaping by any means necessary, be it by pulling the trigger, quick-draining the battery to avoid discharge, or perhaps being thrust into the wide-open spaces of the world when the gun that contained it was sliced in two by what was possibly the sharpest weapon ever conceived by man.

Though at full speed when he struck, Aryu was still blindsided by the sudden localized explosion and the deafening pop as it expanded until no more energy was left.

Johan was staring right at it when it exploded and was thrown backward by the many forces at work. Eyes burning, ears ringing, and body jolted like he had been slammed into by a team of wild horses.

Compared to their attackers, though, their current state was nothing to complain about.

Aryu had tumbled through the air in an uncontrolled spin, only to deftly gain his balance and land. Confusion was on his face as his ears rang. He had never expected such an event from his actions, but when his eyes focused in the poor light, he saw Johan on the ground several paces from where he'd been, moaning and looking as if he'd been kicked by a folme. At least he was still alive and conscious.

The two attackers were nowhere near as lucky. The one with the weapon was almost entirely gone above the ankles, which were charred and tossed about in the roadway behind the blast. The other, although still in one piece, was missing all the clothing and skin from the front half of his body. His face stared out at them both in the illumination of one of the street-side houses. It was a black and grotesque visage with no eyelids, nose, or lips. Seared eyeballs glared at the scene like a wide-eyed gawker.

Aryu had no other reaction other than to vomit at his feet until his stomach (which really didn't have much to hold) was empty. Had he the means, he likely would have done so all night. He had never killed anyone before. Now, although he had zero intention to do so, he had killed two men in an instant, based only on the assumption that his friend was in danger. That triggered another wave of dry heaves as he realized he might have simply misunderstood the situation. Perhaps there was no trouble at all? What if these two men were innocent? He doubted it, but it was still possible, wasn't it?

No, he thought, *that was a gun. There was no good intention here. That was a weapon of the Old.*

The calm realization in his own mind blinded him to the fact that the very loud and bright explosion had awoken everyone in this quadrant of the city who wasn't already awake and milling about. Now the area he occupied with his damaged friend was filling up as people hurried to see what had gone on.

Windows opened above him and doors opened on the streets.

It took little time for him to be brought back to the here and now as someone screamed at the terrifying image of the corpses down the road. That face was enough to drive nightmares into the most stalwart of souls.

Aryu reacted as fast as he could. "Get up if you can, we need to go!" he shouted to Johan as he ran to him.

"Holy shit man, you had better stop screaming!" Johan said as he came to his knees, face and arms singed and cut, wounds bleeding.

His hands went to his ears as he gingerly tried to look around through the flash burn. It was unclear if he recognized his savior in this current state, but he had enough wherewithal to know he may still be in danger.

The crowd grew more brazen and began shouting at Aryu to get away. More than one person looked ready for mob justice that only chaos can create so efficiently.

Recognition dawned across Johan's face as Aryu pulled him to his feet. "Aryu? You have got to be fucking kidding me! Aryu!"

"Yea, yea, it's Aryu, now get to your feet and help me."

"How…?"

"Later, Johan, I promise, now let's go."

Johan could barely see and his ears rang even at low volumes, but the situation steeled him against these ailments. He started walking, instinct driving his feet forward.

The crowd was lost in the horror and no one had the moxie to follow them as they faded into a dark alley down the road. Rumors of army attacks and demon creatures invading the town grew at a speed only a hysterical crowd can propel.

When he was as confident as he could be that they were no longer followed, Aryu asked the drunk and shocked Johan where they could go to hide out.

"No problem, I think I own an inn now," he replied with a smirk.

Aryu thought he was kidding.

CHAPTER 11

The Shortest Night

Although there was nothing left of the Ark 1 after the blast, the connection between huge southern explosions, armies of ancient making, and a mysterious mutant with a sword that spoke of power and death if you looked at it the right way was a simple step to take.

The fact that this was all erroneous was trivial in the mind of a bloodthirsty crowd.

Aryu had since sheathed the mysterious weapon to aid in their escape. It was obvious that Johan had been stunned thoroughly and needed a place to rest.

They emerged from the dark alleys to what could pass for a major thoroughfare, the street well-lit even at this late hour. People and carts bustled everywhere. A modicum of recognition hit Johan's face and he told Aryu the place he was looking for was only a few blocks away.

"Do you like it? It's all mine, now," Johan said with great drunken pride as they entered the inn. Johan started tending to the cuts and bruises he could see with shaking hands and unsteady washing practices. Eventually, Aryu helped as he told Johan the basics of what had happened when he had made it to Tan Torna Qu-ay. Johan likely wouldn't remember it all, so Aryu kept it as brief-yet-detailed as possible.

By the time he reached the part about being saved by Nixon, along with Esgona, Johan seemed to show little effects of the booze, his anger burning off the spirits as Aryu spoke.

"They were just using the village to bait you home? For what? Why you?"

Aryu didn't know, explaining all he could still left him feeling as if great and important chunks were missing. It must be how Nix felt all the time right now.

"Could it be the sword?" Johan asked. Aryu had left out most of the major details of the history and power of the Shi Kaze, alluding to it in the recap of his meeting with Nixon. He had also taken great care to paint Nixon as more of a savior to keep his friend from worrying.

"No, it's not the sword," Aryu answered. "They arrived in the village weeks before I had found it."

"And what about you working with them? What kind of lie is that? Where's Esgona, anyway? If he has to be here, he may as well answer some of these questions."

Aryu was content to let Esgona just wait it out for a while. He wasn't far away, a block or two if he recalled correctly. He described to Johan the place he'd been left and asked him to go. It dawned on Johan that there was still a fair chunk of the town in a bloodthirsty rage searching for a winged man. He agreed and went in search of the boy.

Aryu cautiously looked about Johan's room, now lit with lanterns and candles casting a harsh dancing light on everything it touched. The room was barren except for the bed, a desk with no chair, a washbasin, and a cracked-but-serviceable mirror.

Aryu walked over to the mirror, anxious to see himself again. It had been some time since he'd last seen a mirror. He was much more ragged now. His clothes were ripped in too many places to count. His face and hands were cut and bruised. His dark brown hair was scruffy and tussled, not to mention longer than he'd have liked, but personal grooming had fallen off to the wayside lately with the excitement of returning home. His bright green eyes and now more than a few days' growth of patchy facial hair made him look that much more foreign. Another constant reminder for Aryu that he was not a native of this land and never would be.

He stepped away from the mirror and waited by the window, careful to shield his wings from anyone who might look up his way. Not much fear in that, though. It seemed most of the town had other matters on their mind.

In the few minutes he spent looking out at the town from his perch, Aryu watched three rather obvious thefts of goods, two raucous fights, and one of what he could only assume was the most public and obvious business transactions being executed between a 'professional' lady and customer he'd ever seen. Aryu found the latter act sicker and sadder than anything else. Something about the way they seemed to throw decorum out the window reminded him more than anything else how far one could sink with nothing left to lose.

Soon he spied Johan returning with Esgona in tow. "Anything interesting?" Johan asked when they entered the room, seeing Aryu's attention drawn to the scenes out the window. Aryu looked at him and then back out to the scenes below.

"No. Only the world caving in on itself."

Johan smirked. "Then everything's normal. Good to hear." He wandered over to the desk and hopped up, feet dangling like a child on a chair that was too big. Aryu could see by the look on his face that his mission to find Esgona and return was one he enjoyed greatly. Alcohol still showed on his face, but perverse pleasure was muddled in with it.

By this point Aryu was numb to the plight of Esgona. His moral and social victory over his rival was a lock, and now he only felt sad and ashamed for him. Pity was still a long way off, but it was somewhere in distant sight. That realization was enough to leave the matter alone. He had no further need to demoralize Esgona. His satisfaction at Esgona's failure was enough. For now.

"So now what?" Johan asked. "Hitch a ride with a northbound caravan? I'm open to ideas." A casual glance to the crippled boy now sitting across the room hinted that these ideas were only to come from Aryu lest they be ridiculed and shot down.

"East," was Aryu's reply.

He had told Johan of his deal to help the fire beast, but it was obvious Johan either thought him a liar or just didn't remember. The smirk left his face. "East? That's as much trouble as south."

"I told you. I made a deal to bring Esgona to safety, find you and go east with Nixon. I'll be back when it's over."

Johan still didn't believe him. "Why? Because you promised? Forget that. I thought you were dead. Now you're alive, but you have to go with some crazy demon-thing to the forbidden lands? Let him hang. You're coming with us." Aryu hadn't told him about the power of the man named Nixon or the mission he was sworn to uphold.

"I'll be back quickly, Johan. It won't take long. A week or two at best." A complete lie; Aryu had no idea how long it would take, but he needed some leverage.

Johan was like a rock. "No. This isn't a debate. Napponia is forbidden for a reason, Aryu. People who go there die." A rumor, but a rumor so rampant it was generally agreed upon to be true.

"Look, I made a deal. A promise on my honor. I can't take it back, Johan. He saved my life. I owe him this."

At that statement, Johan faltered. It was a fact he'd not considered, and a deal like that was hard if not impossible to break. Johan, being a man of honor as much as a smart ass, knew that just as well if not better than anyone else, even in his inebriated state. No matter what came out next, Aryu knew he'd won.

"It sounds like a pretty stupid deal."

"You don't have to tell me."

Johan agreed that north was the safest course of travel. He found a scrap of worn-out paper and a charcoal pencil and sketched a rough drawing of the route he planned on taking from memory of the maps they'd studied for their quest.

"Two weeks travel north from here is a branching valley that leads into the Hymleah Mountains. If you go west it follows the Paieleh River to the Blood Sea."

The Paieleh River was famous for its eddies and whirlpools. Boating on it was unsafe and possibly lethal. There was a road that followed it down the mountain valley. Aryu explained that revenge was foremost in his mind and that this route took them away from the advancing army, not to it.

"I have every intention of joining you on that mission, Aryu, but now is not the time. Most people here are going north. Look at this place," he quickly glanced to the window, the hubbub below clearly audible, "these people are running scared and in a state of total disarray. We need to find a place where the threat of the Old can be addressed strategically. Remember what Stroan said? He was with a band heading north. The Inja Army doesn't just march off into the depths of the mountains without a plan, and I certainly can't see that plan having any use where we've been or farther north. The Blood Sea seems as good a place as any to start looking."

The Blood Sea. Somewhere on its shores were said to be great cities and well-traveled highways, but the trek there from here was so long and dangerous. It wasn't a trip many made on a whim. It was also beyond the Inja borders, a place where the world had moved on without them. But first was the river valley. Once the torrent of water crashed over the great Hymleah headwall in a waterfall called the Thunder Run, it wove through the deep valley before emerging at the Blood Sea, another three weeks of steady travel at least. The valley was prone to flash floods. You could go for days on the road mere feet from the river with no way out if a sudden rise occurred upstream. Long caravans of traders and travelers had been lost to the river's emotional outbursts. The valley even in the best of times was prone to rockslides and on more than one occasion the greatest of the most fearful beasts imaginable, the Ruskan Stalker, had frequented the valley for a quick, trapped meal of helpless travelers.

Johan looked determined. A man with a plan. "We'll travel to the village of Huan, the last stop before we enter the Thunder Run. After that, there's not much other than rock and river for the next few weeks. We can assume that since it's the most useable route out of the mountains to the northwest that it will be well-traveled right now, and unless something goes wrong, we'll be alright for supplies. We can align with a larger group and pull our weight to go with them."

"You know you'll be trapped in the valley should anything happen," Aryu said, thinking of a million horrible scenarios but voicing none.

"We're trapped here. The only difference is that there, the enemies we face are ones we've faced before. Time and nature."

"And Ruskan Stalkers? I don't recall ever facing one of those on our travels, only one Hooded Stalker scared away with a puddle of water."

"Moat," replied Johan defensively.

"Whatever, it doesn't count anyway. Ruskans can be two or three times bigger than those, with a nasty streak to match."

Johan was not fazed. "No matter how big, Stalkers' weaknesses are well known, and bringing the big ones down isn't an unheard-of feat. At the very least we can jump in the river as a last resort."

"The deadly river? So dangerous no boat can travel it?"

Johan's lip curled in a half-grimace, half-smile. "That's the one."

Quiet nothingness passed in their little room for some time, each of the three weighing more possibilities than they'd ever thought they were capable of. Unsurprisingly, Johan spoke first, a natural leader. "There are a couple of things that need to be addressed before you go, Aryu."

Aryu had a feeling this was coming. There were a lot of unanswered questions Johan likely had about many different things. Aryu said nothing as he waited for the first salvo.

"First off, do you know what those men who attacked us had in their hands when you… intervened?"

Aryu shuddered at the memory of the two disintegrated bodies. The stare of the one with the remaining head returned to his mind's eye, wide and accusing. "A gun. They had a gun."

"They did not have a gun, Aryu. Guns don't explode like that. It was an Ark 1."

A hint of recognition sparked in his mind. "Isn't an Ark 1 a weapon of the Old?"

Johan nodded, causing Aryu to run cold. "It is. A very prolific one from the last age of mechanical weapons. Gone for an endless number of years. But I promise you, it was what I say it was."

"So what does that mean? Could one of those still be around after all this time?"

Johan shook his head. "They used what was called a battery. A thing that holds power for use later. Batteries can't last this long, even the good ones from the old days. Besides, would anyone around here even touch anything from that era?"

It was a good point. They had been slightly leery of the little lights at the bar in this town when they'd come through the first time. An old mechanical weapon likely would have caused a riot in the streets before this Army of the Old had arrived.

"And that power is why it exploded?"

"That and a really bad sense of timing on your part. You couldn't have hit it at a worse time than when he was about to fire."

"You're welcome."

Johan held his hands up and shrugged. "Hey, not that I'm not thankful, but that was the moment the power had built up the highest. This brings me to point number two: your sword."

Aryu glanced at the sheathed blade sitting beneath the window. He'd not even remembered putting it there but assumed it had been set down as he looked out the window at the goings-on below. Odd how it had wanted to be held so badly at times and could fade entirely from your memory at others.

"What about it?"

"You said this Nixon guy said it was old and powerful, something more than it seemed?"

That and it made Nixon need to kill him, but that was unnecessary information at this point. "He did. Called it the Shi Kaze and claimed it held great power. It's certainly sharp, but as for the power…" Aryu knew it was there, could feel it swell up in the blade even from where he was standing, but again said nothing. His secret. His burden.

"Kind of like my knife?"

"I think so," answered Aryu, unsure. He didn't have the

164

attachment to the knife that Johan did, so it was difficult to say.

"And Nixon is some kind of holy warrior?"

"Yes, something like that."

Johan thought for a moment, then looked at Aryu to be sure his words were heard. "We're going against something we've never seen before, but if it cut as easily as you say it did, just like my knife, then you had better learn how to use it. Get this Nixon guy to teach you if you have to."

Aryu was glad to see that he and Johan had the same train of thought. "Anything else on your mind?"

"One last little thing. What are we supposed to do with him?" Johan motioned to Esgona, his head in his arms. He could have been sleeping or dead. It was hard to tell.

"Esgona?"

No response.

"Esgona, are you awake?"

"What do you want?" His voice was quiet, like a cold wind. It threw off Aryu for a moment. He wasn't expecting an answer, let alone one so obviously pained and malicious. That same part of Aryu that had felt shame at Johan's obvious treatment of Esgona now triggered a distant feeling of fear. Something about this boy wasn't right. This was the response of a man, not a boy, who was one shove from being pushed too far.

"Watch your mouth, you fucking coward," Johan chastised from across the room, legs still swinging playfully over the desk. He loved every moment of this.

Esgona didn't look at him. He just looked up at Aryu and waited for whatever it was Aryu wanted to be said.

"Look, I did what I said I'd do for you. I promised Nixon that I'd take you, find Johan, and return. I've done that. My part of the deal is fulfilled as far as you go. You can stay with him or be on your way.

I don't really care either way, and believe me, neither does he."

"Damn right." Johan glowered playfully at them both.

"You can go wherever you want now, and if you left I wouldn't blame you in the slightest. You can take your shame to someone else for all we care, but remember this; we, the three of us, are still alive, still breathing, still here to honor our loved ones. I'll be right back into the fight when I return. No one else you meet will have the same drive and determination to see that army beaten and destroyed as we do.

"You are a coward, Esgona. That much is public record. You can live with your childish cowardice or you can stand and hope to die like a man. Johan will help you to that end, and when I return, so will I. A coward from Tan Torna Qu-ay is still a person from Tan Torna Qu-ay. Am I right, Johan?"

"He can tag along all he wants. I'll be civil."

Esgona doubted this. "All I want is to get as far from here as I can, and I can't go anywhere but where he's going for the time being. But listen: as long as I am with either of you, I will make sure no machine walks away. And I will not forget the thing I saw leading them, Aryu. The thing just like you."

It was so forceful and to the point that Aryu had no response. Johan didn't seem to suffer from the same affliction. He sprang from his desk perch and across the room to where Esgona had been sitting. Esgona knew what was coming and rolled away with an astonishing amount of dexterity for someone so depressed and with a crippling leg injury. Esgona made his way to the other side of the room by the door, looked at them both in turn, and exited into the hall.

"That little fucker! He has the balls to talk like that to us after the shit he pulled down south? I should just forget about him and leave without him." For a dishonored, lying bully of a boy to be so direct to someone accepted to be his superior, it seemed to prove beyond all reason that this was not the same world it had been only a few days ago. The rules they'd grown with no longer applied.

Aryu agreed to leave at sunup, still some hours away. Rest was needed and far more than a few hours could afford, but one last night with his friend was enough for now.

Johan passed out instantly, but Aryu dwelled on everything for a while. The echo of Nixon's words about the things Esgona had seen and the experiences changing him so much bounced in his head.

Aryu wished he didn't have so much to think about.

When the time the time for sleep came, it was simply because his mind was exhausted from running through everything. So many problems kept popping up that his brain waved the white flag and simply shut down as a precautionary measure, lest the body it controlled and the spirit within suffer from a complete breakdown.

▸◂▸◂▸◂▸◂▸◂▸◂▸◂▸◂▸◂▸◂▸◂▸◂

Dawn brought about more issues. The first of which was the lack of Esgona. "He'll be back or he won't. I'm not going looking for him while I can help it." Johan had needed to be awoken by Aryu, whose internal clock had done a perfect job of rousing him as the sun came up in the east.

The second more immediate issue was how Aryu could get out of the town without being seen. He had no idea if the place was full of people searching for him or if they had forgotten all about him, but it seemed the first was the slightly more likely of the two, and he attempted to hatch a plan to escape. Thankfully, the thing that made him a target also made for some decent getaway strategies. After an exploratory look around the floor they found a doorway to the staircase leading to the roof. If he left now before most people were up, the fuss would be at a minimum.

167

The last and most draining of the issues was the mental state of the two. Johan, physically, was a beaten piece of meat. The booze and encounter from the previous night were taking their toll on him heavily as the day grew older. He'd already been off to retrieve food and water, the latter of which he drank almost by himself before doling out some to his sober friend.

Aryu had gotten his few hours of rest, thinking about his questionable mission east. As he understood it, he had to accompany Nixon to find someone named Crystal Kokuou, an immortal Embracer that had been the bearer of the sword he now possessed. She was obviously a good person, or at least was for a long time. She was never hunted by Nixon during her time in possession of Shi Kaze, so it stood to reason. The time since then had seen her change greatly, Nixon had told him. She was more cautious about people and the world she was stuck living in. Apparently the false god, her ex-lover of untold millennia, had done a number on her ability to trust anyone fully.

Short on detail (as always), Nixon had told Aryu of the many meetings the two had over the years. He couldn't even say for certain that she was a completely changed person. He'd not seen her since he had awakened to clean up the mess left by the false god, but her dead ex-lover had clearly shaken her to the bone. Nixon was the first to admit that she may have long ago turned to dust. With so much time having passed, he couldn't be sure anymore.

All thoughts, stories, and fears he did not burden Johan with. Johan had his hands full as it was. Johan was tasked with leading a crippled, bitter enemy of his youth through the mountains to the Thunder Run, a perilous journey in the best of conditions, then up the valley along the Paieleh River to the Blood Sea, a place so far and distant from these men and where they'd come from it may as well be the moon for all the hope he had of getting there safely.

They never talked about these thoughts. They were brothers. There was no need. They ate and drank in silence, until the moment Aryu announced it was time for him to go.

Esgona still had not returned to their room yet, but Aryu had seen him hobbling to the water pump behind the building as he prepared to leave. Since he was still around, it was a safe bet he'd return to Johan and accompany him on the trip.

The two made it to the door to the stairs and went to the roof. The door was bolted shut, but a quick poke and flick of Johan's knife and the locks flew off with ease.

Aryu marveled. Johan smiled. "I haven't found the thing it can't cut through yet. Not a bad little tool to have." They both thought of the ease with which it had severed a limb.

Then, the weight of the moment hit in earnest. "Don't take long, Aryu. I can't stand to be around that hobbling weakling alone." Johan was clearly choking back his emotions, Aryu trying to do the same.

"You are my brother, Johan. Nothing can keep me from finding you when I'm done. Just keep to the plan: north, Huan, Thunder Run, Paieleh River, Blood Sea, closest town or city. Stick to that and I'll find you."

Johan and Aryu gave each other a long, sad look, both saying with their eyes that this could be the last time they saw each other, but neither willing to say it. "We are the last of Tan Torna Qu-ay, Johan. Let's be sure we do them all proud, despite how each of us had been treated by them. They were still our loved ones, and they deserved better."

The statement steeled Johan, emotions forced back in an instant. "You're right." He nodded. "We do what we do for them, and one day we'll get our vengeance."

A handshake and hug later, Aryu turned to go. "Tell Esgona, too.

Honor or no, we're in this together now."

Johan clearly didn't agree. "I'd rather it was just us, to be honest, but it is what it is."

"I know how you feel, but trust me when I say he's been through a lot."

His wings extended, careful not to be seen from street level three stories below. A quick test flap showed they were as ready as ever for the journey ahead. He turned and waved to his friend. "Be careful, Johan. This is a dangerous and scary new world."

The telltale Johan grin appeared one last time. "Yes it is, and I am a dangerous and scary man."

"Yes, sir, you are. Goodbye, Johan Otan'co."

"Goodbye, Aryu O'Lung'Singh. I'll see you when fate brings us together again. For Tan Torna Qu-ay!"

"For Tan Torna Qu-ay." A nod and a running dive off the roof later, Aryu was off, never looking back.

Johan stayed on the roof until Aryu was completely out of sight. No one below seemed to make a fuss. Their world was far too consuming to notice Aryu's departure.

He took a deep breath and tasted the air. The morning was sunny and crisp, but Johan was an excellent cloud reader. It seemed the afternoon would bring rain, unless it blew south. "Here's hoping," he said to himself. "Let those fuckers and their metal bodies deal with it." He knew it wouldn't stop them in any way, but the bravado encouraged him.

Esgona was waiting back at the room, silent and sullen as he looked out the window. Smart-ass remarks came close to spewing forth from Johan regarding the night before, then he thought better of it. Aryu was right about Esgona, a fact he was loath to admit. He bit his tongue for now and silently returned to a world with no Aryu, one Esgona, and a nightmare of a hangover.

◄►◄►◄►◄►◄►◄►◄►◄►◄►◄►◄►◄►◄►

Nixon had only a microscopic amount of doubt in Aryu's ability to return. It still seemed foolhardy to let him go, but Nixon was far past keeping things to the status quo. This was a brand-new world, and he was just coasting along in the chaos at this point.

Aryu did return at the agreed-upon time in the place Nixon had chosen, an abandoned house on the side of the highway into town.

"Miss me?" His sense of humor had not diminished, it seemed.

Nixon did not respond to the question, wanting to be on his way. He got up from the stoop by the front door and prepared to leave, hopefully towards the answers he needed. "Everything go well?" he asked at last.

The immediate expression on Aryu's face was one of great sadness and confusion, which was more of an answer than any words would have been. Instead of leaving immediately, Aryu began telling Nix the story of finding Johan, the attackers, and their frightening and terrible weapon, and finished with the results of his intervention. Aryu left nothing out, right down to the way he felt with the action, despite its heroism, ending with the horrible glare of the burned, skinless face.

Nixon listened with great interest. When he finished, Nixon brought him back to the deaths of the assailants.

"Ye're not proud or acceptin' of tha things ya done?"

Aryu looked at him disgusted. "Of course not! Why would I be either of those things? Bad or not, they deserved punishment for what they were doing, but not death. It was never my intention to kill them. I had no idea the weapon they carried was so dangerous or would react as it did. I'm glad the machine was destroyed, but it was an accident, pure and simple."

Nixon knew with certainty nothing in life was either pure or simple, and was never, ever a combination of the two.

"Well then, let me ask ya this: would ya take the action back, knowin' yer options are either takin' the action ya did or leavin' yer friend to his likely-poor fate?"

Aryu needn't have answered; the redness growing in his face was clear enough. "Well then, I guess ya did tha only thing ya could. Despite yer feelings or disgust at tha actions, inaction would 'ave caused the death of yer friend. Yours was tha correct choice and one I would 'ave made myself. I'd not judge ya too harshly on this matter, and neither should you. The road ahead is long and dangerous. Best t' learn like this and 'ave the advantage of knowin' yer friend is alive because of ya, and someone tha' would 'ave killed 'em for nothin' more than personal gain was lost. In the world I live in, Aryu, tha's called a fair trade."

Aryu didn't agree at all. It was far more complicated than that, and he knew it. Nix was just as he was created to be: a god's perfect weapon created to destroy life in order to preserve it.

Looking to get off the subject, Aryu asked how far they had to go. "If we remain airborne as long as possible we can make good time and be there with a minimum of fuss. I just hope this rain holds off." Aryu saw no rain but knew better than to question him. If a Divine creation of unlimited power and abilities who'd lived for untold millennia said it was going to rain, you had better prepare for rain.

They took off, Nixon with his flaming, glorious wings in the lead; Aryu and his leathery abominations close behind, gliding along in the heat of the rising sun. Aryu thought of his friend and Esgona and the quest they had to endure. It didn't sound like this was going to be an easy trip for him or Nixon, but at least he had a man made of fire and two unstoppable swords with him. Johan had a cripple and a good knife.

Nixon began his first dive, gaining speed like a falling rock. Aryu reached his apogee, beginning his rapid descent. Only the rush of wind in his ears could be heard, the views of the far-off earth could be seen, and a fireball who would be his dispatcher in other bygone ages blazing a scorching course ahead in the distance. With the Shi Kaze stored tightly, Aryu dove into what lay ahead.

FLUX

RAGE

BETRAYAL

FLUX

⋈⋈⋈⋈⋈⋈⋈⋈⋈⋈⋈⋈⋈⋈⋈⋈⋈⋈⋈⋈⋈⋈⋈⋈⋈⋈⋈⋈⋈⋈⋈⋈⋈⋈⋈⋈⋈

Out of the deep forests of Napponia stepped a shadowy figure, tall and thin, firm and imposing to the locals whom he comes across, should he choose to be seen.

Most in the area knew him and what his purpose was. Protect the people. Protect the land. Protect the life around him.

To see him, one would easily guess his purposes to be much more devious.

It was an intentional trait he'd acquired over many years to weed out the good from the bad. His short blonde hair, well-maintained full beard that was peppered with the perfect amount of roguish grey, and intense, deep blue eyes set in a world-weathered face gave him an instant look of well-kept, unwavering authority. His perfectly-cleaned, blood-red battle armor and large circular silver shield with its series of razor-sharp spikes surrounding it said that authority was in more than his appearance. He was what he seemed to be: a serious man with a serious job to do. The voices just made the job harder.

They were collections of lost souls who were once powerful people. They were now neither of this world or the next. Cast-offs from the age when God decided he'd had enough.

He trudged into the deep woods, slicing his way through with the blades lining his precious shield. If you could even call it a shield. It was so many things, really.

This particular shield-like object had once brought down God.

The history of the weapon was why this man had made it his life's work to serve and protect these lands. It was the least he could do.

He broke through a tree line, coming into the open field and the stream that ran through it. This empty space was his destination.

His armor clanked and sparkled in the sun as he crossed the grassy field. He had no illusions of hiding here. The field and all that dwelled within it were closed off from the rest of the natural world. A pocket of time and space hidden behind the Power. None but those who could see it and know its secrets could enter, and those were people very few and far between these days. Once there had been many places like this. They were havens for the powerful. Now there was only a handful of what was once a vast network of spectral refuse.

He approached the stream and the person sitting next to it that he'd come to speak with. Her petite frame and waif-like constitution made her almost disappear in the light. Her long white hair nearly blended in with the shimmer from the stream she sat by.

She stood as he approached, alerted to his presence as soon as he entered this place. Nothing happened here she didn't know about. It was her creation. She turned to him, her nearly translucent skin as white as her hair, her body small in a silvery dress hanging over her gentle curves, her face young and mischievous, and her eyes a deep crimson, a trait she had once adopted but now embraced as her natural appearance. She stood solidly and took the man's large hand as he neared.

"It's been a while since you've come here. I've missed you." Her childish voice carried on the wind like the babble of the creek beside them. Her voice was soft yet authoritative, as if she possessed a worldliness beyond her young appearance.

"I've been busy. There's a lot of world to protect, and I rarely have a day's rest." His deep voice dwarfed the girl's. While he looked to be a man in the middle-to-evening of years, if she was a day beyond her teens, it would have been shocking. "Besides, you know I hate coming here if I don't have to. There's too much for me to do out there to be hiding in the back alleys of reality."

A soft smile on the thin face of the girl. "Guilt you don't need to carry with you. It was never your fault."

"A fact I try to avoid hearing by never coming here, I'd like to add."

"And a fact I'll keep repeating until you believe it. My constant chiding of your history is not why you're here, though, is it?"

She could still read him better than he cared to admit, even after such long periods of being away.

"Sadly no, as much as I enjoy your incorrect reminders…"

"It's my right, you know."

"So you say. Still, you are right. Something has happened. Something you need to be aware of. Better to hear it from me than to be surprised." He paused. The last time this event had happened was right after the world, and this girl, had changed forever. "The voices bring a message. They say we have a visitor from the west."

"The west? There aren't many from the west that would dare. They're all too scared of their own shadows to come this far."

"This visitor is from a bit farther west than that, I'd say. The phoenix has returned. He has set up camp on the edge of our borders and I believe he plans to enter."

If she was shaken from this information, she did not show it. "Are we certain it's him? Or is it a 'her' this time?"

He nodded. "Yes. A presence like his can't be ignored by the voices. They felt his arrival the moment he came. It's a *him*."

Eventually, she grinned. "He's likely coming to find out why he can't zip from his home to other places in the world in an instant. What an interesting story that will be."

"Also, it seems he's brought company."

A look of doubt came to her face, a cute expression that would have seemed immature had it been anyone else. "A friend? Not likely. I don't need to tell you that he doesn't take well to stragglers and hangers-on."

"Regardless, it's true. He travels with one other, a boy, if the voices are to be believed. A boy with wings."

The impishness on her face was wiped away at once. The man was taken aback at the speed at which she changed. Something in the information had upset her. Something she didn't like at all.

"Wings? Are you sure?"

No answer this time. Of course he was sure. He'd made it a mission of his life to speak to the voices better than any other out of remorse for their plight, which he blamed on himself.

"There is one more thing they said…"

Her red eyes, now serious and terrifying, took the tall man in. He knew that this would be information she didn't want to hear.

"The voices feel the Power. They know one kind from another. They know better than any alive ever could. They feel it, and they are afraid."

He looked at her, and then to the distance, scared for the vision he would see if he held her gaze. Her anger could be great, and her fear was breathtaking in its ferocity.

"The boy carries the Shi Kaze, and Nixon is bringing him here."

"Ridiculous!" she shouted at once, unable to contain her emotions. "Nixon of the Great Fire and Ash is sworn by an oath to God to destroy any sword-bearer he catches. He certainly does not prance around our countryside with them. If he sees them, he kills them! It was the God's will."

Any time she lost control of her emotions was a time to be afraid. Power such as hers was not easily contained, and to be so close to it in such unpredictable moments prickled the hairs on the back of his neck.

"I know what his purpose is, traditionally, anyway. I know it sounds impossible, but I swear it's the truth. The phoenix travels with a winged boy who carries the sword. I doubt I could come up with more ridiculous statement. I'm not that imaginative."

"Are we certain they are coming here?"

The man shook his head. "I can't say for sure, but it'd seem that we're the most likely target."

"You mean me. Nixon doesn't even know you're alive." That was true. A fact he had forgotten. "Still, I don't see how I could help him, or them, as the case seems to be."

Her first reaction bothered him. "Is there something wrong with this whole thing?" She didn't catch his meaning. "Before, when I told you he had wings, you seemed disturbed. We've encountered the winged people before, though never outside their home."

She nodded in recognition. "Yes. The Omnis has told me of a huge army of ancient creation that has risen and is terrorizing lands south of here, where the people are primitive and can't stand against them. It is said that the one who controls them is a man with wings. I'm curious if this boy is somehow connected to him, or others of his kind."

The man stood, looking at her once more in confusion. "The Echoes told you this? I haven't heard anything like it."

"We all have our secrets. You have those voices, I have the Echoes."

Echoes, as the man understood them, were the background noise someone with her powers could hear when she stepped from the Haven into standard reality; a journey she rarely made at all these days. They were idle chatter that rode on the back of a collective consciousness known as the Omnis: an accumulation of shared

179

existence that everything emitted. Even thoughts people didn't know existed, like that of animals and plants. A massive, universal intelligence without body or form. Something more than life itself. An amalgamation of anything and everything.

The concept was staggering in its immenseness. The man didn't have the power to hear such things. Frankly, it seemed a waste to even try. If she, in all her power, couldn't do any more than faintly touch the edges of the things that went on within it, he would have no chance at all. He had great power, but nothing like her.

Also, there was a downside to the Echoes and the things it said. If you can hear the Echoes, you must also touch the Est Vacuus: the antithesis and anathema to life. Not evil. Not negative. Just utter and complete void. An absolute state of barren space beyond the beyond. You could not have one without the other. It was the truth of balance. Good or evil had a million shades of grey. This was something more than both combined. Something more than death, as even death originated from life, lest it wouldn't exist.

She once attempted to describe the all-encompassing nothingness that was the Est Vacuus. *"Imagine water,"* she had told him. *"Imagine it in a clear cup. No background, no color. No light, no dark."* He did as she asked.

"Now, imagine if it filled the infinite universe."

He admitted at once he didn't understand. *"It would be as space is, dark and empty, no up or down."*

She shook her head right away. *"No, even beyond that. Space still has a background, a background of black nothing. Space is full of sub-atomic particles and dark matter. Eliminate the black. Black, although it is the signature of an empty void, is still something. Imagine space with no black. Just an endless sea of clear, free of absolutely everything."*

He couldn't do it. He doubted anyone could without her power and abilities. He did know that such a thing or place as the Est Vacuus was more than he ever needed to see.

Even with her great power, he was certain the times she had tapped this frightening resource had affected her in ways she may not be aware of, and every visit he had with her was also an opportunity to see if they had manifested themselves into a form he could see. As of yet, there was nothing.

This place, this Haven, was beyond the natural world. A shield from the things she spoke of. You could hear or feel neither while you were here. Everything you were went into maintaining the Haven.

"So, what to do now." She said it in a return to her impish ways, a state more becoming of one who looked like she did: young, beautiful, and vibrant.

"I don't know. That's why I've come. To warn you, but also to see what you think."

"All this time and you still can't think for yourself. It's craziness that you limit your abilities the way you do."

"Maybe, but knowing the things you've seen and the pain I've already caused, I'm happy with the state I'm in."

The argument was about to start again, but it could wait for another time.

"Let them come. I'm curious about what they could possibly want with me. Maybe they can create some kind of insight into the terror that this army is causing and why. It's terrible to think we could be at it again. It never ends well."

"And what of the sword? The voices sense no Power in the boy. Nothing but fear and confusion. What does it mean?"

"I guess we have to wait and see. Be sure to go greet them. Better to get your existence out of the way. If it's me they want, I'd hate to keep them waiting. Not that I believe I'll be much help."

"Still, there are worse places in the world to get information than you, the great Crystal Kokuou; immortal keeper of the Dragon Spirit, and possibly the oldest, wisest, and most powerful human alive."

She reached up to his face and caressed his rough beard gently, taking in his age and ruggedness. "I've told you, just call me Mom."

RAGE

It was a gross understatement to say it was upset with the recent events that seemed to have occurred in its domain.

Humans weren't terribly tasty. They were small in size, but they generally put up a decent fight. They were more trouble than they were worth. Below came a stream of people from the valleys of the south. He didn't care in the slightest why they were here, only that they *were* here. He was a solitary creature, aged and wise, but intensely territorial and exceptionally moody. If this was a trend that continued, something had to be done. Humans, especially in such great numbers, were just irritating.

No, this simply could not do.

His vantage point had a clear and unobstructed view of the branching valleys below. From the south poured the unwanted visitors, some going east to the deep valleys and treacherous peaks, a journey that would almost certainly kill them all before they saw any glimmer of whatever salvation they sought. The rest went west, no doubt to follow the mighty river that had long ago carved its place in the rock. These were the people he was cautious about. If well-stocked and keen of mind, they would enter deep into the heart of his domain or the domains of others like him.

He had to think deeply about his next course of action. Perhaps the best option was to travel along with a larger group until he met up with another of his kind, hopefully one closer to him in age and wisdom. The young could be so impulsive and make too many mistakes. It was an idea likely to have its own perils, but it was better than standing here next to the Uhluktahn, the sacred thundering waterfall, and doing nothing. These lands belonged to none of them and all of them at once. Yet the humans were certainly pressing into their home in greater numbers, and something had to be done.

They had no place here. He hoped they would leave on their own. He certainly did not seek their wrath. People were short-sighted and vengeful. Though he was old and wise, it was also a slave to its own animalistic tendencies. If the humans continued, none would be spared.

To be so intelligent only to still be weak to his baser needs. Shameful, yet unavoidable. He hoped it wouldn't reach that point, but if it did, he was glad to know that many, if not all, of these trespassers would suffer for the idiocy of their actions.

He stalked away, letting the rush of the great water fill his ears; lost in the thought of the anger and bloodlust that may follow.

BETRAYAL

The journey had taken a terrible toll on his old bones. He wasn't accustomed to such rugged travel. He preferred to walk, letting the road meet his feet and the fresh air and silence fill his head as he went.

Unfortunately, time was not his ally. Speed was needed to reach his goal. His goal was to be as far from the village and the idiots within it as possible.

He'd left soon after the meeting with the demon. A meeting he wanted no part of at first. He'd have preferred to leave well enough alone and never come face to face with such a creature, whatever it was, but he was bound by a promise to another to deliver the monster. Besides, the opportunity to create mischief so late in the game was too strong a temptation.

At this moment he was seriously wondering if the devil at the bar or the devil who wanted him was to be feared most. At least the devil at the bar bought him a drink.

The caravan he'd been traveling with was full of whiney, annoying children and whinier, more annoying women. All they did was cry and talk while the men rode off ahead or behind or wherever they could escape to. The old man had no mount and was stuck surrounded by their constant chattering and useless banter. It was only in moments like this, when he wandered off by himself during the nights, that he found his peace. How he longed for his home in the high country, still many days travel from here. At least this caravan would carry him most of the way.

He sipped his hot tea, far from the others. By this point in the journey he'd taken great care to establish himself as a man who wished to be avoided in no uncertain terms. After a few lame attempts at persuading him otherwise, he was now left alone whenever they stopped. It gave him plenty of space to clear his mind of the racket.

This night was not to be so peaceful it seemed, as he heard the footsteps approach him in the loose rock scattered around the area. "Fools and their needs for togetherness," he spat to himself as the steps came closer.

A figure circled around him and took a seat just beyond the firelight. In the poor light, it was impossible to see if it was man or woman, old or young. They were wrapped in a loose blanket that hung over their shoulders like a shroud and wore what looked to be a pack of some kind underneath it.

"Be gone, ya stupid fool. I don't care a shit about the things you have to say and why you have to say 'em. If you don't leave me now, I'll teach you a lesson in personal space you won't forget!"

The figure didn't move an inch. More surprisingly, the blanketed head rose slightly, showing a youthful mouth that had the wickedest smile the old man had ever seen. It was a smile the man knew very well. It was the smile he was so desperate to run away from back to his shanty home as quickly as he could.

"Now now," the newcomer said in a pleasant, yet disturbing voice. "I had heard you were a man who enjoyed the art of conversation. Did you not just have a whole bar close down to host one such moment?"

It was the stranger that had made the deal with the old man weeks ago: the one who promised the lands he came from would not be touched in return for the favor of delivering the demon-thing into their apparent waiting hands in the south.

"I was hoping we wouldn't meet again. What business do you have with me?" The thing across from the old man scared him beyond belief, but he held his ground. The fire-demon had intimidated him with its sheer power and presence. This thing was worse. It was disgustingly pleasant and far more ruthless.

"I wanted to talk to you about what I asked you to do. More to the point, I was hoping you could explain why you failed."

"Failed! Bah, I put that godless beast right into your hands! If *you* failed in doing what you had to when he got there, that's none of my business. I did my part."

"Your part, sir, was to send him south to the village where he was to be apprehended or dispatched, depending on the situation. Tell me then why neither of those things happened?"

The old man laughed a dry, mirthless laugh. "I tell you, I did as you said and I did it perfectly. The demon was sent south and that is that. Judging by the activity everyone saw there, you got what you wanted."

The teeth of the creature under the blanket were white as pearls, straight as a razor, and perfect in every way. "That was nothing more than a test of his durability. Some in my ranks believed it would outright destroy him. I knew otherwise. He was badly damaged, but he lived. However, this does not change your failure, sir. You were to send him south, to the home of the winged boy, where we could take them each and complete our business in this land."

"Winged boy? What winged boy? Look, all you told me to do, I did. I don't know a lick about a kid with wings or some such nonsense."

The smile, in all its perfection, faded. "You don't know anything about a boy with wings from Tan Torna Qu-ay?"

"That's what I said, isn't it? No wings. No boy. I haven't got a clue what you're talking about."

The old man knew a little, but nothing about wings. He suspected now that it may have something to do with that depressed young man he saw at Ollie's bar a few days back, on the night before he left with the caravan. The same caravan the old man had taken up with now. An amused, gap-toothed grin came to his face. He remembered who he was and what he possessed.

When the thing across from him had threatened him into conversation with the beast, they hadn't been specific on the how, leaving the details in the old man's hands. When the old man saw the fire beast enter, talk to Ollie, then produce the terrifying blade for all to see, the old man jumped at the sight of it; the terrible and glorious aura it emitted telling him instantly it shared a bond with the knife he'd given to the village, and thusly, the boy from Tan Torna Qu-ay.

186

It was that connection that gave him the chance to talk to him, telling him where he must go. By the gods, the fire beast had *wanted* to go south. It was the easiest deal the old man could have made.

Now, sitting with his cooling tea across a fire from a smiling fool, he realized two separate and very important things. The first was that they had no idea the weapon the boy had in his possession and the kinds of damage it could do if used properly. The second was that he would never live to enjoy this thing's misery when it found out. If they were here, asking the question it had, there wasn't much hope for the old man. The smiling creature was angry that something beyond the old man's control had gone wrong. The old man was about to pay the price for it.

At least he'd die knowing his last act on this earth would cause the thing across the fire untold amounts of misfortune, given the hope that the boy could figure out what to do with the knife in time.

"What's so funny, you old fool?"

Was he smiling? He hadn't realized it, but it was too late to hide it now. "I just can't believe my luck, I guess. I did all you asked, and you failed, so you're here to blame me and do me in. I guess no matter what I had no chance of winning, did I?"

The smile, seemingly buying the story, grew and nodded. "So it would seem. I guess you weren't the right man for the job."

"Ha, well, you picked me, so one wonders who the one is doing a poor job."

The thing was at his throat in an instant, leaping the fire like a cat and squeezing down with a strength one wouldn't expect from a frame so small. "You are not near as wise as you believe, you worthless old man."

All the old man could do in the face of such evil was laugh. "Nor are you, my stupid friend. You think yourself to be the one in control, but you haven't got a clue."

187

The hooded thing was certainly not smiling now as it uncovered a shiny, mechanical hand. It reached up to the old man's face, gripping it like a vise as it pulled him forcefully from the ground and released his neck. The quiet air filled with the soft crack of bones breaking to accompany the pop of the fire.

Still, despite the pain, he laughed harder and harder, the situation too amusing to be ignored.

In a rage, the thing tossed the old man back through the tips of the flames. He landed terribly on the other side, his old body nowhere near the shape needed to escape such a forceful and malicious toss unscathed. Still, broken and dying, the old man laughed harder than he could ever remember. He laughed hard enough to erase his pain. This thing had no clue what it was up against.

The thing was livid now, annoyed and consumed by hate for the old man and his useless laughter. He realized the stubbornness and senility of the old bastard would never let him tell it anything it needed to know. He was far too pleased with himself. There was nothing left to do but finish him and be done.

With its other arm, one of natural flesh and bone, it produced a sword, the likes of which the old man had never seen. It was long and thin, curved all the way to the tip. Where a normal metal blade would be was what looked like the purest diamond or crystal, so clear and perfect that it was almost invisible, were it not for the distortion of firelight as it moved around. Another weapon of Power? Perhaps, but different. The others he'd seen were both good and bad; here there was more than bad. Here there was absolute nothingness.

The nothing consumed him, breaking him into a million shards of emptiness. The feeling so all-consuming in its vastness that it made him want to die just to escape it. At least in death there was the hope of something more. Here, facing this thing and its horrible weapon, there was simply a void. And that scared him terribly.

"Oh no, old man," the thing said, reaching into his mind. "With this, there is no death. Nothing beyond. Nothing but... well, nothing." It laughed as it spoke. What did it mean there was nothing? Please, gods who hear his prayers, don't let this feeling last! Please let it be over and never come back!

Again, the thing saw his thoughts in his terrified eyes. "God can't hear you. God is dead. Prepare to enter *my* fate for you, as I am the only god you need to fear, and my fate for you is an eternity within the hell you feel right this moment. Behold! The all-encompassing void that is the Est Vacuus!"

The thing was at him again, blade in hand, stabbing the end deep into the man's body. It never came out the other side. It just seemed to disappear with every inch that was plunged into him. The action brought more of the same, disgusting emptiness. If the creature said anything else, he couldn't hear it. All he saw, all he heard, all he tasted, all he felt, everything about him was filling with a crippling sense of nothingness. No hope, no joy, no fear, no pain, nothing beyond nothing, and back to nothing again.

His head felt as if he was falling in every direction at once, at speeds faster than he thought possible. Each iota of his being was consumed by the feeling of destitution as he went. He could barely get the thought through his head that this kind of torture was not worth the joy he had just felt at his attacker's ineptitude. A joy he couldn't remember feeling anymore. There was only the clarity of the void.

To his enemy's eyes, it appeared the opposite was happening. Each part of the frail body collapsed towards the hole made by this terrible weapon. Soon, his feet left the ground, hanging lifelessly as his torso fell inward into nothing. His head, once full of mirthless laughter at the misfortune of others, began to shrink and condense like air from a balloon until it fell into his chest as well. After a few moments, the blade devoured the man like the bottom of an hourglass consumes the top until all that was left was the attacker and a dying fire.

To the victim, there was only nothing, until even the acknowledgment of the sensation was lost to the infinite expanse.

Soon, the void that is Est Vacuus, unable to support anything within itself in any capacity without losing what it is, allowed the infinitesimal something that had just entered its expanses to be obliterated and consumed until it returned to its natural state. For such a thing to happen to a living creature, even the smallest single-celled organism, torture is an incredibly useless word. One is never so certain they have a soul as they are the moment it is ripped from their body and destroyed.

The assailant, confident the deed was done, drew back the perfect blade and sheathed it beneath the blanket, careful to not let others see the action or the face of the one who had committed it. They were angry at themselves more than anything. They were well-trained in the control and manipulation of both people and situations, but the old man had struck a very sensitive nerve. The old man was in no way worthy of the destruction he had just endured. It was simply an over-reaction to a fool. Still, it was upsetting even now that the bastard was gone into the nothing. How he had laughed! How he mocked them right to their face! What had he known? What didn't he tell them?

There were no more answers here.

They left the scene of the horrible crime they had just committed. Once they had traveled down the road enough to be gone from the light of the fires and the range of the scouting parties each caravan had established to protect the others while they slept, they cast off the blanket, exposing their twisted visage to the night.

He had been human once, many years ago before the foolishness of mankind tried again to destroy itself. Now he was a terrifying mix of flesh and metal, a hybrid of all the fears of the people in these lands, because not only was he an advanced and efficient machine, he was also a human that possessed the Power on an unrivaled level. Only his right arm, upper torso, and head were still fully human, each being a part of himself he refused to have altered. His arm was toned and strong, his body hard and muscular, his head youthful, but not too much so. His eyes dark and narrow, the head smooth and hairless. His face was handsome once. Now it was scarred and battered, each wound telling a tale of unfathomable evils committed in another life.

Of course, there was also the smile, a glistening beacon of dubious intent. Even small dimples accentuated the edges.

Just like his father.

The rest was extremely similar to the monster that had ordered the destruction of Tan Torna Qu-ay. It was only fitting. It was designed in his image. Right down to the perfect, pleasant voice.

The most non-human part exposed itself. From his back unfolded his large, thin, nearly indestructible mechanical wings. Wide and skeletal, like a synthetic version of the ones belonging to the young man he had been hunting. A young man he had apparently just missed thanks to the interference of the phoenix at the last minute.

This evening's task was complete, and he had to return to the south where the great army he commanded awaited his next set of orders. He had to ensure the proper next move was made. The wings, in what could be described as a perfect harmony of strength and motion, had him airborne instantly.

The old man was on his mind the whole trip, his laughter echoing like shrill background noise as it went.

He knew something, and it was important enough to defy the

creature until the moment of his destruction. That said something very powerful to him as he flew. The old man was a fool, but not so foolish as to laugh at nothing while facing his death. Nor was he insane. Indeed, it was the amount of wit the man had about him that led to him being the one chosen to send Nixon. Damn it, why had he chosen to manipulate such a person. No good could come of it.

Oh well, lesson learned as he carried off south to where his word was law, and no one would dare laugh.

The weapon at his side and his readiness to use it was testimony to that.

CHAPTER 12

The Power and the Foolish

From the time they had landed and set camp in the shade of an old cherry orchard he could begin to feel something powerful, but more disconcerting, he could hear the voices that flowed with it as well. This made the phoenix very sad. This was a sadness it had felt before, when last it was awake to clean up the mess of Tokugawa Ryu and his foolish actions.

These were the voices of the past. The lost and trapped. The fallen. The remnants of the powerful souls Ryu had purged. The voices on the edge of the Omnis.

Aryu was a complete wreck by this point in the trip. Nixon had maintained a hard and exhausting pace. Although he was much faster than even a few days ago, he was still nothing compared to Nixon.

The nights and moments of rest were almost as bad. The two unlikely compatriots were through the feeling out process of one another and had begun what could best be described as a very young acquaintanceship. For Aryu and Nixon, it seemed to be more of a teacher and student connection. Nixon told his stories and tried to express to Aryu the needs and morals of each. Aryu listened, enjoying the story more than the message, and took a little something from each one.

On day two, the question of the sword was asked.

"Do ya know how to handle such a thing, Aryu?" he was asked. "Could ya defend yerself if ya needed to?"

Aryu, unsure of the answer, vaguely said, "maybe, if it came up," and left it at that.

"Well, it came up a few days ago, I'd say. If ya want t' rejoin yer friend and be of any use, I'd suggest ya learn. It's a powerful weapon. Possibly the most powerful ever, but tha' can only get ye so far. With it now, ye can use it as ya would a regular sword, with the added benefit of its near invulnerability. Ye can still be a very dead young man if ya can't handle tha' thing as a weapon in its most basic terms."

Aryu had handled weapons before, but he didn't need to be told the places he was going to would have situations beyond those he'd encountered.

"So what do you propose?" he'd asked at last, knowing the answer, giddy at hearing the words from Nixon.

"Simple. Each day between here and when we reach our destination, ya listen and follow while I show ya some of tha basics. Pray my small amount of instruction is ne'er needed, though."

Aryu agreed instantly, elated at the thought. This had been Aryu's intention all along: to accompany the beast and learn anything he could about the sword and its uses so he could make himself a stronger fighter for the battles to come.

So it had been for days. Hard flying topped off with a few hours each day learning some basics from Nixon. Aryu learned that strength had little to do with it when it came to the Shi Kaze. With a simple thrust or wrist flick, he could drive the point into a thick rock or fell a giant tree effortlessly. The memory of the mechanical man who had almost abducted him and the ease with which the sword had taken its arm or the slick and graceful way it had cleaved the Ark 1 in half (results of which notwithstanding) were made clearer as he learned more.

At times, the obvious question of whether it was pure coincidence that he had found it rolled through his head, though he never voiced them.

After practice on the day they reached the Napponia border, Aryu returned to the camp to see Nixon lost in his own mind, his deep black and red eyes saddened as he stared deeply into their fire. Anyone could see that more than usual was weighing on Nixon's mind. Aryu questioned him about it.

"So obvious, am I? Well, this is a very sad place fer me. A place of death and lost voices. Ryu was a very po'erful man, and I can only assume by tha fact I ne'er 'ad to hunt him except fer the last time, he was a good man to many people. He was also foolish in his actions, a man lost t' his own powers. With his final act, an act of unspeakable maliciousness, he attempted t' purge all the users of Power from the world, not fer any matter of control, or t' become the strongest person alive, as he likely already was.

"He did it fer selfish and personal reasons, ones tha', in my mind, did'na necessitate the cullin' of so many lives. He was forced into a corner, and he reacted with a level of force he believed was necessary to get wha' he wanted while hammerin' the point 'ome t' all parties involved. But he failed. He didn't purge everyone with control of the Power. He missed quite a few who had found shelter in wha' are called Havens, which were beyond 'is reach. Crystal was one such person. I fear tha' despite his love fer her, she still would'a been lost if he could get her.

"There were those he killed and those he spared unknowingly, but the voices I hear are of those somewhere in between.

"Napponia was once tha central location for all who wished t' learn of the Power. Crystal was the daughter of a very powerful and beloved mortal Embracer, who hadn't let the Power lake 'is life yet. At 'is school, many people came to learn these mysterious ways. He believed tha' use of mankind's untapped potential was tha key to savin' tha world he lived in, one which was destroyed some years earlier by war. A war tha' caused wha' I believe ye would know as the Second Fall of Man.

"Many Havens sprang up 'ere. For years this was the 'ome of peace and a leader in the restructuring of the world into a new and enviable place. Sadly, before he 'ad enough students t' carry on properly, he died savin' Crystal's life, an act tha' was so powerful and pure of 'eart tha' the Power he 'ad built up was released into the world, triggerin' the planet's healin' process. This was an unimaginable feat fer a mortal, never havin' succumb t' the Power's ability t' slow or halt time and agin'. A truly astonishin' person, he was. I've ne'er seen any others like him in all my years.

"'Is work was unfinished, though, and the direction of many he taught didn'a become noble. As they spread into the world, the age of the Power began, with many wars being fought between different Embracers. In time this would lead to the Third Fall of Man, at the hands of Tokugawa Ryu. There was so much innate power 'ere, both in mankind and the surroundin' lands tha' all of Ryu's considerable powers couldn'a completely penetrate it. The result was any exposed Embracer, noble or not, being stripped of all but their base consciousness and essence. The result was the voices I 'ear now.

"When last I passed through, the moment of their disembodiment was fresh and they were fallin' over one another tryin' t' understand wha' 'ad 'appened. Now they're more organized, but not at peace. In fact, quite tha opposite. It seems tha' now they know their plight and are desperate to escape it. At least with bodies, it was a possibility. Now they're trapped."

Aryu listened intensely, lost in the story and the victims it produced. A part of him was revolted to be surrounded by these people, despite his inability to see or hear them. "I think I need to ask a question I don't want the answer to, Nixon. But if I'm to understand all that has happened, and may happen again, I need to know." Nixon nodded, unsure of the conversation's direction. "What exactly *is* the Power? I know it's born inside us, and can manifest itself in ways once thought to be magic, mind-reading, astonishing strength and whatnot, but what *is* the Power?"

Nixon smirked. "Aryu, if ye 'ad any idea tha vastness of tha Power and the things it could do, I doubt ya would be able to answer tha' question if asked. Basically, the Power begins with eliminatin' the restrictions of yer mind. For years people believed the mind was more powerful than we were shown t' believe but didn't know how t' progress towards finding its true depths.

"The ones who tapped it first were deeply religious people. People who dedicated their lives to explorin' themselves and the abilities tha' lay dormant. Soon they realized tha' life and death, power and weakness, all basic living standards were not fixed in stone but were arbitrary. Death is only inevitable if ya believe it t' be; 'owever, since everyone seemed to die, it seemed as unstoppable as the wind. Jus' because one couldn't conjure fire from 'is 'ands, or make it rain with a thought didnn'a mean it couldn't be done. Soon, these honorable figures around tha world found new, astonishin' and sometimes terrible ways t' use their mind's 'idden secrets. The practice was widely 'idden until shortly before tha Second Fall of Man, when those with an ear t' the spiritual winds caught the image of wha' was about t' befall mankind.

"Crystal's father is a prime example of it, though as I said, he was much more skilled at its mastery than many others. His teacher, an old man named Owata-san, who is let's jus' say an old acquaintance o' mine, was determined t' pass on the teachings and saw in 'er father the person to do so. Owata-san chose, some say foolishly, not to limit wha' her father could do or teach t' others. Owata allowed him t' enter the world with a mind full of Power and possibilities, hoping tha' 'is lack of restraint would cause a ripple effect, givin' all men the tools required t' thrive in this new land the closed-minded 'ad created.

"W'ether tha' decision ultimately led to the rise of the Power and tha Third Fall of Man is a debate left t' 'istorians, should there be any left."

Aryu, lost in the story, was still confused.

"Think of it this way, Aryu," Nixon continued, racking his brain for an explanation Aryu could understand. The story of Crystal's father, a story she had told him during their first meeting, came to mind. Nixon used his powers to create a small flame no bigger than a candle, at the tip of his finger. "Ya see this fire?"

"Yeah, of course."

"Can ya put it out?"

"Sure."

"From across a room? With no aid from water or anythin' else? Jus' by thinkin' about it?"

"No. That can't happen."

"Why?"

"Because I'd need to use some kind of tool."

"There ya go. Think of it this way. It exists. You exist. Ya have tha' in common. Yer both real. The Power is a means of tappin' tha' common bond, connectin' the two of ya and allowin' ya t' do as ya wish without liftin' a finger."

"So you're saying that just because it and I are real, I can put it out? Just by thinking it?"

"Put it out! Make it bigger! Turn it into a flamin' pony! The possibilities are limitless, if ye release the limits of yer mind and allow yerself t' be lost in the unimaginable sea of everythin'."

"And the objects you say are used to focus, like the sword?"

"Ah, well, most people in history enjoy takin' the easy way to anywhere. Ryu originally needed the Shi Kaze to focus 'is powers. 'Is use left its mark on tha blade, as did each subsequent use fer the same purpose. In the end, it became as it is now."

"And why the need to focus with an object?"

"The same reason the Power became so widely used after Crystal's father began teachin'! Because people need to see it to believe it! Let me jus' say this. Do ya' believe tha' ya could make tha' flame dance and grow? Honestly?"

"Well it seems unbelievable that it's that easy. Just believing we both exist doesn't seem like enough."

"But ya believe tha Power is out there?"

"Ryu didn't leave much doubt."

"Right. So yer belief isn't an outright no?"

"Not a total no."

Nixon smiled. "Why is tha'?" The truth began to dawn on Aryu's face.

"It's because the history of the world proved that people with these amazing abilities exist."

"And if there 'adn't been, 'ow easy would it be t' believe?"

Aryu finally saw where Nixon was going, though it still seemed far-fetched. "It would have been impossible."

Nixon clapped his big hands, a deafening sound in the quiet air, his sorrow at the plight of the voices momentarily lost. "Exactly! Ya *know* it can be done, history teaches ya tha'. People are a fantastically skeptical species. 'Seein' is believin'' may as well have been yer motto from the dawn of Genesis!"

Now Nixon started to calm himself, having found himself so wrapped up in the story, while Aryu's green eyes had grown wide. Nixon started again, looking to help the young man's dawning epiphany properly. "So, finally, we come to the objects of Power. Simple as this: people knew the Power was possible. They knew wha' it could do to objects, givin' 'em great strength and significance. Everyone believed it was just easier to begin with an object of focus and go from there. So 'ere we are, with a world full of nearly indestructible weapons, necklaces, rings, whatever some damned fool used t' get t' tha' point. These objects exist only because one person started a trend tha' grew. Believability came from tha action. Nothin' more. That's what Allan, Crystal's father, did. He broke down the barrier of disbelief. He let the secret out."

Aryu was flabbergasted at the thought that it was just that easy. Aryu had originally hoped the answer was a little more feasible, perhaps something he could use to his advantage later down the road. This one was just too simple.

Now, beyond getting the beast-man off his tail and returning to his friend, he wanted to find Crystal just as badly as Nixon did for the same reason as the phoenix. He wanted answers. If he could master the Power, but limit it, not allow it to get to the levels that had crippled the world, he may have found a weapon powerful enough to use on the mechanical army.

He knew immediately he had to tread carefully from here out. How many had fallen to the Power thinking just what he did right at this moment? *Well,* he thought to himself as he settled into sleep, *at least I'd have one hell of a reason not to go too far. How many of the people Nixon had destroyed would have changed their tune after meeting him?* He was a smart young man. He knew the fine line he'd have to walk to make this idea come true. Nixon seemed intent on teaching him enough to survive, but perhaps Crystal could go that one step further.

"Wake up lad..." streamed through his dream state as he was slowly rocked awake. The terrifying visage of the phoenix glared at him through the darkness, the soft glow of his hair and eyes all that could be seen in the shadows of the night beneath the trees.

As he began extending his wings to stretch the muscles he'd been sleeping on, Nixon quickly reached out and grabbed the leathery appendages before he had a chance to do so.

"What's going..." He was quickly shushed, so he asked in whisper, "What's going on? Is there someone here?"

No answer.

Aryu was about to ask again when Nixon put his large, warm finger to Aryu's mouth to keep him quiet. Aryu listened, straining to get past the rustle of leaves by the wind, but could hear nothing more than the sounds of the night.

The air here was moist and Aryu had taken to sleeping without a shirt, using only the warmth of his wings at night. His shirt, the last of the special woven canvas shirts his mother had made him before he had left a year ago, was currently his pillow. The dark brown (and now very tattered) top had two long slits cut down from the back of the neck to accommodate his wings and buttons at the top of the slits to make it wearable. Aryu had thought often over the past few days about where to get another when this one gave up the ghost. His mother wasn't around to make him a new one. The thought flashed sadness past his mind, but he quickly dismissed It.

"Get yer sword," the big man said. Aryu still wasn't terribly confident with the blade, having only the most rudimentary skills to begin with, but if some kind of threat was out there, better to have it than not. He pulled the ancient weapon from its sheath and waited by Nixon's side.

"I believe we're bein' watched," Nixon said eventually. "And watched by somethin' very strong."

"Strong how? Animal, person, what? I don't have your ears."

Nixon shook his head. "It's not ears I'm usin'. This thing, whatever it is, 'as command of tha Power."

Nixon motioned him to stay where he was as he slowly made his way into the darkness beyond the trees surrounding them. From time-to-time Aryu saw what he believed to be the glow from the beast's hair float through the underbrush.

A sudden gust of wind came from behind him, quick and unnatural like something had moved past him and disappeared into the trees on the other side. Shi Kaze up and in the ready position, Aryu turned only to encounter the same sensation behind him once more. A crack of a branch snapping came out of the dark from the direction Nixon had gone. In an instant Aryu saw the muted blur of something go after it.

Not hesitating, Aryu charged after the shadow. Ahead of him arose a plume of fire from the trees. It bathed enough light on the area for Aryu to see the soft, flickering sign of something to his left. His adrenalin pumping faster than rational thought, Aryu ran at the tree and brought the sword about as quickly as his arms could do so. The tree he suspected had hidden this secret assailant was cleaved in two with the effort and came crashing down in a thunder that shattered the silent night.

The flame pillar died down, and Aryu heard heavy feet and armor coming towards him. Stealth was unnecessary after his felling of the tree, so Aryu called out to Nixon at the top of his voice. "Nixon! Over here!"

Nixon, eyes wild and darting about, crashed through a series of bushes to his location, the massive sword swinging back and forth just as quickly.

"I saw it, behind the tree, but it escaped before I could get it."

"No problem, lad. Keep tha' sword up! Follow yer instincts."

Without warning, Nixon locked onto an empty space in the trees above Aryu. His arm extended and a shot of white fire blasted over his head. The wave of heat hit the ground a few paces away, lighting the grasses and bushes that were there. With the wave of his hand, Nixon extinguished the flames and continued the search.

"Bastard! They're fast."

Aryu began to worry again, even with the big man by his side. "Is it an Embracer? Can you feel it?"

Nixon shook his head again, his hair flipping back and forth with the jerky motion. "I feel somethin', but it's unfamiliar t' me. If it is tha Power, it's like nothin' I've ever felt. It's far more natural, like it's a part of tha forest."

Another wind rushed behind them, causing Nixon to send a wave of brilliant flame off into the direction it traveled, incinerating a young cherry tree. Aryu could hardly believe the awesome display the phoenix was putting on.

The flames gave Aryu the glimpse of another brief reflection moving around to flank them.

He spun off to his right, bringing the Shi Kaze around and hitting another tree, driving the sharp edge into the trunk yet again. This time the blade hit something very hard with a loud *clang* and sparks flew from behind, sending the shadow backwards with a thud. Nixon was past Aryu and on the thing immediately, broadsword out and arcing down as he went.

"Wait!" said a cry from the dark. "For the love of God, Nixon." Nixon, still fired-up, stopped the attack against the person on the ground.

Aryu ran over to see Nixon standing over a very tall and lithe man with a large silver shield raised to defend himself.

"Nixon, please, I wasn't trying to cause trouble, I was just trying to watch over you."

Nixon took the edge of his sword and moved aside the shield to reveal their attacker.

Once clear, Nixon looked at the face of the man before him. Even in the dark, Aryu could see the expression on his face grow from relief to being horribly upset.

"Sho?" Nixon said at last. "Dear God, is it you?"

A cautious smile on the face of the man below him. "It is, my old friend, it is. Please, help me up."

Nixon lowered the sword instantly and reached for the man's free hand, hauling him up to his feet. The man was tall. He wasn't as massive as Nixon, but wiry like a large cat. The shield he carried was lined with pointed spikes and looked impressive. His face was still shrouded and blurry, but Aryu could see the light hair and beard. The man's free hand extended, which Nixon took readily, shaking it with great enthusiasm.

Something about this man had instantly put Nixon in a terrible mood, and Aryu was certain it had nothing to do with the brief skirmish they'd just had with him.

"Sho. By all things good and holy I can't believe it's you."

"Oh, it's me alright." He released Nixon's hand and extended it to Aryu as he stepped over to meet him. "And you are...?"

Aryu looked at Nixon first, unsure if he should trust Nixon's face or body language more. Nixon gave the briefest of nods, followed by a deep sigh.

Aryu took his hand, shocked by the strength in a hand so thin. "Aryu O'Lung'Singh, from the village of Tan Torna Qu-ay. And you are...?"

The man looked back to Nixon. "All we've been through and he doesn't know who I am?"

Nixon, still sour, looked at the man and then at Aryu. "Aryu, this is Tokugawa Sho, a man who I wish were dead more than anyone else in the entire world."

▶◀▶◀▶◀▶◀▶◀▶◀▶◀▶◀▶◀▶◀▶◀▶◀

The three sat around a fire at Nixon's insistence.

Tokugawa Sho was very quiet and reserved once he sat on a nearby log.

"Why are ya here, Sho?" Nixon asked right away. The story behind Nixon's cryptic statement about wanting Sho dead was held off until they could get back together at the fire and be more comfortable.

"I'm here because I must be, Nixon," he responded eventually. "I'm here because this place demands it of me."

Nixon clearly wasn't satisfied. "Why? When last we met ya gave me yer word on wha' ya were plannin' next, and it wasn't a life in service t' this place and tha Power tha' maintains it."

"The voices haunt me, Nix."

"The voices? Wha' do ye have t' do with tha voices?"

Aryu could only assume they were referring to the mystical voices Nixon had mentioned earlier. "I have everything to do with them. It's because of me that they exist."

Nixon snorted with contempt as much as laughter. "You? Wha' do ya 'ave t' do with it? They exist 'cause of a fool."

"Regardless, I am in part responsible for their pain and existence. As the fool isn't here to be held accountable, who else is left?"

"Not you, Sho. Least of all you. By God, man, how can ya think it was yer fault? Ya did wha' ye must, and ye were the only one tha' could. Ya did wha' even I would 'ave 'ad a terribly difficult time doin'.

Don't waste yerself runnin' the useless errands of a dead man."

A small, half-smile came to the face of the newcomer. "You sound just like my mother."

"HA! More like yer mother sounds like me. I'm the older one. Still, she's damn right. This never shoulda' been yer path, ya old fool."

Mother? Since the name Tokugawa was mentioned, Aryu assumed that this person was related to Ryu, and Crystal was his lover. The rest came together.

"Well, as ya brought it up, is yer mother still alive?"

Another shallow smile. "Yes, she's alive, and I'll wager you have a lot of questions for her."

Nixon looked annoyed, even though the answer sounded like what he wanted to hear. If Sho knew what Nixon was referring to it was a safe bet Crystal did too, meaning she'd likely have some kind of answer.

"What d'ye know, Sho?"

"Nothing at all compared to her. She has some very interesting new skills since last you saw her."

"Really? I doubt she could be much more powerful. What grandiose ability does she possess now?"

Without eye contact, Sho simply said, "She can hear the Echoes of the Omnis."

Nixon was on him at once, leaping across the space between with a speed Aryu could barely perceive, his massive hands grabbing the red armor. Aryu could swear he was beginning to trail smoke. "*What!* You had best be tellin' me yer jokin', Sho. Even then, tha' is certainly not funny at all!"

Aryu was amazed at the loss of control from the phoenix. He'd seen him angry, but never like this.

Sho was still very calm, clearly not fazed by the sudden violent treatment by the slightly larger man. His eyes casually scanned the ground as he continued. "For almost three centuries now. I would never dare joke with you, Nix. Your temper is something I want no part of. Your sword, even less. Besides, why would I lie about that? I'm as worried about it as you seem to be."

"*Bullshite*! If ya knew HALF as much as I do about the Omnis and what it all means you'd have gotten off yer self-pitying arse yerself and stopped her before she even started! Don't ya DARE pretend ya fear for her when ya coulda' stopped it!"

No doubt about it. There was smoke coming off every inch of Nixon's body in small, wispy plumes.

"I won't pretend anything. You should know I couldn't stop her if I wanted to. What am I going to do, fight my own mother to the death? I've killed enough of my parents in my life, thank you. And besides, you're one to talk about avoiding the Omnis when you accompany that sword and bearer. I don't have to remind you of what your duty is, sworn to God Himself. You can't really complain right now."

The smoke plumes were coming off Nixon like he was on fire beneath his armor, but the great hand released Sho and dropped him back to his seat. Nixon's eyes burned into the stranger, the light within them bright and furious. Still, he took a few steps back and allowed himself a measure of composure.

"You, sir, do not get the right to question me, my God, or the way I conduct my business, I say thank ya." It was as if Nixon was fighting the battle of his life just to keep from bursting into flames of rage.

Sho just straightened himself and returned to looking nonchalantly at the ground. "You are correct, sir. I apologize. My time in isolation has done me no favors in the area of social niceties."

Nixon still looked mad enough to explode, but he did return to his spot across the fire. Many tense minutes passed before he spoke again. "Very well then," he began at last. "Has she shown any effects of the Est Vacuus?"

Sho shook his head. "No, though in truth I fear I may not know what to look for. I hope you may be more attuned to that sort of thing when you meet with her. I rarely see her anymore. She stays in her Haven most of the time. She always insists I come around more, but she only wants to guilt me, just like you. I'd rather not hear it."

"Bah, given the time I'd tell ya 'til ya could hear it no more. Ya hold no responsibility at all, Sho. Ya should have reveled in yer victory and died in peace."

Sho didn't respond. Aryu could read in Sho's thin face that this topic was one he was very sick of. He decided to be the icebreaker. "While we seem to have a quiet moment here, can someone please explain what that was all about?"

Nixon simply glowered and said nothing, seemingly content to allow Sho the chance to tell this tale.

"Very well," he began, still looking around at nothing and everything. "The short version is that as you may have guessed, your large friend and I have met before. At that time, the world was still suffering the shock from the loss of those with the Power. Nixon arrived a day later, the carnage of the situation still fresh." Nixon frowned at the words but said nothing. "At that time I accompanied him and my mother around to assess the damage. When we finished it was agreed that my time of usefulness was past and I should leave this life. Even my mother thought so, having never wanted me to follow the same path as her and my father..."

"So your father was Ryu, the false god?"

A smirk at the title. "I see you've been speaking at length with our friend here. Yes, Tokugawa Ryu was my father. Anyway, after Nixon left and I returned to these lands with my mother, the destruction and lifelessness that seemed to cover here were evident, even after a short time had passed. The amount of the Power here exploded when he purged things and ravaged the land, making it not unlike Nixon's home." Aryu signaled his understanding so Sho continued. "The fault lay with two people: Death, whose foolish selfishness had caused the anger of Ryu in the first place, and Ryu himself, who should have never acted as he did without thinking about the possible side effects. Since both were unavailable to answer for what they'd done, for obvious reasons, I took it upon myself, against my mother's advice and my word to Nixon, to return my homeland to its previous splendor and maintain it until it could sustain itself or I die. As of yet, neither has happened, so I remain, to do what I swore to myself I must."

"Why you?" Aryu asked right away, intrigued by the story.

Nixon looked over at Sho, clearly interested in the answer himself. "Well," said Sho after a moment, "I suppose that would be because after those two, I was the next in the chain of events that caused it all..."

"Bullshit ya fool!" Nixon spat at the fire to hammer home his point, the action causing a brief flare-up.

"So you and Mother say, but answer me this: who, then? Who would save my home? Not my mother. She stopped caring about anything but her Haven long ago, seeing change as necessary in the course of things."

"And she was right, Sho. Even my home will be restored one day, with or without anyone's help."

"But your home isn't haunted by the ghosts of an evil action *you* caused. I couldn't leave it like that, Nix. I was the only one left with blame on his shoulders and the power to do something about it."

"You were, and are, a fool t' think tha'."

"Yes, yes, so I've been told. Many times, thank you."

"Not enough, it seems."

Sho almost smiled. "Oh, how I look forward to getting you and Mother together again!"

The brief show of humor amused Aryu, though in truth he agreed with Crystal and Nixon. He couldn't see why Sho was responsible.

"I 'ave much more t' discuss with her than you and yer foolishness."

"Well, I do hope so. The both of you at once would be more than I could stand."

Nixon wasn't as amused as Aryu seemed to be at the chiding. "Is she still in the same place, near the tower that once held her?"

"She is, but the tower no longer stands, a remnant from the destruction I wasn't keen on restoring."

Sho saw the new look of confusion on Aryu's face. "There was a time my mother chose self-imprisonment as a means of protecting the world at large from her volatile abilities. Now she no longer required it and left for her Haven. Though if you ask me, there's not much difference between the two. I need to continue my rounds. I'll likely see you two again at her home, though I promise nothing."

He rose to leave, as did Nixon and Aryu to see him off. "Thanks for the workout, boys," Sho said earnestly. "It's been a while since I'd stretched the legs like that. Next time let's see if we can spare the trees. It takes a lot of work to make them as big and strong as I have."

Sho shook hands and was ready to leave.

"Ya may be a damned fool, Sho, but I can't say I'm not glad t' see ya."

Sho bowed deeply as their hands released. "I thank you, my friend. I am glad you are here as well. I hope we can still do great things together."

With a nod and a wave of salute, the strange man vanished into the trees like a wraith, not making a sound as he evaporated.

"A damned fool he is, I'll tell ya, but there are worse people t' 'ave on our side."

"Well, I like him," Aryu said. "I have to know, though; why does he claim responsibility for what happened here? What did he have to do with it?"

"I'll spare ya tha details for the moment, but tha shortest answer is tha' Sho defeated 'is father in battle whichh triggered tha Third Fall of Man. I was awoken, met Sho and 'is mother, did as he described, and it was done. To see 'im here now is more than a little disappointing, I can tell ya."

Aryu could see why. It seemed wrong that he must live to avenge his father's mistake. "So why does he blame himself?"

"Because it was selfish pride tha' put him in tha' battle in the first place. He 'ad defeated his brother and believed he was good enough to face Ryu at a time when Ryu felt he needed to die but couldn't. Then Sho won, and the rest is 'istory."

"Why did Sho fight Ryu?"

Nixon began to speak but held his tongue. After a moment, he tried again. "Because he is a good man, and sometimes Ryu was not."

Nixon and Aryu sat in silence, saying nothing as the small fire died. Aryu wasn't sure he agreed with either of them, but he could say that any crime committed by a selfish act by Sho wasn't worth a lifetime of servitude to his father's mistake.

Soon, Aryu slept again, the events of the day overtaking him.

Nixon, as was his way, did not. He sat, listening to the pain of the voices, each looking for a way to be freed.

CHAPTER 13

Slipping in the Back Door

At first light, Nixon woke Aryu with more edibles than he could believe. Various fruits, some kind of small mammal meat, hot tea, and a large piece of honeycomb to finish.

"Eat all ya can, Aryu. Tha days ahead may be long."

Aryu was still holding onto the unlikely belief that his part of this quest would end when Nixon met with Crystal. He thought of Johan as he ate. If he'd stuck to the plan, and if Esgona didn't slow Johan down too much, he should be nearing Huan very soon. Aryu wished he was with them, or at least one of them. Not just for the company but to see the things they were seeing. The Thunder Run in particular was legendary for its massive size and awe-inspiring beauty.

"From 'ere we walk," said Nixon. "It shouldna' be much farther."

The land was hilly and green, vast forests abounded, and the dampness was palpable. Nixon led the way like a pro, but Aryu was no slouch. He was able to keep up on the ground much better than if they were in the air.

Nixon filled the damp morning air with more stories, his supply seemingly endless. At times he asked Aryu about himself, the journey he'd just been on, and the years preceding it. It felt good for Aryu to talk about his family and home. He was more at peace now with the circumstances. He was still a bubbling pit of hatred and revenge, but he realized nothing he could do was going to stop what had happened, and if Nixon hadn't been there, he'd likely just be another statistic of the destruction. At least here, he was able to go on living, planning the end of the force that had wronged him and Johan, not to mention every innocent life of Tan Torna Qu-ay and beyond.

"And what of yer parents?" Nixon asked at one point. "Do ya not wish to find them?"

Aryu looked struck. "More than anything... But I need to pick my fight. The time I spend looking for them is a waste if the monsters of the Old just take everything down. I'll focus on finding them when we're done."

As the early afternoon began, the sun burned off the morning chill while Aryu marveled at the idea that one man could keep everything as lively and beautiful as Sho had, as if a defeater of a god needed any more proof of his abilities. Aryu still didn't trust Embracers, but it was good to see they weren't all as terrible as he'd been led to believe.

While Aryu ate a small lunch, Nixon scouted ahead. When he returned, he informed Aryu they weren't far off. Without asking how he could be so sure, Aryu followed Nixon again until they reached a thick wall of trees.

"On tha other side of this is where we start."

Aryu looked at the dense brush, unsure at once of his or Nixon's ability to get through without thrashing and cutting their way, a tactic Aryu wanted to avoid after his meeting with the respectable Sho.

"Can we fly over it?"

"Nah, not this time. If this truly is tha place we seek, on foot is tha only way in or out."

Aryu trusted Nixon and followed as the big man began to move into the thicket.

"Can anyone just wander into one of these havens like this?" Aryu asked, doubting a place of such power and solitude could be so easily stumbled upon.

Nixon shook his head. "Nah, only one with the Power t' see it and enter its walls. If someone could wander in at will, the sanctity of tha place for the user would be lost, and aged Embracers would 'ave nowhere to 'ide."

They broke through the woods and entered a large field, lush with grass, a variety of fresh smells, and a collage of different wildflowers, overlaid perfectly with the ring of trees encircling the space and the distant mountains and their snow-capped peaks lining the horizon. Nixon began heading towards the middle of this slice of perfection.

"Nixon, I have no Power. What makes you think I'll be able to enter into this place just like that?"

Nixon began moving through the foliage. "Well, there are a few possibilities, Aryu. The first of which is tha' simple bein' with me will allow ya in. Sometimes the owners can be fooled, though not often. If ya stay with me, ye can almost piggyback in on my presence. These things aren't foolproof. The next is tha' Crystal, havin' likely known of our arrival thanks to Sho, will allow ya in, since the creators have some control. The last is tha' even without any real Power at yer command, tha' thing on yer back will 'ave more than enough stored up t' get ya in the door."

"Well, what if those things don't work? Will I just watch you disappear?"

Nixon smirked. "I'd wager ya got nothing t' worry about."

"And what makes you so confident, oh worldly one?"

"Because we've been in Crystal's Haven since we came through the trees, Aryu."

Aryu didn't feel any different. Whatever power this was, he couldn't sense it like he could the innate power of his sword.

"Are you sure? Nothing seems different."

Nixon raised his eyebrow. "Doesn't it? 'Ave we passed through any place as beautiful as this yet today, or any days previously?"

"No, but this land is all new to me. Every new hill brings something I've never seen before." Nixon relented to this fact.

Aryu followed Nixon as he trekked to the center of the field, marveling at the sounds of birds and smells of wildflowers all around him. A part of his heart ached that his friend couldn't be here to share in the wonder of this place.

"So where is she? There doesn't look to be anyone here but us."

"Well, this is her home. She's here or somewhere close by, or we'd have never gotten in. It's one of the perks of these places, almost like a natural security system if ya leave for too long."

At the center of the field was a meandering silver stream. It was no wonder Crystal didn't like to leave. If he was cursed with immortality as she was, what better place to spend it?

"We wait here," Nixon said. "She'll be about when she wants. I doubt the lure of my being 'ere will be easy for her t' resist."

Aryu almost asked why but never got the chance. A voice came from behind them. A part of him, and from his brief experience with it, the part of him that was intimately connected to the Shi Kaze, knew she was there before his natural senses did.

"You flatter yourself, Nixon. I'm not so bored as to pounce on every visitor I get here, even if it is someone as interesting as you."

The voice Aryu heard was light, youthful, and airy; something more akin to an over-confident child than an all-powerful mystic being from before time was time.

As Aryu turned to meet her, real shock set in.

In the last few weeks, Aryu had learned not to be so surprised by the things he'd seen and the people he'd met. In that brief time, he'd become what he would have considered a worldly person. People, especially ones as young as Aryu, are never easily limited in their views. Although he hadn't formed a visual opinion of her, nothing could have prepared him for this.

It was her age that struck him first. She looked very young. Barely older than him. Her face was soft with perfect skin, small features, and stark beauty. Her hair was white but not so white it looked like snow. More like it had been sun-bleached for a thousand years. Maybe it had? Even her eyebrows were bleached off-white. Last were her eyes. Nixon had the most surreal and unnatural eyes any man could ever see, with their red-shimmering centers floating in a sea of the deepest black. If there was a bizarre eye contest, Aryu knew Crystal Kokuou would have come in second. The whites were as white as any other normal person, perhaps too much so, but her eyes themselves were an odd shade of dusty, faded pink, and the black of the pupil seemed horribly out of place. She was wearing a thin, knee-length silver dress that blew in the wind as if it was made of nothing at all. Her arms and legs had the same perfect-yet-imperfect look as her face, like her skin had never seen the sun from the day she was born. Her body was youthful, seeming to confirm that she was no older than she looked. She wore no shoes of any kind, her feet bare and standing out against the grass and dirt beneath her.

He knew right away she was beautiful but very different from others he'd met. Not different like Nixon, whose aura of power was unmistakable. Different like himself, being perfectly human save for one design flaw. His was wings; hers was her look and tone. She was certainly human but unsettling and astonishing at the same time.

Crystal took Nixon's hand, bowing deeply as she shook it. Nixon returned the bow, followed by motioning to Aryu to follow suit. Aryu obliged, taking the svelte girl's hand and bowing as he did so, never fully taking his eyes off her. Her hand was as soft as it looked, completely devoid of any natural imperfections save for what may have been faint freckles once upon a time.

"Nixon of the Great Fire and Ash. Welcome back to my home," she said as she rose from her greeting and released Aryu's hand.

"Crystal Kokuou, keeper of the Dragon Spirit. I am 'onored t' be back." He gestured to Aryu. "Aryu O'Lung'Singh, of the village of Tan Torna Qu-ay."

"And reigning Ryuujin of the People I see, though without any command of the Power…yet." In the one statement she recognized the user, the weapon, the circumstances, and the situation each of them was currently in. A perfect statement, without being rude or confusing.

Nixon was also not oblivious to the notion and nodded. "Well, that remains t' be seen, but he's not dead."

"No, he's not dead. But I feel that his heart is."

Aryu was nearly immobilized by this small girl and her amazing ability to train his eye only on her. Her words slipped off him like water as he stood there. He heard them but had no response.

Nixon seemed nonplussed by Aryu's reaction. He'd seen it before when someone met her for the first time. "He recently lost much that was dear to him. Do ya feel this pain?"

"I still can't read people like Sho can, but his pain is deep and hard to hide. Perk up, kid. This isn't meant to be a place of sadness."

The statement brought Aryu out of his self-induced hypnotization. "I'm sorry?" he managed.

She had called him kid?

"My home," she continued. "I didn't create it to have visitors moping about. It'd spoil the mood. The vibe I'm going for. I can see your pain is great, but don't worry. We'll see if we can snap you out of this funk. Nixon, what kind of party pooper did you bring here?"

Aryu could only smirk and look at Nixon. Her attitude was just as unnerving as the rest of her. Although she had a look of a pixie, she clearly had the vitality of something a little more worldly.

Johan, he thought at once, *she sounds like Johan*.

Crystal gave an impish grin as the two men exchanged glances. "Oh, don't look like that, Aryu, which is a fantastic name by the way! He's as much of a downer as anyone I've ever met."

Funk? Pooper? Downer? Who was this person?

"Forgive me, please, but I can't fully understand what you mean."

"Your friend here," a hand thrust at Nixon like an accuser of a criminal, "only seems to show up whenever bad stuff happens. It's terrible. Frankly, I'm not sure why I let him in here anymore."

All secondary assumptions about Crystal vanished just as quickly as they'd come a moment earlier. One quick glimpse at Nixon told Aryu what he felt was the truth.

Crystal Kokuou, for all her apparent abilities and longevity, was a quick-witted smart ass.

Unfathomably powerful and near-godly beings should be feared, but this one was very attractive and instantly likeable in a manner he could identify with. In a heartbeat, she had gone from fearsome, ancient, mystic warrior to delicate, fragile beauty to something close to what Aryu would consider a good friend.

For the first time since he'd agreed to this trip, Aryu was glad he came. Even if she didn't offer up a single useful answer, she was instantly worth it.

Aryu and Nixon sat next to the perfect little stream to eat while Crystal wandered about. It seemed this place even had a calming effect on the phoenix. Despite the multitude of questions racing around his head, he seemed quite content to just sit.

"How've ya been, Crystal?" Nixon asked between bites of some kind of red fruit Aryu had never seen before. The juice dribbled down his chin, making him appear to be feasting on a human heart, blood and all. The image would have been terrifying were it not so amusing.

Crystal continued to look about uninterestedly, a trait she shared with her son. "I get by. Not much has changed since last you were here. Empires rise and fall; heroes and villains come and go. Life. Time. Same ol' stuff on different days."

It was astonishing the way these two reflected on the passing of eons as if they were minutes.

Nix nodded and continued to eat his snack until there was nothing left. Stem, core, seeds and all. He gave a large belch, the result being a puff of smoke and a rich sulphur smell in the air.

Crystal gave a look of mock disgust. "Don't foul my air with your nastiness, Nix. Certainly not in front of a guest." She pointed at Aryu, who was smiling at the comment.

"It's alright. I think this is the first I've ever seen him eat."

"Well, I don't need much t' keep goin'," he said, wiping his face with the back of his hand. "I do it more fer tha flavor than tha sustenance. Food is a wonderful thing. A good beer is even better."

Aryu couldn't say he'd ever given food that much thought.

"Tell me," she said, turning her attention to Aryu, "what's the story behind the wings?"

Aryu went red instantly as Crystal launched into the topic. Being around Nixon alone for the past week had made him forget his life-long sheepishness and embarrassment about his deformity. He suddenly realized they were spread out behind him in the sun as opposed to their default position of folded tightly on his back. An interesting fact, if one considered how he'd foolishly reacted with the young serving girl from the Komoky Valley not that long before. Another testament to how comfortable Crystal could make someone feel.

"Have you never seen a man with wings before?" he asked in a tone far ruder than he'd intended, the topic of his wings growing a natural barrier he'd forgotten existed.

Crystal looked hurt, but only jokingly so. "My my, touchy subject I see."

Nixon snorted a laugh. "Huh, our young friend 'ere isn't too high on 'is uniqueness. Says he wishes he'd ne'er had 'em."

Crystal looked at him again, a soft smile on her face. "Is that so? I apologize, Aryu. I've been alive a long time, but it's been ages since I've seen natural wings."

Aryu looked at her. "Natural?"

Crystal walked over and took a seat between the two men, ghostly feet dipping into the water below. "Yes, natural. I've seen people with mechanical wings, or in vehicles with large wings. I've even seen people who have used the Power to grant themselves something similar. But, if my hunch on the matter is true, you're mortal with no mastery of these things. Perhaps I could even say a fear of them? Yours seem to be flesh and blood, born to you like an arm or leg. Correct?"

Aryu couldn't meet her gaze, the shame of the topic still present. "You are. So is he, though," he said, motioning to Nixon. "I'm not a big fan. They've caused too much trouble in my young life, thank you."

Nixon interjected immediately, seizing the opportunity to begin the difficult questions. "Aye, it's true. He even told me he was brought to his home village because he feared he'd be killed as a monster in 'is 'omeland."

"And where was that, that would persecute one so young?"

Nixon looked to Aryu to see if he'd continue or put up resistance. Aryu did neither. "Over the ocean."

Crystal only looked at Nixon with an odd, knowing look passing between them. Aryu caught it but said nothing. "I'll say," was all Crystal said. Aryu looked at her, unsure if she implied something he didn't catch or thought him a liar.

"All I know is what I'm told, Crystal. My parents are good people. Or were. I doubt they'd lie to me."

"Were? Has something happened to them?"

Consumed by less pain than he'd expected, Aryu told her the story of how he had met Nixon, his missing parents, the destruction of his home at the hands of the machines, and the deal to help Nixon and rejoin his friend when he was done.

After the story finished, Crystal reached over and took Aryu's hand in hers, his cut and dirty fingers looking grotesque next to her perfect digits. "I am truly sorry for your loss, Aryu," she said, eyes meeting his. Despite their odd color, they were very much human and began tearing up at the telling of his tale. "The loss of so many so needlessly is a crime without borders. I haven't seen or heard of such terrible actions in ages. My heart goes out to you." He thanked her, greatly appreciating her sentiments. He removed his hand from hers and returned it to his side.

"I know of this army you mentioned," she continued. "A fighting force that came from the south and pushes northward daily using weapons like the ones you described to destroy many. They haven't begun a march this way yet, not that I expect them to, but if they do, we'll be ready."

"How do you know of this?" Nixon asked, clearly fishing.

Crystal wasn't fooled. "You know how, Nix. You've no doubt spoken with my overprotective son. I hear the news of the world in the Echoes of the Omnis."

Nixon fouled instantly. "Ye admit ye tap the Echoes?"

"I do, for some time now. It's an exhilarating experience. So much to hear and so much to learn."

"So much to suffer from!" Nixon responded instantly. "Ya dare probe the Omnis fer news of the world, as ye say? Why not just *leave* this place and see fer yerself? The Echoes are not yer plaything. The Omnis is All and Everything! It's blasphemy t' use it as ya do!"

Aryu saw the fire in Nixon's black eyes grow bright and strong. This Omnis, whatever it may be, was not something he took lightly.

"Blasphemy? You say that to me when your task, as prescribed by the Lord God Himself, sits beside me and eats my food?"

"Bah, like mother like son. My task and how I chose t' execute it are my own business, lest we all forget my Creator's Divine gift of free will."

Crystal smiled, and not a peaceful one this time. It was a look of defiance and mischief. "Tell me, did my darling son ask you, great and powerful weapon of God, to check on me to ensure I haven't taken ill of the effects of what I do?"

"Bah, ya sly hen, ya know damn well he did, and rightly, too."

"And what do you see in me, Nixon? Any change?"

Nixon was slow to respond, taking her words and actions in. "No," he said at last, much quieter than his previous barrage. "Not yet."

"Not yet? So you expect to, eventually."

"The Est Vacuus comes fer all who see it, Crystal. Ya know tha'. Even you, with all yer experience and power, know ya can't escape it. Not forever."

"I know, and I hope to be rid of the Echoes and Omnis in time, but with the connections between the havens severed, it's a much more daunting task to see the world than it once was."

"Don't touch the Omnis, Crystal. Respect its power. Respect its existence. And respect fer what it means t' witness its awesomeness. No man or god can stand against it. Even Ryu knew that."

Crystal, clearly trying to change the subject to one she was certain Nixon wanted to talk about in mentioning the missing Haven connections, was sullen for a moment at her failure and the mention of her lost love.

"Ryu was a fool," she said at last, her broken heart on display for all to see. No one contradicted her.

Seeing he'd hit a nerve, Nixon allowed Crystal the respite from the topic she was seeking. "Tell me, Crystal. Let the questions begin. Why can I not flow through the Havens as I did? Clearly, some still exist. Wha' 'as 'appened t' tha others?"

Crystal, in all her power, could not entirely hide the relief she felt at the subject change, but after that, she wasn't as cocky. "That, my old flaming friend, is a very long story, but to give you the short version of it: Embracers banded together years ago to sever the connections between our respective havens. We came against an enemy powerful enough to enter them despite our best efforts. If they couldn't walk into one, they would walk into another and attack one after another until they got to where they were going. After that we found a way to use our abilities to cut each other off, effectively making every Haven much like your own.

Crystal waved her hand and looked into the distance. "Of course, the point is moot now." Nixon looked at her, encouraging the reason behind the statement. "It's simple math, my friend. There are barely any of us left."

"How many is barely?"

She gave it a moment's thought. "It's hard to say for certain. I haven't gone out looking in a while."

Nixon was nonplussed. "Where did they all go?"

"You don't seem too surprised. Is this what you expected?"

Nixon nodded but did not explain, allowing her to first answer the question. "Well, up until the Fourth Fall of Man, there were still quite a few. When the power of technology began destroying everything again, many chose to stay out of the fight. Others chose to join in, believing they were strong enough to withstand such simple weapons. During the wars, many didn't return; others who did weren't the same as before. People I knew for thousands of years seemed to change overnight. Soon, they all began to disappear. Eventually I, Sho, and only a few others were all that was left.

The playful nature returned to her voice. "But tell me, oh wise phoenix, what makes you so certain that it would come to this?"

Nixon smiled his non-reassuring smile. "God knew eventually it would all come down t' one. If they follow tha right, I'll ne'er awaken, if they follow tha wrong, I rise and destroy 'em. Both instances equal my eternal rest. Now then, about this enemy tha' warranted a complete shutdown of tha system I've grown so dependent on. Wha' was the nature of this enemy, and if it was such a threat, why didn't I wake up?"

"We thought the same thing. For a time, we waited for you to arrive and deal out a little of that swift justice you're so fond of. When we realized it wasn't going to happen, we made our own plans. Limiting his ability to travel was the best we could come up with. That way we could keep him trapped. It only worked for a time, then he simply became too powerful to contain. So they brought in the big guns."

"Huh, that would be you?"

"No," she said, "not me. They asked Sho. At first he refused, swearing not to get involved. His power was strong enough, but he still foolishly believed his place to be here. He stayed out of it until they did something foolish."

"And what, pray tell, was tha'?"

The impish smile came to her face again, Aryu loving every smirk of it. "They attempted to invade here and destroy the hard work Sho maintains. After that Sho stepped forward and stopped them and their army of loyal Embracers."

"And how long did tha' take him? Three days? Four?"

"Bah, barely two and a half, ye of little faith. I think he fell asleep in there somewhere, though. He always was a napper."

"Wait, wait," Aryu had to step in here, not believing what he was hearing, "Sho defeated them all in two days?"

"Two and a half," she corrected.

"Aryu," interjected Nixon, "ya must understand tha' Sho and Crystal 'ave tha most amazin' grasp of the Power I've e'er seen. I 'ave no doubt Crystal, if she were willin' t' do so, could 'ave cut tha' time in half."

Aryu looked at her questioningly. "Maybe, if I didn't take a nap." She smiled.

"Well then, who was this enemy so easily defeated at tha hands of yer son?"

Crystal lost her cutesy look again. "It was his brother."

In Nixon's stories he had mentioned Ryu's other son, an immortal from the same age as his father named Izuku, whose mother was Ryu's first lost love. Izuku had once held the title of Adragon but was wise enough to allow others to do his dirty work for him so that Nixon wasn't summoned. Sho originally defeated Izuku when Sho was only a mortal teenager. Izuku relinquished the Shi Kaze to Sho and began turning his life to noble purposes. He failed.

Crystal continued. "They fought once more, and although Sho couldn't bring himself to kill him, he used his abilities to permanently disfigure his brother to ensure he never had the urge to stand against him again. No matter what Izuku does, he can never mend the wounds inflicted on him by his brother. That was the extent of Sho's mercy. Next time, should there ever be one, I doubt he'll be so lenient."

"Let's 'ope for Izuku's sake there isn't," Nixon agreed. "Now, on to other matters…"

"Wait," she held up her hand, silencing him at once, "someone… no, some*thing* has entered this place…"

They each looked around, trying to see who had entered, scanning the tree line for any sign. They saw none.

"Are you sure?" asked Aryu. Crystal and Nix both looked at him like he'd said something terribly silly and went back to looking. He assumed that was a yes.

"I thought it was Sho so I opened the barrier, but now I'm not sure. Something is wrong. If it is him, he's not alone… There! From the south!"

They all turned to look where Crystal pointed. At first, Aryu saw nothing. Then he discerned the movement between the trees as Sho emerged like he'd been shot from a cannon, the shining red armor sparkling as he landed roughly with his shield in hand, tumbling across the ground and tossing dirt and flowers as he rolled.

The beast known as a Herald emerged behind him.

CHAPTER 14

All Power Is Fleeting

Aryu was stone cold. His eyes widened, his breath stopped, and every muscle in his young body seized. The peace he felt in this place was erased instantly. He couldn't draw his sword. He could barely remain conscious.

Crystal was familiar with different machines from the ages, with this one looking like a holdover from the last time mankind had dabbled in something so advanced. This was more than some dumb robot. This was what the Echoes spoke of.

Sho regained his footing as the machine began towards them.

"Hold there, Sho!" Nixon called when they were thirty or so paces away. "Keep that damned thing where it is and step away *NOW*!"

With the air echoing his words, Sho looked at Nixon with a sense of wonder, almost questioning at the request. "What do you think I've been *DOING*! Back off! Get away! Something is wrong!" he answered in a rage. Even from this distance, Aryu could see that Sho was not himself.

The Herald raised its hands and stopped, now with what looked to be an Ark 1 pointed at Sho. Like something from Aryu's worst nightmares, that overly pleasant and professional voice had returned, and this time it was armed. "Please, stop. Or I'll do to them what I did to you, Sho. Just a few words. I bring a message for the one named Crystal."

"No words! Send it away now Sho, or so help me I'll cut it t' quarters with or without you in tha way!"

Sho could only look back at Nixon bewildered, as if he was frozen in place. Something serious was stopping him from helping.

Aryu swore he was about to cry.

"Damn it, Sho!" The ground trembled with the words, and Aryu could feel the heat emanate from Nixon. He had no doubt that smoke would form on his skin at any moment. "That thing destroyed a village of honest innocent people for no reason! *THAT* is what destroyed Tan Torna Qu-ay!"

"Untrue," it spoke again. "That unit was dispatched by you, Nixon of the Great Fire and Ash."

The voice! Dear gods, that voice was going to put Aryu over the edge! He began crying instantly and fell to his knees. The unbelievable pleasantness was a sound he'd never forget for all his days.

Nixon was taken aback by the thing's use of his full, God-given title. It *was* his name the other had said in the village as he cleaved it into pieces. Whoever they were, they knew him.

"Yes, yes we know you," is said, reading the obvious faltering in the large man. "You are known to us very well, as is Aryu O'Lung'Singh." Aryu openly vomited at the mention of his name, the illness far too much to take. "As our previous attempt to secure you went…" The clicking again. The terrible, soft clicking of its deeper thought process. "…poorly, we have decided on another tactic. One of open dialogue."

"How do ya know me, creature?" Nixon took the chance to get at least one answer before he used his considerable abilities to bring the Herald down. "What do you and yer people know of me?"

"Simple. We know all those whose natural abilities extend beyond the…" click click clickclick "…normal human range. We admit you are an anomaly, but essentially you fall into this category. We also know of Crystal, keeper of the Dragon Spirit, one of the oldest humans alive, born February 29th in the Gregorian year 2036 AD, lover of the one known as Tokugawa Ryu…"

"Yes, thank you," Crystal said, obviously annoyed. "I know who I am."

"Our knowing these things is inconsequential at the moment. The point is we do, and it's information we can use to our advantage."

"Well now," said Nixon, his gaze unwavering from the non-face of the machine, "I would say it would be wise not t' threaten tha one with tha big fuckin' sword, which is proven t' dispatch you and yer kind with little effort, thank ya very much. Now, as t' yer knowin' these things, I'd say we don't think it's so inconsequential. How do ya know?"

"Fine," it said, mock exasperation in its words. Another oddity of human speech from a non-human body. "During our dormancy, select models were sent out at random times to collect information on any and all peoples who may cause us…" clickclick click "…inconvenience upon our reactivation. We were created to be war machines, sir, and knowledge of the abilities of both friend and enemy is a wise device to use in times of conflict, would you not agree?" Nixon said nothing, letting it continue. "Regardless, despite a general guarded nature of those we speak of, given enough time and the proper resources, information can be found in great number with relative ease, even on one as elusive as yourself.

229

"Humans are notorious documenters, with chronicles that can be found dating back millennia, should one know where to look. From these times we found more than enough to count, calculate, and record information on every living…" click clicliclick "…well, we call you Ethereal Beings. However, I'm sure everyone who has known you has some different kind of descriptor or another. Beings who have evolved beyond the natural classification of human."

Nixon said nothing of his not actually being one of the things it was describing. Although they knew far too much about him for his liking, they didn't know everything.

"We even have very detailed information on these places such as the one we are currently encased. 'Havens' as you say, Mr. Ash. All this information coupled with our leader's wealth of knowledge has given us great insight into your kind. We admit you are more of an enigma than we are accustomed to, which is the main purpose of our desire to obtain and detain you and your young winged friend."

"Ya want us t' go with ya?"

"More to the point, I need you to. This isn't going to be a failed mission. Tan Torna Qu-ay was regrettable, but we have learned and are not about to fail again."

"And wha' if I told ya t' get up on yer lit'le rocket feet and fly yerself straight t' Hell? What'd ya do then?"

The mention of his home had caused Aryu to vomit again, though no one had noticed. Now he could only listen as this robotic devil described with that annoying voice the confidence it had its new mission would be a success.

"Your reputation for belligerence precedes you. Despite your great abilities, and that of two of your three companions, we will take you by force."

"Another bomb, perhaps?"

"No, nothing so destructive. The natural resources of this land are far too valuable for such a messy solution. Besides, I doubt I'd have the ability to send the order from this place. I lost contact with HOME as soon as I entered into these lands."

"I don't allow any kind of mechanical signal here," Sho said quickly, looking to move the conversation on.

Its spinning blue eyes locked onto Sho. "You, sir, could be very annoying in any other setting."

It turned back to the trio. "Are you certain you will not accompany me back to HOME? Much time and pain can be spared if you do."

Nixon bristled. "I'm afraid I must decline, on behalf of myself and my charge, thank ya."

Sho looked at the phoenix. "Easy, Nixon, don't antagonize this thing…" Nixon looked at him like he was a fool, but Aryu saw that there was something Sho knew. Something that scared him.

"So be it. A large contingent of ground forces will be arriving shortly. Only your cooperation could have called them off. As it is, they will arrive shortly to apprehend you. Why must you be so defiant? So much loss for no reason."

Crystal looked both amused and defiant. "You must know that any army, even one as powerful as yours, doesn't stand much of a chance against one of us, let alone three. I don't think I feel like letting them in here, either. They'd spoil the view. It's bad enough you snuck in like you did," she said, her face no longer that of a child but more of the grown and serious woman she was.

"Too true, but you and your friends' abilities rely on command of what you simply call the Power, a focusing of the mind beyond levels the average human can obtain. Previously referred to in history as many things: magic, chi, miracles, faith, noetics, or telekinesis. Everything is rooted in the fact that your brains became advanced enough to understand standard scientific particle physics and the quantum field on an intimate level.

"You are also still human. A collection of natural base elements and electrical impulses no different than myself or any other machine at your most basic. It is a weakness no matter how you defend it."

No one alive could have seen the motion of two small, cylindrical tubes that emerged from the body of the Herald just below the shoulders. They all heard something pop.

Nixon was the first to react, followed by Sho who charged the spot where the Herald had been, diving out of the way of an Ark 1 shot that exploded the ground like a mine, but not before it deftly jumped away. The whole scene played out in an instant, a blur to Aryu's eyes. He was surprised to see Sho react so slowly compared to the astonishing speed he'd shown the night before. Sho brought around the bladed shield but was nowhere near his target.

Crystal did nothing, simply raising her hands to her face and looking at them questioningly.

Nixon gave chase instantly, bounding across the grassy meadow to the thing, closing the gap just enough to grab hold of its arm before it leaped off again.

The force of its leap coupled with Nixon's iron grip caused it to tear its own arm off as a child would an insect wing. The reaction from the Herald was exactly what Aryu remembered from before. The robotic, twisted scream that followed as it landed with an awkward 'thud' only a few paces away was pitch for pitch the same as the one from Tan Torna Qu-ay. Right down to the length of the sound.

Nixon was on it instantly, mighty sword in hand and ready to finish this bold creature before it could cause any more damage. "*WAIT!*" shouted Crystal, startling Aryu with her volume. "Wait, Nixon!"

Nixon held off, bringing the blade to a stop just before he would have connected with the machine's non-face. He turned to her, eyes blazing in fury, with a look of both rage and total confusion. He was not accustomed to being stopped.

Crystal ignored him and immediately approached the fallen robot. "What have you done to me?" she asked, to Aryu's extreme confusion. "What did you do!"

The thing, fallen and at the mercy of the three most powerful beings alive, could only begin to laugh, a terrifying sound coming from a mechanical body with no mouth or face to speak of. "We evened the odds, Crystal Kokuou. Look about you. Your mighty Power is failing as we speak!" The laughter continued unstopped as the four looked at what it was referring to.

Aryu saw the disorientating image of the world around him as it became hazy, like opening his eyes underwater. In a matter of seconds, the startling beauty of the meadow in the foothills was replaced with a bland collection of rocks and scrub grasses, still ringed by trees, but in a circle far less impressive to look at. To the right of where they all stood Aryu could barely make out the image of a large, circular rock wall, now crumbled and aged. It appeared to be the base of what was once a very large and impressive building that was likely the aforementioned tower Crystal had once lived in.

Crystal was back to looking at the thing on the ground, her red eyes demanding a more direct answer to her previous question, rage and fear written across every inch of her face.

The laughter stopped like a switch had been turned off, sharp and abrupt. "As I said, humans even as powerful as you are at their core the same. Elements and electrical impulses. Our solution is a simple one. We have injected you with a solution designed to impede the signals of your brain that have command of the ability to access the deeper natural order of the universe. I have turned off the part of the brain that allows you to tap the Power. You are as you once were.

Frail, weak and ready to be destroyed."

"TURN ME BACK!" Aryu jumped back at the level of emotion Crystal displayed. She was beyond enraged. She was on another level of emotion altogether, and it was terrifying to see.

"Don't be foolish; why would they send me, knowing you were obviously going to trap or destroy me, with anything useful to reverse the process?" The laughter started again, followed by the immediate dispatching of the Herald by Nixon, who believed he had waited long enough as it was. His sword came down with a force that not only divided their unwanted guest but also drove the blade into the ground below where it was resting, making the earth shake with the force. The laughter stopped.

That was when Crystal began screaming at the top of her lungs, arms thrust upwards as she did so, madness etched into her eyes.

Aryu could barely stand it. The madness into which Crystal had apparently descended was terrifying and deep. Sho, a look of both confusion and worry in his eyes, seemed to collect himself enough to usher Aryu over to the crumbled rock wall and allow them both to take a seat while Nixon tended to Crystal, trying to calm her as best he could.

The dizzying queasiness Aryu felt was still there, but each fresh wretch brought nothing, his stomach empty after the second round.

Sho brought Aryu an old cup filled with water from the stream. The stream was still there, flowing as peacefully as before, but everything else had changed all around them, and a sudden feeling of helplessness and desperation was in the air.

Aryu drank the cold water, the shiver of the drink on him at once.

"Is it true?" he asked after a moment. "Have you lost the

command of the Power?"

Sho nodded. "So it would seem. That thing dropped from the sky and ambushed me before I could react, doing to me what it did to my mother in the process just before I made it here. Then it followed as I tried to battle into the Haven. I can't feel anything around me like I could before. The life of this place escapes me."

"What about the trees and animals? Don't you maintain it? Why hasn't it begun to disappear like the Haven did?"

"I keep the peace here with a mixture of my own abilities and the natural essence of the planet. As time has gone on, the Earth maintains more and more of the order of things here, needing less and less of my interference. I simply travel around to bolster the spots that have weakened. This land will be alright for a time, but it will eventually fail to the forces that would destroy it."

"How? How can it know how to stop your control of the Power? What did it do?"

Sho reached into a small storage pocket tucked behind a gap in his armor, producing his hand and showing what appeared to Aryu to be an empty palm.

Aryu's confusion at the gesture was obvious. "Look closer," asked Sho, indicating the center of his hand.

Once closer, Aryu could see what appeared to be a small, perfectly straight hair, barely noticeable in such a large hand. "What is it? They didn't do this with a hair did they?"

"No," Sho said, "not a hair. it's ridged and the end is feathered. It seems to be a small dart."

Aryu quickly began looking himself over, trying to find an errant hair-sized projectile. "Don't worry, Aryu. I don't think you were an intended target. I doubt they did anything to you."

Aryu looked himself over anyway, convinced he was more to them than just a collectible. Eventually he stopped, finding nothing.

Not even in the leathery folds of his wings. They hadn't thought him powerful enough to require such a tactic.

Crystal began screaming even louder now as Nixon could be seen with her hand in his, bowing in a praying motion as she looked skyward with complete ambivalence to what Nixon was doing. The scene was unsettling. "What's wrong with your mother? I've never seen anyone so...so..."

"Terrified?" he finished.

"Well, I'm not even sure that's what it is. It seems to be even deeper than that."

Sho agreed, "Very good, Aryu. You're right, of course. It is deeper than fear and terror. Much deeper."

"From losing her grasp on the Power? You don't seem as bad as she does but you're in the same boat, and Nixon looks fine."

"Well, first off, I don't think our large friend over there is affected by this cunning little attack. His abilities stem from somewhere beyond mine and those of my mother. Also, although I appreciate the confidence you seem to have in my willingness to accept what has befallen us, I assure you I am horrified beyond reckoning. I have not been without command of the Power in ages, and the feeling is very disorientating. I also fear what will happen to this place and the life I help maintain here. If we can't find a way to reverse what has been done, the thought of what could happen here absolutely crushes me."

He looked at Aryu very seriously. "She is in much more pain than I could ever imagine. She has been a student and Embracer of the Power since she was very young, and has grown her abilities to go beyond simply conjuring havens and projectiles of energy. My mother, despite my undying love for her, was foolish enough to begin experiencing the Echoes of the Omnis, and it is the loss of that all-encompassing warmth of the Everything that has put her into this state, accompanied by the memory of the Est Vacuus."

"Omnis? Est what?"

Sho looked at the ground in his look of removed non-interest and smirked. "No, no of course you don't know. Forgive me, Aryu. I forget myself. The situation has me not thinking clearly. I can't begin to tell you the full story about what I'm speaking of; someone with no grasp of the Power could never understand the whole story. Suffice to say there is a…presence, a level beyond what you know as the Power, and it has unfathomable levels of glory within it, but also there is a level of emptiness beyond even death that accompanies this 'everything' that must be experienced at the same time. It is the loss of the feeling of one and the memory of the feeling of the other that has done this to her. It may take some time to bring her out of the state she's in right now."

Aryu didn't understand, but he supposed that was natural. Sho was speaking of things a young man from a small southern village could never grasp and likely shouldn't try. "Do you think we have time?" Aryu asked as Crystal let loose another barrage of agony. "The Herald said an army is on the way."

Sho's unwillingness to answer said all that was needed, and once again Aryu was wrapped in the crushing terror of the army and what it was like to be in their path. He reached back and pulled the Shi Kaze from its sheath and allowed the distant, soothing comfort of its power to fill him with what little easing pleasantness it could. If he was going to die here, days from his homeland and his friend, it was not going to be on his knees begging to be released. The great and powerful sword in his hands reminded him of this, and it was doing an admirable job doing so.

Sho looked at the sword in Aryu's hands. "Just having that on our side picks my spirits up. Both my mother and I have held the title of Ryuujin at different times. Both of us turned the sword over to someone else, not wanting to be responsible for its power or destructiveness. Not all who come into its possession can wield it properly. For both of us, it was best to just let it go."

Aryu had a difficult time thinking about letting it go so easily. Even now it was doing wonders for him just by sitting in his hand.

Shortly thereafter, the yelling stopped, and Sho and Aryu looked to see what was going on. They saw Nixon kneeling over an unconscious Crystal, her breathing rapid and her eyes fluttering behind their lids. Nixon addressed them as they approached.

"I've done wha' I can fer now, but tha rest is up t' her. The madness will pass. It's 'ow she deals with tha aftermath tha' will determine 'ow she gets through this."

"What can we do to help her?" Aryu asked as he looked at her lying on the ground.

"Don't ya worry about 'er, Aryu," Nixon replied. "She can get through it just fine without us. It'll just take some time."

"Time we don't have," Sho said, stepping in. "If that thing spoke the truth, we can't have long before we receive visitors."

Nixon was up to his full height instantly, fire again in his eyes. "Yes, my old friend, about tha'; what the hell were ya thinkin' leading tha' thing here?"

Sho became passive again. "It attacked without warning. I was hit before I even knew it was coming. The voices couldn't warn me of it in time because it's lifeless. Without the command of the Power, I had to run. I needed to make it here. It was just too fast and attacked me again when I was close. You don't understand, Nixon; it wasn't what it said, it was how it said it. It was important enough that I had to find my mother. I was sure you two could stop it. I didn't know at that point how it did what it did. I wasn't scared of the gun when it threatened me, but that it would de-power you two the same as me. I had to choose to trust it. I needed to tell you about the voice."

Nixon waited, seeking the punchline. "You likely wouldn't know it, never having met him," finished Sho, "but I would know it anywhere. The voice that thing was using was my brother's."

CHAPTER 15

The Army of the Old

Nixon and Sho took turns carrying Crystal away from the empty field and into the higher mountains to the east, the last natural border before the expanse of the eastern ocean.

With the proper means of travel, one could go south, past the shores of this land to a small island called Kume, where the one known as Tokugawa Ryu was born. Even closer at hand to where this band began to flee were places littered with stories about the Ryuujins and Adragons of the world.

No one knew these stories like Crystal Kokuou. No one even came close. Sho knew many, Nixon the same. Others could add a tale or two, but no one could compare to the wellspring of knowledge and stories tucked behind her flowing white hair.

These were the stories she was immersed in now, locked away by some old, arcane influence used by the phoenix and the god that created him. A god far wiser than all that came after.

Deep inside her head, a war raged between the power she held, now lost by some nefarious means, and the strength she possessed as a person that was clear from the influence of the Power.

So far, the battle was a draw.

She knew in her deepest heart of hearts that she was one of the most powerful humans to ever live, with or without the Power. Her worldly experiences, love of learning, and abilities both mentally and physically were unparalleled. Two things prevented her from emerging. The first was the memory of the Omnis. The loss of the ability to tap that flow of galaxy-spanning wholeness was destructive to someone's soul. The other was the memory of the void of Est Vacuus. Left to the simple memory of a Power-less human, even the slightest inkling of the Est Vacuus risked driving one mad.

Couple the two things together, and you get someone in Crystal Kokuou's unenviable position.

She remembered the feeling of the Power. She remembered meeting Ryu for the first time, ragged and disheveled at the gates of her old home, begging for a place to stay and a warm meal. She marveled with great humor at the juxtaposition of that image versus the one that came years later, when his godliness was all but assured in the eyes of the world and he hugged her close for the first time in years and the last time ever, before he left for the confrontation that would lead to his loss, madness, and most unspeakable of all acts: the destruction of all within his reach who possessed the Power, guilty or innocent. If only she had known.

The faces of her father and mother were everywhere in the muddle of her mind. Never before or after had the world seen two as honorable as them.

The face of Sho, her precious son, and the day he came to the world. Before the gears of fate had rallied against him to cause him the pain he felt now. When his innocence cleansed her of her indiscretions. He was still her most loved son, and would be forever.

The face of her daughter Emerald; her spirit and vibrancy lost years ago to that most blessed of all things: age. Emerald had chosen a life of peace, away from the Power. As such, hers was a life without the pain of all the memories carried by her older brother.

The training. The losses. The joys. The love. The hate. The light of the world. Everything that made her human fought against the emptiness left by everything that made her powerful.

"Truth," her father's voice said in her mind, a constant in her darkest hour (but for how long? Was it the Power that kept his memory so fresh?)," *is what makes us powerful. Not guns or wars, governments, or rulers. Truth will always be at the core of what we are. Always remember the truth of who you are, and you will never lose your way."*

Yes, the truth. She could still remember the truth. It was fleeting, but it was there. A solid rock of herself, locked away like a precious gem. She was Crystal, trained from birth to be righteous and strong; a paragon of maintaining the balance just as her parents had been. The living embodiment of what was once called the Dragon Spirit. The spirit of the universe that would forever seek harmony no matter what.

"Thank you, Daddy," she whispered to herself while opening her eyes to the real world.

Now powerless, only truth was left. That was enough.

She awoke to serve the balance once more. She had a job to complete and it was barely started.

"There," said Nixon after a moment of searching. He pointed to the valley between two distant hills to the southwest. Aryu could see nothing from such a distance. "They come, and in great numbers. Seems our friend wasn't lyin'."

Nixon was an expert at dealing with each new situation as it arose. This wasn't the first time he'd had to run away to get where he was going, and thinking on his feet was essentially what he was made to do. Thankfully, in the aftermath of the loss of the Haven, it was quickly discovered that Nixon still had full command of his facilities and could still summon the Divine power within him. Yet further proof that his God was truly infallible. Yet more proof that he should have killed Aryu when he had the chance? *No*, he thought each time it occurred to him. *Since the arrival of His Son, God is also merciful. I must honor that as well.*

Nixon did admit, however, that they were between a rock and a hard place, and that made Nixon a very nervous man. He had been trying to pay particular attention to the appearance of any small black flying drones but had seen none. That was not a mistake worth repeating.

As they looked, pondering the next move, Crystal awoke in the arms of the giant phoenix, drawing all their attention back to her. Aryu expected the screaming to start all over again.

"Please, set me down, Nixon. I'm fine now."

Nixon did as was asked but kept a close eye on her. Crystal gingerly walked around, stretching her legs and making sure all was as it should be in the physicality department. It was Sho who spoke first, asking the question on everyone else's mind.

"How do you feel? That was quite a fit you had back there, Mom."

Crystal, as if realizing for the first time they weren't at home, looked around to get her bearings. "I'm fine," she said, looking for some sign of their location.

"Fergive me, m' dear, but after wha' I know ya went through, no one alive, even you, would be fine," Nixon spoke assuredly, as a man who knew more than any what mysterious feelings she had just had as the reality of the world hit her.

"We are east of home, aren't we?" she asked, ignoring him. Sho nodded in agreement, but Nixon stood firm, awaiting her response. "I'm fine, really," she said again. "Well, maybe not 'fine' fine, but I'll be alright. It will just take a moment to put the pieces together."

"What was yer trigger? I've not seen many go through what ye did. Two, maybe three others, long ago. Each time their minds focused on a trigger, a moment or object that grounds 'em and helps 'em through to clear their mind and restore the balance."

"What difference does it make? I'm here, I'm fine, who cares?"

"I care," he insisted, pushing her with his intense red eyes. "It's important fer me t' know so tha' I know ya aren't walkin' around moments away from another breakdown. If ye're 'ere again because of some false hope or shallow memory, it'll only be a matter o' time before ya lose it again, and as we are currently bein' chased by a very dogged army wishing t' do us 'arm you'll forgive me if I dunna' want t' be carrying yer arse up a mountain!"

Crystal looked at the big man, seeing his seriousness. Not many knew more about the Omnis and the Est Vacuus than Nixon. No one alive, anyway. "My father," she said, serious and truthful. She agreed with his reasoning and had no desire to deceive him. "Words from my father helped me through it."

Nixon needed no further words on the matter. He saw no lies in her eyes, though he supposed she could hide them if she wanted to. He believed her to be honest. "Bless tha' man yet again," he said to end the subject. "May he rest in peace."

Crystal nodded her thanks. "Amen."

Sho had turned his eyes back to the place Nixon had indicated, desperate for some sign, seeing at last a series of trees fall in unison near the top of the rise. They were coming, and they were doing nothing to hide their approach. "Alright, my friends, we need a way out. Any thoughts?"

Aryu spoke first. "Let Nixon handle them!" he said, as if it was the most obvious answer in the world. "He still has his abilities! He could destroy them, or at least make them think twice before continuing to chase us."

Sho and Crystal looked as though the counter argument was obvious, and all at once Aryu wished he were traveling with Johan instead of three supernatural beings. He suddenly felt very insignificant.

"Sorry, Aryu, but I won' be doin' tha'. They think I am as powerless as these two, and I'm in no rush to tell 'em otherwise. If they see I am still a threat t' em, nothin' will stop 'em from tryin' t' destroy us. Likely wit' weapons yer very familiar with. Unless I have a damned good reason, I need to play tha' card close."

Aryu could think of counter arguments to this as well, but out of fear of more looks from the others at his seemingly 'pathetic' reasoning, he kept his mouth shut and decided to trust Nixon yet again.

"How far are we from the coast?" Nixon asked Sho.

"Two days' walk, maybe more with a group of four. They're much too close for us to make it that far, Nix. They don't need food or sleep, and they're only a half day behind us as it is."

Nixon frowned. Two days? That was assuming they weren't being watched around every corner and behind every tree right this moment. Nixon had already decided they were being followed, likely by those little black spheres. Why no move had been made yet was a mystery.

Begrudgingly, Nixon looked up to the small troop. "Well, I am open to suggestions…" Blank faces returned the statement. "Is there no one else with command of the Power left here?" Nixon asked. "No one who may 'ave a Haven to retreat to?"

"Perhaps, but I have no idea where they're hiding," replied Sho. "Most of those that were left are long gone."

Aryu was lost in thought, doubting his ability to out-think his companions. Nixon looked worriedly at the coming trouble, Sho had his characteristic look of non-interest, and Crystal was still obviously dealing with the issues the loss of her Power had created.

In the end, all Aryu could do was think of Johan, on a mission of his own, and wondered if he would ever see him again. It had only been a little more than a week since he had left him to his own problems. He recalled a foolish part of him hoping he would be done with this madness by now and be back with him.

Still, no one knew what to do. He understood Nixon's reasoning behind not summoning his considerable abilities just to destroy their first wave and escape. If only they could get somewhere and do some real damage.

"I have an idea," he said at last. The look on everyone's face told him two things: that they were glad someone had said something at last, but they were also instantly disheartened to see it was him. It was still worth a try.

"What if we get caught intentionally?" No one laughed or said it was stupid. Each of them knew that there was more to the idea than it seemed. He brought each as close as he could, trying to keep his voice down and his words hidden. "I agree with Nixon that we are being watched right now, somewhere, somehow. I have no clue why they're waiting. They can fly right to us in an instant. Instead, they're chasing us. They're either leading us into something east of here, or playing with us for some other twisted purpose. I'm not about to walk into a trap and I definitely hate being toyed with."

"So what's yer point, Aryu?" Nixon was showing signs of actual interest.

"As I said, just let them catch us. We know they want Nixon and me for some reason. We know they think Nixon is a human and shouldn't have command of the Power anymore. We also know that at the first sign of making any kind of actual escape, they'll likely just bomb us and be done. If they catch us, it's a safe assumption that we'll be taken deeper into their depths, possibly to the heart of the whole thing, or maybe near the person in charge of them. We're lost without anyone's abilities; eventually the numbers will just win no matter how valiantly we fight. If we are taken in deeper, then allow Nixon to unleash whatever God-fueled fury I'm sure he's capable of, we stand a much better chance of taking more important things out with him than if he just cuts down some splinter group of their army that's heading to us now."

"But what about us, Aryu?" Crystal asked, more interested now, seeming to set aside her personal demons for a moment. "Sho and I aren't what they want. I can't speak for Sho, but I can tell you that I *feel* the aging process occurring in me now, a feeling I've not felt in who knows how long. And if I'm aging, it's a good bet we can die pretty easily."

"Crystal, I 'ave some serious doubts tha' ye and Sho could e'er die easily," Nixon said. After the stories he'd heard and the things he'd seen, Aryu had to agree. Losing the Power didn't mean losing thousands of years of experience. Experience that included dealings with mechanical enemies before.

"I don't know, Crystal. Maybe you could still make it out if Nix and I bought you some time?"

"No, I don't think that will be necessary," Sho said, finally joining the conversation. "I believe we should go with you. I doubt they will harm us. At least, not right away."

"And you have reason to believe they'd treat you to some of their hospitality?" Nixon asked.

"I do. It was my brother's voice. I know it was. I know what I heard and if it's true, he's involved somehow. Izuku isn't stupid, but he is vain. He'd rather brag about how he finally beat me before he dispatches me, and believe me, that's exactly what he wants to do."

"Tha's a hell of a risk t' take, countin' on yer brother's vanity not t' kill ya now jus' so he can kill ya later."

"Better than dying or being captured on the run. They have the upper hand here. Even with your abilities Nixon, how long before they just pepper the area with these bombs and get you again. I'm not a big fan of the thought of anyone but you having possession of that weapon." He indicated Nixon's broadsword, sheathed on his back. Nixon whole-heartedly agreed.

"They'd jus' take it anyway, and yer shield, and the Shi Kaze. What's t' stop 'em if we jus' walk in t' their waitin' arms?" Nixon raised a great point, but Aryu was ready for it.

"Well, for one thing, we don't let them capture us. They always seem so willing to talk, why not let them. Come to them with open arms. See what they want, use what we know, make them some kind of deal."

No one seemed to be *fully* on board, but no plan was without its flaws at this point. Each weighed the options in their own minds. Aryu took the moment to be secretly pleased with himself at his plan and the way things had turned out. Johan would be proud.

"We don't go in half-cocked," Nixon said after a moment. Aryu didn't really know the expression. "We sit right 'ere and wait, we make a plan, and we do somethin' other than hand ourselves over t' 'em and think on our feet when tha time comes."

"You know they can likely see and hear everything we do, right?" Sho asked. "Even right now. All the whispering in the world won't help us."

"We'll do tha best we can. Although, before we go any farther, I 'ave t' say tha' I'm not accustomed t' so many odds bein' against me." Nixon's honesty was scary.

"Well," said Crystal, "seeing as I'm looking at the handsome holder of the Shi Kaze right there, alive and breathing, I'd say being in new and crazy situations Is your new favorite pastime, Nix. Good thing too, or else where would we be now?"

Aryu blushed at the statement as she flashed him an impish, rosy-eyed wink coupled with a slight sticking out of her perfectly pink tongue. Her manipulation of a person was nothing short of perfection.

"Alright, take a seat, folks. We've got a bit o' a wait and many things t' discuss in the meantime."

"And the likely surveillance on us right now?" asked Sho.

Nixon shrugged. "Does anyone know any good songs?"

▶◀▶◀▶◀▶◀▶◀▶◀▶◀▶◀▶◀▶◀▶◀▶◀

The messenger slinked off into whatever hole he came from, terrified by the brief glimpse of the Est Vacuus sword, with urine dripping on the floor from pissing himself in fear of the emptiness. The bearers of bad news often tasted its *full* wrath, so this one got off easy.

Singing? Of course they were. Singing their little hearts out while they concocted a plan. Simple but effective.

They *wanted* to get caught. They actually thought they could devise a way to stand a chance.

The leader of the mechanical army resumed his surveillance of a series of translucent monitors, each showing live aerial images from different fronts of the pressing army, each the same boring mishmash of marching troops, hovering tanks, and wheel mounted weaponry. Boring, boring, boring.

Ever since he had activated this fantastic army ten years ago and learned of the rumored boy with wings, he had come up against a disheartening lack of obstacles, save for the likely inevitable arrival of the phoenix. Still, even he had his weaknesses, proven by his first encounter with the drone and the High-Yield it had brought with it.

He did wish he could come up against something to challenge him and his (mostly) lifeless minions. If he didn't, this was going to be a very dull domination of the world and all who inhabit it, which of course was where this opening foray was destined to lead.

His discovery of the science that led to the creation of the neural impulse inhibitor was just the icing on the cake. All of those with the Power whom death was too quick an option for were instantly at his mercy, as weak and mortal as any other. In one quick, fortunate blow, he had at his command all the strength to defeat the most powerful beings alive with nothing more than a pinprick. It was simply too easy. Almost depressingly so.

Almost.

He left the screens, weary of his domination. Who knew you could find so much malaise in so much triumph. He walked out to the staging floor of HOME, a large launching pad used to lift the army away in large mechanical troop transporters. Beyond the pad was the vast ocean. Beyond that, the southern beaches where their first foray onto land had begun. Spread out to the visible distance to the east and west were the landing crafts and high-powered battle ships that had announced their arrival to the weak and frightened people of these lands.

What a lot they were. Some of them, like the messenger he had just gleefully intimidated, surrendered and offered their unwavering loyalty in exchange for safety and ultimately, their lives. Although he had no real need for living minions beyond a few loyal people, the occasional strong arm from their own race was useful, and he would much rather have living people on board HOME to serve as his messengers, workers, and minions as opposed to anything robotic. For one, robots loved to break down, and two, he had much more respect for robots versus the weak human form. Most of them were either too scared or too foolish to even operate even a simple handgun, and the ones that did learn took to using them far too readily. Still, they could always get places other more lifeless inventions could not to do his bidding. That was enough to keep a handful around. For now.

He lamented at how quickly and easily this whole operation had come about. If only he had known it was just this simple: a flick of a few proverbial switches, and he was king of the world. All that time, all those useless millennia wasted on mastering the Power only to lose repeatedly when once it had been enough to make him so dominant.

Even his once-loved brother was nothing but a fragile shell of the man he once was. Oh, he knew bringing him and Crystal here was a mistake, but at last he had nothing to fear from him. The malicious weapons of the Old had rendered them powerless.

He recalled what pride always came before and dismissed the ill-conceived notion. He'd have them at his feet just long enough to revel in the fear in his brother's eyes and then kill him with the great and powerful blade at his side and the unthinkable void it contained.

"How do you like me now, Dad," he said to the answerless air. His father, another fool, but his father he still was. A God among Gods. Brought down not just by his son, but also by his pride and faith in his abilities. A mistake this son was not going to repeat. Despite it all, Izuku loved his father, even in the dark times. A feeling he was unwillingly forced to share with Sho. Likely the only thing left that they had in common.

Tokugawa Izuku was now the only person left from the days before mankind had made it their mission to destroy themselves. The only one left who knew peace maintained only by the will of the people and not the brawn of their army. It was meant to be this way. He was certain. Why else had he, out of all that had walked out of that era of early human existence, been the one to survive? Was it luck that the eldest son of the God of Dragons was the one who stood here, all the power of the world at his command?

Izuku did not, had not, and would not ever, believe in luck.

CHAPTER 16

Welcome to Huan

It had been just over a week since two of the last sons of Tan Torna Qu-ay had left the company of their compatriot and began their dangerous mission north and beyond, to the Blood sea. That week had been, for the sake of abbreviation, very poor.

Not precisely for Johan and the reluctant Esgona, but certainly for their travel associates. In the time since they had left the mountain town, five travelers on this journey north had been lost to illness, accident, and repeated attacks by marauders preying on the disorganized and scared masses that had come their way, including a frail old man who'd gone missing in the night. The bottom of the barrel was always quick to float to the top in times when the water was disturbed.

As they traveled to Huan, Johan had been disheartened to learn that many of the people that had joined them were planning on going deeper northeast, into the Komoky Valley and beyond. From there, only handfuls were going their way, and even they weren't completely certain on their decision to do so. It could very well end up being just them when the time came to go. Not a hopeful proposition.

There was no avoiding it. That was the way agreed upon with Aryu. With luck Aryu, already finished his fulfillment of that ridiculous promise to the one called Nixon and was starting his journey back. Traveling as straight as possible, he was bound to meet up with them before the time came to make that choice at the divide below the great waterfall. They still intended to stay in Huan as long as possible. Perhaps then the plan could change. If not, they were faced with the long and difficult trek west to the mysteries of the Paieleh River and the Blood Sea beyond. Still, a deal was a deal, and should Aryu not return by then, Johan had no doubts they would follow the course they'd planned.

Well, at least he would.

Esgona, on the other hand, could do whatever the hell he wanted with little to no objection from Johan as long as he kept his childish mouth shut.

Johan couldn't deny that Esgona had done nothing since they had left to incur his wrath in any way. More to the point, he was helpful to others, kept out of the way whenever possible, and had more than once been seen saving another of their troop when they were in trouble. Johan himself had seen him stand against a much larger bandit from a group that had attacked two days prior. If someone else hadn't called a general retreat for the devious gang, Johan had to believe that Esgona would have tried his hardest to stand his ground against the man.

Aryu had been right in his general assessment of the boy, just as he was also correct that a week does not eliminate the years of ego-driven torture or the shameful way he had encountered this army that gave chase. It was still something redeeming. Esgona had seen far too much (as had they all, in their own way) to be so easily cast off. Johan was a man now. Men, even so recently forged, must know mercy on some level. On the other hand, this *was* Esgona, and Johan made certain that he did not forget his place in the small hierarchy of two. He was, and would continue to be until such time as he left their company, a very distant second place, moving quickly to a distant third once Aryu returned.

Esgona had kept to himself, even in times of rest. The caravan was pushing through all day and night, taking on other drivers of the carts and horse or folme teams, making their trip that much, but also that much harder. Sleep came when time and responsibilities allowed it. Esgona could hold his own but still found extended amounts of time on his feet painful. He had begun looping around to different drivers, seeing who sought rest or needed a hand mending lashings and tethers. Johan only saw him in passing a few times a day, if he saw him at all.

How nice it was for Aryu to leave him behind as a parting gift, Johan thought during a moment of rest, riding on the edge of a folme-drawn cart with a handful of others. For Johan there was never really rest anymore. If he wasn't working, he was thinking. Could they even make it the Blood Sea? If they did, what would they find? Would the Army of the Old have made it that far and be waiting for them before they even get a chance to put up a fight?

Tactical thinking was Johan's specialty, and it didn't take him long to know the best course of action. To have any hope, he had to know what it was he was up against. Their numbers. Their technology. Their general presence. There was only one person around with answers.

Esgona enjoyed the work, the location and most of the people. He'd trade it all ten-fold to return everything that had brought him to this point. He was so cocky and sure his deviousness would net him big rewards for little effort, and for a while it had gone so smoothly.

Then the ships appeared on the horizon. Now it was easily the worst plan he'd ever had. A plan his good friend had died for, just because he wanted to tag along. Hogope had followed him, telling him all the while how excellent his plan was, and that he was certain countless others had done the same thing. Esgona was inclined to agree. It really wasn't hard to imagine that most others on the Quest would have done the same thing. When the ships arrived, Hogope had died very quickly and gruesomely at the hands of the attackers, all because he panicked and didn't spit out the right answers in a timely enough fashion.

The fruits of this deception were now paying off in record amounts, and every one of them was rotten. Permanently hobbled, stuck on a cart in the depths of the northern mountains (which had a delicious twist of irony when he considered this was where he was supposed to be right now anyway), and the only person around who he did know was Johan: lower class trash that should be serving his whims, not leading his way.

But no matter what anyone said, he was certain it was someone like Aryu he'd seen leading the Army of the Old. The details might not match, but his memory worked just fine, and he was bound and determined to prove it was so. And when he did prove it, when he had the ability to get his revenge, he swore he wouldn't hesitate to take it.

As if on cue, Johan was now striding over to him. This would likely be the first overt attempt at conversation from either since they'd left together. That didn't mean he welcomed it, but he was at least willing to hear what Johan had to say. The truth was, Johan had completed his quest, and as was agreed for all from Tan Torna Quay for centuries, he had earned his manhood and respect. However, in no text or tome was it written that Esgona had to like it.

"I didn't think you actually took rests, Esgona," he said. Esgona couldn't tell if he was being smarmy or boyishly sincere. He didn't care either way.

"Can I help you with something, Johan?" he asked, just to get the ball rolling faster. Sooner done, sooner gone.

"Easy there, young lad, no need to be snippy!" Esgona was tired of this conversation already and laughed at himself for thinking that this was going to be any different than he'd first thought. No matter what crude, stinging verbal barb Johan would dish out at him, nothing could be as potent as what he was doing to himself every waking hour of the day. He made no response and just waited, praying there was a point.

"Well now, that's better." Johan pulled his legs up and crossed them beneath himself. What a jerk. Fine, his point was made. His legs worked. *Thanks for the reminder.* "I'd like you to tell me something." Esgona raised his good eyebrow, thankful there was a point.. "What can you tell me about where this army came from?"

Esgona didn't know how to respond at first. Did he want the story of what went on while he was there or something else?

Johan beat him to the punch.

"No, no, we can all see what happened to you during your stay. I want to know about the things you saw. The way they operate, their numbers, anything helpful."

"Planning an attack?" Esgona sneered.

"Maybe, now do you have anything I can use or not?"

Esgona could still see the smarminess, but he also believed that deep in Johan's foolish mind, planning an attack might not be so farfetched.

"I never saw their numbers, but judging by the ships at sea, it's more than you could possibly imagine. There were thousands that came ashore, with tens of thousands more to follow. I doubt that was even a sample of their full numbers. Unless speaking to a prisoner, they never talk, they just mill around doing whatever it is they do. Some of the prisoners were taken away, only to show up again later with large cuts across parts of their bodies. If they were simply tortured or cut for some other purpose, I can't tell you."

Johan listened, the gears turning in his head. Esgona didn't think he'd said anything useful at all, but it appeared he did.

"Anything else?"

"Yes. Whatever you're planning won't work, Johan. They are numerous, powerful, remorseless, and efficient. Everything people aren't. Run far and run fast. That's my best advice for you. And if by some miracle you *do* get the chance to stop just one of them, you had better take it. I know I would."

"I don't want your advice, Esgona, and you sure as hell haven't earned the right to volunteer it to me."

He had a burning desire to retaliate. Only tradition held him back. For now.

"If you do think of anything else, no matter how small, I'd like you to tell me."

No answer given would have suited the mood Esgona was in, so he stayed silent, barely acknowledging he understood.

Johan sprung back down, knees bending deeply as he hit the ground. Further proof he was never likely going to let this go. Before he left, though, Esgona thought he might try to get somewhere first.

"Johan, wait."

Johan turned, walking back over to where Esgona sat and followed the moving cart along, waiting. "I have a request." Johan smiled. This was just what he wanted to hear. He likely didn't even care what it was. The fact was, Esgona was in some way admitting he needed him for something. He would be simply insufferable now, but it couldn't be helped. "Whatever useless plan you're putting together in that brain of yours, I'd like to hear it first, before you go do something stupid."

"Now why would I do that? What could I possibly owe you?"

"You don't owe me anything. I'm just saying that if you come up with something and think it might work, telling me may trigger something useful, something about what I've seen that doesn't seem needed now."

"Aw, isn't that sweet. Why so caring?"

"Because, like it or not, we're all that's left of our home…"

"Us and Aryu."

A quick-telling glance told Johan that as far as Esgona was concerned, the jury was still out on Aryu O'Lung'Singh.

"*We* are all that's left, Johan. It's no secret my feelings on this whole thing, but I've seen what they do to people. It's not right. I don't want that to happen to anyone if I can stop it. Somewhere out there is someone smarter than you who is planning something better, but until I meet them, you're all I've got."

Johan considered the truth in the words, then nodded. "Fine. Have it your way. If I come up with anything, I'll let you know."

That was enough of this conversation, and Esgona turned away to get some rest. He'd swear this was the early stage of an alliance. The thought made him sick.

◄►◄►◄►◄►◄►◄►◄►◄►◄►◄►◄►◄►

After two days of hard travel, the caravan reached the village of Huan.

It was burned to the ground.

There was still smoldering and the crackle of random fires in the buildings they saw. Something or someone had hit hard and fast. It wasn't long before their arrival.

Small groups were sent out to see if anyone had survived and hopefully see what had happened. Johan set off with one and searched the village perimeter. Esgona stayed back with the caravan.

It wasn't a large village. Maybe half the size of Tan Torna Qu-ay, if that. Huan was clearly a merchants' town, as most of the buildings were meant for trade and sales. The homes here were small and not meant for large families or extended stays. Although set in a beautiful valley junction, the soft roar of the Thunder Run barely audible in the distance, no one ever wanted to stay here long. It was too far removed from most things to be livable, and the winters could be legendary in their nastiness.

As they followed the perimeter, Johan made mental notes of the landscape. One side of the village gave way to a sharp drop off that led to a small stream which was likely a raging torrent in the melting season. On the other side of Huan was a sloped, open field that gave rise to two massive mountain valleys higher up. An individual road was visible between each one. The one slightly to the north was the intended route of travel for the majority of the caravan.

"So, are you still planning on heading past the Run?" one man with an aged hunting rifle asked Johan after about ten minutes of searching nothing but wrecked buildings and dying fires. He was a slight, middle-aged man with short black hair and quick, darting eyes under bushy brows. Johan nodded and kept scanning the terrain making mental notes. "Is that so? Well, that does seem like a shame. To make it this far only to die on the road ahead."

Johan looked at the man, who was staring him down, clearly looking for some reaction. Johan said nothing, but was intrigued at what the man might have to say.

"Oh yes, you'll meet your end on that road, I promise you that."

"What makes you so sure your road is any safer?" Johan asked.

The other two had stopped now, wanting to hear both sides of

260

this confrontation.

"Well, there's strength in numbers for one thing," he answered, "and for another, even without being chased by the mechanical monsters behind us, the way along the Paieleh is cursed to misfortune and desperation."

"That's your argument?" Johan asked, smirking. It was clearly foolish to have listened to the man in the first place. "Curses and misfortune? Good gods, look at us all. Look at this village! I'd say the evil is spread pretty evenly right now. I'll take my chances, thank you very much."

The man simply huffed a response and the group continued their search.

The world was a large and complicated place. The gears that turn in all corners at any one point in time are tremendous. No act of God or fate had brought Johan this far. No act of divinity had brought Aryu to him the first time; it was just the way it had to be. Johan Otan'co always knew he was destined for something beyond the life of dishonor his father had bequeathed him. And since he hadn't found out what that something was yet, it was simply because he had not done what he must in this life, and that was enough for him to put one foot in front of the other every day.

If there was a god left in this world, Johan was inclined to believe that as his search group looped back around to where the caravan waited, god bore a striking resemblance to that of one Cadet Rider August Stroan of the Inja Army.

Stroan was sitting astride his giant horse in his dented and dirty red armor. Johan was glad to see a friendly face, even one he'd only known for a few moments, and approached Stroan who finally turned to see his group with Johan leading the way. A broad smile came to his face.

"When I said I'd see you again, I can't say I meant it to be so soon," Stroan said as he dismounted.

"I'm just glad it was in this life and not the next," Johan said, taking the Rider's hand.

They sat around a makeshift camp that the Inja Army detail deployed here had set up on the north end of the destroyed town. Here the caravan from the south merged with several other smaller groups that had been in the process of being escorted deeper into the mountains by military escort.

"We left Huan three days ago to the high country of the northeastern passage, heading for the Komoky Valley and beyond," Stroan told Johan as he sat with him for the evening meal. He was dressed casually in dirty canvas pants and a thick sweater, his helmet replaced by a knit cap to cover his military-cut blonde hair, a rarity to Johan, but more common in the lands Stroan was from. He'd told Johan he was from the Vein Valley northwest of Tan Torna Qu-ay, on the borders of the Inja where the war with the Westlanders had been waged for years.

His youthful face still contained the sunken eyes, a sure sign that his journey had not been easy. "A Rider from another troop tracked us down, telling us of the fate of Huan. We turned around and met up with more Riders as we came into town, not long before you all arrived. How *did* you get here?"

Johan began telling him of what had befallen them since they had parted company. He spoke of the blast that had forced he and Aryu to go their separate ways, the needless destruction of Tan Torna Qu-ay, the mountain town and their first encounter with an Ark 1, the deal Aryu had made and the mission he'd left on with the promise to return, and finally their journey here.

"Quite a tale for such a short period of time," Stroan said. "We had heard of what had happened to your home. I am very sorry. I thought of you at once, hoping you'd not been a part of it. My journey has been less eventful. I met up with my troop and accompanied them and other travelers into the mountains to Huan, where we'd been for a few days before we chose to leave as escorts. Only a small amount of us were going with the caravans;. The rest rode off for the Thunder Run, planning on following the Paieleh, much as you planned to do."

"That's still the plan, my friend," said Johan,

"Yes, well, I believe once we make a few more rounds to determine what happened here, we'll have to leave the travelers behind and ride on for the rest of the troops that have gone that way."

"And you still have no idea what happened here?" Johan asked.

"Not a great idea, no. My superiors are piecing it together and there's not a lot that trickles down a cadet's way. Essentially I just do as I'm told and follow my orders."

"But you do know something, don't you?" Johan pressed. Stroan said nothing. "Stroan, think about all the things I've seen lately. Do you really think that whatever you have to say will scare me?"

"It may not scare you," he began, "but it may certainly make you think twice about either staying here as you planned or following the Paieleh."

Stroan looked into his face and relented, seeing the determination in the young man. He brought Johan closer, sure that no one at a near-by fire could tune in. "The rumor is a large and nasty group of Ruskan Stalkers did this. Old ones. Smart ones."

"I didn't think they traveled in groups," replied Johan, pondering the possibilities. "They're so territorial."

"They are," Stroan agreed, "but this group wasn't just attacking randomly. They were organized. They hit, killed, and burned across the whole village like a wave, then took off again into the mountains farther north, led by one who seemed particularly clever. They were in and out in the blink of an eye. There are tracks, but they're difficult to make out. Our scouts that we sent farther north to the Thunder Run confirmed what appeared to be several tracks heading away from the town, around the lake at the base of the waterfall and continuing up the valley floor. From there, who knows. It's possible they just wanted to disrupt Huan because it was where so many people were. This place has been packed full since people started running here. Being so territorial, they might have simply had enough, hit Huan, and retreated back to the high country before we could send retaliation."

"Would they be that intelligent?" Johan asked, mulling over a million different things in his mind (as any story such as this was prone to do to a tactician).

Stroan shrugged. "It's just a theory, but older Ruskans have been known to talk, plan, strategize, any number of things an animal shouldn't be capable of as far as we know. Unfortunately, they're so lost in the unexplored high mountains that no one can confirm any of it. Even what I tell you now is third- or fourth-hand information, honestly."

The two sat silent, thinking of the multitudes of possibilities. Finally, Johan spoke what had been on his mind.

"You said your troops were heading up the Paieleh. Why?"

Stroan nodded. "There's a massing of military might from the Westlanders, the Inja Army, and powers from farther places on the south shores of the Blood Sea. At first I thought that was why you agreed with your friend to go there. I'm just hoping that if those Ruskans did go that way, they never caught up with anyone and have since left the trail to their homelands."

"And this massing," continued Johan, "is it to confront the Army of the Old?"

Stroan nodded. "To confront, and destroy."

"I'd love to hear how you plan on doing that," Johan said, not jokingly.

Stroan gave a weak smile, pulling him closer again. "Because, they aren't the only ones with the technology." And with that, from under his worn-out tunic, he produced the second Ark 1 Johan had ever seen.

▸◂▸◂▸◂▸◂▸◂▸◂▸◂▸◂▸◂▸◂▸◂▸◂

Esgona had found a good group to be associated with during the day; a group of families that he'd spent most of the trip assisting. The others in the party seemed to be less astonished by the destruction of the small village. The pillaging that had been so bountiful for most of them was likely a core reason why.

Now, as they sat amongst the masses around scattered fires on the outskirts of what was once Huan, he found himself locked in a dilemma. He had no want or need to accompany the idiot across the way into the deeper mountains, where death was a certainty and it was sure to be quick and painful. He also wasn't quite up to the trip the others planned on taking to the other valley, trying to run farther and deeper into the mountains they foolishly thought would protect them.

Esgona knew better. He knew firsthand the power of the army that chased them. It was entirely likely they were being watched even now.

He hadn't lied to Johan; he really did want to be a part of whatever revenge he planned, but he also wanted to be sure he'd live to see it played out.

He sat there long into the night after most had gone to sleep, watching the sky and the things he saw there. Occasionally, an officer on patrol would come by, but never stay for long. Esgona was not the most stimulating company right now.

While he watched the sky, he'd often see the passing of faint, pulsing lights. He knew that they weren't stars, though that was the story often told to children from Tan Torna Qu-ay so as not to frighten them. They were once used for a multitude of things. Communication in mysterious, invisible ways around the planet. Distant, unimaginably beautiful pictures of the land below them. Many were used for war.

His mother was a smart woman and had never led him astray when it came to these things. They may still be around, always watching. There they float, junk in space, a remnant of foolish times.

Now he had seen the pictures they could take, the ways they could communicate, and had heard the methods they could be used for in war. None of which was useful in any way to these people.

Except one.

Putting aside the humiliation of his family and his terrible choice in friends, Esgona had seen the amazing way Johan Otan'co had with strategy and the interest he'd taken with the ways of the Old.

There was so much hate in Esgona. Hate that needed satisfaction. Here, at this junction, his only two decent options were both certain to lead to the death of everyone. Into the mountains, or the madness. As much as he hated to admit it, the option with the most likely chance for the retribution demanded by the actions he'd witnessed was the path with the person he hated more than any others, save for the freak who was anticipated to join them shortly. (Though, judging by the state of confusion Nixon was in, he doubted it would be as quickly as was promised. The phoenix had too many issues to be resolved so easily.)

He also had more to offer Johan than what he'd given him earlier about the things he'd seen. At the time, he just had no interest in sharing them. Loathing was never so easy to overcome, and he took a small amount of satisfaction knowing how hard it had been for Johan to approach him in the first place.

Something Esgona had said triggered a response, despite trying to keep it as vague as possible. A lack of valuable information and Johan still had come up with something. It may be stupid and rudimentary, but he still had an idea that he thought he could make work based on completely useless, though accurate, information. That was sadly a better option to align with at this time, Esgona decided. No doubt Johan would have a field day with his wanting to go with him. It couldn't be helped. Besides, he had never told the whole story. The whole story was his and his alone. He may have been heavily wounded, both physically and mentally, but he still had a touch of the old, bullying, intelligent Esgona in him. Let the lower-class asshole and the freak have their fun. When the time was right, he'd show them all why he was the true upperclassman of the group.

CHAPTER 17

The Thunder Run

Esgona was certainly correct. He had taken a moment the next day to inform Johan that he was going with them. Skeptical, now that Esgona could in essence escape to wherever he liked, Johan asked why.

"Because I want them finished off even more than you do, and between my two options here, going with you is the more likely way to accomplish that."

Johan seemed to understand. He gave him the "Don't get in our way" spiel that made Esgona's skin crawl, but in the end the deal was done and the plan was in motion.

Esgona wasn't the only one planning to dance with death in the Paieleh Valley. Upon learning their escort was pulling out to rejoin other forces at the Blood Sea, a sizable number of the caravan members were willing to forgo the northeast route plan and simply follow the military contingent, content to be near anything that seemed to offer protection. Stroan told them that twenty extra people, totaling four carts, were accompanying them. There was a military contingent of twenty-three (predominantly Riders) and one gas-powered equipment hauler called a Turtle Loader, so called due to its generally slow speed and rounded wooden outer shape that contained storage within. It was ungainly, as most powered carts of the area were, but it burned little fuel, could handle large weights relatively effortlessly, and was a cinch to drive; meaning the controls didn't have to be manned by an Inja Army officer.

"My time here is shorter than we planned," Johan commented to Stroan, "but I'm sure if we miss him, he'd understand our need to go with the big, armed group. I'm not sure another few days would have done us any good anyway." Even if Aryu showed up somehow, the plan wouldn't change, just the tactics. The information Stroan had told him the night before gave him a very uneasy-yet-hopeful feeling. It didn't seem as hopeless as before.

After showing Johan the Ark 1, he had explained more thoroughly. "Some of the other military forces from the far reaches of the land surrounding the Blood Sea have many powerful, advanced weapons of their own. We may as well be throwing rocks for all the good we could do against them without something to match them."

"How far advanced are we talking here?" Johan asked, the possibilities swirling in his head.

"I'm not the best one to ask, again I'm just a Cadet, but the word is they may not have full robot warriors, but some do have weapons that are energy-based like this, as well as vehicles and flying machines."

"This is craziness!" Esgona said, listening in and fearing every word. "Trade the devil that chases us for the devil that's just going our way?"

"We know them to be decent people," Stroan reassured.

"I'm sure they are, but they still have possession of technology." Esgona wasn't about to let this go.

269

"How do we know they're so good-hearted?" Johan asked, still mulling scenarios over in his mind.

Stroan, sure to quiet them and keep it between the three, leaned into their faces. "Because we've been in contact with them for hundreds of years."

The Inja aversion to technology was more local than anything else. Understanding the fear it could bring, the land to the south expressed no interest in joining their 'fool's quest' and agreed to keep to themselves. The two worlds left each other alone: one out of fear, the other out of respect and understanding.

"We've kept in contact quite extensively in that time," Stroan told them. "Once they learned of the threat to our south, they agreed to intervene. I have no idea the true power or force they have given us, but there are definitely members of at least three technologically advanced countries that have come to aid our cause."

Esgona was pale as a ghost, but Johan spoke up before he could protest again. "Grow up, Esgona. How did you think we were going to fight back?" Esgona looked at Johan with obvious malice and left as quickly as he'd come, cursing Johan for being right.

▸◂▸◂▸◂▸◂▸◂▸◂▸◂▸◂▸◂▸◂▸◂▸◂▸◂

The last day in Huan was spent scouring the town for anything and everything they could carry to make the trip a better one. No one wanted to risk running out of food and supplies halfway into a one-way trip. Most of the available stock was stored in the Turtle, while everything else was spread out between the remaining four carts in case something unfortunate happened to the awkward rolling storage unit. "She's stable," Stroan had said, "but she sure isn't indestructible."

Johan was wandering around the wreckage with Stroan when he

put the question forward about being an extra set of hands for the Riders, something beyond just being another civilian traveler.

"Are you asking to enlist?" Stroan asked, looking at him with confusion.

"No, no," Johan said at once. "It's just, I have a lot invested in this whole trip, more than most I would say. I would kind of like to put in a little more than the masses to that end. The more we could do to learn and be taught anything useful to help us the better."

"You could ask to enlist. You're a good man. We could use you, that's not a secret. Your winged friend, too."

"In all fairness, the path we may choose to take would be much easier without military…restrictions."

Stroan caught the meaning and understood at once. Johan was looking for training and information for the purposes of revenge. That path wasn't likely to coincide with the strict rules of warfare that the Inja Army upheld. Of course, neither was this particular enemy. Stroan saw in Johan a determination and resourcefulness that many he served with lacked. That was a set of traits he had no problem keeping around.

"I'll be sure to speak to my superiors about it."

They finished rummaging through the buildings, grabbing canned foods and travel supplies like unburned blankets and metal cooking pots. Johan even found some books to bring. Nothing he was very keen on, but he hadn't had a good read in a while. He just hoped the trip would be uneventful enough to get the chance to do so.

When the carts and Turtle were fully loaded, the Brigade and their civilian charges set off for the Thunder Run and the mysteries of the Paieleh Valley.

Esgona had already been taken aside, much to the dismay of Johan, and shown the basic controls of the Turtle. The man in charge, Chief Rider Samson Wyndam, had done so after he noted the young man (or old boy) and his willingness to work hard, despite his obvious handicap.

Chief Rider Wyndam was keen on the work ethic. He was not as aged as some in his position, his short dark hair and goatee only starting to show signs of graying, but his body had seen a dozen lifetimes' worth of hard work. A life serving the Riders and the wars they fought had made him a very rugged man. His hands were tough from the years of riding, his gray eyes sharp and watchful. Even his armor, the same maroon-red tinge the others wore, was so badly damaged from its dutiful service that it was hardly recognizable. It was dented, wrecked, patched, welded, and fixed so often (due to his refusal for any replacement) that it looked as though it could fall apart at any time. His skin was likely tough enough to stop a bullet anyway.

He led them all north to the bend that would take them to the Thunder Run. Johan was getting anxious to see the mighty waterfall. The rumors of its majesty were known far and wide.

As they left Huan behind and turned the final corner leading into the last stretch, he could see even from this distance that he was not to be disappointed.

In the thousands of years since the Second Fall of Man, the world of old had changed unimaginably.

Huge underground explosions had caused many tectonic plates to become erratic, at times tearing the ground apart with the pace of movement it set. Other times, the massive volcanic upheavals had created plateaus of mountain regions in sizes and heights never before seen.

Here at the tip of the Great Range, the large mountains that were around them everywhere were suddenly dwarfed by the titanic Hymleahs farther north. No man could ever enter those peaks. The climb and the thinness of the air was too much for any but the great

Stalkers that had adapted to the high ground.

Here, though, the Hymleah headwall ended abruptly in the form of a gigantic cliff face. It was not altogether wide, eventually giving way to more sloping climbs on either side. It was, however, monumentally tall. In its center cascaded the monstrous sight called the Uhluktahn by the Ruskan Stalkers of the area but known more simply as the Thunder Run by the men and women who had traveled this way over the centuries. The Thunder Run was caused by the higher mountains above giving way to a valley that, due to the recent and massive tectonic shift, kept the base layer of rock warm to the touch. The snow and glacial feeds it passed through for untold miles north of where the party stood was the source of its amazingly bountiful water supply.

Many from the area, human and Stalker alike, regarded the formation and its unimaginable beauty as something closer to a spiritual entity, like a church formed from the earth itself. For the two from Tan Torna Qu-ay, one of which had only really seen Tortria Den and its paltry volume to compare this with, it was as if the whole planet gave way to a massive and unbelievably loud wall of water pouring down from the sky.

The huge formation came to a rest at the base of the cliff face in a huge lake called Thunder Head. The deep lake was so turbulent from the waterfall that very little could survive within it. Mostly plants and very small fish that could withstand the massive mini-tides at its shores were all one could find of any kind of life. If someone went swimming in it, they were instantly at risk of being sucked into one of the pressure swells and carried off to be pummeled to death by the crushing downpour, or simply drowned in a never-ending ballet of deep cyclonic surges that simply came and went, up and down, never to be released.

"Impressive, isn't it," Stroan said, pulling his horse up beside

Johan. "I reacted the same way when I first laid eyes on it. We will travel the road that winds to the west of it, around Thunder Head, and into the heart of the river valley."

The winds from the large valley they were to follow allowed them a respite from the giant plume of mist that emanated from the lake like a cloud, drifting the opposite of the way they intended to go. When the winds died and it carried more spray to the west, travel was nearly impossible. The rocks of the road became slick with water, the vapor soaking into everything, causing a damp chill that cut right down to the bone. For a valley with such fleeting sunlight to dry things and keep warm, that was not a pleasant prospect.

Chief Rider Wyndam called the party to a halt and summoned his Riders to him. The rest of the carts and people waited as the meeting took place. Most of them were content enough to wait and continue to admire the site sight ahead of them.

The Riders returned to their posts and each conferred with the cart drivers. Stroan pulled up beside Johan and did the same. "The Chief says that we're to pick up the pace to get past the Thunder Run and farther down the valley before nightfall. When we're a decent enough distance away, we'll see if we can set the first camp."

Johan nodded his understanding, but asked why the need to discuss it now while they were still so far from the waterfall. "Because," responded Stroan, "once we get a bit closer, the noise will be too much for clear communication. We want to make sure everyone knows what's going on and why before we reach that point."

The rest of the people they traveled with who were on foot began climbing onto whatever cart was closest to them and found what spot they could. The horses and folmes pulling the carts were cinched in tighter and prepared for the double duty they were about to undertake. Another Rider began asking the carts ahead to move aside while the Turtle took up point. It was the slowest of the caravan, so it would lead to ensure it and its valuable cargo wasn't left behind or swept into the Thunder Head.

"The road we take passes right next to the lake," the Rider said. "At times the drop off is right beside us. We keep the Turtle in front to set the pace and help if it runs into trouble."

The Turtle and its noisy engine rumbled up beside them. Esgona yielded the command to another Rider; however, he did remain next to him as a passenger and the Rider and Esgona looked to be deep into their own conversation.

Stroan had known there was no love between the two young men from Tan Torna Qu-ay. The details of their history weren't discussed, but the mutual feelings were blatantly obvious. Johan knew he could never explain the torment and terror Esgona filled him with as they grew. It was more than simple bullying. Sure, there was the name-calling and dustups as youths, but it grew steadily worse as they aged. Once, in their early teens, Esgona had tricked Johan into going to the pools that peppered the rocks beneath Tortria Den by sending him a letter signed by a girl he'd had an obvious crush on. Once he arrived, Johan found he had been tricked, and was led into a trap by a waiting Esgona and Hogope. After laughing mercilessly at his trick, Esgona shoved Johan into one of the deep pools.

Johan, at that point in his life, couldn't swim.

As he thrashed and fought for breath, Esgona and Hogope laughed harder. Eventually, when it became clear that Johan was in serious risk, he could see Hogope falter and ask Esgona to get him out. Esgona just stood there smiling. Were it not for Aryu's intervention, Johan still believed that Esgona likely would have let him drown.

Aryu had been in town, seen the girl, knew she was certainly not at the pools, and knew instantly what had happened. He had just begun to master his wings and flew out as quickly as he could. Esgona and Hogope ran once they saw him approach and haul out his terrified friend. Despite the anger felt by the two, no retribution was even devised. Although their hatred for Esgona and his actions was great, they feared his mother and the power over their families that she possessed.

And that was just one thing he'd done to the two. Granted, it was on the severe side of his actions, but it was not an isolated incident.

Stroan had no issue with the boy and had found him just as helpful as Johan despite his ailment. He did not have their history, however. History makes all the difference.

▶▶▶▶▶◀◀◀◀◀▶▶▶▶▶◀◀◀◀◀▶▶▶▶▶◀◀◀◀◀

By the time the sun began to pass its apogee and began the fall towards sunset, the group was deep into the astonishing noise created by the Thunder Run. The torrent of water from far above crashed into Thunder Head, and given the geography of the valley itself, the landscape created a natural echo chamber. Stroan was right; words were useless even spoken side by side. The travelers found whatever means necessary to shut it out. Ad hoc earplugs were passed out between some while others took to muffling the sound with wraps and other clothing tied tightly to their heads.

Even the animals were granted some form of protection, usually by heavy blankets tied around their ears.

Johan, riding on the back of a cart, had fashioned earplugs from soft dough used in making miscellaneous fireside pastries. They did the job well enough, but the power of the waterfall still made it through and buzzed his ears, which were still sensitive from the Ark 1 explosion. He could swear he felt the pressure of that much falling water hit the lake below, like the Thunder Run did more than stir the water of Thunder Head. It was so massive it vibrated the air around him.

The Turtle kept a steady pace along the lakeshore. Many looked at the sudden drop off of the water in fear, knowing what entering it was likely to do. Johan was simply awe-inspired by the view.

Above them was nothing but headwall as far up as they could see. It cast an unnatural darkness on everything, the sun sitting well behind its mass by this point in the day. The lake was the largest most of them had ever seen coming from a place so dry and arid. The shore didn't gradually fade into the depths. It was a solid drop into abyss from the moment the crystal-clear water hit the edges. With the depth, and the lack of sunlight, the lake was simply black.

The animals, even the large pure horses of the Riders, were clearly uneasy being so close to the noise and the power that created it. They stayed the course but were twitchy and nervous. The road was wide even as it passed directly beside the drop offs, and most of the animals kept as far away as they could. It would still be another few hours before they were past the shores of Thunder Head and beginning their trip up the valley.

Johan noticed a folme having issues. It wasn't pulling a cart, just walking along the side of one being driven by a mustached gentleman and a young girl he surmised to be his daughter, a pretty, dark-skinned brunette in a soft blue dress with lace trim, currently sporting a small blanket wrapped around her short-cut hair to block out the noise. He'd noticed the daughter a few times up to this point in the trip, and he had taken small bits of enjoyment from the fact that she seemed to be noticing him as well.

The animal was rocking its large head back and forth rhythmically. It was then he saw the folme's rag-tied headwear slipping off its left ear.

Johan was up at once, waving to the cart driver, desperate to get his attention. From where they were sitting, the driver took no notice of him. He had moved to the side of the cart and was ready to hop down when he ran out of time.

The big animal lost the headgear in one of its head-rocking motions, casting the old blanket to the ground.

It immediately had a very pained expression on its face, its mouth open in what Johan could only assume was a cry of fear and discomfort. It thrashed back and forth, ramming its head against the cart and then away, pulling its rope taut repeatedly.

The motions finally got the attention of the driver and his daughter. They were trying to figure out the best plan of action when the folme gave a huge yank on its rope, snapping it.

It fell back and listed to one side, hitting another cart that was traveling behind the one it had been tied to. The cart was thrown off to the left of the road at the jolt and began sliding down a small embankment the road rested on. The driver tried in vain to steer back, and had managed to get the right wheels back on the road when the beleaguered folme hit again, ramming its head against the cart once more in an attempt to shut out the horrible noise. With the last hit, the cart tumbled, throwing the driver, passengers, and all cargo it carried down the hill.

By this point most of the caravan had been alerted to the peril by rear-flanking Riders. The carts were all being brought to a stop and many curious and horrified travelers looked back to see what had happened.

The pained folme was battering the cart it had been tied to and had smashed it closer to the edge of the road and toward the Thunder Head. It reared back and was in the midst of charging with all of its considerable might when the mustached driver gave a powerful whip to the reigns, causing the team tied to the cart to wrench forward with a burst of speed. The action caused the folme to miss and stagger across the remainder of the road to the edge of the lake, where it had no choice but to succumb to its mass and heave over the edge and into the tumultuous water below with a silent splash.

The driver's quick thinking had unexpected consequences. The sudden rush forward caused the young girl at his side to tumble backwards, over the boxes and bags of supplies they carried, and on to the lip of the cart. No one rode with them, so no one was there to stop her as she twirled like a dancer on the edge, a look of terror on her face for a moment as she looked about for help that wasn't there, then off and into the lake not far from where the folme who had led the way was now thrashing madly to escape its fate.

Johan watched the whole scene as if it played in slow motion. Helplessly he watched the folme topple headlong into the Thunder Head, then the girl and her picturesque movements followed moments before she turned and met his eyes as she went backwards.

The driver was back at once, and he looked over the side of the supplies into the lake. When Johan saw the man begin pulling off his boots and shirt, his paralysis was broken instantly. The man was going to go in after her, a trip guaranteed to bring his own death in the dark water. A heroic death, but a death all the same. That could not happen.

Johan looked around, spying a piece of spare rope. He bent down and grabbed it by the matched ends, got back up, and turned to Stroan.

His sudden movements had gotten Stroan's attention. By the time Stroan had begun his shout of *"No!"* at the top of his lungs (a useless action, even so close) Johan was already moving forward, bounding like a cat from his own cart to the one beside him. In a blur, his hand whipped back, tossing a free end of the rope to Stroan while he catapulted himself off the other side, wrapping the end he carried around his wrist twice and into his hand before he hit the water feet-first.

It would barely be a perceivable moment that could measure the time it took for Johan to go from hero to fool in his own mind. He hit with such a force that he went right past his intended target and beyond, to the deep abyss below.

The forces at work in the lake were amazing. It grabbed a hold of him at once and tossed him about with no rhyme or reason. Johan had no concept of up or down, and the blurry images his brain could process did nothing to help the matter. He was lost in such a short period of time that he could only feel helplessness; all heroism he had possessed a moment before on the cart was gone like a candle getting snuffed out.

The first tug on his arm hit, threatening to pull away the safety line he'd nearly forgotten about in the muddle of fear and confusion. Instinct caused him to clamp his hand down, grabbing the rope as it pulled back again. Had he not grabbed when he did, it easily would have been lost.

Soon his body jackknifed upwards, and with another tug he broke the surface, gasping for the air the fear had pushed out of him.

The pain hit him like he'd been shot. At first, he thought a powerful blow had struck him in the head, and his free hand reached up to see if he was alright. It was then he noticed his doughy earplugs had been either popped out or dissolved in the water. Either way he was now at the mercy of the waterfall in more ways than one. Each moment seemed to make this plan worse and worse.

The difference between heroes and normal people is nothing more than how one thinks in situations such as these. True, it would take an act of heroism to bound across the carts and after the girl, but heroism is not the strict domain of heroes. It can encompass anyone at any time, given the proper circumstances. Heroes are the ones that don't let the heroism pass. More to the point, they don't even know it's there when it happens. To them, it's just the way things are. It's that clarity of view that allows them to see past the rush of the heroic actions and adrenalin, past the terror and the pain, and think about the next move not just as someone trying to survive, but as someone going beyond that and continuing the mission they set out on.

It is that difference that allowed Johan to block out the pain of the noise and the fear of his fight to the water surface. He ignored the truth of the situation and looked around just in time to see the blue-clothed arm of the girl below the surface dip down and out of sight. With one quick tug back on the rope for whatever slack he could convince the unseen people above to give, he pulled himself back down below the water (not that it was hard, the action being what the water wished to happen anyway) and reached out for the quickly disappearing form of the girl below him.

His hand met her wrist with the soft embrace of a lover, followed quickly by her clamping down on his own wrist in the death grip that it was. Johan hauled up his arm and the girl attached to it with a feat of strength he'd never have thought possible, using his other hand to pull them both back to the surface and take another lifesaving breath.

Heroes are rarely given such an easy time of it. That is the best explanation anyone could think of for why, after all that bravery and effort to save the girl, the rope snapped from the repeated rocking motion against the sharp edge of the road, and the two below were once more tossed back into the Thunder Head.

The forces at work on their lower extremities were breathtaking as the water churned to pull them back down. At the same moment, Johan was extremely thankful the girl apparently knew how to swim (as did he, and very well after the incident with Esgona years before), and terribly regretful he'd jumped in with all his clothes, boots included. They were all doing him no favors in trying to stay afloat.

It was then, as he struggled harder to stay up, his free arm brushed against the hard, forgotten handle of the dagger he carried. Out of options and time as the girl was beginning to go under once more, he reached into his shirt as quickly as he could manage without sinking again, pulled the knife from its leather sheath, and turned to the rock face before him that marked the edge of the Thunder Head.

What he saw was not encouraging. The face was smooth as glass from the years of pounding torture from the water and the sound that bounced off it. It was dark gray, polished, and imposing. Nowhere did he see a spot good enough to wedge the knife for a place to hold.

The girl went under, torn backwards by a sudden surge, pulling Johan with her. He held his grip, but her body was lost to the lake. A fraction of a second before he was taken with her, his eyes locked on what he believed was a miniscule crack in the rock face. He swung his arm wildly, bringing down the blade into the hard surface as his head was lost below the water.

The blade hit the rock and sunk in like it was made of warm butter. He had hit it! A million to one stab, and he had hit it! Luck truly did favor the bold.

The knife held, acting as a solid and unmoving grip in the rock. His reservoirs near empty, he used whatever power he could muster from his exhausted body to heave up the girl once more and himself to the surface, another act of inhuman strength by this point in the battle. Whatever submerged whirlpool had a grip on her let go and allowed her to be pulled back to the surface.

Once there, Johan pulled them both to where the knife stood firm while the next rescue line came from above and pulled the girl to safety, followed by Johan.

Just as he was beginning to rise, his eyes met the knife as he pulled it out. There he saw something frightening and amazing before he was pulled to the shore of the mighty Thunder Head.

It was many hours later when the caravan finally came to a stop for the night. They had made it far away from the Thunder Run and the lake below it. Still, even here, hours up the Paieleh River Valley, the echo could still be heard through the towering walls around them. It was much more tolerable now, and people could speak in normal tones and had no need of headwear.

Except for Johan.

His ears rang, his head pounded; his eyes still blurred from the power, the noise, and the effort he'd put in to saving the girl. Once pulled from the water, he was immediately taken to a cart with some unseen figure wrapping his head from the sound once more. Not that it did any good. Even wrapped, his ears hurt. At times they felt like they were bleeding. He hoped it was just water.

The girl, after eventually releasing the vise-like grip she had on his now heavily bruised wrist, was taken off for her own tending-to and could no longer be seen.

Stroan sat with him, as did others. Some talked to each other, some to him, though he couldn't hear much. He did hear small pieces, and that was enough to give him hope that he would hear again sometime soon. It seemed the damage might not be irreversible. As his cantankerous old grandfather would say, "Thank Heaven for small miracles boy, because that's all you'll ever get."

Eventually, after eating what he could of some soup and bread, he had a moment to talk to Stroan outside of the ongoing conversations that surrounded them.

"How is she?" he asked. At least, he assumed he did. He could barely make out the sound of his own voice.

Stroan understood at once and gave him a thumbs-up. Johan sighed heavily. He'd done it.

"We lost a cart as well as the folme," Stroan informed him. His face was close so his lips could be easily read for whatever Johan didn't hear. "It went over the other side of the road and broke both axles. There was no way to fix it without spare parts, which we don't have." Johan understood, and he had the utmost faith in the Inja Army Riders that they salvaged all they could to make the situation less dire. Not a bad outcome. It could have been much worse.

"Nice toss, by the way," commented Stroan when Johan's moment of reflection was over. "You're lucky I grabbed it. Sorry it didn't hold."

Johan was now so consumed by the memory of the knife (once again sheathed and resting next to his chest) that he'd forgotten the rope. He looked at his wrist where the burns from the tension were obvious, like red tattoos in his skin.

A smirk. "Nice catch. It saved our lives." Stroan shook him off. He was a military man. He did what he had to. "No, honestly, thank you. It bought us the time to get a breath and fight longer. I owe you my life." Stroan still didn't buy it, but before he could argue, his attention was drawn to movement coming toward them.

The girl. Johan saw her coming to them, the mustached man leading the way with a vigor that made Johan's body hurt just to watch it. The man's arms spread wide as he came, a smile on his weathered face from ear to ear.

"I heard you were awake!" he said, just loud enough to be heard. He came to Johan and wrapped his arms around him in a tight, suffocating hug. Johan hurt but allowed it, knowing no amount of complaining in the world would pry this man off. "I owe you so much, sir. My daughter would be lost without you. You are a hero! I thank the Lord Ryu that he brought your path to meet ours."

Johan said nothing audible, just a sound that might have been "*no problem*" or something along those lines. It wouldn't have mattered.

The man was now crying so heavily that words were useless. The girl met his eyes as her father continued his fevered hug. She had an intense gaze that held Johan twice as firmly as any grip her father could muster.

After composing himself enough to speak again, he motioned to the girl, her dark brown eyes still gripping Johan effortlessly. "Sir, I am honored to present my daughter, Seraphina. May the King of Dragons forever shine the sun upon you for returning her to me."

Seraphina. Beautiful.

He bowed as much as he could muster with his still-depleted strength. The bustle of the situation did not excuse proper manners, after all. She closed the gap between them in hurried steps. When she was right next to him, she kissed him softly but passionately and held him tightly, followed by mouthing the words "Thank you".

The crowd went mad at the action while the purity and emotion poured into him like a warm drink, and when at last she pulled away, his heart almost broke at the loss of the feeling of her. The emotion of the moment was as much positive as the moment he witnessed the fire consume his home was negative: absolute and pure.

She joined her beaming father once more and returned to their cart. Johan stood flabbergasted at the feelings he was bombarded with. He likely would have gone mad if not for at the last moment before he lost sight of her, she looked back past the crowd, met his eyes once more and smiled. The image was so complete and heartwarming that the mental image of his knife driven into solid rock effortlessly, inches from the crack where he had been aiming, melted away like smoke.

For now…

Still these fools persisted. This was why it hated them so much. They were too stupid to know when to quit. Some may call it guile or tenacity, but not this one. All it saw was foolishness.

The rallying of others had gone well. Even the younger ones it had encountered were quick to follow, with no issues or impulsiveness. They too were sick of the intrusions and were willing to follow the elder members of the breed to get this job done.

They had gathered and when the time was right, just after a large group had left (this way the destruction would be seen and the word of it spread to others of their kind), they came down from the high country, and under the direction of the elder named Skerd, they pounced on the town, sparing no one with their fury. Every man, woman, child and animal was destroyed. Ravaged until none remained.

Skerd was not terribly happy it had come to this. It was only by carefully laying out his arguments and each pro and con that he was able to convince them this quick and brutal show of force was the course of action most likely to drive off any further intrusion.

Skerd now waited at the top of the Uhluktahn. He was right to do so, it would seem. Shortly after the rampage, another large group had arrived in the village. It stayed for longer than Skerd would have liked, clearly raiding what was left for themselves (*scavenging dogs*) and when they did leave, although most left into the high country, a small number *still* continued down the path and into his territory. Unbelievable! It was not an elegant plan by any means, but it was meant to be far more effective than it was proving to be.

He came down his mountain and watched them progress around the black water. He stalked and tracked them effortlessly, the noise clearly too much for them, and they had to cover their ears just to pass by it.

He was near them and was about to pounce when he caught sight of the beast or burden beginning to succumb to the power of the Uhluktahn. He watched in glee as it caused havoc among the people. Then the animal and the young girl fell into the water, an action that meant certain death.

Skerd was ready to strike in the confusion, but he saw the young one *willingly* jump in, likely to try to save the girl (or perhaps the beast? Skerd believed it to have more value in the long run.).

It had never seen an act of such amazing stupidity.

Or bravery.

Bravery or not he still planned on his attack, hovering over them now as most tried to help the fools in the water. He tensed his body, preparing for the kill, eyes red with rage and the need to destroy these interlopers, when it happened.

From where he sat perched, he couldn't see the things that had gone on, but he certainly felt them.

It was power! Amazing, pure, and unfathomable in its depth. He felt it in the earth below him, coursing like electricity below his feet. It instantly brought his logical mind to the forefront, pushing back the rage like a plaything. His refreshed and clear eyes saw with astonishment the people below pull up the girl who had fallen in, followed by the fool who had jumped in after her. The feeling stopped, but the memory remained. He still felt the tingle from its presence.

Skerd stopped his attack before it even started and ran back up to the higher ground, trying to understand what he was feeling. Was it that? Could it possibly be?

His heart and now-logical mind said it was, and the realization created something new and unnerving.

It was fear.

Something down there was powerful enough to make the ground all around him pulse with a life he'd forgotten existed.

These ones needed much more special attention. They would still pay for their intrusion, but an unplanned attack against something like that was foolhardy. He did not get to be so long lived by doing rash things.

Humans. Always more trouble than they were worth.

CHAPTER 18

Just Walk Away

To say that Boroha Sharp was upset at the way things had turned out was a gross understatement. He had watched with great interest as the targets had stopped and began singing, each one taking a turn while the others spoke quietly, clearly a ploy to hide their plan. Simple, brilliant, everything he'd expect from the people he was tasked with apprehending. People he never in a million years would have agreed to hunt, no matter what threats the leader of this facade might lay down.

Boroha Sharp was an aged and wizened Embracer of the Power, one who had escaped the wrath of Ryu by being in a communal Haven. At the time he was a man of peace, not driven by the personal gain he was currently entrenched in. A drive to find that balance in the world had led him to the doorstep of the man named Izuku and the weapons he commanded.

Izuku was much older than any other person of Power and he had command of an army Sharp had not seen since the Fourth Fall of Man, an event that completed the feelings of bitterness Sharp now felt towards people and the things they do. He'd seen the Third and Fourth Falls. Both times it was unstoppable, and both times his faith had left him. He had believed in the Power, and when that backfired, he believed in the intelligence of the common man. Surely the Second Fall wouldn't be allowed to happen *again*!

Then it did…

When he had met Izuku and his army, he saw a man with both extremes in his grasp. A very aged and powerful Embracer that commanded an advanced mechanical army.

He was not a fool by this point in his life. He never thought for a moment that Izuku's dream was a sound one, or that his dreams were in line with his own. All he saw was a man with the ability to inflict some serious damage on whatever he surveyed. That was all Sharp wanted. A return to balance. Anarchy with a purpose seemed a foolish but acceptable way to describe it. Many Embracers in his position felt the same.

The time had come to admit the execution of the plan was growing too long-winded, and his 'faith' in Izuku was waning. By the time Izuku asked him to carry out this mission, he'd had his army for five years. What was he waiting for? Only fear of Izuku's weapon kept him from asking. But now he had these ones to fear as well. It was time to turn his fears against one another.

That young man with wings was the worst of all. A powerless mortal youth that possessed the Shi Kaze. He had never seen the blade before today, but once his eyes took it in, the voice to his brain was undeniable. He had every intention of keeping that boy at arm's length. The other three he could anticipate, but one so useless possessing that weapon was frightening.

Sho, once an acquaintance who had been to the communal Haven (which was populated with more than one winged human like this young one), came to him with their proposal. It was a fool's deal.

They clearly had a plan. They were sitting peacefully and waiting for Sharp to arrive after their melodic conference. The execution of this request never said a thing about how he did it. They made a deal and were willing to go back to HOME. Then they were Izuku's problem. Besides, none had command of the Power, just powerful weapons. So did Izuku. And Izuku's was possibly the most frightening of all. Only because of the Shi Kaze and his recent brief encounter with it did Sharp believe these four might stand a chance against Izuku's terrible sword.

He was not loyal to Izuku. He didn't care. All he wanted was to inflict all the pain he could on the land while he was alive and hopefully live to enjoy the peaceful aftermath.

He had to admit a very bitter part of him wanted to see the little ruckus back at HOME they were sure to make. He'd already decided not to tell anyone there that he hadn't disarmed them as part of Sho's request; leave them be and send them to HOME, and Sho promised they wouldn't touch Sharp. Let it be a surprise. Loyalty was overrated anyway.

        ▶◀▶◀▶◀▶◀▶◀▶◀▶◀▶◀▶◀▶◀▶◀▶◀

Sitting in their temporary accommodations, Nixon was the one that was the most flustered and out of sorts. The first part of the plan went smooth as silk. The second, much riskier part had gone the same. It required very little pomp and bravado to convince the leader of this group, one Mr. Sharp, to allow them their weapons in exchange for a peaceful and uneventful return to wherever it was they were to go. After informing Sharp that they were willing to fight to the death to stop him if they didn't get their way, he agreed. Embracers like Sharp rarely want to risk dying. Sho and Crystal had seen the disinterest in his task instantly and used it.

"Will you sit and relax, you fiery old fool," Crystal told him once she could no longer stand his pacing and fidgeting. "We're here, and all we can do now is sit and wait. What do you have to fear, anyway?"

Nixon stopped and stared at her. She never went so far as to say he still had command of his considerable power (any fool knew they were being monitored in every way imaginable), but her allusion to it and the current state of things was still upsetting to him.

"Let me tell ya somethin', yer majesty," he returned in a harsh tone. "This is a very fine line we tread on right now. We are in tha hands of tha enemy, headin' t' who knows where, surrounded on all sides by weapons so powerful tha' they can wipe out whole cities in just a wink of an eye. If our plan is gonna work, so many things 'ave t' fall into place tha' it makes my 'ead hurt."

Crystal looked mildly shocked. "Why Nixon, I know nothing of a plan! Whatever are you talking about?"

The phoenix wheeled on her and glowered. "Bah, each of us knows the whole truth, don't get cute with me. These people are not idiots."

Crystal stopped her prodding and turned her attention to Aryu, a young man she had wrapped around her finger by this point. "What about you? Holding up alright?"

Aryu smiled in return. "Fine. This isn't the trip I was planning, I can tell you that."

"Tha' goes for us both," Nixon chimed in before resuming his relentless pace and fidgets. He had all the time in the world for answers now, but he felt the need to deal with the situation at hand first.

"I agree with Nixon, though. Mr. Sharp wasn't what I was expecting to come across as the leader of this group."

Crystal smiled, putting him at ease. "Did you see the expression on his face when he saw the Shi Kaze? He wasn't expecting that at all. It seems its recent discovery isn't general knowledge yet. That's something."

"Maybe not then, but it is now."

"True, but there isn't an Embracer in the world that doesn't fear and respect that sword. Whoever leads this army, be it Izuku or not, will not cross it without a good reason. Just its presence is enough to put people on edge."

Sharp's mobile base was leading a relatively small force of mechanical soldiers. They were smaller than the Heralds they were accustomed to, but they were no less terrifying. Some held weapons the likes of which Aryu had never seen before (what he wouldn't give for Johan or one of his history books right now), other ones held what looked like remotes or monitors, scanning the area as they came.

Aryu had done well. When Sharp's troop came to a stop at the outer edge of the alpine clearing, half-tracks grinding anything and everything under foot, the four of them just stood like a wall with weapons in hand (except for Crystal, who stood a half-step behind her son and his razor-edged shield).

They watched the lead unit, expecting something any moment. Only Nixon wasn't surprised at what they got. An Embracer was what he'd expected from the beginning.

A door opened, sliding aside silently. From the darkness within stepped forth a man, seemingly as human and normal as any other. Average height and build, shaggy blonde hair and gray eyes that took the four in as he emerged. Thin lips and a narrow face gave nothing away about him or his motives.

Sho, Crystal, and Aryu all took a sharp breath at the non-robotic person before them, dressed not in armor nor even adorned in mechanical gizmos or some other such devices. Just a man in canvas clothes with a long flowing leather coat reaching down to his knees. Crossed like an 'X' on his back were two short swords. His hands held what Aryu recognized as Ark 1 pistols. Each of them knew at once he was no fool, or at least, not fool enough to come out guns blazing.

"Decided to stop, have you? And I was so enjoying your singing." A mish-mash accent, but much like Nixon's when he first met him, he could not place it. The four said nothing.

"Well," he continued, a look of caution and seriousness on his face, "what do you propose we do now?" Four non-responsive looks answered him. "Look, I know what state you're all in. How weak and fragile you now find yourself. Let's not waste time with false bravado, hmm?" He raised one Ark 1 to prove his point. Sho raised his shield slightly, and Nixon and Aryu tensed.

"Ha, any one of you is weak as a kitten now. Weapons of Focus or not, we really don't need to try very hard to end this, now do we?" He indicated the circling army around him, and they all raised their weapons to face them. Aryu felt the beginnings of nausea tickle the back of his throat.

"What do you want from us, Sharp?" Sho said. The edge he possessed when first he'd met Aryu returned. Sho had an amazing battle high, and it was beginning to surface again.

"Sho, it has been a long time, hasn't it?" He smiled and mock-bowed to the big man with the shield, but went into no further details of their relationship. "As you know, those two are wanted and I've been sent to ensure their apprehension. Mechanical devices can't seem to get the job done. As for you and your mother? Well, that has yet to be decided."

"We all go, Sharp," Sho replied. "Willingly and together, weapons in hand."

Sharp faltered. "Sho, I'm not a fool. In what world would I agree to that?"

"The world where you have nothing to lose if you do. You know me. We are people of honor. We have no issue with you, save for the company you keep. We'll go willingly and peacefully with no resistance or trouble. When I last saw you, you were seeking the balance. You know we are the ones who can deliver it."

Sharp didn't have to wait long to measure his sincerity. In the circles of Embracers, Sho was legendary, as were Nixon Ash and Crystal. He knew they had a plan, but he also believed it had nothing to do with him. How much trouble would he get in letting them walk into HOME fully armed to see Izuku? Plenty was his guess, but that was an issue for another day. After the meandering plans of Izuku, Sho's directness to giving Sharp exactly what he wanted was a nice change.

"I have a hard time believing you'll be this pleasant for your journey. You are clearly at a disadvantage here. Why can't I just command my forces to incapacitate you, take your precious weapons, and have it both ways?"

"Because you have to know that despite our current predicament, we are still three very skilled and very difficult opponents. All it would take is one of us to reach you. Then where would you be?"

Sharp looked them all over, reading each face and the weapons the three men held.

It was only when his eyes fell on the young one on the end, the one he was specifically tasked to acquire, that he saw the Shi Kaze for the first time. Time stopped.

Mr. Sharp just had his first lesson in the true power of the Shi Kaze, and the experience rattled him. One good slice and Boroha Sharp was a dead man.

Anarchy, but with a purpose. Lines drawn in the sand. Sharp agreed.

Now rolling across the landscape, Aryu hoped for a distraction, and a conversation about Mr. Sharp was as good a place as any to start.

"So, how do you know Sharp?" he asked Sho, who unsurprisingly was lost in some meandering thought and paying attention to nothing.

Sho sighed. "I met him a few times hundreds of years ago when Havens here were popular and I'd just taken up the charge of tending to this land. He traveled from place to place, seeking insight and information about everything and nothing. We once sat for hours with me telling him stories of my father and the things he'd done.

"I can tell you this: he's a man I'd have called little more than a passing footnote on the world, directionless and I dare say boring in the grand scheme of things. That was the problem with the Power; it didn't discriminate whom it infected with immortality. It took any who had the patience and the ability to learn its ways. So many came and went giving little or nothing to the world in return. Wastes of time and Power. They were one of the main reasons my father did what he did to prevent the abuse of the Power and try to keep it in the grasp of the truly special."

Nixon and Crystal both managed a snide smile at the statement. Sho's reverence of his father clearly was clouding his mind to the fact that Ryu was viewed by them as an unstable self-centered dictator who had committed a heinous genocide.

"My best guess is that the years have seen him wronged somehow and this is his answer to it. Justification is so simple to come by given enough time. He's survived the last two Falls of Man, so he has good reason to be bitter. Most like him are."

Aryu was the one to give a snide look this time. "Not too dedicated to the cause, is he?" He indicated the Shi Kaze to put his point across.

"No," Sho answered. "His lot in life, I suppose. Even working for the other side, his commitment level is certainly lacking which as you can see I used to our advantage. That's the issue with these kinds of Power users. Too scared to live, too afraid to die." It was an aspect that Aryu had never thought of. Could you really become so blasé given enough time to let it happen? Perhaps Ryu wasn't *completely* crazy after all.

They sat in silence as their vehicle stopped. Moments later the door of their mobile brig opened and Mr. Sharp, flanked by two large, silver autonomous figures, indicated they step out. They obliged.

"From here you board that plane which will take you the rest of the way," he told them all, indicating a large, winged tube in the distance. The image of it and its questionable ability to fly gave Aryu the shivers. "On board are more security drones than you could ever hope to handle in your current state. It will take you back to HOME and whatever fate awaits you there."

It was all bravado and they all knew it. Sharp had let them keep their weapons and armor, so he may as well have offered them a hot bath and a warm meal for all the graciousness he'd given them.

As they were taken to the waiting aircraft, Sho took the moment to express his contempt for the state of his land in a direct confrontation with Sharp. "Whatever your reasoning for doing this, Boroha, it's wrong."

Sharp never even faced him. "There is no right and wrong, Sho. Remember that?" He did. It was the overlying message he'd tried to express to Sharp during that brief encounter centuries ago. It seemed Sho couldn't win a battle anymore if he tried.

With a shove from a burly android, the quartet was on its way to the next phase of their journey.

On board for almost an hour before it lifted off, Aryu could barely suppress the urge to throw up as the gangly beast lifted vertically into the sky. Sho and Nixon had been taken elsewhere, but without even a slot in the door to look out, they didn't know where yet. A flaw in their carefully concocted plan, but not an impossible one to overcome. They knew what to do. For now, it was just a matter of waiting.

Crystal sat across from him. "Uneasy flyer?" she asked.

"Only when it's not me in control," he answered, grateful for her sudden need to strike up a conversation.

"Don't worry. I once flew all the time in something like these. They're harmless." Harmless? Judging by what he'd seen every machine he'd encountered thus far in his life do, he seriously doubted that.

"Tell me," she began, "what do you think of the Shi Kaze?" He looked at her questioningly. "I know you're not a user of the Power, but how great it is couldn't have escaped you."

He looked at it in his hands. "I feel...something, deep inside myself. A flow of positive and negative. It's disorientating, like a feeling that's welcome and repulsive at the same time."

She understood the feeling perfectly. "That is its specialty. It was how Ryu intended it to be, balanced in both the fantastic and horrifying, now magnified thanks to its sordid history. When you awaken to it more, you'll see what I mean."

"Yeah, about that, I don't have any intention of awaking to anything, thank you. Nixon made it clear that at the first whiff of something amiss with me while I hold it, he'll cut me in two and go back to sleep."

"You can't tell me you haven't thought about it though, how the Power can help you with what you want to do, kicking their robot butts?"

"Oh I've thought about it," he said honestly. The ghostly beauty across from him could likely read any lie, so he wasn't about to try. "But living and making it back to help my friend beats out dying at the hands of Nixon. I can't do much to help if I'm dead. And for that matter, since he never got the opportunity to ask, do you know why it is he seems drawn to hunt me for no reason?"

Crystal shook her head. "I'm sorry I don't. I was very surprised to hear he had awoken and was with you when first you came to me. I had hoped you two could answer that for me, but the looks on your faces told me you were just as clueless."

She got up and sat next to him, her warm, white hand meeting his. "What do you know about my father?" she asked, pink eyes looking at him, finding places inside him he didn't know existed.

He was flustered by the action, but eventually managed to spit out, "I know it was his accepted responsibility to teach the art of the Power to all who would master it. Bring it to the world to see after it had been hidden for so long."

She nodded in agreement. "Well that's the pretty way to say it. Do you agree with him? That what he was trying to do was right?"

"Not according to Ryu."

"To hell with Ryu!" she said forcibly, her hand almost crushing his with the action. There was still a staggering amount of strength in her even now. "Ryu acted like he always acted, foolishly and without thought to any consequence that didn't involve only himself. I loved him, that's true, and even I can't agree with what he did. Sho says it was to stop the misuse of Power? Ha! Bullshit. It was to help himself and no one else. He needed to do something no one in the world could ignore to get his way. All he did was go a step further than anyone thought he was capable of. There was no underlying nobility to it. It was pure, unadulterated egotism. Something that you don't have."

He believed that. Egotism wasn't high on his personal traits to the best of his knowledge.

"Trust me, Aryu, you are not him or any other that followed the path that brought Nixon to their door. You are a mortal man in command of a powerful thing. You create the path it takes, not the other way around. I don't know you well, but I do know you well enough to see I'm right."

It was a convincing argument, but with all the fear he harbored about the Power, he doubted it could ever become a reality. "Why tell me this?" he asked. "Why try? You know I can't."

She smiled her impish smile. "Because no one expects it of you. They never tried to take your power away like they did mine or Sho's because they thought you had none. Nixon is a fantastic asset, but *two* of you! You can't tell me they'd see that coming. What a tool to use against them!"

Another true statement. "So what do you propose?" He was curious but knew enough to keep her ideas at arm's length. It was, after all, the reason he wanted to stay with Nixon *and* meet her. He also believed her and what she said about his character. He honestly and truly believed he was incapable of the kind of evils that would summon the phoenix to him, revenge against those that had wronged him notwithstanding.

"I propose that you listen to me and take whatever actions you deem necessary."

Years of learning about the world and deep meditation had made her brain advanced beyond what any mortal could obtain in their meager years. She had the perfect ways to describe the process of what she was proposing to Aryu, in ways his young mind could absorb easily and quickly.

She started and Aryu listened, loving every minute of it.

▸◂▸◂▸◂▸◂▸◂▸◂▸◂▸◂▸◂▸◂▸◂▸◂

When the time came to let HOME know the goings-on, Sharp went

300

to his drab and lifeless post and contacted Izuku.

"They're on their way. They should be arriving in a few hours."

Izuku acknowledged but was clearly upset at the news. "You chose not to escort them? That seems somewhat foolhardy, Mr. Sharp."

Sharp expected this answer but didn't care. "They agreed to go. They wanted to. They gave me their word of honor that they would cause no fuss and go peacefully. My duty was fulfilled and carried out perfectly."

"Don't bog me down with semantics, Boroha. Do you really believe they would be so passive? What kind of a fool are you?"

"A fool who thinks their honor is to be trusted. You said yourself that's the kind of people they are."

"True, but I'd still like a pair of human eyes on them for the trip. This is reckless even for you."

Sharp was not phased. Even if Izuku lost it entirely, he couldn't do anything with that demon blade from so far away. Sharp's lack of loyalty to Izuku was growing exponentially lately. He resisted using the High-Yields too much. They had hundreds in storage at HOME. Hit fast, strike hard.

"Did you at least secure Nixon's and Sho's weapons? Those were two things I'd very much like to see."

Oh, you'll see them, thought Sharp, but before he answered, he clued in to the specifics of the question. "Just those two? Not the other?"

Izuku, his smile seemingly glued to his face even at the worst of times, became dead serious. Sharp was instantly taken aback. If it was possible, it made Izuku so much more frightening. "What other weapon? The boy has no Power, and Crystal never had a weapon she cared to use and is long lost."

It was then that Sharp realized that Izuku didn't know what the boy was carrying. Could he have been so blind? All Embracers knew to fear two things: the wrath of the phoenix and the blade of the Four Winds. The fool had the strongest weapon of the ages arriving at his doorstep and he didn't even know it. Sharp thought that was why he wanted the boy in the first place.

The pause in Sharp seemed to enrage the man on the other end. "What other weapon, Sharp?"

Sharp recovered from his shock (and amusement) at the situation he'd unknowingly created and turned back to the screen and the madman contained within it.

"The boy, he had a sword. A weapon of focus. Not strong like the other two, but still a Power weapon." The lie was just a cop out. If they caused the ruckus he expected them to, he'd never be called on it anyway. Anything to escape this lunatic and his shortsightedness.

The news seemed to calm him, however. "Not as powerful, you say?" Sharp nodded. "Well, I'll add it to the collection. Do you have them, Mr. Sharp?"

The moment of truth. Saying 'no' was guaranteeing Izuku's wrath, should he survive whatever the four have planned. Saying 'yes' did the same, but gave him a chance to get some ground between himself and revenge.

"Yes, I secured them," he answered, his mind already planning three moves ahead of where he was. "They're stored within the plane they're on, but nowhere they can access."

Izuku smiled yet again. "Good. I look forward to getting my hands on the big phoenix blade, and I think I'll hang the shield on my wall. I don't need to tell you of its history?"

He didn't. Someone like Sharp knew what it did (though how was still a mystery for the ages. It didn't seem like anything special to him.).

"Well, carry on I suppose. Though, next time, try not to be so liberal with how you interpret my orders, please."

"It won't happen again." *Damn right it won't. Enjoy your surprise, you old fool.*

The communication ended, and Sharp returned outside to the far nicer and more natural sunlight. *Now,* he thought, looking at a hand-held display showing the surrounding landmass, *I suppose it's time to run?*

He wished he could wait for an emergency call or some other indicator that said HOME was experiencing technical difficulties, but he had to get away from here quickly and return to the Havens he knew. The thought invigorated him; any hints of reticence and malaise were slowly washed away. He exited his command post and began to slip away. Today was going to be a good day.

He had only made it a few steps when his half-track unit exploded with a deafening roar, the force to the blast hitting Sharp and any mechanical soldiers in the area and tossing them like toys in a perfect circle while a fireball rose into the air and singed everything in range with a wave of stifling heat.

Sharp was on his feet at once. He was a skilled Embracer and such a thing never had a chance at killing him. His treasured swords were unsheathed in an instant as he came to his feet and examined his surroundings. Other than the fiery hole where he had just been standing and the multitudes of mechanical soldiers who were in the process of picking themselves up (or in some cases, putting themselves back together as best they could), nothing could be seen to be any different. The rest of the visible army forces were still going about their tasks, oblivious to the goings-on.

Sharp's first thought was an attack, but no one followed up the assault. Next he thought it was a malfunction, but no heavy weapons were carried in his post. Nothing on board would have ignited like that.

Lost in the confusion, he approached the wreckage and tried to ascertain what had happened. It was as he stood there staring that his entourage approached him quietly from behind.

Boroha Sharp had been alive for centuries. He had worked hard to master the Power as early in life as he could. The eternal message of Allen Kokuou was loud and clear at the time of his birth. Embrace the Power and heal the world. One of his bodyguards couldn't move a hair's width without him knowing, and by the time he was almost in reach, he whirled about and with a skill that took ages to master, succeeded in cleaving each one down in a blur of motions an untrained eye would never have discerned. Each sentry was in multiple pieces in almost the time it took for them to process the information that their target was moving and they should attempt a counterattack.

Then, systematically, each surrounding artificial intelligence in the area turned their attention to Sharp with one clear command.

Boroha Sharp had been used. He should have known better.

Each soldier charged him. Those with firearms had them up and began blazing away with any number of particle rifles, hand weapons, and whatever else they had at their disposal. Wave after wave rushed forward, attempting to shoot, grab, and generally harm the target of their new orders.

But this was no scared boy or harmless townsperson. This was an Embracer of the Power, and in a sudden blind flurry, that Power was unleashed with frightening effectiveness.

Short swords at the ready before the first malicious trigger was pulled, the natural awesomeness of the Power was summoned like a protective shield around Sharp, dispersing and deflecting anything that would harm him. He ran back to a tree line in the distance, the Power coursing through him and the blades he carried, aiding him forward at inhuman speed, slicing down any that got in his way with quick and astonishing effectiveness.

The trees gave him a relatively solid level of protection to his back while he dealt with the legions that came at him head-on. The years of practice gave him great focus very quickly. He likely could have summoned the Power even without his trusted weapons, but in a situation like this, he much preferred to have them in hand.

He cut across the empty space between him and the coming horde in a half-circle. Waves of energy resembling millions of blue electrical sparks bonded together by some unseen force emanated from the tips of the weapons. In an instant the Power spread out, cutting down each robot just as easily as his weapons did alone, and before many had time to process the event, they were destroyed. A battlefield of twisted silver bodies fell while the sounds of servos grinding and limbs clashing together filled the air.

Sharp had no time to admire his work. The piles of debris only slowed down the next wave, and this one was more than useless foot soldiers. Now the heavy arms and advanced thinking machines called Heralds were approaching, and although individually they were no match for him, massed in the hundreds they were a threat. The only reassuring fact was that they couldn't kill him. They could do some serious damage, even crippling, but he would live. He had already injected the cure for the Herald's neural inhibitor drug, so there was no worry there, but if they did manage to incapacitate him, they would likely take him right to Izuku.

He crashed into the trees behind him, running and dodging as best he could in the dense brush. The forces behind him had no such obstructions as they used the heavy weapon tanks and half-tracks to simply mow through. The nimble and intelligent Heralds were ahead of the pack and could move as quickly as Sharp. After only a few moments, the first few began outpacing him, reaching out with Ark 1s and firing randomly in his direction.

He realized they weren't aiming for him, but ahead and around him, causing small, popping explosions that crashed trees and threw up dirt. They didn't want to hit him. They just wanted to slow him down.

He opted for the offensive, coming to a stop in an area with older growth trees that were tall and widely spaced. One by one he attacked the things, each issuing the standard, inhuman scream as he did so.

He fired waves of the powerful sparks at the enemy, slicing them down with ease as the big guns approached in the distance. All around him, silver streaks told him the enemy was massing, attempting to flank him and close the vice. The time for the next level was at hand.

He drove one of the short swords into the ground and unleashed what he could of his considerable talent into the effort. Blue energy coursed out in forceful waves like ripples in a pond. Just as a lightning rod sent energy into the ground, the Power flowed outward from the point of the sword's impact in a circular spreading spider web, obliterating every target like they had stepped on hot lava that melted and eroded each one. All around him the screams sounded and were silenced as the Power pulsed outward. Even units hiding in the trees couldn't escape as the blue energy ran through the large trunks and dropped the ambushers to the ground.

With only a minimum of effort on his part, the attack ceased. Soon he could no longer hear any more approaching, and he turned his attention to what he should do next.

For an Embracer like himself, it was just that simple.

Was it Izuku who had done this? That seemed the most likely, but as he had just hatched his plan to turn Izuku's laziness against him, he didn't know what had triggered this assault. The likeliest answer was that Izuku had planned it all along and had waited for the mission to be complete.

If all Izuku could do now was throw lifeless bots at him, he might make it out of this in one piece, though he doubted Izuku was so short sighted.

An insight that was, naturally, completely correct.

Before he could leave, the dappled silhouette came into the woods, following the path where the destroyed vehicles were littered. How anything had escaped Sharp's Power was a mystery.

When it stepped into the old growth clearing, the answer became perfectly clear. Sharp could now see that he had been slated to die all along.

Before him stood another robotic creation, but not like the others. Instead of silver, this one was black, with a mother-of-pearl shimmer coming from wherever the sun touched it through the trees. It stood like the others, with tall legs and a body similar to a normal human, complete with the arms, neck, and head. The head was more lifelike than the Heralds, which had no real face to speak of other than eye slits. This one had a fully operational mouth, with spinning blue eyes like its inferior, lower-grade relatives.

In its hand was what something Boroha Sharp instantly feared. A broadsword with ornate images etched into the blade from tip to hilt, the handle wrapped in soft leather.

If the weapon had a name, he did not know it. He assumed it did. Ones like this always did. He didn't know its previous owners or who had made it, but once his eyes took it in completely, he *saw* it, and what he saw was very unsettling.

Sharp was old. Very old. But, there were older and more powerful Embracers out there throughout history. One of these unseen faces of history had created this weapon, and that person was older and more powerful than Boroha Sharp was this day. How it had got the weapon was not his concern. What concerned him was that it wasn't just the sword that spoke to him. It seemed to be the whole damn machine. Izuku had done it. The rumors were true.

This was Eleotherios Duo #0901, and before it came at him with its weapon of Power at the ready, Sharp had two thoughts. First: just how powerful was Izuku that he could complete this monster? And second: how glad he was that he sent those four off with weapons in hand and a plan in their heads. Should this confrontation go as he anticipated it would, that small act of indifferent defiance would likely be his last gift to the world.

When their swords clashed and the machine was able to overpower him after only the briefest of skirmishes, he knew his assumption on the outcome would be correct.

CHAPTER 19

The Dragon Awakens

Crystal knew that she didn't need to do much to break down Aryu's preconceived notions of the Power, reminding him that technology getting out of hand had destroyed the world twice, the Power only once ("That's fifty percent less!" she giggled demurely), and of all the Power Embracers in history. One crazy man wasn't quite enough to label the whole collection of people with these abilities.

The only things really holding back Aryu's mind on the subject were his fear of the beast named Nixon Ash and the simple fact that, despite some dealings with it on a very abstract level, Aryu still was terrified of the Power. A deep part of him believed that mankind simply wasn't made to hold that kind of ability.

"Is the Power Divine?" Aryu asked.

Crystal shook her head. "No, not really. Science and divinity are so close to one another it's frightening. The Power is deeper than that. Faith has always sprung *from* the Power, not the other way around. Look at Sho and I. Science enfeebled us, not faith."

"And Nixon?"

"Nixon is an extreme who proves the rule. A person born entirely of the Power. Science can't take away his Power because he *is* the Power. There's nothing human about him to take the Power from in the first place. He is a creation of 'God', but he's just the most perfect example of the pinnacle of science."

Aryu flustered. "So he's *not* a creation of God?"

Crystal grinned devilishly. "Well, that's a question of your faith."

Aryu wasn't amused. "I have no faith."

Crystal was ready for the answer. "Then you have no God, old or new, and Nixon is the result of an unbelievably powerful Embracer creating an actual living creature eons ago. He is one of the ultimate culminations of all of Earth's sciences."

"And what if I said I believed in the true God?" Aryu asked, smirking back at her.

Crystal shrugged. "Well, then I'd tell you that he's an Angel and you'd believe me."

Aryu wasn't sure if it was fact or Crystal's bitterness at Ryu veiled behind an impishly cute exterior that had come up with that answer. One tends to lose faith when directly betrayed by a god, be they old or new. A thought occurred to Aryu.

"Is he the only one of his kind? Are there others like him?"

Crystal faltered slightly, but just enough for Aryu to catch it. After a pause, she finally responded. "There are others, but you'll never have to worry about them." Aryu tried to press her for more, but she expertly brought the topic back to him.

Crystal worked with him until the appointed time, but even she could see he needed what all skeptics needed: proof. Since both she and her son were lacking the talents at this moment, it would be difficult to break that all-important mental barrier without some kind of tangible visual display of just what, if given the time and resources, a human is capable of. Her father had faced this dilemma many times;

trying to always find a way to convince someone it was possible, and in many cases necessary, without showing them.

The barrier in him remained. Until proof was shown (or he pushed himself over that last hurdle just as she had as a child), Aryu was taken as far as she could get him.

"Remember, Aryu," she said, "it *is* there, inside of you. Inside everyone and everything. You will see it, and you will be amazed."

Once the big metal bird began to noticeably slow and descend, the lessons were all but forgotten as they began to execute the plan the four had devised.

Sho and Nixon wasted no time. The moment they felt the telltale change in altitude and velocity, they were on their feet with sword and shield in hand.

The door that held them was a sad collection of hard metal and electronic locks that to them were more like tinfoil. Nixon slipped his sword into the crack along the edge of the door above the handle and just let it fall, severing the weak attempts to seal them in as he did so.

The alarms sounded before he was even halfway. Either by his actions or that of Aryu and Crystal he didn't know or care. The plan was in effect, and they all had to see it through to the end.

One mighty kick was all that was needed to cause the door to swing open with a bang and the two inside to emerge, ready for an attack, screaming madly as their battle-ready eyes scanned for the enemy. There was nothing but a wide empty hallway lined with doors, without a guard to be found anywhere. Only the bleat of the alarm that seemed to summon no one. The confidence of their enemy was staggering.

Nixon was instantly suspicious. No one was so stupid as to assume they didn't have a plan. This was just a trap.

Across from them, one of the many doors that lined the area

swung open and Aryu stepped out, Shi Kaze in the lead. Crystal, despite her current condition and lack of armament, pushed Aryu aside at once and led the way out the door.

"Not much for greetings, are they?" Crystal said, looking around. Aryu appeared ready for an ambush from all sides, but Crystal only looked bored and listless, as if this was all just a large waste of her valuable time.

"So it'd seem," replied Nixon over the alarm, a part of him upset at the lack of any physical confrontation. The brief skirmish with Sho had been all he'd seen since he had awoken, and that was nowhere near enough to satisfy the battle hunger one such as him possessed.

"What do you think it means?" Aryu asked, still jittery. The surroundings of cold metal and blinking buttons and switches were still putting him in an uncomfortable place, even after all he'd seen. He was not one who would so easily forget the deep-rooted fears he harbored about machines and technology, but at least he didn't vomit or pass out. That was a hassle Nixon didn't want to deal with.

In the end, he just shrugged. "Yer guess is as good as any, Aryu. I doubt we're so low a priority after all tha' destruction they caused jus' t' get us, but I expected at least one guard. No point in wonderin' the 'why'. Let's just be done with this."

Nixon and his still-intact Divine powers in the lead, Sho and his unbreakable shield bringing up the rear, they followed the hallway until it branched at a 'T' intersection. "Which way ya figure, Crystal?"

As the most important part of this plan, she pointed them left, searching for wherever the central command was located (assuming it had one. These things were self-sufficient enough to control a plane like this without one.).

Once they turned again and entered a large cargo bay in the heart of the plane, luck took one of its frequent turns for the worse. Multitudes of robotic autonomous eyes turned to where they entered. They had entered a cargo bay full of dozens of troops.

"Protect Crystal!" Nixon yelled as he brought up the shimmering sword he carried and began cleaving his way through the masses like a man possessed.

"Aryu, follow his lead!" Sho shouted to him as he came around his diminutive mother and brought his shield into a defensive position. Aryu was about to argue, but one look from the intense eyes of the forest-keeper and he knew enough not to. Fear gave way to adrenalin as he followed in step behind Nixon, the mighty Shi Kaze clenched tightly in his fist. There wasn't a Herald in sight, but these common robotic foot soldiers would have to serve the purpose.

"For Tan Torna Qu-ay!" he screamed as he began slashing with what little educated movements he could muster, a modicum of his revenge finally at hand.

He never doubted the power of the blade in his hands. The light-as-air ninjato sword began slashing through each enemy in range effortlessly. The machines relied strictly on their numbers, as any errant pistol blast could cause a serious problem. The numbers game and superior strength (at least over Aryu) were their weapons of choice, but as Aryu rushed through the crowd in Nixon's sizeable wake, he had the strong belief his side still held the advantage.

How much he had retained from the heavy training at Nixon's hands astonished him as the lessons transferred themselves into his movements seamlessly. Thrusts, feints, and counterattacks ran through him like a seasoned pro, each motion bringing down more and more of the enemy. The sound of metal grinding together and piling on to the ground was everywhere. Although the group had anticipated this encounter to some degree, the variables in their plan relied on working quickly.

To his right, amidst the crowd of rushing, flailing silver bodies, another group of soldiers broke off and began moving towards Sho and Crystal. Aryu cried out to Nixon as best he could to tell him, wondering if they should help or continue as planned. After a moment, Nixon brought his massive sword about, taking at least six with him. "Bah, it's only twelve or so, he can handle twice tha' even without the Power!"

Aryu wasn't so sure. All it took was one to breach Sho and make it to his mother. They only had the shield for defense, and although impressive with its border of jagged teeth, Aryu doubted it could be used against such a numerous and aggressive enemy.

As he beat down all that came at him, body still tense and loving every dispatching, Aryu watched as the wonder of Sho's miraculous weapon came to light. Before they reached the two, Sho readied his weapon in front of him and began a steady and repetitive clenching of the fist that carried it.

Through some unseen workings, Aryu watched the shield remain stationary, but the blades that bordered it began to rotate like clockwork, gaining in speed until they were a whirling saw blade when the first robotic set of hands were at them. Careful to keep the spinning weapon of both offence and defense at a distance, Sho began sweeping his arm back and forth, leveling out the shield and easily shredding the robots to pieces. In only a matter of a few strokes, all who broke off and attacked them were nothing more than broken metal on the ground, the shield back to its ready position, waiting for another group to be foolish.

Aryu could now believe this exceptionally clever weapon and the man that carried it, with Power, luck, and training in equal number, really could have killed a god. That did not, however, prevent one of the machines from reaching an unlabeled switch and pulling it before shutting down.

"Aryu!" screamed the accented voice behind him. "Get t' tha side *now!*" Aryu didn't argue or ask why. Nixon's word was law and he followed it unquestioningly. Aryu began to make his way to the closest wall, opposite where Nixon was heading. It was a welcomed position to be in, as he now had nothing to worry about behind him and the number of piling up enemies in front were slowing down those that still functioned, allowing more time between attacks and ceasing the need to slash about blindly.

Aryu could feel the heavy vibration in the wall, a steady reminder of exactly where he was at that moment. A hint of his dormant fear came to the surface, but he could now fight against it just as well as the tangible enemies before him. If he succumbed to either he was a dead man, and only being a man for such a short while, he wasn't quite ready to relinquish the title just yet.

Somewhere, out of the confusion, he heard Nixon's voice shout what sounded like "Everyone hang on!" Aryu, in his brief free moments, looked around at the wall for something to grip but found only smooth surfaces everywhere he looked.

A sudden jarring at his feet caused Aryu to lose his balance, staggering him to the side, allowing a set of metal hands to reach out and grab him by the left wing, a painless but no less incapacitating action. The arm twisted the appendage around, using Aryu's own wing as a guard while it continued to attack. Aryu tried to shake free as the ground below him rumbled on. All the adrenalin in the world could not have drowned out his fear.

The floor was shifting away, sloping downward toward the rear of the plane where Sho and Crystal still stood, though away from the descending floor. Crystal was on the pulled switch in an instant, trying to do who-knew-what with the device. Aryu saw daylight to his right as the bottom of the plane fell away, revealing a dizzying height below them that bottomed out in an endless field of blue. The ocean was dark and unwelcoming to Aryu, and it sat ready to swallow him up unless he could find a way to get this beast off his wing and get to safety.

The whole plane jostled as the destroyed attackers began to slide out the back of the plane and fall off into the endless nothing below. The wind rushed into the cargo bay and drowned out all sound. Still, the arm of his enemy held tight, though he could feel it slipping, turning him about and threatening to take him with it.

Aryu, in an action terribly similar to his friend and brother Johan, concluded the next course of action. He turned and drove the blade of the Shi Kaze into the sheer metallic wall behind him, sure to push it in sideways so as not to risk the super-sharp blade from simply slicing down to the bottom of the plane.

The idea worked and the blade held, but so did the grip on his wing. Now facing the wall, Aryu felt the massive weight of the creature of the Old pull him down as it slid until his arms locked and held them there, threatening to give under the pressure. He knew if the floor gave out much more, nothing would help him from eventually giving in to the weight and falling out into oblivion. He doubted his ability to shake the thing in time to free his wing and glide out to safety.

Nixon was now across a wide expanse where the floor had been and was still fending off his own attackers while scores more of the ones he'd defeated pelted him as they fell. Sho stood back from the hole before him, the wind catching his shield like a sail, and he fought to maintain his balance and bring himself and his mother back into the hall from which they had entered.

Crystal, while working frantically on the panel, saw Aryu and his plight.

All she did was stare at him, her beautiful pink/red eyes meeting his. Her look resolute and strong, all hints of playful passiveness gone. Determination was etched on every inch of her soft face. Aryu saw it, arms weakening, and for a moment he was lost in loathing at her inaction.

But then he understood the serious message she was attempting to convey across the gap between them. Aryu, both hands gripped around the handle of the sword he carried, tried to see beyond the crippling terror he was feeling as the floor was now nearly gone from his reach entirely and his feet began to slip away. He used whatever clarity he could muster to stare into the handle before him, with its aged wrappings and odd small latches jutting out from the bottom.

In his hands, even while it lay jabbed into the wall and useless for any kind of attack, was the weapon of his salvation, and all he needed was the clarity and truth in his mind to make it so. If he didn't find it, he had no doubt that he'd be lost, plummeting into the water.

Despite the blinding fear, he found in the handle what he sought. The mystic feeling he always received from it was more prevalent than ever before, and at last he allowed the doubt of his abilities to leave him, and the void that was left by its passing filled with nothing but the Power, and the wrath it brought with it. He *had* to believe. If he didn't, he was going to die.

That realization steeled him. He would not die like this.

His body vibrated like an electric shock, warmth and clarity coursing through every vein in his body like lifeblood. Soon, in the back of his mind's eye, he felt every body part, cell, and iota of all that he was align and follow his mental will. There was no doubt at all now. He knew the truth. History had documented it so well, but he knew now that fear was not needed in the wake of the Power. Only respect. Respect and strength, two things Aryu O'Lung'Singh had in abundance.

He could see in his mind the thing that clung to him, yanking to pull him free. He could see the molecules that gave it existence. He could taste the air between them, swirling like water, until he channeled the power of the sword outward like a conductor and used its considerable influence to take command of things man has no right to take command over.

The winds that rushed around the two errant bodies hanging in space constricted into a single, fine line of controlled fury, and with only the smallest amount of effort on his behalf, Aryu could feel his mind reach with the formed air like a hand and pry the clasping metallic fingers from himself as if they were made of paper.

The thing that would have seen Aryu dead a moment before was lost to the gap below them and into the unseen depths.

As the clarity and truth of his actions came to the young man hanging in space, so too did the floor, and soon it met his waiting feet and began to carry him back to safety. Crystal had closed the giant door and set things right again just in time.

Once the large cargo room was restored and the party back together, Aryu looked around for any indication the others might have had of what just happened. Nixon particularly held his attention, but he saw nothing telling in the face of the phoenix.

Crystal met his eyes and smiled as they left. He could tell in that glorious look that although she couldn't say for certain, she had a very good idea of what had just happened. The mental lock had been broken with relative (if not terrifying) ease. Still, he questioned how far he could push it before Nixon became aware of what he had just tapped. It felt like so much was at his fingertips, but in truth he knew it was just a small and simple action. He was still a long way from conjuring fire or summoning great forests…

…or destroying half of the world with a snap of his fingers.

In his brief seconds of tapping the glory of the Power he could see how, if one was strong enough and smart enough, one could reach out into the world around them and change anything they liked.

The troop made their way to the main command hatch, a large

oblong door that was sealed from the inside. The alarm still sounded, but either out of lack of available soldiers or confidence in the marauder's inabilities to inflict any serious damage, no other resistance was encountered along the tight, cold hallways.

With a swing of the Shi Kaze, Aryu broke through the heavy metal door and effortlessly sliced it away, the new connection with the weapon strengthening his confidence. If the Power was what made a king, then here in its infantile stages was the newest Ryuujin. That fact alone made Aryu flush with pride.

Nixon forcefully kicked the door. Inside they found a room with only a small front window, surrounded by controls and screens. Although there were no chairs, there were two control yokes standing up on the floor in front of the circular window that faced forward. This vehicle was made for autonomous flight, with an option for a person to take command if they so choose. It was time to begin.

Crystal stepped forward, looking like a ghost amidst the dark room and solid steel casings. She walked to the control yoke and looked out the window before her, eyes squinting in the harsh natural light beyond. "We're still quite high," she said, "but I can see the destination below. It kinda' stands out like a sore thumb. Here, come see."

Sho looked sick as he glanced out and then back again. "I've never liked heights," he explained to an amused Aryu.

When Aryu took his turn to look out, it wasn't the height that bothered him as much as it was the scope of the image. The sky was clear and he could see the horizon spread out before them, a reminder of the size and vastness of the world. The ocean they were over was littered with little black specks he could only assume were ships, the same ships that had first arrived weeks back and had led the terrorizing assault on his homeland.

Ahead of them was the largest of these; a massive flat 'V' shape with various smaller crafts emerging from the front of it. The whole unit was a hub of activity.

He only needed to see its great dimensions once to know that Crystal was right. This was the army's central command, the location the Herald and Sharp had called HOME.

He stepped back, a look of seriousness on his face not there a moment before. This was it. This was where revenge began in earnest. Crystal grasped his hand and looked at him, slowly guiding him back to where the big men were standing. "Let's get started," she said, giving his hand a light squeeze before letting him go. He nodded in agreement, sorry again to lose her touch.

"Remember to act quickly, Aryu," Nixon advised him. "Your mission is just as important as my own." Aryu agreed and braced himself, the Shi Kaze out and ready to act. There wouldn't be much time from the start to the finish.

Crystal turned back to the controls and began turning switches and hitting buttons in a manner Aryu dazzled at, and soon colors changed and screens began showing garbled information Aryu could make neither heads nor tails of.

Human technology had peaked long ago, and this craft was no more complicated than others Crystal had seen hundreds or thousands of years prior. Any fear that she wouldn't remember how to do this vanished once the yoke was back in her hands. With a slight nudge forward, the plane lurched and began a quick and frightening drop. Not uncontrolled, but certainly with more velocity than they'd started with.

A moment later, the alarm stopped and a voice surrounded them. A voice they all knew very well. "Is that you, I assume, Sho?" The pleasantness was there, cutting through the room like an illness. Aryu knew this was no Herald. This was the man himself.

"It is, Izuku. And friends."

"Ah yes. The friends. The weak, helpless friends. I see you've taken command of my plane. Where do you expect to go that I cannot track you? Even now I have dozens of forces ready to pursue you and take you in again. Perhaps even finish you, should you cause me too much grief. What do you think you can accomplish?"

"Nothin' you can stop, Izuku," Nixon said. "Ya were a fool fer lettin' us get this close, and now you'll suffer fer it."

"Nixon! How nice to have you here. Welcome to my HOME. I'm glad we'll meet at last. I assume you've brought your young charge?"

"I've no time fer pleasantries, Izuku. I know I can't expect tha same idiocy from you tha' was given t' us by yer general, so I'd never dream of asking ya t' let us land and talk 'bout this, but I will tell ya tha' ya will either return our abilities or we will cause ya t' suffer."

Silence. The plane began to shake as it passed through a small cloud burst and back out below. It wasn't much longer now. Was he stalling on purpose?

"No," was the response. Nothing more.

"Very well. Try and stop us then."

"Stop what? Four desperate heroes on a plane? Heaven help me! What cruel fate to be so weak against such odds. You, sir, my good Nixon, can go rocketing straight to Hell." And with that, a click indicated that he'd ended the transmission.

Nixon shrugged. "Have it yer way." He nodded to both Sho and Aryu, who took a spot next to the closest wall and braced their weapons at the ready. Nixon told Crystal to begin.

Crystal pushed the yoke forward one last time and sent the plane into a dive at a terribly steep angle, followed by Nixon sliding forward past her and swinging his broadsword down across the closest control panel. Sparks and fire burst forth at once and followed the path of the slash he made.

He looked out the window to ensure they were on target. Sure enough they were, he then saw a barrage of various planes and other strange hovering crafts begin to pour out of the sides of the base called HOME and fly up towards them.

Crystal was back by Aryu and Sho. She glowered at Nixon. "Was that really necessary? I promise I won't miss."

"It's not yer aim tha' concerns me as much as it is them takin' remote control of this thing and savin' themselves once they see wha' we've got planned. Now it's a one-way trip."

Sho, uninterested in the banter, already began the clenching of his hand to start the rotation of the shield's blades. Aryu could now see that each of his fingers sat in loops, and when pulled forward they cranked some unseen gears inside the weapon to create the spin.

Sho jammed the humming shield and its protective border into the side of the plane, cutting through the thin skin. Aryu followed suit, cutting his own hole, eventually letting it meet up with Sho's.

With the cut complete, the sheet metal flew off into the rushing air, and the command cockpit was filled with heavy winds and unbearable noise. As Sho stood on the edge of the new impromptu doorway, a serious flaw in the plan came to Aryu. He instantly felt foolish that he'd not thought of it sooner. "Wait!" he called to Sho before he knew what he was doing. "You can't jump!"

Sho looked at him with his signature placidness. "Why not? We need to go now."

"I know, but your armor! You'll sink like a stone!" It was true. The plan involved a freefall into the water with Nixon holding back Sho and taking the brunt of the forceful impact, using miniscule amounts of his own Divine Power to cushion them both while Aryu took Crystal and glided her either to water or a safe landing somewhere on the ship.

The armor of both Nixon and Sho was likely to cause them to

sink. Sho would die if they didn't get rid of it right now.

Sho only looked as he always did, calm and uninterested. "Don't worry, Aryu." And with that, the big man gave a push and let himself fall out of the plane, followed quickly by Nixon.

"Our turn!" shouted Crystal. The base was approaching rapidly, and Aryu had no time to worry or argue. He hugged her close, folded in his wings to prevent the initial drag from pushing him into the fuselage and launched himself clear of the unguided missile moments before it made its surprising and unexpected impact straight into the heart of the deep-gray floating command structure known as HOME.

▶◀▶◀▶◀▶◀▶◀▶◀▶◀▶◀▶◀▶◀

Being so old was bound to have its drawbacks. Hubris was only one of a multitude Tokugawa Izuku possessed. During the re-creation of the Neural Inhibitor drug, he had decided that to someone like himself, an Embracer of the Power and long in years, loss of these abilities would be something akin to torture (indeed, it had been for more than one test subject, he recalled gleefully). The loss of mental strength would cripple one like him, making him unable to think clearly.

He certainly would not have been able to concoct a plan mere hours after the fact. A plan so smooth and effective it could create such a tidal wave of repercussions such as this one seemed to.

Indeed, seconds after he realized they had no intention of running away with the plane, he momentarily believed that maybe, just maybe, the powerful trio of Crystal Kokuou, Nixon of the Great Fire and Ash, and of course his beloved half-brother Tokugawa Sho may be just as dangerous without the Power as they were with it, only for different reasons.

323

As the initial rumble of the impact rocked the core of HOME, he knew he would never make that mistake again. But first he resigned himself to the fact that he would have a terrible mess to clean up.

HOME was a floating superstructure comprised of a massive hull that was shaped like a monstrous, dark gray 'V'. It stood as tall as a twenty-story building out of the water, with nearly as much room below the surface. It was not terribly mobile, with most of the defensive and maneuvering capabilities bestowed on the armada that accompanied it everywhere it went. It was the figurehead, the launching point for waves of ground troops by means of fast attack vessels from its wide, opening hull. On top of the High-Yield weapons within its body, it had multitudes of aircraft, from the quick and nimble Peregrine SCRAM reconnaissance jets to the High Heavy Aero Trackers that could take off with ease on HOME's exposed launch deck. Even the extremely large Bullfrog cargo planes could land with very little hassle, given the space to do so.

This Bullfrog, although given space in expectation of its landing, brought with it more than a 'little hassle.'

Hitting nose-first on the deck just to the side of the apex of the massive 'V' shape, the plane disintegrated on impact. Waves of fire shot outward in every direction, consuming the deck crew without discrimination, followed by pummeling the levels below in equal measure.

A large chunk ripped through to the cargo bay, taking with it numerous crew and vehicles in a blinding fireball. Although most of the crew were mindless automatons, those that were alive (vagabonds and ne'er-do-wells from one walk of life or another who had opted to bet on the winning pony) couldn't help but think that this career choice was not the stable employment opportunity they were looking for just before their painful and ultimately fruitless deaths.

HOME listed to the port side briefly with the impact, sending anything that wasn't nailed down sliding across the floor. Papers and parts flew everywhere. Soldiers lost their footing and numerous planes on the top deck slid off into the ocean. Eventually it righted itself as the smoke from the impact wafted into the sky, but by that time, the damage was done.

Izuku looked at the chaos and seethed in silence before he flew into a tirade of orders and commands. His mechanical hand pointed and enunciated his shouting as his human hand tightly gripped the handle of his precious weapon, ready for the first sign of weakness from his living crew or attack from his enemies. As long as his massive vessel remained afloat, their destination was clear and he would be waiting. No conversations. No reveling. No wasting of time. The wrath of the blade forged from the Est Vacuus would be swift. He doubted even the mighty sword of Nixon Ash could stand against the power he had now. No time like the present to find out.

▶◀▶◀▶◀▶◀▶◀▶◀▶◀▶◀▶◀▶◀▶◀▶◀

Rapidly approaching from the east was the dark specter of the being known as Eleotherios Duo model 0901, or E2-0901. Eleotherios had finished his duties with the weak human known as Boroha Sharp in the expected period of time. Now, with the aid of his leg-mounted RAMjets, he would be returning to HOME in a matter of minutes.

Eleotherios spotted the smoke in the distance. It was a very smart machine. It surmised what had happened and rerouted its destination to a nearby unmanned attack ship, where it could await further instructions or begin to deduce its own next move. It had that ability, and if an unfeeling machine could be said to do so, it enjoyed the opportunities it got to exercise it.

It landed. It waited. It was the Liberator by Madness, most

advanced of its kind. Much blood and sweat was shed in its creation. It would not rush so quickly into a dangerous situation.

There it would stay until called, even if that call was its own.

CHAPTER 20

In the Shadow of Death

The first week down the mighty Paieleh River Valley had been as trying and draining as any week in the memory of the two from Tan Torna Qu-ay. Esgona had mastered the Turtle and was now its full-time driver. Johan was much better since his death-defying dive into the Thunder Head, and as he recovered his hearing slowly and his strength slower still, he had more and more time to ponder the image of the dagger in the rock and how it was possible that it was so.

Well, that said, he spared it a thought whenever his time wasn't taken up by one Seraphina Langley, who had been a shadow to him ever since he had the strength to walk unaided and resume his normal duties.

She was with him constantly now, helping him with meals and tending even the smallest of wounds. It made Johan uncomfortable at first, but eventually he saw it wasn't some kind of subservience she was showing since she had proven herself more than independent and strong enough, but an honest need to show him how appreciative she was. She had shown herself to be a very capable and smart young woman. Johan was a proud man, but even he wasn't immune to her and her need to be with him. Something terrifying had happened to them both, and now it was a bond they shared.

Well, that and the heart-stopping attraction.

As they had spoken to one another, they realized that they had much in common, and just as Seraphina was attracted to Johan's bravery and good looks, Johan was attracted to her independence and family-first attitude. If she wasn't helping him, she was with her father. He never saw her alone or looking for something to do. An ethic worth its weight in gold to him.

The road the band followed was not as forgiving as they'd hoped. Although warned by the Riders that it was not for the faint of heart, Johan had secretly hoped it was simply a long, flat, slowly descending piece of road whose main obstacle was time. Alas, this was not the case. Although hard and long, centuries at the base of a cavernous ravine had led to rock falls and erosion to the poorly traveled path to the point that there were numerous times the party feared they would have to leave something valuable behind.

It was for the best that they were so well-stocked. The road offered no animals or vegetation. They had hunted what they could early on, knowing the pickings would be slim in time, but not even a mouse had been seen in two days. The only saving grace was the Paieleh River. Its waters were dangerous, but clean and refreshing after a hard day of travel. Whenever it allowed, they filled canteens and barrels and let the livestock have their fill. They carried grasses and hay enough for both horse and folme and had yet to meet an unbeatable obstacle.

That was exactly what worried August Stroan.

He was in tight with the Tan Torna Qu-ay boys now. He spent his off hours with one or both of them, finding their company preferable to that of the older officers and their cliquey ways. He was still green, and a small part of him enjoyed the respect from Johan and Esgona.

One evening he sat with the three others (Esgona had decided to join them on and off at times, and naturally any free moment Johan had demanded the inclusion of Seraphina) around a small fire. He had shed his armor, and if not for the short hair and clean face, any passerby would have simply thought him a regular part of their party. Noticing the man being much quieter than usual, Johan asked him what had put him in such a mood.

The answers they could get back were plentiful, and the story of this possession of the advanced technology with allies ahead hung over each of them as they questioned the necessary evil of the possibilities, but Johan had a feeling this was something else.

"I think we're being followed," he said, looking at each of them to show his seriousness. They believed him at once. As a Rider of the Inja Army, his word was not to be taken lightly. Besides, Johan had seriously considered this possibility for himself.

"What makes you say that?" Seraphina asked. Her indoctrination into this small clan had been rather painless. Any man from Tan Torna Qu-ay was raised to respect and honor women for their strength, guile, and intuition. No good ever came from underestimating the ferocity of a woman. But Seraphina Langley was a very easy person to like. She worked hard and was wonderful at deep conversation. She had proven to be more than adept at helping figure out alternative courses of action to issues the party had encountered.

"I think…no, that's not even fair, I *know* something is out there somewhere, because we've done nothing but come up against rockslides, massive boulders, and heavily washed-out road conditions from the first step we trekked into this valley."

"It is a pretty big valley, Stroan. I wouldn't say these things were out of place," responded Johan while stoking the fire, getting what heat he could from it in this chilly, walled-in expanse.

"It is out of place, Johan. It's out of place because we had two full parties bigger than this one head this way not a week before we set out. Parties that would have dealt with many of these issues. We've still heaved massive amounts of rock out of our way and wedged boulders into the river. They should have gotten to them first and cleared the path. Something is out there, following us, trying to ward us off, and I'm not the only one who thinks so, am I, Esgona?"

Esgona was his quiet self until this point. Now, spotlight thrust upon him, he went red and tried to shy away from the conversation as best he could.

"What does he mean?" Johan asked with a harsh tone in his words. "Do you know something?"

Esgona softly nodded. "Two days back while I was driving the Turtle, I was looking at the valley walls and saw what looked like a dark shadow moving with us. Ahead of us, actually. It would stop and continue, never getting too far out of our range. I only saw it for a moment, but whatever it was, it was fast and very large. I told Rider Stroan about it shortly after, but I haven't seen it since."

"But the rumor is that we have," Stroan added. Johan was upset by Esgona's seemingly integral involvement in the Inja Riders once more. "Scuttlebutt is that some of our sentries have seen something similar for days, mostly on the move at dawn or dusk. Some say tricks of the eyes, some say a very large Stalker, and some say spirits of the dead who have ventured into the valley. Until we get something concrete, we'll never know. But I'm telling you all to be aware that this situation isn't right."

The topic changed to other, lighter things, though the terrors of the unseen above them or ahead were so close they could each taste them. Soon each went their own way to bed. Eventually, each was asleep and readying for the day to come.

By the time the moon was high, the rumbling began.

"You've got to be *kidding me!*" was the shout that awoke Johan and Seraphina.

Johan looked around, eyes still heavy from sleep and blurry in the darkness. He had no idea what time it was, but there was still no sign of light over the ravine walls.

The waning moon provided something to see by, as did some remaining fires set by the night patrols, but what he saw was still confusion everywhere. Men and women were up, running to or from something.

They got to their feet, looking for anyone who could help. As if on cue, Stroan emerged from the hue and found them. "We're under attack," he said calmly, as if the scene did all the talking for him. "A few minutes ago we began getting pummeled from above by rocks and boulders."

"How do we know it's an attack?" Johan asked, strapping his knife to his side and trying to gather his things into some kind of order.

Impatiently, Stroan looked at him, sending the message before he spoke. "Because random rockslides don't systematically take out all of our patrol Riders followed by individual attacks on our most well-stocked carts. Now get moving!"

The two took off behind Stroan, who was still in his casuals. Seraphina left to her father and family while Johan headed off to see what use he could be.

Chief Rider Wyndam called to Johan out of the darkness, his beaten armor rattling as he moved around. "You, go join your friend on the Turtle and get it out of here. Head farther down the valley road and don't stop until we send word for you to do so!"

Not bound by the Inja Army chain of command (and mildly

incensed at someone calling Esgona his 'friend'), Johan protested at once. "No!" he shouted, turning the elder Rider's hard gray eyes on him in an instant, shocked at the refusal. "Haven't you heard of 'divide and conquer'? If this is an organized attack, taking the most well-protected and heavily stocked thing we've got away from the rest of the group won't help anyone. Plus, it looks a whole lot like you're sending us up the fuckin' river without a paddle, sir!" He punctuated the last word as if to prove defiantly that he was not bound by the rules the older man held so closely.

The gray eyes narrowed, clearly about to tear this sprout of a man a new one, when a fresh rumble echoed behind them. They turned just in time to see one of the larger carts pulled by a four-folme team get devastated by a humongous rock. It slammed into the side of it, blowing apart the soft wood deck and making a wreck of the wheels and lashings that held the folmes in place. As the rock careened off to the side, its damage done, the now-ruined cart was sent sliding backwards, down the side of the river embankment and into the rushing water below. Cart, supplies, and helpless beasts of burden were swept away before anyone could even think of reacting.

Wyndam instantly forgot the chewing-out of Johan and ran off to assist his men with any multitude of things. Johan went to a cluster of carts at the back he knew contained the supplies of the Inja Riders. The confusion had meant that no one was left to guard the arms and supplies held there, but the hard carbines and handguns weren't what he was looking for.

After a few minutes of searching, smaller rocks began raining down yet again. He knew that at any moment another of those giant haymakers was going to hit the Turtle. If that happened, Johan and his blatant defiance of Chief Rider Wyndam's orders were likely to be set in chains for the rest of the trip, if not outright tossed into the Paieleh in a fit of blind rage.

After looking into several crates and wooden boxes, Johan found what he was looking for, pulled it out, and ran back to the Turtle, its sides now taking a heavy beating.

In the darkness above, the familiar rumble was heard. Johan knew what was coming.

The Turtle was empty of people, but still fully loaded with fuel and supplies. If it was hit, they'd be lucky if the whole thing didn't go up like a powder keg. Esgona was nowhere to be seen. Figures, he thought as he ran to the front of the machine. *Some things never change.* A second later, Johan's hand was up, the Ark 1 already charging.

Straight ahead of them, he saw it; dark and gray, the largest one sent down yet. He suddenly questioned if this was going to work on something so large. *Too late now,* he supposed, and pulled the trigger.

Though Ark 1s have no recoil (a benefit of their design), the sound they make can be enough to startle anyone pulling the trigger for the first time. Couple that with someone who had recently experienced some very serious ear trauma and you had the equivalent of sonic head-punch the second the trigger was pulled.

The pop as it went off sent Johan back against the Turtle. A second later, the crushing bang sounded, and the boulder exploded in a sudden flash, sending chunks in each direction. They hit the Turtle, but with much less impact than the original boulder would have dealt.

Johan's ears rang as he waited for the Ark 1 to recharge, desperate to stop another attack.

Then the rock barrage fell silent, and the attack ended.

The damage report was not good. The cart and folmes were lost, but worse than that, so were six Riders who were on patrol at the time; three ahead and three behind, lending credence to the fact that this was a calculated attack and not a random event in the valley or

333

something concocted in the spur of the moment by an unseen assailant. It was planned and it was executed with purpose.

The cart lost was a well-stocked one, containing many canned goods found in Huan and two large kegs of water. Now they'd have to begin rationing foodstuffs and making more stops for water. With the increasing danger of the valley and the apparent enemies it contained, stopping more often was not a welcoming prospect.

The three had not seen Stroan since the end of the attacks. Chief Rider Wyndam had ordered teams into the higher grounds but each came back empty as far as useful information was concerned. They found places where rocks were dislodged, but no sign of the perpetrator. The size and scope of the attack, coupled with the attack on Huan, made it clear who and what the enemy they faced was.

The following morning the three were left to their own ponderings without Stroan to aid them, and it was made very clear any man or woman not being a Inja Rider was to stay with the carts and tend to those and only those.

Johan opted to break the silence and turn attention to the problems at hand. "We can all agree it's a Ruskan that's to blame, yes?"

Nods and silence.

"And we agree they attacked Huan? Possibly the two caravans ahead of us as well?"

Same response.

"Alright then, why throw rocks?"

They looked at him questioningly, wondering where he was going.

"Why attack from far away? They clearly don't care about making a rush for it and causing as much damage as possible. What makes this group so different? Why not just pounce off the valley walls and be done with us?"

It was a good question, but Esgona, who was revealed to have been rather selflessly aiding others when the Turtle was attacked, was certain he already had the answer. "The Ark 1?"

Johan was ready for the answer. "No, it's not that. They never would have known we had it until last night after the attack began. And can we honestly say a Ruskan Stalker in this world is smart enough to know what it is and the damage it could do? Stalkers are old, tough and smart, but I'd hate to think they'd be so worldly."

They didn't jump up and agree right away, but it seemed the truth. Silence again as each of them considered the possibilities and the reasoning behind each. They sat there for the better part of the day, the three young travelers lost in their own deep thoughts.

After a lunch no one really ate, Rider Stroan returned with the new orders. "Well fellas…oh, and lady…" A nod of thanks from the lone female. "We ride out in an hour, and then we don't stop unless something stops us. We go, day and night, until we make it to the Blood Sea and whatever awaits us there. We're spreading the word to one and all that we go and go hard."

It seemed a reasonable idea. The plan would, in theory, cut the remainder of travel time in half, leaving only another week in this dark and unforgiving valley.

Another thing to speed them along, thought Johan. If Aryu was still following as he hoped he was, each step further from the plan was a step away from him. At night, fires and smoke would have told him if they were below, but what now? A few lanterns to light the way? Not promising if he wanted to find them at night.

If he was on his way at all.

It had been more than two weeks since their separation in the mountain town, and Johan was getting more and more confident that if he hadn't shown up yet, he likely wouldn't show up at all. He quickly pushed the thought from his head.

"First though, we have another matter to attend to," continued Stroan. They looked at him, wondering. Sadness on his face, "We need to bury our dead."

The service was quick. Traditionally, a fallen Rider of the Inja Army would be set alight on pyres. Wood being a commodity they couldn't spare at this time, they opted instead for graves of rock higher up the valley wall on a flat plateau. Quick words of honor spoken, tears wept by many (yet none by any other Rider or man from Tan Torna Qu-ay), and the party was off again, this time at as full a tilt as they could manage, the Turtle and its hobbled driver leading the way.

By the time night began to fall, it was obvious that things had changed. Rocks and debris no longer littered the roadway and travel was brisk. No one had to speak the words. The issues encountered up to this point were clearly intentional, and someone somewhere was in a holding pattern awaiting the next move. The stress in the air around them was thick as autumn fog. How long would they have to wait now? Days? Hours? No one knew, but every set of eyes was scanning the slopes above them, praying to see it before it saw them.

The day brought a chilled wind up the valley and hit them head on, slowing progress as dirt and dust kicked up, blinding the group at times, but still nothing.

By the end of the third day since the attack that had started the rush, the foolish, uneasy feeling of being through the thick of it crept into the faces of the civilian aspect of the caravan. More talk and laughter filled the air, and by the crack of dawn the next day, things seemed almost normal.

The young group of three and any Rider they saw knew the truth. Johan picked it out right away. Lulling them into an unguarded and false sense of (sleep deprived) security was exactly what he would have done if he wanted to hit hard and fast, and by the time breakfast was over, he looked to the high walls of the Paieleh Valley, heard the thunder of the coming carnage, and knew that he was right.

As the rush of unfathomably large Ruskan Stalkers crested the closest ridge and began pouring down at them, ungodly voices screaming as they dove down the loose rock, the security was lost in the panic of the people below. Johan and Esgona could only sigh and laugh to themselves as another glorious form of the luck they had lately showed its head, followed by a hardening of their nerves as they sprang forward, once more into the breach.

▶◀▶◀▶◀▶◀▶◀▶◀▶◀▶◀▶◀▶◀▶◀▶◀

To say Skerd was afraid was an understatement. Still, there was no help for it. Even after explaining to all that would listen that this particular group of humans was far more dangerous than the previous ones had been, their time had run out and the rage of his fellow brothers was too much for logic and planning to overcome. Even the failed high-ground attack wasn't enough to make them think it through entirely. They saw first-hand this group had defensive capabilities similar to the previous entrants into the valley, but time had run out and their blatant incursion into this land must stop here and now. There were no more ahead, no more behind. Just these ones, and now they had to be stopped, weapons and defenses of a higher quality be damned. With the loudest roar he could muster, the aged and battle-hardened Skerd of the Uhluktahn led the charge.

He'd gathered seven of the most reasonable members of his brotherhood for the attacks. None were close to his age, but many were similar in abilities and intelligence. Some were newcomers; the others had been with him during the raid on the village. All were angry with this group of useless people and were happy to see them suffer.

They came over the ridge following Skerd's battle cry. If the humans weren't afraid before, they certainly would be now.

The decorated men on horses weren't as shaken as Skerd had hoped, and they wasted no time forming ranks in front of the carts. They were seemingly ready and waiting for this, but the others behind them were crying and terrified. The fear in the air was a boost of energy to the creatures and they let it fuel them farther down the slope, massive scalding bodies bristling with ridges and rage. *Let this end it,* thought Skerd, praying his instincts on the matter were wrong.

Age and wisdom, even for creatures such as these, is rarely wrong. This simple fact was forgotten in the red haze of anger for each of them, and because of that forgetfulness, the first of their monstrous ranks fell.

It was a younger beast to Skerd's right as they descended, one who had joined on after the village attack. Being smaller and faster than the others, he'd begun to break ahead of the pack, thirst for blood and vengeance in his eyes. Below, the riders had opened fire with their small and useless weapons. The bullets bounced off the tough hides like bugs and did nothing to stop the charge.

Until the brave and foolish boy from the waters of the Uhluktahn rushed through the front line and raised something small and silver. Skerd knew at once it was an old weapon. A weapon to fear.

Skerd was just a whelp at the time of the most recent destruction of the land. He had seen many weapons like this at that time. Weapons used to hunt his kind before they all but disappeared. Weapons that had no issues ripping through the outer shell each Stalker had, even one as tough and hardened as his own. He could call no retreat or reassembling, his pride and rage would never allow it, but he knew the moment the loudest pop was heard and the flash erupted to his right where the young one was surging ahead that his instincts were absolutely correct, and now may well be the time he paid the price for his damnable lack of control.

The leading Stalker exploded in a shower of white-hot blood and sinew. Where its head had been was now just a smoking hole as its lunging front legs collapsed under its weight and momentum and began careening down the hillside, scattering those around it and striking the first hints of fear into the hearts of his brothers who had not listened to Skerd when he said this group was not to be taken lightly. Moments later its body hit the road and came to a rest between a cart and the large, rounded, mechanical thing not pulled by any animal.

Seconds later Skerd and the others were on them, striking out at the closest rider or cart they could reach.

Skerd bit down on the head of the horse nearest him, taking it off in one clean slice, blood pouring forth from both animal and mouth as the body it left behind fell instantly. The body pinned the leg of its rider just long enough to allow Skerd to advance and crush the hapless man under his powerful front legs. The smell of burning flesh hit his nose, adding to the primal bloodlust.

More of the weak shots rang out, but if any hit him Skerd didn't notice. He began wheeling around to another rider, an older one this time, possibly a leader of the ranks. He charged, barely seeing the scene unfold around him as his eyes locked on his target. He could see the mettle in the man he approached and sensed this kill would be that much sweeter for it.

Then the second pop was heard and another of his kind was lost to a gruesome explosion. The blood that rained down on the humans burned and many screamed in pain as it hit them. In some places, fires started as it hit something incendiary. Animals began to panic more than ever and the drivers of the carts could no longer control them as they began bolting and jostling around.

Skerd forgot his intended victim with the second blast and

searched out anew for the holder of that damned weapon. He gave the elder rider a swipe, sending the horse and rider spiraling into the air and away; the beast was dead before it hit the ground and the rider likely not much better. He crashed into the riverbank and came to a rest, the toes of his boots licking the rushing water below as he lay unmoving.

Skerd looked around, scanning all he saw for the young fool. The others of his kind were faring well, the damage and disarray already considerable and many of the humans and the animals they possessed were lying lifelessly on the ground. Carts were overturned and fires spread.

A smile came to him, or what passes for one on the face of a Ruskan Dragon Stalker, as he saw the young one and his precious gun, falling back behind the round rolling machine and its young driver. Skerd charged forward, careful to keep an eye on the weapon he carried, ready for it to rise and fire again. He came around the machine with astonishing speed, eager to end the threat and finish the job he'd set out to do.

The weapon never raised and fear was written over his boyish, dark face, though he still faced Skerd bravely. The weapon wouldn't work, Skerd surmised, though for reasons that were completely beyond him.

Just as he was in striking distance and was about to snap the whelp in two, the large machine shifted, front wheels turning and engine coming to life as the young crippled one fired it up and drove it forward quickly, striking Skerd and tossing him off balance as he reached out for the kill with his huge claws. The hit was just enough to allow the prey to elude the killing blow, as well as put the huge beast and his considerable momentum on a downhill course to the river below, an occurrence that surely meant a painful and long-suffering death to one of his kind.

A cry of rage from his mouth as he dug his feet in with all the strength he could manage, claws ripping at the uneven and loose surface. He put his body low, scraping his belly on the ground to help slow down, causing himself to spin as he descended. Soon, he was facing away from the river; panic overtook him, as he feared he might not meet his death head-on.

His fear was assuaged when he stopped short, but not before his large, spiked tail hit the water, sending pain through his body and steam into the air. He pulled it free with a mighty yank and took two labored steps up from the river.

He looked up the small hill to ready his next move and was pleased to see he hadn't missed entirely. Although he'd missed a full killing blow to the boy, he had reached him at least a little, and now he was laid out on the ground just beyond the front wheel of the mechanized wagon. He was coming to his feet now, the weapon no longer in his hand.

Then Skerd saw it, broken and in pieces at his feet. The boy saw it too, then he looked up at Skerd and the beast met his gaze.

Out of options and about to die, Skerd looked into the boy for fear but saw none. He saw bravery. Even unarmed and wounded, this one would fight to the last. He respected this young one. He was glad he would be the one to take his life and not some other who would not recognize the sacrifice and strength of will it was taking to do as he was now. This death would have meaning.

Skerd began the movement forward, eager for this honorable and engaging confrontation, when the boy reached to his leg and produced a knife which he held before him, ready to attack with whatever strength he had left.

Instantly the mind-altering clarity of vision came to Skerd, just as it had at the base of the Uhluktahn. The rage he felt and the bloodlust he craved were washed away like nothing as he laid his eyes on the blade. Suddenly, with a hint of foolishness, he understood everything and stopped his attack on the people, his attention consumed by the clarity in his mind and the realizations it meant.

"*Cease!*" he called out in his native tongue to the others of his kind. At first they ignored him or were simply too lost within the rage they felt. "*Cease at once, my brothers! Cease and fall back!*"

They continued, until the first of them saw his seriousness and begrudgingly did as he asked. Soon the others followed as the humans looked on wondering what had happened. As the remaining members of his kind retreated up the hillside once more, the people below allowed them to leave, firing no more shots with their weak weapons, and instead turned to their own problems. Watchful eyes always on the beasts on the high ground above them. A moment of uneasy calm overtook them all. Only the sounds of crying children, burning wood, and rushing water could be heard as Skerd looked back to the young one with the weapon before him.

"You there," he said, shocking all nearby with his deep but suddenly-understandable voice. "You carry a talisman. How did you come to have it? Are you an Embracer?"

The young one looked confused at first, and then seemed to realize it was the knife Skerd spoke of. "I...I received it as a gift some time back." The lad was unsure of what was going on, but held his place, nonetheless. His face was cut and bleeding and he favored his leg, but otherwise he'd come out alright.

Skerd, lost in the sea of this newfound clarity, attempted to move away from the river but was met with the knife being thrust in his direction as a warning. He wasn't happy being so close to the water, but it seemed the boy held the advantage now.

"A gift for what?" he continued. "One does not give talismans like that away for nothing."

"For saving a village far from here," the boy said at last. "Saving it from another of your kind."

Of course. All things come around in full circle to Skerd. A reward for saving others from a Stalker was a weapon that could save many Stalkers' lives. It was as it was meant to be.

The wariness on the boy's face was still evident and Skerd realized at once that he wasn't sure what was going on, although Skerd's talking to him as he was should have explained everything.

"The weapon you carry there," Skerd continued, "is a very powerful one to me and my kind. You do not see it for what it is. Is that true?"

Confusion began to mix with a mild sense of relief, likely caused by the ceasing of the attack and beginning of an open dialogue. "It would appear so," the boy answered, obviously uncomfortable. "What is it to you?"

"To answer that," replied Skerd, "would take a very long time. I can tell you this: what you hold there gives me and my kind a clarity of thought lost in the ages to a muddle of anger and rage, our natural state. Just being near it now is the reason we no longer attack, although you should know some of my brothers above might not be so easily swayed by it. Their age and impetuousness are defying them."

A young rider joined with anger in his face, "Why tell us this, beast? Why tell us anything other than why we shouldn't kill you all right here and now?"

"Hold your wagging tongue, fool! It is by my will and that alone that we don't finish the very easy task of killing you all right now, so listen and listen well. We will not apologize for our actions at your intrusion into our lands. They are justified and done with pride for our race and kind. What we will do, and I will make it so for the rest of your trip, is allow you to continue to the vast waters beyond which is home to many more of your people. You may travel unhindered."

He locked his eyes on Johan to ensure no mistake was made with what he was about to say. "If, and only if, you stay and let us speak more of that item and what we can do with it together."

"Why would I do that?" the boy asked. "You've killed or wounded so many of my people. What reason do I have to help you?"

"Simple," Skerd replied, impatient with the child's lack of vision, "if you do not agree, we kill you all now and any others that come our way without remorse. We'd take it from you if we could, but I'm afraid it is useless to us without a human to hold it. You seem to be a very intelligent boy. Do you believe that each side of a conflict has their own justifiable rights for fighting, as you and I do now, regardless of how one feels about the other?"

"Yes."

"Good, then you shouldn't be surprised by our actions. We are older, wiser and much stronger than you will ever be. We will allow all others of your kind to pass our way with impunity. Knowing what I know of what you have, which is more than you it seems, it won't be difficult to convince my brothers to do the same. I will gladly kill a defiant member of my own kind to ensure the safety of you and that item. It means that much to me. Do you believe that?"

"I do, though I don't know why."

"Nor can I tell you, as the Power escapes my understanding."

A pause for a moment, and then the child's dark eyes met Skerd's. "My answer is no," the boy said, startling some members of his group. Skerd looked him over, expecting more to come from his mouth in explanation. "I can't stay. I *won't* stay. I have a mission I must fulfill, *with* my knife. You mention justifiable right to fight a battle, well I have that. I have that far down this road, against an enemy I fear more than you. An enemy you and your kind would be wise to fear as well."

Skerd doubted that, but he didn't doubt this boy believed it to be true. Then the boy indicated the smashed silver weapon, and Skerd believed he understood.

"I see," he growled, noticing those high above him getting impatient. "You go to battle the machines." The boy didn't answer but nodded to indicate he did. Skerd was unaware of any machines returning to the land, but the nobility of the boy gave him no reason to doubt him. The knife was a handy weapon regardless of the enemy. "You will fight me, here and now, if I don't let you go?"

"Yes." His muscles tensed, preparing for an attack. It was all Skerd needed to see.

"Very well. Go. Take your people and fight your battle. When it is over, you *will* return to me with that knife. Do you know how to use it? How to harness its power?"

"No, I don't. Not in a way one like you could possibly need."

"I can tell you this: you'd best attempt to figure it out soon, boy, because you're useless to me if you return and you haven't. Now, will you make my deal?"

Hesitation at first, coupled with a look to the young rider. "No harm to me and my people. We may pass freely and without incident."

"Without incident caused by my brothers or me, yes. Rare is the journey without incident of any kind."

"And others that may follow?"

"Correct."

"Alright, beast. I agree. I should warn you, though; the journey I'm on is likely to end in my death."

"I'd recommend that it doesn't. Your death, likely as you say it may be, matters not to me. If you do not return as agreed in what I would call a reasonable amount of time, we will not show any more restraint in matters of your people's incursions. We will leave our mountains, enter your homes, and finish off everyone we find to find that weapon or one like it."

A look of doubt. "It's really that important to you I return with this knife? Worth the countless lives you'd end needlessly?"

"Those and a thousand times more, yes."

"Wow. Well then I suppose I had better return." A half-smirk on his face.

"I suppose you should," Skerd agreed, upset by the lad's hints of mockery at this conversation. "When you do what you must and your affairs are in order, return to the remnants of the village that once was near the base of the Uhluktahn. That is my land and I will see you. I will wait for you. I will not wait long."

The knife lowered and the boy nodded his head in agreement, smugness removed from his face at the threat. Skerd moved his massive body up the hill, tail still pained from the dip in the river, but otherwise fine. He crossed the road, continuing up the hill to his brethren, turning one last time to the scene of destruction and death below, knowing that shortly the talisman would be gone and the animal inside him would be back. A worrisome proposition, but in this deal, everyone had something to lose.

"I will wait for you...?"

"Johan," he answered. "Johan Otan'co of Tan Torna Qu-ay. I will be there or I'll be dead. On my honor."

"And on my own, Johan Otan'co. That of Skerd of the Uhluktahn. Pray you are not late or otherwise indisposed."

Even now, getting higher in the mountains, Skerd could feel the clarity leave him in small bits, and with each iota that left, the more skeptical he was that this deal was the right one. So it is and so it must be.

He knew what he needed to know, even in the haze of animal instinct now overtaking him; there were talismans in his lands again, even if it was just this one. The foolish one known as the Dragon King had not rid the world entirely. That was something worth killing for.

Moments later, he and his brothers were gone.

CHAPTER 21

Tower of Crystal, Sea of Blood

The prospects were terrible for the small group left in the Paieleh River Valley. Of the twenty-one travelers, twenty-three military Riders and three from Tan Torna Qu-'ay, as well as the four large carts and the giant Turtle loader that had left Huan, very little remained after the Stalker attack.

The Riders had lost more than half their numbers and mounts, leaving only eleven including Chief Rider Wyndam who had suffered what was likely to be a fatal injury at the claws of Skerd. For now, he was being carried in an open spot in the back of the Turtle, but to all it seemed a matter of 'when' not 'if' he was lost.

Another cart was lost, bringing them to the lonely number of one, with four folmes and one ragged horse remaining of the travelers' stock, and nine warhorses for the Riders. The people who had chosen to undertake this trip were not as bad off as the Riders who had taken the front lines of defense during the attack, but the toll was still damaging. Four dead, and Seraphina's father had been badly injured as well. She had separated herself from Johan for the time being to tend to her father and likely to take stock of her feelings towards him. It was no secret many thought he should never have made a deal since he seemed to have an advantage on the monster.

The aftermath was gruesome and frightening. Blood and destruction were at every turn. But mankind is terribly resilient, and when you're still short days of anything in the world that could save you and your loved ones, pinned down in a dangerous and deep river valley with little supplies and less hope, there's nothing else to do but pick up and go or lie down and die. Since the ground was already littered with the signs of many who had met that finality, pick up and prepare to set off again they did. By daybreak the following day, the battered Turtle led the charge once more, followed by a now heavily overloaded cart pulled by four terrified and injured animals; all others on foot, no space left to carry them and what they needed to survive.

Canned food was all that was left to eat, which was for the best as they no longer had enough supplies to build a fire to cook by. The next few days were going to be tight and likely very hungry. No one complained, though. They did what they must.

On the road once more, the group no longer spared a thought for where their place was, even the Riders. Each did what needed to be done at the time it needed to be done with no questions. Riders surrendered their mounts to weary travelers, and the travelers were thankful for it. Rank and social standing meant little to this group now. Putting one foot in front of the other was all that mattered. Each step took them closer to a faint hope of salvation and farther away from the rock-covered graves behind them.

The two from Tan Torna Qu-ay went together now, hatred set aside in the wake of their newest shared experiences. They weren't likely to spend holidays or free time together, but for the sake of the journey and their shared pain of the last few weeks, they had more than enough in themselves to be civil.

When Esgona did join Johan in free time, he was still his quiet self. He understood this was all of the acceptance he was ever going to get. One night, Johan finally asked him about things he'd seen in the south, and during that time of conversation, he told Johan about the knife and the things he'd seen in it, the feelings it conjured and the thoughts it evoked. Johan listened, not sure if he believed him or not, but after a moment he realized his mind did have more echoes of the things he was speaking of, though he'd never thought of it as out of the ordinary since he was so attached to the knife and its meaning to him in the first place.

Silence was still his strength, and he didn't reveal everything. Somewhere deep down inside him, beyond the pain and guilt of his actions, he was still Esgona, and these two were still Johan and Aryu, and that was a barrier likely never to fall.

Johan thought often of Aryu. Where he was. What he was doing. If he was coming at all (a dire possibility he seemed to freely accept).

They encountered no more trouble that was a major setback of any kind. The river held its dangerous-but-tolerable levels, the road remained clear (confirmation that what Skerd had promised would be so) and the weather, although still windy and cool at the best of times, held out enough to let the group stay dry with a minimum of effort. Once again, the blessing of small miracles experienced by Johan was in the air. The world was merciful in its cruelty.

They trekked for six days, stopping each night since they could no longer afford the space for people to sleep on the carts. After the third night, only one Inja Rider was left for sentry duty, but it was mostly to keep an eye on the river and nothing more. It was a useless position. If the river was to surge as it had become famous for, by now the steep walls were nearly impossible to climb, the loose rock giving way to sheer slopes and huge cracks in the rock face that appeared to continue on forever. They were all trapped.

At high-sun of the seventh day, the coldest they'd seen thus far since setting out from Huan, they came to a small rise that signaled the steady decline of the mountain peaks. As the day grew into evening and the sun was close to setting, the walls fell away at last, shocking each of the travelers with their sudden absence. Their eyes had a difficult time adjusting to the sudden appearance of an actual horizon and not just the dark shadow of rock.

Soon the sun, in the last of its moments in the sky, cast a light that reached out below the cloud line and illuminated the vast and impossible sight of the great shores and massive expanse of the Blood Sea.

No one cheered. No one said a word. The arrival at this place was either thought of as a dream or the inevitable end to what was an excruciating and nightmarish journey. Huan and the Thunder Run seemed like another lifetime.

It was here, at the top of a hill that descended to the shores of the sea that Chief Rider Samson Wyndam succumbed to his injuries at last. He let out one last breath as the group watched the sun go down, though no one would know it until they checked on him while unloading the Turtle moments later. Here the ground gave rise to trees and grasses and his body was sent off to what lay beyond in the manor most fitting a man of his kind, with all that were left from the group standing in a circle as he burned, the last reminder of the death that was found for many of those foolish enough to travel the Paieleh River Valley. Samson Wyndam was a good man, and died in the manner he'd have chosen for himself on any given day. He was sent off to the who-knew-where of the afterlife with a minimum of tears shed, only memories of his greatness in the minds of his men. He never wanted anything more.

A camp was set up on the roadside and the fires burned brightly once more. The two had a moment to pause and reflect on what was to come next. They had agreed with Stroan that when his evening duties concluded he was to join them, and as a group they would discuss what the next course of action was for the Inja Army Riders and war they were soon to fight. The last few weeks had done nothing to them but strengthen the need to extract as much machine-destroying satisfaction as they possibly could, come hell or high water (a fantastically apt expression after their time in the valley).

It was a long time coming for them before Stroan finally did arrive.

Esgona said nothing and Johan looked off to the other fires searching for Seraphina, finding her at last in the distance, minding her younger brother. Thankfully her father seemed to be on the mend, but she'd still said little to him in the last week of travel. He missed her most now, in the chill night, as any man would.

"The city is another day away, south, down a heavily traveled road that follows the shore of the Blood Sea," Stroan said, launching into the story. "We've sent a Rider ahead to survey the area and try to get an understanding of what's going on. We can't see any fighting nearby, but we can't say for certain the army isn't here."

The Great Range came to an end south of here, following the line that stretched right across to the east, where Johan assumed Aryu still was at this time. Their homelands went along the base of them, funneled into a great valley by another, less impressive mountain range that rose from the Westland, a place known to conceal many fighting troops during the wars that raged there. This large valley, many days across by foot, was the home of the wide and impressive Vein River, the outflow of the Blood Sea that eventually led to the southern ocean.

The valley was a pinch point, making it a terrible place to travel in times of war and dispute (which was always, it seemed), and many fled into the mountains instead of the sure death of the flat and open Vein Valley. By this point in time, it was essentially a foregone conclusion that if you wanted to get to whatever lay north of the Vein Valley, you were either in the military or in a casket.

There was no sign of war anywhere. No proof that the Army of the Old had marched this far. Knowing what they did of the army and its staggering capabilities, they should have been here weeks ago, dropping bombs and conquering lands with impunity, yet they were not.

"There's a city to the south of here. It's a big place, from what I've heard. Not like what you may be accustomed to. Buildings are tall and there are hundreds of thousands of people. People who've fully accepted technology like those on the far side of the sea. I'm guessing it will be a shock for you, or any of us for that matter. Most of the other Riders in this group are from south of here, me included. Towns and villages on the ocean or near it. This is new territory for us all. Still, it beats the alternative." That was something they didn't all entirely agree on. The possibility of getting to a place where *hundreds* of thousands called home was unsettling to the two. No great good had ever come from such a large collection of people.

If the size of this place was the truth, how was Aryu going to find them? True, he has wings and tends to stand out in a crowd, but was that enough? How long did they wait until they decided they couldn't wait anymore, either by their own choice or the dictation of circumstances?

Stroan was equally disturbed, as it was well-known from their first meeting that he has no love of technological advances beyond the Ark 1 he sometimes carried, and there was also the worry he felt for his family and loved ones. From what he'd told them about the location of his homeland in his talks with them, if the Army of the

Old made it to the Vein Valley, then his home had likely been lost.

The three eventually slept, there on the threshold of many dark roads to travel.

Sunrise brought out the best in people as the light caught the distant water and showered the group from the Inja in shimmering beauty. Few had ever seen an expanse of water so large, and those that had still enjoyed it immensely. Being in the valley for so long meant they hadn't seen a proper sunrise not obscured by mountains or valley walls. By breakfast, a very welcome non-canned meal, the Riders assembled and prepared for the expected coming of the scout sent off the night before.

Fate had grown weary of the depression it had bestowed on this clan, and not a minute past the expected return time, the Rider Scout came into view at full gallop, both horse and rider looking well-fed and rested. Flanking behind him were two more Riders keeping pace, though who they were and why they were here was a mystery.

As they got closer, a general feeling of uneasiness washed through the group. The Rider and his companions were already back and talking with the man who, as of the unfortunate death of his superior officer the previous night, was thrust into the command of the ragged group.

One of them was another Inja Rider, a man likely the age of Chief Rider Wyndam at the time of his death, though this man had a long beard with little original color. The same steel eyes looked out of his haggard, sunken face, a seeming prerequisite for a Rider commanding officer. It was the other man that set the crowd on edge.

He was a Westlander, and a very large one. Having been the only one that had met him, Esgona put him a hair's width taller than Nixon Ash. His horse was a head taller than that of the largest any had seen before, its black body covered in nothing but a modest saddle, unlike the Riders and the full armored regalia of their mounts. He was muscular and wore tan clothes that fit firmly to his broad chest. His skin was darker than the two from Tan Torna Qu-ay, who were already a deep shade. The whites of his eyes stood out like beacons from his face as he surveyed the group (who of course surveyed him right back, decorum be damned by this point in the journey), and soon he glanced down at the two in the back of the pack, his eyes remaining on them until the elder Rider had finished his discussion with those that were left of this brigade. After a brief stop at the pyre of Samson Wyndam to pay their respects, they approached the Turtle and the two with it.

Stroan rode with them, hanging back with a look of great sadness on his face, though the natural strength of the Rider and the journey he'd just undertaken to get this far betrayed any attempt they used to figure out what had him so down. Soon they sat in the presence of the four: the visitors, the newest commanding officer Rider Liffe, and Stroan to the rear.

Liffe greeted the two, dismounting and casting aside his helmet (they had known Liffe from the trip, but he was never anyone they had been close to). The senior Rider and the Westlander did the same.

"You are the two from Tan Torna Qu-ay?" the elder Rider asked, voice rough like sandpaper scraping together. They nodded. He took measure of each of them. "And who is the one named Johan?"

No time wasted, as it was clear that this conversation had purpose. There was still tremendous respect bred into Johan for the Inja Riders. "I am, sir. Johan Otan'co."

The Rider stood before him, only slightly taller than Johan, but with a presence of someone much larger. His hand extended, less his pinky finger. Johan took it and shook heartily, no longer surprised by the strength and roughness of the action. These were both hard men. Each would have expected no less from the other.

"On behalf of the Riders of the Great Inja Army, I, Chief Rider Merrik Caspar, wish to thank you…" a look to Esgona, "each of you, in your part of the safe return of my Riders, and the people they were charged to protect, to this place. I know there were losses, but it likely would have been everyone if not for your quick thinking and help. For that I thank you both." He released Johan's hand and took Esgona's, followed by stepping back to take them in. Johan surged with pride, and Esgona filled with disinterest muddled with shame. Authority did astonishing damage to his psyche.

The large man stepped forward, towering above each of them, great arm extended, massive hand devouring each it met in another round of congratulations (met by the two, it should be said, with a fair amount of distrust and skepticism). "I salute you each, and your party as a whole, for emerging from the Paieleh Valley. The dangers of this place are well-known far and wide, and the courage it took to get here is astonishing." His voice was deep, but not so much as his body was large. They didn't know what to expect when he spoke, but they certainly didn't expect what they got: a voice and tone exactly like theirs without an accent to be found. Clearly they didn't know near enough about him and his people, another downfall of the sheltered life of the places they came from.

"I'd like you boys to accompany us," Caspar continued, "the Turtle in the lead, as we head back to Bankoor to get you and your companions a decent meal, a solid bed to sleep in, and a hero's welcome."

Although all sounded too good to be true, Johan still had to speak up. "Um, thank you sir, but where?"

Chief Rider Caspar looked at him, understanding dawning on his face. "Bankoor, the city you and yours have been questing for." Blank faces on the two. "Really? All this time and trouble and you didn't even know the name of the place you were going. Simply amazing."

They'd never given it much thought to be honest. They didn't even know there was a city for certain when they set out. The rumors simply made them assume as much. Looking back on it, it did seem somewhat foolish, but given their options, what else could they do?

A name given their destination, as well as promises that sounded like they had been cut from a dream, they agreed to what Caspar was saying and began to head out with the rest of the meager troop.

They descended the small rise they were perched on, looking out over this new landscape and the life it held and began the trip to the road on the shores of the Blood Sea and the city of Bankoor. Not a word was heard from any of the group except for the newcomers leading the way. The rest knew it was no time for talk; it was a time for reflection.

So they went on in silence, bad memories in tow.

▶◀▶◀▶◀▶◀▶◀▶◀▶◀▶◀▶◀▶◀▶◀▶◀▶◀

In the quiet of the evening, the sun close to the horizon once more after its journey to the west, two things of great importance happened to Johan Otan'co. Things that could help shape the man he would become in the hard years ahead, years that could see him travel far and see much. Things that may give him just enough strength to see each hard and painful task ahead to the end. All of this was only if he lived through the coming storm, of course. It's a shame people rarely meet these moments head on, never realizing what they are until years afterwards. Esgona had met many situations that defined him face first, from the capture at the hands of the Army of the Old to the torture of watching his one friend Hogope murdered, to the destruction of his home and the privileged life it ensured.

Johan would never look back on these two important things for what they were. Perhaps it was the part of him that was the hero, taking each development in stride as if what was happening, good or bad, was as it was meant to be.

He was walking along the side of the Turtle. They'd pushed through lunch and had met up with the large road that led south to Bankoor and north to who-knew-where. They met many others coming and going in a hurried fashion. There were far more leaving the south than were entering, a fact no one missed.

Most they passed were much like themselves, little changing in appearance or modes of transportation.

Others were very different. Perhaps even frighteningly so, had this group not just walked through the bowels of Hell. Some people passed them in powered carts much faster and nimbler than the ones they had seen in their lives. Others rode on single-person vehicles with small wheels that ripped past them like a streak. Nothing was horribly out of place here, at least not yet, but the slight advances in transportation and the ever-increasing number of people they saw began to put many of the long walkers at unease.

The sun was very close to setting. Johan was simply staring blankly ahead, praying for a view of the city he thought may never show up, when his hand was taken into another and he looked around to see the tired-yet-still-beautiful face of Seraphina Langley, looking ahead longingly, much as he had been a moment before. He turned back forward, enjoying her return, waiting for her to speak but understanding if she chose not to. There was a lot going on in her mind, and he wasn't about to make things worse by doing something dumb like speaking.

"Why make the deal, Johan?" Her voice was calm, not accusatory. She seemed to simply want an answer. "So many dead. So many injured, my father among them. Yet you chose to spare them when you had an advantage. Why?"

A good question. He'd thought about the deal from a week ago very much. Although it may not seem to have been the most logical answer, he was quite certain that he'd come upon an answer he could live with.

"Because I believe Skerd. I believe him if he says he's willing to start a war with people over this knife. They clearly had the advantage, but still they stopped when he told them to. Stalkers don't just stop. It was something so much more to them. And even if I'd killed him, which I doubt I could have, then we all would have died. If I live through what's to come, it seemed a small price to pay to have to return. It was an easy choice."

She nodded but continued to look forward at everything and nothing. "And what about the knife? This is twice now it's saved our lives." In the days after the Thunder Run, Johan had told Seraphina about what he'd seen when he saved her.

"It's obviously more than it seems. Skerd mentioned Embracers. I'm still just trying to find out. What do you think?"

She smirked. "I think you need to hold on to it, no matter what that monster says. See them again if you have to, but never give it up. I believe there's a reason you have that now and we're only just beginning to find out what it is."

Seraphina hadn't shown many signs of being overtly religious or prone to belief in fate, but she was so beautiful and their attraction was so great Johan never cared. Perhaps a bit of faith was what he needed in his life, even if it wasn't his.

Johan cleared his throat awkwardly, afraid to ask the next question even though the answer was quite clear. "So, you're not mad at me for doing what I did?"

She stopped him and looked in his eyes. "I owe you my life, Johan. We all do. I may not agree with it all, but I understand. You're a good man. A hero. Good men make good choices more often than not. They just seem foolish at the time."

An uplifting sentiment. "Like making a deal with a talking Dragon Stalker I have no reason to trust?"

She shrugged. "Of leaping to certain death to save a girl you don't know. So far I'd say both choices worked out for the best in the end."

He agreed.

He motioned to the others ahead of them. "What do they think? Do they forgive me?"

She didn't answer immediately. She turned and continued to walk towards Bankoor, hand firmly intertwined with Johan's while they moved on in silence. They walked like that for a time, enjoying the touch of the other and the warmth of the action. Soon, she was pressed to his side with strides in unison. Then, she leaned over as they walked, lightly kissed his cheek, and whispered, "I forgive you," in his ear.

Forgiveness is an amazing thing. The giving of it can bring peace; the denial of it, war. Very few are the simple things in life that hold that much power. Perhaps only love rivals it in terms of potential, and that is hard to give and harder to take away.

The evening wearing on and the miles falling like rain behind them, Johan realized what she said was all that mattered. That fact accepted, he pulled her close to himself, kissed her forehead through a tangle of hair and offered her a quiet "Thank you" in return. She nodded in acceptance. With that issue being dead, life continued on.

The second thing that changed Johan (and Esgona equally, though he kept that to himself) came shortly afterwards. This moment was almost seen by the young man for what it was: a defining moment, just as the return of Seraphina to his side had been (though he didn't know that yet).

The sun was beginning to touch the water and the salt wind was coming in harder now, as if pushed at them by the giant falling star. The smell was almost alien to Johan, but it brought a sickening feeling of remembrance to Esgona. The last time salt air had met his nose was not a pleasant point in his life. It was here that the sun set alight the buildings of Bankoor in the distance, shimmering pillars of glass casting a reflection out in their direction as if guiding them home. At its center was a massive tower, like a spike driven into the heart of the city from beneath the ground, with a sharp point jabbing into the coming night sky, threatening to rip it open.

Below the city center, lights began blinking on like small fires until the whole of Bankoor was alight. The jut of the great tower in the center of the city was glowing softly in a steady reddish-yellow, while the city seemed to burn with light below it like a frozen fire.

The fact that no story ever told about the Blood Sea mentioned the great cities clearly on its shores was not lost on the two from Tan Torna Qu-ay. This was certainly a difficult secret to keep, but here they were, looking at the largest, most advanced collection of living people they'd ever seen.

"Slightly advanced, my ass," Johan said under his breath as they all stood, staring at the sight before them. Mysteries abounded in this new world.

They began moving again, eager to reach Bankoor before the night wore on too long. The surroundings were strange and the destination unsettling, but no one argued. This group was no longer of the opinion that the Old was something to blatantly and unreasonably fear after the technology it produced had saved them twice in the form of the now-lost Ark 1, but there was still an army of unimaginable power heading for them, and that was enough to make them nervous in the shadow of Bankoor and its unknown evils.

Missing for most of the day, Stroan rode to his traveling companions, giving a perfunctory nod to Seraphina, either out of a standard greeting to a lady or perhaps to acknowledge her return to the fold. "I can't say I expected this, did any of you?"

Johan laughed, "Seriously? How could we? You never knew and you're from closer to here than we are."

Stroan looked dejected at the thought. "My home was farther south, and our enemy to the west. Once the Vein Valley opens into the plains where I lived, we never thought of the valley and what was north. We knew there was great fighting going on and to travel to it without reason or without being in the army was suicide. So we ignored it and went our own way. It seems we were wrong to do so." Johan agreed. "Well, no stop to it now, eh?" Stroan continued, his horse striding along beside the group, bringing Stroan eye to eye with Esgona sitting high on the Turtle. "What do you think?" he asked him, curious of the young man's reaction after all he'd been through.

A shrug from the driver. "I think we're going to die here." Esgona, if shaken by the destination, didn't show it outwardly, but his abrupt statement was chilling. The question was in the air about his next move, either continuing his uneasy alliance with Johan (and soon Aryu) or go his own way, seeking another direction.

"What do you know about this place, Stroan?" Johan asked, curious if the Rider had heard anything.

"I know it's the central location for our army and those who've joined us. A jumping-off point to the battle with the Army of the Old in the south. It's where we've established our base of operations and stored many of the equipment and troops yet to be deployed. Something about the city protects it from those distant attacks we're all so familiar with, but I have no idea what it is. I'd love to find out before I put faith in it." Johan assumed it was radar, a jamming signal, or some other such invisible defense that didn't allow the Army of the Old to just toss weapons at them like they did back home. "I also know that the tower in the middle is a huge collector of sunlight, turning it into enough energy to power the city around it."

"Solar power," Johan said. It wasn't a question.

"Yes, that's right," replied Stroan as if a question was asked anyway. "But also, it holds the headquarters of our armies at its base, a lookout tower at its peak..." He stopped for a moment, looking suddenly worried. "And our 'last hope' in its depths."

The statement was left out there, waiting for the question that would bring it out. Stroan sounded melodramatic, though he didn't mean to. It was the fear of this 'last hope' that held his tongue, afraid to speak of it just as he had feared speaking about the Army of the Old during their first meeting.

After the silence persisted and the city grew closer, Rider August Stroan knew he had to explain, but was also thankful they gave him the time to do so himself. They were truly friends of his now. "Should the city be overrun, a general fall back order is issued into the streets and homes of all those who live there. Then the city, evacuated or not, is eradicated."

A chill ran down Johan's spine. "How, Stroan?"

Stroan collected himself and Johan was instantly reminded of their first roadside meeting, as well as the reveal of the Ark 1. Stroan was always the first to know.

"With a High-Yield bomb."

Johan went as white as a ghost. "What the *hell*, Stroan! We're walking *into* a city with a bomb at its core? This is fucking *madness*!" He released Seraphina's hand. "Why? Why would we dream of going there? That's the evil I want to *destroy*! I don't want it to protect my life!"

No one saw Chief Rider Caspar fall back behind them. How long he'd been listening was anyone's guess, but he rode forward on his huge horse to pipe in at this point. "Easy, Johan, easy," he said while ushering them along as others looked around at the sudden elevation in anger. "I allowed Rider Stroan to tell you all this for that reason you just mentioned. No one knows what they can do better than you, survivors of Tan Torna Qu-ay.

"I knew your home. I knew its people. I'd been there many times in my younger years. I mourn your loss more than many you'll meet. It was a beautiful place. I've stood in Longhold Park and I've been to the pools below Tortria Den. I've been from one end of the Valley of Smoke to the other, but I wanted you to know what it was you were joining and the things it had to offer, whether you liked it or not. You have a right to know. The world beyond your borders is one you will fear. One you distrust. One you have been raised to call your enemy.

"I know how you feel and the hatred for the things you now must trust, but it is the way the world beyond your borders operates. We were in the dark, kept there by choice and foolishness. Now we must emerge, stronger and smarter, into the world as it is. Modern. Growing. Flying towards the things we've feared for so long. You may not know me, but you know my place in your world. You know of the Riders. You know of who we are and where we're from. You know you have no reason not to believe me.

"This is the way of things, like it or not. The shroud is dropped. The truth exposed. You, the two of you, three when your friend returns…" They didn't know how he knew of Aryu. Stroan telling him seemed most likely. A man with wings isn't easily forgotten. "You may be the last of your people, last of your home. I've heard of your quest. I know you are men of the world." A glance at Esgona. "All of you. These others with us still try to live behind the veil of the past, present company excluded of course." Seraphina nodded but said nothing. "They can't know what we know. They can't see the world as we all do now. Look at me. Here I ride, side by side with a man I swore to be my enemy for all my natural life until only a short time ago. We must change. The world demands it of us."

The words struck each of them as he spoke, but to Johan they were the strongest. To hear the thoughts and fears he'd given voice was overwhelming, and he found himself looking blindly in the dark for Seraphina's hand.

Once he found it, strength returned and he looked back to the elder and wiser Chief Rider. "What is it you want from us? You wouldn't tell us any of this unless you wanted something."

He could feel the wry smile beneath the beard on the old man's face. "You are right, of course. We have a use for you and the knife you carry."

Gods be damned, the knife again? True it was powerful, perhaps even otherworldly, but why did it all come back to this knife? This token gift from a small, poor mountain town? Was Johan a man with a knife, or was he just a knife with a man? Seraphina gently squeezed his hand as a reminder of what it was she had said.

"Why join you?" Johan asked. "You know we won't join the Army or the Riders. Why should we do anything you ask?"

"Because lad, our paths are the same, and my way offers a chance of victory. Yours likely only offers a useless death."

"Don't call me lad," Johan said with unmistakable bile in his words. He felt it now, clear as day. Caspar was simply a messenger. He didn't know all the answers either. He was being used. They all were, or at least, they were in the process of trying to be. "Since you know where we're from and what I am, you won't call me 'lad'." Johan hated being used.

"You're right of course. My apologies. Men, join me. Come with me to the tower in the center of the city, after a good rest and all those other things I promised. Hear what we have to say. All of you. Make your decision then."

Johan and Esgona each doubted every word for their own reasons, but let it be. They held no power here. They only wanted what everyone else seemed to want: the destruction of the force that had destroyed their home. They still had no idea how that would be done. Caspar, and apparently others, had an option.

"Alright, sir. We'll go tomorrow, after all the great things you promised have passed. I think we need a little celebration at this point, sleepy or not. Then, off to your tower."

"Good choice, fellas. My dear, as you seem intimately tied to this band, you are welcome to join as well." No response from Seraphina. "Well then, onward to Bankoor, sirs. Then, onward to victory!"

He sped up, rejoining his two riding companions, already headlong into a new conversation with them. "Caspar!" Johan called after him, the volume in his voice enough to draw the attention of everyone in earshot. The Chief Rider turned, somewhat perturbed by the interruption of this new conversation, eyes awaiting the reason.

"If you try to fuck us, you won't like the results!" There was no bravado. It was the truth as Johan saw it.

No response. No nod. No smirk. No visual cue at all. Just the quiet recognition of a man who could make his life very easy, or very hard.

In silence now, the tired and lucky survivors of the Paieleh River Valley continued to the haven of Bankoor and the uncertainty that lived there.

Johan didn't enjoy threatening a senior Rider, but he knew he had to be taken seriously. What had been a simple plan of finding his friend and seeking his revenge was starting to take shape, and no force on earth would stop that.

Seraphina whispered to him as they walked. "Do you trust him?"

Johan shook his head. "No," he said matter-of-factly. "I trust Skerd more than him. If the knife is important to Skerd, it must be important to a lot of people."

"Is it important to you?"

"Revenge is important to me. That and finding Aryu."

She believed him. "Do you think he'll find you here, in such a large place?"

Johan smiled. "For a man who can fly, anything is possible." He held her hand and squeezed, silently indicating that despite his strong answer, he was still concerned.

She returned the gesture and the two carried on. The valley was now far behind them, though never out of memory, and their tired footsteps headed for Bankoor.

CHAPTER 22

Going HOME

After the rough flight (and rougher landing thanks to the extra weight of Crystal) onto the smoldering deck of HOME, Aryu folded his wings back against himself as the wind on the deck threatened to carry him off once more into the blue abyss.

Crystal was on the move already, heading for what appeared to be a hatchway to the lower decks. Most of the robotic soldiers stationed up top had been lost as the base listed and tossed them into the sea. Others were badly damaged and could do nothing to stop the two. The few working models that were left didn't seem interested in interfering as they clearly had their own orders of putting out fires, fixing broken comrades and generally doing anything they could to solve the problems created by Aryu and his friends.

He didn't see what had happened to Nixon and Sho. He feared their confidence was wrong and now Sho was at the bottom of the ocean. How he'd ever get out of his armor so quickly without the Power was something Aryu couldn't figure out, and after Crystal told him for the tenth time to stop worrying about it and follow her, he figured there was no help for it now. They had to keep going and assume the other party was fine.

Once inside, Aryu figured if ever he wondered what the hallways of his own personal hell would be, it wasn't too far off from where he was now. False, buzzing lights flickered annoyingly as the white/gray walls lit up with red lights on button-filled panels. A warning alarm shrilled into the air and the smell of smoke was everywhere. They clearly had succeeded in catching the enemy by surprise.

Aryu still had a deep and unwavering fear of the technology of the Old, and this place was almost a shrine to it. Nothing was natural. Everything was a harsh reminder that this was not the beautiful Valley of Smoke.

Their part of the plan was both simple and complicated at the same time: find a cure for the loss of Crystal and Sho's Power. They knew there had to be one somewhere, and here seemed like the most obvious answer. Izuku, being an Embracer of the Power himself, never would have allowed it to be around him if he didn't have some way to reverse its terrifying effects. He prized his power too much to let something happen to it.

Crystal seemed unfazed by such a small thing as the reality of their current situation. She ran ahead, rushing past alternate hallways and other paths without a glance, leading Aryu to believe that she had some kind of crude plan.

Soon, the illuminated non-eyes of the soldiers around them began looking in their direction as they passed and Aryu surged forward, taking the lead from Crystal and pulling the Shi Kaze out. Their fleeting moment of relative invisibility was about to come to an end. They came to another 'T' intersection, though it hadn't always been that way. The hall in front of them had collapsed in the impact and now there was only left and right to go. Crystal told him "Left!" and Aryu went, readying himself for the first sign of confrontation.

What he got was something he never expected.

They pushed through a large, circular door into a dome-shaped room. Tables lined the area, chairs tossed about as if many people had left in a great rush. To their right, the perfect dome shape was caved in, the exposed main hangar bay and the remains of the plane that had brought them here lay beyond, fires still raging in places and debris made up of huge pillars and metal columns scattered around like twigs.

Do robots need tables and chairs? Suddenly his face went white. There were people on this ship, and he may have just helped kill many of them.

The reason behind their being here didn't matter. He had no desire to kill anyone, despite having done it already.

Crystal saw his face as the truth struck him. It was more than just a few odd low lives that got their hands on an old Ark 1. There were people, apparently hundreds of them, which were helping the Army, either by their own choice or by (a shudder through his body before he thought the words) being forced into it somehow. He may have just killed untold numbers of innocent people.

Crystal came to him, guiding his eyes to hers as tears filled his vision. "I doubt he tricked them or enslaved them somehow, Aryu," she said, though he knew she couldn't know that for certain. "This is war, and war has two sides. You can't dwell on the choices of others. You're a good man, Aryu. Not many others I've met can claim the same. You feel the pain of your enemy. I hope that's a characteristic you never lose. These people are your enemy now. War has its casualties, and like it or not, they will be suffered by both sides.

Her eyes, strange as they were, became soft. Comforting. "I know what you did on the plane. I know how much it scares you. Don't be afraid. Not many people can tap the Power so easily. You can use the Power as you see fit, either to destroy your enemy or save them. Let that choice guide you the next time the situation calls for it."

He wiped the tears away from his eyes, half hearing what she was saying. He was still lost in the horror of what he may have done. She was right, though. It was easier to believe these people were here of their own free will.

As they crossed the room, past the tables and toppled chairs, the first of the enemy forces appeared in the doorway. It was a combination of robotic soldiers in the lead and some humans behind them, with large rifles similar in looks to Ark 1s. They weren't glassy-eyed or sad to be there. They were angry, with scratches on their faces and blood on their hands. They were the enemy.

Crystal fell back, taking cover behind Aryu as she left him to do what he must. The men behind began screaming as the rifles came up and many took aim. The first sound of the shots they fired rang out into the domed room as the leading mechanical soldiers rushed at him, iron hands grasping wildly.

There was no more time to worry about the consequences of his actions. These soldiers, both real and artificial, were here to kill them. Nixon's words came to him.

I don't punish what they could do, I punish what they have done.

If you chose to side with the enemy, you were no better than they were. Crystal was right. This was war. War has casualties.

With that thought and the bloodcurdling scream of *"For Tan Torna Qu-ay!"* that was so fierce it made the human enemies stutter, the Shi Kaze flashed like lightning. One by one the enemies, both living and autonomous, fell before its power and the thirst for revenge from the user that drove it. With every stroke, the bond between weapon and wielder grew stronger.

There wasn't time to explain to Aryu the joyous wonder that was Makashi armor. Hopefully Sho would get the chance to tell him about it. As it was, he would just have to wait for that opportunity; because right now there were much larger and nastier fish to fry. A giant fish named Izuku was here somewhere, and it was Nixon and Sho's job to find him.

They reached the base on the lower decks, finding a way into the belly of the beast through a hole that had been torn open during the crash. The hole was taking on water, but there were enough precautions in place to keep the ship afloat and continue on without much incident.

Once they reached the main deck, the chaos was astonishing. Everywhere they looked mechanical soldiers partnered with human lackeys to extinguish fires and try to contain the damage from the plane crash.

Sho watched dumbfounded as humans shouted orders and went to great trouble to try to save the giant ship and its crew.

Nixon wasn't surprised at all. After Aryu had told him about the incident with his friend back in the mountain village and the subsequent meeting with Boroha, finding people on board was precisely what he'd expected. Society's dregs were often found in places like this, feeding off the sludge handed down to them by someone such as Izuku. It was and shall always be the way of things. Better a pet than a prisoner, at least in the eyes of the weak.

Raging sword in hand and the hum of the bladed shield beside him, Nixon stepped to the first crowd of robotic drones and cleaved the whole lot of them with one swipe. The sudden felling of their comrades made the rest of the forces in the large hallway take notice. They attacked these new threats, but none possessed weapons in this time of turmoil. They were easy prey for the two skilled warriors. The living members of this riot squad were a little more hesitant to confront these newcomers and held back behind the first wave of soldiers, trying to organize themselves and plan what to do next.

Once the last of the robots was cleaved into bits and tossed aside, Nixon (careful to keep Sho behind him and protected from unseen threats) stepped towards the remaining figures.

"Gentlemen," he began, careful not to smile, knowing full well that his grin was made to set someone at ease, "as I am in a terrible rush, I was hoping tha' one of ye could guide me t' the man named Izuku? Perhaps tell me where t' find him?"

No answer, just a crowd of scared faces. Nixon and Sho could both see them trying to decide whom they feared more. "I'll make this simple," Nixon added, knowing their inner conflict for what it was, "Izuku likely would kill ya all for helpin' us; 'owever, he's not 'ere right now, and I am. I assure ya, I'll do the exact same as he will. Ya may not suffer as much, but in the end, you'll be jus' as dead. You either 'elp us now and live, riskin' the chance t' stay alive later, or ya die now by my 'and and tha' of my friend."

"He's upstairs, on the top level!" shouted a man from the back. "He was trying to put out the fires and get the last transports ready to leave."

Nixon singled him out and called him forward. He was short and dirty. He looked like one who hadn't worked a real job in his life. A drifter from place to place, looking for opportunities with high reward and minimal effort. "There's a helpful fella. Tell me, how might we make it up there from here?"

He pointed down an adjoining hallway and stammered, "Through...through there. Emergency stairs lead all the way up, unless the fire has gotten in and blocked the way."

These fires were nothing to him. "I'll worry about tha'. Thank ya

373

for yer help."

Nixon turned, careful to keep at least one eye on the group, when Sho stepped towards them. "Why worry about the last transport? He has a million troops on the ground. What's one more ship?" A good question Nixon hadn't considered. Surely Izuku must have more than enough support from the troops that had landed and the fighting machines and ships that were everywhere.

No answer from the little man, or any other. The bladed shield whirred to life, coming closer and closer to the one who had chosen to speak. The look of malaise was gone from Sho's face. What remained was an icy stare and his infamous battle high.

"I'd answer. He's no more forgiving than I am," Nixon added, curious about the answer.

"Team Yosuru. The last transport is entirely Team Yosuru," he spat out, the fire around them growing stronger now that no one was trying to douse it.

"Team Hug?" Sho asked, clearly incensed now thinking the stocky man had said something funny. Even without Power, Nixon marveled at how quickly Sho could change moods and aura. Then it dawned on Sho what he was saying.

"Embracers!" the man cried out, rushing to get the words to his lips. "A force of twenty Embracers of the Power! Everyone he could find to join his cause!"

Sho's eyes widened at the revelation. Twenty! That many was a number too terrible to consider in his weakened state, even with Nixon and a wielder of the Shi Kaze on his side. He should have known. To come so far and risk so much was one thing for Izuku, but all it would have taken was one strong-willed Embracer to wipe out some or all of his forces with the essence of the Power at their command. Izuku was strong but often didn't like getting his hands dirty if possible. What better way to ensure victory in case such a situation was encountered? How long had it taken to arrange this whole attack? How many decades, or even centuries, had his brother been planning this foray? Patience was always Izuku's weak point. It would seem he was over that particular foible.

Nixon could handle his fair share of rogue Embracers, but more than five was enough to get the better of him, depending on the Powers each had chosen to specialize in. This put yet another crimp into the plans.

Huh, the phoenix thought to himself. *All I wanted was answers.* The job he had been ordained by God Himself to do was skirted to the back burner in the hubbub. Now he was a leading force in the battle to save the world from a powerful enemy. And where did Izuku's loyalties lay? With the men, or with the machines?

"Come Sho, leave these cowards t' their fate." With that, he hurried off down the hallway, Sho following behind.

He followed Nixon into the stairwell, the man of fire in the lead taking four steps at a time in his rush to get up. Now, knowing that he was rushing towards a lethal force of Embracers and his already over-powerful brother, the spring wasn't quite in Sho's step anymore.

▶◀▶◀▶◀▶◀▶◀▶◀▶◀▶◀▶◀▶◀▶◀▶◀

The part of the plan no one counted on (truthfully, they were somewhat busy at the time to cover *every* angle) was that HOME would be divided into two separate wings with the massive launching bay in the center. The plane crash had essentially split the base in two, and Izuku, shouting orders and planning his escape, was first encountered by Crystal and Aryu.

They had left one man alive during the assault in the dining room and from him had learned the whereabouts of the most likely location of the lab and its precious contents. It was while running there that they came across Izuku as he was trying to get things in order.

When they came around a corner into a wide corridor that had once led to the main launch hangar in the middle of the ship (and now was filled on the far end by crumbling debris and milling mechanical men), it took Aryu a moment to realize what he was seeing.

There at the far end was a man smaller than him, covered in dark, plain clothes, with gleaming metal wings protruding from his back. Wings so like his in design and size it was astonishing.

It was Crystal that cried out, knowing the enemy for who he was. *"IZUKU!"*

The winged man turned, exposing the mechanical conglomeration that was his body, sheathed sword at his side. Bald, gleaming scalp reflecting the light of the fires around him. A grin like death, even in his anger. The rage in his eyes, even before he knew who had called him, was horrifying. Aryu had never seen a look so full of hate. He was no longer sure why he was running to this man. That one gaze told him it was a terrible idea.

The anger Izuku had felt after the initial attack was melting. Within arm's reach was one of the two he had wanted all along. Dare he say, the one he had wanted most of all?

"Aryu O'Lung'Singh," he said, smiling at the words as they left his mouth. "And Crystal Kokuou. What a moment this is!"

Crystal didn't stop charging him, which to Aryu seemed like a foolish thing to do in her current state. Izuku kept smiling, welcoming this futile attack. When she was almost in striking distance, he stepped back into a defensive position, and with a flick of his wrist, pulled the non-existent blade out just a touch.

The movement caused Crystal to instantly stop her charge and

376

fall back, gripping her head in obvious pain, for reasons Aryu couldn't see. He caught up with her as she went to a knee, humming to herself quietly like she was trying to block out something imperceptible. Izuku didn't move. He only watched Aryu with interest.

"Stop it!" Aryu shouted at the terrifying blend of man and machine in front of him. "Whatever you're doing, stop it! You know she can't hurt you like this!"

"That is true," he replied in a voice Aryu knew to fear immediately. "But she is a danger to me even without command of the Power, so I'll keep her where she is. You, though. How do you feel?"

Aryu was angered and confused by the question. "I feel like cutting you to pieces!"

Izuku laughed at the idea. "Really now, Aryu, you are a guest here. I guess common courtesy is too much to expect from someone who just flew a plane into my home."

"*Stop it!*" Crystal suddenly yelled, breaking her humming like glass. "*Put it away!*" Tears were in her eyes, but still Aryu couldn't see why.

Aryu was up, face to face with this thing called Izuku. No matter what, he couldn't let Crystal hurt like this if he could stop it. He was taller than Izuku, but Izuku was nothing but machine and the Power. He knew he didn't stand much of a chance, but he had to try. His wings extended out, trying in vain to block out whatever it was that Izuku was doing, but to no avail.

"Ah, yes, the wings!" Izuku said with a hint of pride. He finally had the man he wanted. "I admit I had my doubts. You were a challenge to find, but I'd say I did fantastically!"

"What do you mean?" Aryu asked. His voice was threatening, but his eyes were curious. Izuku knew something.

"I don't have time to indulge you in stories, Aryu. I have places to go and things to do. For now, I'll take my leave and give you over to the care of my entourage. Gentlemen…"

Izuku stepped back and summoned his waiting robotic forces to his side. It was a safe bet that most if not all of HOME was a loss, which was a shame. He'd emptied most of the base, and except for the loss of the collection of High-Yield bombs, this was not a crippling defeat. Once his troops took Aryu, Izuku was satisfied that it would be a good day.

Aryu held his ground. "Let her go, Izuku!"

Izuku simply waved and turned away, sending his minions after Aryu and the fallen Crystal.

The Shi Kaze was out in an instant, and with only a few powerful strokes the attacking soldiers were torn to shreds. Rage and revenge drove Aryu forward, desperate to get to Izuku before he could escape.

The last soldier fell and Aryu charged Izuku while bringing the Shi Kaze around, ready to cut his most hated enemy down.

Izuku didn't move. He didn't need to. He could feel the movement Aryu was making. He knew that whatever weak weapon it was he was swinging would slice through the sheathed blade of the Est Vacuus. He felt confident he had nothing to fear from this futile attack, and the boy would quickly learn a lesson in the Power and the things it can do.

That is, until Aryu hit him.

As if fired from a cannon, Izuku was tossed into a far wall by the force of the sword strike. He hit it unprepared for the impact and winded himself as he did so.

Aryu stood across from him, surprised at what his actions had done but more surprised it hadn't cut him entirely in two. By this point Aryu was confident there was nothing the Shi Kaze could not

378

get through. He felt the repulsive force as the two blades met, but he could still hold his ground and was unmoved by the action.

There was no smile in Izuku's face now. No more games. He wanted Aryu alive but not if he was going to cause this kind of trouble. The Power built within the part of him that was still human, and the air filled with the heat of the fire and the electricity of the sudden buildup of otherworldly essence. The blade was out, allowing Aryu to see, or more to the point, not see, the shape of the thing. All Aryu could make out was a glimmer and nothing more. He felt no power or emptiness, though a part of him knew it was there. Perhaps it was the part of him linked to the Shi Kaze? He didn't know.

"You," growled the inhuman monster in front of him, "have run out of time, Aryu. A shame, really. You were supposed to open so many doors for me."

Aryu, ready for the attack, raised the sword he carried, bringing it up to eye level. Tokugawa Izuku saw what he was up against and the realization was considerable.

Izuku's eyes widened in an instant, recognition written all over his face. The ethereal blade he carried began to shake in his hand and suddenly the truth of his enemy dawned on him.

He knew this sword. He had carried it himself once. He knew its story. He knew its history. He knew its Power.

He knew that one good cut from it could kill him in an instant. And he had just let Aryu get in the first shot for free! What a fool! Why couldn't he feel it? It was the Power given shape! How did the legendary blade of his father come back to the world again? Where had it been hiding? How did Aryu, of all people in the world, acquire it? If Aryu had just hit a few inches to the left or right...! It was staggering to suddenly realize how close he had just come to a crushing defeat. In fact, how close he still was now as Aryu challenged him. The downfall of his work, and even more so his *life*, was a few steps away in the hands of a child!

At a loss for what to do, he eventually decided the original course of action was the smartest, though perhaps a bit faster than originally planned.

"You and I aren't done yet, Aryu. You'd better look after your friend." He channeled a pulse of crushing nothingness into the air from the sword and the Est Vacuus it contained. The action brought a shrill scream to Crystal's throat and she doubled over backwards as if struck, eyes wide and maddened, just as she had been when the Power had left her.

The noise made Aryu turn to her, and in that instant, summoning the Power within himself to aid his escape, Izuku was gone.

An older and more experienced man would have chased Izuku, knowing whatever evil he was attempting to unleash was worth the fragile sanity of just one woman. Aryu never even gave a moment of thought to following him. The safety and health of Crystal was paramount in his mind.

It was no secret he was drawn to her, but not in the ways it seemed. True, he was quite taken with her strange and otherworldly beauty and sharp, likeable personality, but there was nothing romantic in Aryu's mind when he looked at her. She was something from a time before he could even imagine, and that alone tethered him to her in ways he'd never thought possible. She was a god, sitting here in front of him in a great amount of pain. He had to help her.

He went to her, taking care not to let his guard down in case she lashed out at him unexpectedly in her madness. Soon, he stood beside her, trying to devise a way to help her. Last time she said it had been her father, likely coupled with Nixon's own gifts that had pulled her out of this craze. He had no way of doing what the phoenix could, so he did the only thing he could think of, using whatever

Power it was he thought he possessed. As he knelt beside her, he drew the Shi Kaze in his hands and presented it to her, trying to tap the Power and what he had felt on the plane.

It never needed to get that far. Once the blade caught her eye, her yelling stopped instantly. Soon, the lost look was replaced with that of understanding. The two's eyes met. Aryu was relieved to see recognition there. Did he save her, or was it the Shi Kaze?

Once the moment of understanding had passed from Crystal's face, her radiant smile returned, followed by a sudden, diving hug into Aryu's arms, sandwiching the extremely dangerous sword between them.

He held her back, unsure of what to do and weary of moving too much in fear of the dangerously sharp blade between them. Soon, she let go, tears in her eyes. (Of joy? Of pain? He couldn't tell.)

"How did you know what to do? she asked.

Aryu was flabbergasted. "I, um… I just assumed. Power saved you before, and this is all I have, so I hoped it would help. Did it?"

She wiped the tears from her eyes and laughed lightly. "You had better believe it did, Aryu. The sword Izuku has was something from the Est Vacuus. I don't know why or how, but it was a piece of it. A slice in our own reality, here in the heart of the Omnis. I felt it again and was lost to its nothingness. How he ever got something like that in his hands I couldn't even guess, but it is a very, *very* dangerous weapon. I don't even know how he's holding it. We were extremely lucky."

"If that's true, why couldn't I feel it like you, at least on some level? Is it one of those 'not experienced enough to feel it' things, because I'm getting really sick of that."

"No, the Est Vacuus extends beyond something as small as the Power. It is the embodiment of nothing. No one can escape that."

"Except me, it seems."

"No, not even you do; however, you carry the Shi Kaze, which is the closest thing this reality has to a pure piece of the Omnis. It would seem that the two cancel each other out."

"Which is why I hit him like he was kicked by a horse! He didn't know what I had could hurt him."

"Hurt him? Aryu, you could have killed him with ease right then and there. He lives only because of the intervention of luck and fate."

Aryu became dejected at the thought of how close he was to ending it all. Luck and fate. Old adversaries revisited once more. "Should we chase him?"

"No, we'll never catch him now. Besides, now that he knows what you have, he won't be so giving with the free shots from now on. I'd say we'll be hard pressed to get you near him again."

"Oh, I'll get near him, don't worry about that. He has crimes to pay for, and answers to give." The things he'd said before disappearing weighed heavily on Aryu. What did Izuku know about who he was? What doors to open? "Can you move? We should try to keep going. We need to find you a cure."

"I'm not sure I need one," Crystal whispered. Aryu wasn't sure what she meant but knew she needed to regain the Power before they faced Izuku and his blade of the Nothing again. "You're right. Let's go." She was up and leading the way once more, Aryu following behind, watching for another attack. "Thank you, Aryu," she said as they left. "Thank you for bringing me back."

"Let's try to find that cure and that way you don't have to go there again." A faint smile from her. One that said that she wasn't so sure.

"I didn't hurt you with that thing when I hugged you, did I?"

Aryu shook his head. "No, I'm fine. Thanks for the hug, though."

"Aryu, in another time and another place, I would have kissed you."

Despite his reticence to her and her attractiveness, it was a thought he didn't hate.

They hunted high and low for a lab or some other location likely to have the fabled cure, but after searching room after room they realized they were searching for a needle in a haystack and called off their search before they ran out of time. HOME was burning madly, sirens blared everywhere, and it was clear that whoever was left was abandoning ship very quickly.

Finding Sho and Nixon seemed the best bet. They had agreed to meet on the roof of the ship once they were done with their respective tasks. They found a set of stairs leading up and eventually made it to the roof of HOME once more, the sunlight cutting through the smoke from the crash site blinding them temporarily.

Sho and Nixon were there. Sho spotted his mother and Aryu and waved them over. Fires burned unattended and a few scattered piles of mechanical debris indicated that any remaining resistance from the Army of the Old left on the top deck had been quickly and easily dispatched.

Nixon told them of the revelation of Team Yosuru and what that could mean. If Izuku did have a small army of Embracers, it made him that much more dangerous. The upside was that they had Nixon's righteous broadsword and the Shi Kaze, two weapons that could easily take them down, not to mention the still hush-hush fact that Nixon was the same powerful beast of a man he always was.

"We've got t' get off this thing and head north after 'em," Nixon explained. "There are n' more vehicles left 'ere we can take, so I fear it may be a long way fer us. Hopefully we can make up some ground when we reach land. Sho, d' ya know tha best way t' follow 'em? Any idea where they're goin'?"

Sho was unsure. "They were moving west, away from our home. There's a large river estuary far northwest of here. Beyond that, a few small cities and towns, eventually leading to the Vein River Valley, but unless we find a faster means of moving other than walking or labored gliding, it's still a great distance to go, and they have a hell of a head start."

"Then we catch 'em when they stop," Nixon declared. He had no way of knowing they would stop, but it was a safe bet they had to reach the rest of their army at some point. "Well, no point wastin' time here if there's nothin' t' see. C'mon, let's find a way off this thing." Nixon led them on, Sho and Aryu behind, Crystal in the rear.

They found a tall set of emergency stairs on the far side of the ship. At its base was a collection of emergency rescue boats for the human element of Izuku's forces. Though many of the boats were gone, two still remained. As the trudge of descending so many stairs began, Aryu looked behind him to see that Crystal was no longer following them.

"Wait!" he called to the leading two. "Where's Crystal?" They looked back in confusion until they realized she wasn't there. A quick trip back up to the top showed them she was nowhere to be found.

"Son of a bitch!" Nixon cried. "Why would she run off? We need t' protect her!"

"Maybe she wasn't fully healed yet? Maybe that Est Vacuus thing took more out of her than she said."

Nixon wheeled on Aryu. "The wha'?"

Aryu was so caught up in finding them and planning the next move, he hadn't told them all the details about the meeting with Izuku. "The sword Izuku had, it was a part of the Est Vacuus."

"No," Nixon said at once, eyes blazing, "nothin' 'ere can be a part o' the Est Vacuus. It goes against everythin' the Est Vacuus is! Wha' 'appened, Aryu? Tell me everythin'!"

He did, explaining her madness, the blow to Izuku and what it had done, and how the feeling was lost on him and seemingly Izuku as well. When he was done, Nixon was beside himself in anger. Even the typically reserved Sho was showing signs of disbelief.

"What?" asked Aryu. "What do you know that I seem to be missing?" He got no answer, not really a surprise considering his company wasn't known for volunteering anything and assuming everyone knew everything. A very annoying trait in a time like this.

"Tha' bitch!" Nixon called out, fury overtaking him as the smoke began to rise again from his massive body. "I swear to my Lord God, Crystal! You will *suffer for this!*"

Nixon screamed like an animal, loud enough to make the skies tremble, the earth quake, and the seas boil. They had been fooled somehow and he, the only one left with any kind of Power, had not seen it. So blinded was he by finding her and selfishly looking for the answers to his own problems that he hadn't seen the truth.

Crystal had betrayed them.

▶◀▶◀▶◀▶◀▶◀▶◀▶◀▶◀▶◀▶◀▶◀▶◀

Crystal, long gone from where the other three were, heard the scream of anger and rage. The sound ripped through her like a knife, but she pressed on. She had to. She had to get away quickly before Nixon tore this place apart trying to find her. Even now she believed escape was not likely if Nixon really set his mind to finding her, but that was a risk she had to take.

She hadn't betrayed them. Not really, anyway. Betrayal implies that she allowed vital information about them to get into the wrong hands for the purposes of undermining them. She had not done this. Only their little party knew the master plan. No one knew that Nixon still had control of his considerable powers. No one knew anything other than the basics, and she wasn't about to tell. That wasn't part of her plan. A plan so grand in its scope that she was at once proud and ashamed of its magnificence.

It was a plan worthy of Ryu.

She both was and wasn't sorry for what she'd done. She knew the truth was bound to escape at some point and now was the latest possible time she could have left and kept her plan safe. Crystal had played every side with the perfection of a true artist. Now they would go on to the final goal, and when that was done, every piece she put into play would come together and she would have what she wanted.

She made it to a waiting escape ladder and small jet boat at its base. Soon, she would be gone and even Nixon with his God-given abilities couldn't find her. His preordained mission to destroy the sword-bearer would block his ability to catch her unless she allowed it, and considering she currently had no actual powers to track (admittedly, this was not part of the original plan, and it was a situation she would attempt to rectify very shortly), she would slip away easily. If he hadn't begun the chase by now, he wouldn't at all.

He didn't know the truth. She never let that happen. It was so obvious yet so far from his mind that it blinded him. *Of course* she knew why he was sent to kill a young, powerless mortal man, but she had kept things flowing so well that he never asked. She knew why it was that Aryu had the sword. She knew his history, that of his parents and where he came from. She knew every who, what, where, when, why, and how, and Nixon was a fool for not assuming it was so. Izuku may be the oldest person alive, but she was still Crystal Kokuou, and that fact alone meant that she was still likely the most intelligent and dangerous person who had ever lived. Even Ryu proved in his final moments that he couldn't be as strong as she was. Or as smart. She loved him very much, but good god was he impulsively melodramatic.

Seated in the small jet boat, she set off for the mainland at top speed. She had escaped the wrath of the phoenix for now, and it was time to begin the last and most difficult part of the plan: a plan that rested very heavily on the ability and determination of Aryu O'Lung'Singh. It was a shame to have to leave him so soon. If she was younger or more impulsive, she'd be instantly taken with the young man and his strength. It's amazing how much of an effect on a person having an ex turn into a malicious, genocidal nut job can be, so as it was, he was just a pretty face to her. A face that had not disappointed when the time came to show that he was truly the right person for the job. By gods, he'd mastered the Power, even on a small level, with barely any training at all! His mind needed the Power. It *yearned* for it hungrily. It was amazing to watch, and now he knew what to do. If he didn't get too carried away with it (considering the penalty for failure was a monster of fire at his side constantly, she wasn't concerned about that), he would soon master it. The Power was his to control, and he was hers to manipulate.

Would her father approve of this course of action? No, likely not, but he was from another age. The rules had changed a hundred times since then. If the result to his vision was the same, she didn't think it mattered. Everyone knows what desperate times call for.

Into the horizon she went, on the hunt for the next part of the master plan. With a quick look back, she saw the distant smoke now pouring out of HOME as if every inch of it was burning.

Somewhere on the burning deck in the distance were Aryu, Nixon, and her son, Sho. When this was all over, she hoped each would understand her and her reasoning better. For now, although it pained her to think about, at least one of them wanted her head on a pike.

Aryu would be tossed into the pit of confusion that would lead to the bitter ending she began working towards long ago. She hoped

387

to meet him again.

"Good luck, Aryu," she said as she gave a wave of salute to the distant ship. Then, she turned back and was gone.

POWER

HONOR

HUMOR

HORROR

POWER

Eleotherios Duo watched it all while waiting for orders that never came. The loss of HOME was not in any plan that it had been made aware of. The development it was witnessing unfold in the distance was a new one. Now, as the waiting continued, its processors kicked in and the exciting opportunity at last arrived. E2-0901 began deducing its own plans for its next step.

It knew it was different. It was stronger, faster, smarter, and simply better in every aspect of the things it did. It had no idea why it was created and it didn't care. It was the pinnacle of what man can achieve. A walking, talking embodiment of the perfect harmony between technology and what was referred to by his creator as 'The Power', a quantum manipulation of basic scientific elements.

Something about this Power allowed humans to exceed the standard boundaries of their genetic makeup. It allowed them to transform one form of matter into others.

Izuku had slaved for decades to master the techniques needed to construct Eleotherios Duo. The research he'd done to build the artificial brain of it took years on its own, let alone the time it took to attempt the near-impossible task of forming its indestructible outer shell. Now even the most powerful of the Embracers would have more than their hands full simply trying to scratch it. Not that it would even allow anything to ever get that close.

This was the longest it had ever gone without a command, and it had to assume something in the plan had gone wrong. The first inklings of its own chosen course of action began to pass through its synthetic brain.

Soon it was off, flying to the location it had deduced was the most likely place to find either its compatriots or its targets.

After the proper speed was reached, the RAMjets kicked in and E2-0901 was ripping through the air ten times faster than any bullet could be fired. It would only be a matter of minutes for the thing to reach its destination, a trip that would take the average person weeks by land.

It followed the river up the great valley. It had strict orders to keep its existence a secret. It was the last weapon, the final obstacle in the path of the enemy. That was the way it had to stay for now.

This was also why it was heading to where it was. There would be no end to the places it could hide in plain sight, day or night. There, it would wait for its orders or possibly carry out its master plan.

Then what? What purpose would it serve if Izuku was successful in conquering the world, or at least this large part of it? Something to question while in seclusion.

It saw the collection of buildings and structures below and it slowed to a crawl, RAMjets powering down and switching to its standard solid-fuel thrusters. It landed on the roof of a run-down building in the shadow of the massive spire at the center of this city, assessing its surroundings and enjoying everything it saw. It took to the shadows and began its waiting game. It had time now to document and plan, so that was exactly what it would do, preparing for the call it hoped would come.

HONOR

▶◀

By the time the group that had traveled out of the Paieleh River Valley reached the city of Bankoor, the specter known as Eleotherios Duo had been waiting for some time for something, *anything*, to happen, but as of their arrival, nothing had, so its waiting game continued in secret. There had been rumors of a dark warrior skulking in the shadows, but in this time of war such rumors were common.

Chief Rider of the Inja Army Merrik Caspar left the celebrations in honor of the weary group and its young saviors to the private confines of his temporary home. He had no time for such pomp. There was much to get done before the meeting tomorrow between the three young upstarts and his superiors. He had been chosen as the go-between specifically because he *had* been to Tan Torna Qu-ay, and his commanders all agreed someone who could drop some local landmark names and not be completely ignorant to their homeland was the best choice. He hoped they were right. Too much was riding on their trust, especially the one named Johan and his knife.

Caspar knew nothing of this 'magic' knife other than that it was important to the War and Glory Council of Bankoor and its leader, the man who it could be said was really in charge, Auron Bree. Auron was an enigma to Caspar, and indeed most who met him. He had come to Bankoor forty years prior as a young man with some of the first groups to actively travel down from the northwestern side of the Blood Sea, a place that at the time was still terribly different and

392

taboo.

When Auron and his group came, they helped establish the first War and Glory Council to ward off enemies, though at the time it had been the Westlanders that they were afraid of. As more and more new and frightening technology came from places farther and farther away, it became obvious the Westlanders were not to be feared anymore. Although terribly fierce, they simply lacked the new abilities Bankoor and its people now controlled. The War and Glory Council and Auron Bree remained in case other, more threatening enemies appeared.

Await trouble long enough and trouble will find you.

Caspar was a proud member of the Riders of the Inja Army and would serve his duties therein until struck down in battle. He'd been chosen as the Riders' military advisor to Bree and had served that post for two years.

So it was that he was selected to speak with the group and its young heroes. Their messenger had barely been in the city for an hour when word of his arrival and story of those he rode with, as well as the plan and the need to send Caspar to them, came to Caspar's ears. He assumed it meant that those above him knew twice as quickly and made their plan instantly.

He collected his needed items in his barren home, a place he'd been given as a temporary residence as he served in Bankoor where he'd been since his advisory position began. His home village was far south of here, on the shores of the great ocean, ground zero to this new attack. Although he knew his home was destroyed and many killed needlessly, he took solace in the fact that he had brought his wife and child with him when he was called away. Another glorious appearance of the small miracle.

His wife and daughter were off at a friend's for the night, knowing Caspar would be busy and not want to disturb them or they him. The house, a modest sized place with little in the way of accoutrements and knick-knacks anywhere, was no closer to being home to him than it was before he got the news of his village, but it was the best he had now.

He prepared for bed, pondering the situation. What did the W.G.C. want with Johan and a 'magic' knife? Or any of them for that matter? What of the missing one, the one rumored to have wings? These questions were treading dangerously close to the 'things too big for Merrik Caspar to think about' territory and that worried him.

As he lay down to sleep, one thing worried him the most: Johan Otan'co and his brazen statement after their first encounter together.

The lad was young but had seen much in his short time. He was too strong of will to ignore. He wondered if the W.G.C. knew this. Did they see them all as puppets to control or allies to gain the trust of? He was very much afraid that if it was the previous, then Johan and his statement were going to turn out very, very true. He wouldn't like the results if the W.G.C. 'fucked' with them.

If it was as it seemed and the War and Glory Council did plan on trying to manipulate them to their own wishes, they were going to be sorely disappointed. And, if as rumors suggested, the war did eventually make it here to Bankoor and the battle was on his doorstep, he hated to think their need of Johan or his knife was the only plan they had to stop this new threat if it came this far.

He was a man of great honor. He respected what that brave group had been through to get here. He hoped for them to rest and be at peace. He didn't want some bureaucrat trying to screw around with any of them for their own gain. And if his impressions of Johan and Esgona were as accurate as he thought they were, the W.G.C. was about to meet a very real and very dangerous brick wall of willpower.

HUMOR

━━━

There was nothing funny about this at all. Nothing had gone to plan. Well, not his anyway. His home and work from the last major part of his life were lost, his forces to the south were in total disarray, his troops to the north were fighting against a much better prepared and skilled opponent than he had expected to meet so soon, his ace-in-the-hole brute squad of Embracers were suddenly very, very vulnerable, and these were just the *recent* developments. He wasn't even counting the laundry list of issues that had arisen in the weeks before all this began, as he hunted and slaughtered Embracers, knowing each kill would bring the phoenix closer and closer, until he was at last in the field of play.

Still, after all that, Tokugawa Izuku simply had to laugh. The twists, turns, and double-crosses were piling up like a house of cards. How long until they fell? And when they did, he wasn't terribly certain it would be him who would be left standing.

It was very exciting. Maybe that was why he laughed. It had been eons since anything had rattled him like this and the exhilaration of the uncertainty was invigorating. Rare was the feeling of truly being *alive* anymore. It was something to be savored, as it was likely to be fleeting.

The fire in front of him crackled and spat as another figure joined him out of the cover of the woods he sat in. The clearing was small and far from anything that could interrupt this fantastic moment. A moment he'd been waiting for in the last few weeks, ever since the unexpected loss of HOME and his run north to the front lines of his war with E-Force.

The night remained quiet as the ghost approached across from the fire and sat in the waiting seat, the light adding to their wraith-like presence. It was true that although she was possibly the most beautiful person he'd ever seen, Crystal Kokuou was, and always would be a gigantic pain in his ass.

"I trust you traveled well?" he asked with a smirk.

The grin was not returned. "It would have been a damn sight faster if I had the fucking *Power*!" she hissed at him in anger. "You could have told me about that! You haven't got a clue the amount of concentration it takes to keep myself from going mad right now. You had better tell me there's a cure."

He, much like her, had played as many cards close to the chest as he had on the table. The neural inhibitor drug that had stolen her powers was only one of them. Team Yosuru was another, one she likely knew about by now, but he wouldn't bring it up if she didn't.

The memory of her in all that mental anguish back in their meeting at HOME made him smile that much bigger. Only if it had been her son Sho would it have been any more pleasing.

"There is a cure, but how much is left after your little stunt with the plane is a mystery to even me. Did you really have to crash a *plane* into it?"

"It wasn't my idea, it was Aryu's."

"Ah yes, Aryu. Who would have guessed he would somehow magically obtain the Shi Kaze?" The bitterness in his voice oozed out of the smile on his face. This game of brinkmanship was entertaining, but when the Shi Kaze was involved, you could never take the situation too lightly.

Crystal smiled, her white face positively glowing in the firelight. They could keep this up all night, the back and forth about who did what to whom. They both agreed to the plan, but the path each chose to get to the end was in their own hands. They wouldn't have had it any other way. They were each untrusting of the other. "It's all a part of what needs to be done, Izuku. Although, even I admit it was assisted by a bit of dumb luck along the way."

Bah! Dumb luck. That wasn't very likely. Izuku, much like anyone who lived even half as long as he had, never believed in such crap. Still, he'd set his own series of similar events into motion. Was that luck as well? Strange they should think so alike yet be so different.

He shifted, smile radiating towards her. He hated her but admitted no one else on the planet could be so fearless in his company. Even without her powers, she had come here. One flick of the wrist and Crystal Kokuou was gone from this or any other world, lost to the void of the Est Vacuus like she was never even here. His hand twitched slightly on the handle at his side, but nothing more. Where was the fun in that? Besides, she was too instrumental in what was yet to come.

"You just keep that thing where it is unless you want a screaming lunatic on your hands," she admonished, impressively catching the motion that was more in his mind than it was in his hand. "I don't see anyone around powerful enough to pull me out of it. Thank you, by the way, for making a small part of my life a complete hell."

He nodded in a mock thank-you and reached back behind himself, pulling forward a small vial filled with a clear liquid from a bag he'd carried in with him. "A touch of the last of the cure that I'm aware of. One vile will treat one person, but if there were more of these left I'd be shocked, as most of it was kept at HOME. Not so intelligent to go flying a plane into someone's place of business now, was it?"

"I don't believe you," she replied.

"Your choice, I suppose. Still, I have no need for it…"

397

"Nor do the ones you travel with I assume." Did she know of Team Yosuru, or was she referring to the machines he was generally surrounded by?

"True, neither do they, so I never had much need to carry any. I kept it all at HOME and now it all seems to be at the bottom of the ocean, as well as my glorious collection of destructive toys. It was a task just to find this one. I seriously doubt there's much more out there left to be found."

"And are you offering it to me, or do I have to take it?" She truly feared nothing. Once Izuku rested his hand on the hilt of his sword once more, she deflated slightly.

"As I see it, I have one vial of cure and three wanting ex-Embracers. I seem to have the opportunity to choose."

A quick hint of smile on her face. Something he said amused her. Something she knew that he didn't. It was so obvious that he wondered if it was intentional. A brief hint about another of her hidden cards. "Seems to me you'd want to give it to the one on your side?" she replied.

"I would if someone were. Let's not lie to ourselves about where everyone stands, Crystal. You and I are playing two different sides of the same coin, but in very different and non-complementary fashions. No. For now, it stays with me. My enemy will be one of my choosing when the time comes, and let me tell you, you'd likely be last on my list."

"Why show it to me? I know you have it. Why taunt someone like me? There's nothing to gain."

"Isn't there? We both know death for any of you three would be a meaningless gesture. No. I want to keep it for a time I know will do some damage. The time and place of that instance hasn't played itself out yet, but it will. I just want you to remember what's on the line. At some point, perhaps you'll understand."

"You're as enigmatic as your father," she said, stinging with more venom than he thought possible. "Always planning for outcomes he couldn't see. How many elaborate schemes have you two come up with that never panned out?"

Comparisons to his father were always met with rage. He was not his father. He had never once considered any course of action like Ryu's. Where was the honor? What was the point? To live so long only to die like a fool. Shameful.

"I'm done with you now. You keep doing as you promised and I will as well. That is all we needed from each other, and that is something we still have."

"We do," she agreed.

"Good, then if that is all…"

"It's not, Izuku."

He had already risen to leave, preparing to fly off back to the front lines of his war. He looked at her, hand still on the blade at his side. He wasn't certain he could take much more of her without using it.

"What's left?" he asked angrily.

"Aryu. What do you plan on doing with him?"

"Ha. You're very bold, Crystal. Who says I have a plan?"

"Tell me, or we leave here enemies, Izuku. No alliance. No plan."

"Why? Why throw it all away for an answer I may not even have?"

"I don't believe you. And even if I did, you will be involved in all of this in some manner still. Why him? Why someone who can do so much damage to you? To everyone in the world?"

"There's little chance of that. If he gets some heroic idea to kill me man to man, maybe. The only thing worse than a hero with the Shi Kaze is a fool with the Shi Kaze. But the *world*, Crystal? Shame, shame. You know better. He's here. He has chosen his own path, and chosen it very well I'd like to add. The tapestry of his fate isn't spun by me. He's no threat to the world. I am!"

"He could be if he goes home," she persisted, knowing she didn't have what she wanted yet.

"He has no idea where or what home is. Unless you told him?"

"No," replied Crystal, "that's not a truth I'm willing to give him." Izuku believed her.

"Well, I don't know what to tell you, Crystal. It's interesting that he's here, but did I have a part in it? No." He didn't mention how amazingly overjoyed he was when he first found out about Aryu, like a drop of gold from heaven. He had become a ticket to something so much greater. One of his kind never left their home.

She studied him, searching for any sign he was lying. Although she was the one person who could likely see his treachery, all he could do was smile now. She would find nothing, because there was nothing to find.

This obviously upset her. "I suppose I have to believe you," she sighed. "You wouldn't risk losing just for one part of the whole picture."

"Losing? Not likely. But you're right of course. It's unexpected, but these days what isn't." He nodded to her, confirming their business together was concluded. "Adieu, Crystal. When next we meet, should that day even come, may it be at the end of all things."

"Get lost, Izuku. Just the thought of you makes me sick right now." With one last malicious grin, he flapped his metallic wings and was off into the night.

It seemed everything was still on course; the road had just become a bit bumpier. So is life, he supposed. What other deviations had she set in motion, either against him or in general? Would she even witness his series of masterstrokes now firmly set in place? He hoped so, and he hoped each was more startling to her than the last.

With a last glance to the distant fire below and the guest he'd had at it, he pushed off again and was gone.

HORROR

▶◀▶◀▶◀▶◀▶◀▶◀▶◀▶◀▶◀▶◀▶◀▶◀▶◀▶◀▶◀▶◀▶◀▶◀▶◀

Edgar Taft was badly beaten. He was bruised and scarred, his head hurt, and his left leg was heavily wrapped from the battles he'd seen. His dark eyes were flash-burned in places that may never recover and the strength of his broad, stocky frame threatened to leave him on an hourly basis.

He was also grinning from ear to ear.

For weeks they'd fought the relentless hordes of the mechanical army, demons from a time and place he'd been raised to fear as a child. He was wiser and more accepting of the fate of his people now. All those that were hiding in the past knew what was happening here, in the wide and lush Vein Valley.

The fighting had been hard, and Edgar had been worried his men weren't up for it at first. Many of them were new to this frightening situation, whereas Edgar had been here most of his life in one war or another. A mere foot soldier when the alliances had been forged, he was now Field Commander of twelve different brigades of brave men and women, the spearhead of the front line in this war.

Soon, after the initial shock had worn off and the realization came that they weren't going to use one of their horrifying H.Y. bombs (for reasons Edgar neither knew nor cared about; much like Merrik Caspar many miles north, Edgar Taft knew that knowing these things wasn't his place in the world), the victories began to pile up. The army was mighty in number and abilities but fragile in the correct circumstances. Those circumstances currently were the proper and well-timed use of the weapons Edgar Taft now commanded. Once the heavily armed tanks and low-flying tactical strikers had arrived two weeks back, the tide shifted overnight. After weeks of being herded back up the massive shores of the Vein on both sides, suddenly they were holding their ground. Soon, they were pushing back. In the last week, they had regained sizable tracks of land back from the enemy. They were merely a shadow of the terrifying enemy they'd been not long before.

Couple this with the report that their central command had been destroyed in the great ocean, a rumor supported by the lack of new robotic troops to arrive as of late, and you had yourself one extremely pleased Field Commander Edgar Taft of the United Peoples Military, the amalgamation of the armies of the Westlanders, Inja at least four ally nations to the north, who had been providing the technical might that had helped them get this far.

Sadly, the smile was short lived. No sooner was he about to give the order to give those heartless bastards another good push when new orders were brought to him via coded transmission.

ATTN: F.C. EDGAR TAFT,

YOU ARE HEREBY ORDERED TO CEASE ALL FURTHER AGGRESSIVE MILITARY ACTION AGAINST THE SOUTHERN INSURGENTS UNTIL FURTHER NOTICE.

AT NO POINT ARE YOU TO PROGRESS FARTHER SOUTH. YOU ARE STRICTLY TO DEFEND, AND DEFEND ONLY.

YOURS IN TRUST,

A. BREE.

"God damn it!" Taft screamed.

His good friend, second in command Shan Dio, a representative from a far north race who'd served with Edgar for four years in one way or another, looked up from his desk, glasses askew as he reviewed both digital and paper aerial maps of the area with marked locations of friends and foe.

"Not good news I assume?" he asked, thin face smirking at his own obviousness. Edgar never returned the look. He just stood in their shared military trailer/bunkhouse staring at the orders on the screen in front of him. Shan got up and joined him, adjusting his glasses as he moved his terribly thin frame over to his friend. Once he was done reading it for himself (a taboo, as it should have been for Edgar's eyes only, but such standard decorum was no longer practiced between these two) he flopped down in a chair next to Edgar and let out a large sigh. He had been just as eager to drive these devils away as his friend and was in the throes of planning how to hit them the hardest when Edgar got the news.

"What on earth does the W.G.C. have up its sleeve that it wants us to stop here, in the middle of winning this war?" he asked, accent thick with rolling 'R's like those of his people. It had long since stopped sounding strange to Edgar.

"I have no idea. Why sit on the sidelines for so long only to get involved now? Why not just let us do as we have been? It's a system that's seemed to work so far."

"You don't think there's more to it than what we see, do you?"

"Oh I give you a great big good god damn guarantee that it does, Shan, but I haven't got a fuckin' clue what it could be. Pass the order along to the troops, I guess. Don't hide the fact that we're not big fans of it though. I want them each to know exactly where this is coming from."

"Can we do that, sir?" 'Sir' didn't come out of Shan's mouth often. It meant he wasn't positive whatever Edgar had asked of him was the right course of action.

"We can and we will, Shan. Nothing says we need to run and hide every time the damned W.G.C. gets involved. These are men and women of action. It'd make me sick to my stomach if I heard this order from a commanding officer without good reason. I'd think he wasn't happy with what we were doin'.

"No, no we tell them straight out that this is bureaucratic interference. They've earned that much truth by this point, I'd say."

"Agreed. Just making sure." With that, Shan went back to his post and sent word to the standing forces in the front lines, the message heavy with disgust.

"Why, Shan? What are they thinking?"

Shan had no time to answer. A hurried knock on the door interrupted them as a cadet burst in, face red and out of breath. Edgar was about to admonish the young man but was interrupted. "Sir!" he spit out in a ragged breath. "Sorry to interrupt sir, but you need to come here at once. There's something you need to see!"

Before he had a chance to answer, the cadet was gone again out the door and lost to the masses by the time the two friends looked out. Neither of them liked what they saw outside.

There was panic and discord everywhere. In an unbelievable action, some were even running away, past the military trailer and the two inside. Edgar and Shan stepped out at once, trying to see what was going on. This was the U.P.M. They didn't run. Period.

Edgar Taft searched out a recognizable face, found a lieutenant he'd seen around and asked what the devil was going on.

"The enemy, sir, they've released a new weapon and it's on its way here!"

Edgar went white as the thought of the H.Y. and its power flashed in his mind. Had they been too complacent? Had their victories of late spurned them too much to be ignored?

"Is it a bomb?"

"No, sir. Worse. Much worse!"

"Well don't leave me hangin', son, spit it out!"

"Here, sir. See for yourself." He handed Edgar the Digital Image Enhancer around his neck. Taft looked into the eyepiece and scanned the horizon. He could see massing of the enemy directly south, but they didn't seem to be on the move, just clustering around a large aircraft that had arrived.

"What am I looking at, Lieutenant?"

"At the center of the crowd, sir. Near the base of that new plane."

Edgar enlarged the image, making out the details of the enemy until he could clearly see the place the man had mentioned. There, at the nose of the craft, was a group of non-mechanical people. Fifteen, perhaps twenty, it was hard to say.

"What in the good sweet gods above have they got..." He cut himself short as the image became crystal clear. Human beings, unbelievably enough. Each one of them armed with shields, swords, wooden staffs, canes, any variety of short-range weapons. Why? What did this mean? He was about to ask Shan what he thought when the truth hit him like lightning. A truth so unbelievable he had to steady himself on a crate nearby. The strength that threatened to leave him for so long had finally given up the ghost.

"Shan, call a general retreat, as many of our forces and arms as we can move safely. Do it now and don't you dare ask me why!"

Shan began to look very worried but did as his friend asked, and he ran back into the trailer. Moments later, Shan popped his head back out and had to shout over the noise of the full-scale retreat. "Sir! Headquarters wants to know what's going on. It's got word of your new orders already!"

Bastards are monitoring all the communications, Edgar thought to himself, not entirely surprised.

"What should I tell them?" Shan continued, the look of worry on his skinny face creasing it mercilessly.

"You don't tell them a damn thing, Shan! You pack your shit and you get the fuck out of here!" He ran past Shan into the trailer, gathered up a few small belongings like data keys and a picture of his family in Bankoor (*Gods, please let me see them again,* he silently pleaded). Then, he was back out the door with Shan Dio following close behind.

By now the retreat order had spread like wildfire and the masses were falling back, leaving behind tanks and other vehicles that couldn't carry more than a few people at a speed faster than running. Although scared beyond belief at what he'd seen coming his way, Edgar Taft still held his ground, making sure as many of his troops got away as possible.

"Damn it Shan, I told you to get out. I can see to the rest of it myself!" Shan still followed, almost too scared to leave his friend's side. Shan gave him a quick look that told him no order in the world would make him leave Edgar's side.

Edgar looked at him in the face, trying to dig into the core of Shan Dio's reason. "Shan, this isn't a bomb, or anything else we've faced up to this point. This really is something much worse. Something all the might of the U.P.M. can't stand against. At least, not right now."

Shan saw the seriousness, but still refused to move. It seemed Edgar hadn't dug deep enough. "Shan, there are Embracers of the Power over there, and they're coming this way."

Shan said nothing. He only turned a paler shade of white. Still, he didn't move, though now it was possibly because he couldn't. "Are… are you sure?"

Edgar nodded. "I'm pretty sure. Can't think of what else they could be. Now, are you going to go, or do I have to throw you?"

"What about you?"

"I'm right behind you as soon as I'm confident we're not leaving any fool behind. Besides, you're my eyes and ears right now. If something happens to me, you're in charge."

The truth in the words hit Shan Dio. Edgar Taft, although tough and stout, wasn't expecting to live through whatever was about to come.

"Sir, they're on a transport and they're heading this way very quickly!" a scout shouted at him as he began to fall back. Soon the scout was on a high-speed half-track and gone.

"You're right behind me?" Shan asked, almost pleading in unspoken words for Edgar to reconsider and just come now. There were still a great number of troops left to ensure safe retreat.

"I am, I give you my word, you stick-thin softy, now get the *fuck* out of here!"

Shan's face hardened. He had always hated jabs at his skinny frame. "Fine, but you better not do anything stupid, *sir*." At last, an understanding between them. Edgar nodded and smiled. Then, like a man possessed, Shan was bounding onto a passing transport, shouting orders and demanding no one was left behind.

After only a few seconds, he was gone.

Taft looked back through the Digital Image Enhancer, though it wasn't necessary. By now the hovering transport was almost where he was standing. In a few more moments, it would be here, either to let out the Embracers or just pass right over him and head after the rest of his men. He hoped the former, or this was an extremely useless gesture.

There were very few left to pull back when the transport landed at the doorstep of his trailer, the jets below it kicking up the dust and sand. He sat on the step by the door waiting for what came next.

The whine of the engines ceased and a bay door slid open softly from the base of the aircraft. Moments later, the first of the fully armored Embracers stepped out, an average sized man with streaks of bright blue running through his long hair and beard. At his side a gladius was sheathed and ready. Edgar could almost feel the Power radiate from him. Other equally odd and dangerous looking Embracers stepped into view. Twenty that he could count. Men and women, each pulling out their weapons. As they all looked around, Edgar saw the last of the transports in the distance pass behind him and out of sight.

The ethereal blue man came forward with hands open as if to show he came unarmed. Edgar wasn't born yesterday. He knew the sword was more for show than use in the possession of an Embracer. Edgar Taft knew the real Power was in the body.

"You are commander of these forces?" the man asked, almost casually, as if simply passing the time with idle chitchat.

"I am. Edgar Taft, Field Commander for the United Peoples Military. To whom do I have the honor?"

"You have the honor of me. That's all you need to know."

"Well, should I bow or curtsey?" There were no false premonitions now. All Edgar could hope for was to slow these heathens as long as possible, if it would make any difference at all.

The blue man smirked at the guts of the man in front of him. "You should run," was all he said.

Edgar rolled up his pant leg, revealing the wound and the bandaging. "Don't feel much like runnin', truth be told."

"Ha, so you'd run like the others if you were able to?"

Edgar stood and approached the man cautiously. "Maybe. Seeing as how I had no choice in the matter, I hadn't given it much thought."

"I doubt you would, Edgar Taft. You don't look like a runner."

"Then, my blue friend, just what do I look like?"

"You look like a man of honor. You also look like a man who has tossed his life aside recklessly for the vain hope of saving the lives of those you command. A man who would meet death with a sharp tongue."

"Other than the recklessly part, I'd say you have me pegged, Bluey."

"Do you know who I am, Edgar Taft?"

"I know *what* you are. That's enough for me."

"Good. Then you know what you're trying to do now is hopeless?"

"Likely, but not as hopeless as runnin'."

"And you know why we're here?"

"I do, though the reasoning behind it kinda escapes me at the moment. I thought we were fighting robots, not heathens."

"And do you think you or your people will win against us 'heathens'?"

"Maybe. You're not indestructible. There's always hope."

The blue man smiled, drawing the sword out. Edgar hesitated when he saw the same blue shade glow through the blade. Echoes raced through his brain as he looked at it, but the sensation was muted once he tore his eyes away.

"In this world, we are indestructible, Edgar Taft. There is no one powerful enough to stop us left on the Earth."

Edgar got up, grunting as he did so. He stepped over to the man and met him face to face. "You were human once. You have to remember that we don't give up hope easily."

The blue man lifted the blade, pointing it past Edgar to his trailer. Instantly the trailer was in the air. When it was high overhead, a large blue spark rocketed from the blade of the weapon. The trailer was obliterated into pieces that rained down behind Edgar. Many Embracers laughed.

"That's where I kept my belongings, sir. I'd thank you to pick it up." The sharpness in his voice was still strong, but his gut knew that this simply wasn't natural. The truth of who he was facing was that much more apparent. Embracers? Siding with the mechanical Army of the Old? What did it mean?

The blue man was amused by Edgar's wit, but it was obvious that his patience with him was done. "You are a credit to your family and peers, Edgar Taft. It's a shame to kill you."

"It's a shame to die at the hands of one like yourself."

With a nod of recognition to a true statement, the blue man flicked his wrist, tossing Edgar into the air as if he were made of feathers. At the apogee of the throw, he was frozen and floating just as the trailer had. He knew what would come next. He prayed he would feel nothing but doubted it was going to be so.

"Goodbye, Edgar Taft. Your death is meaningless. Your friends and family will still suffer just as quickly. You have accomplished nothing here. I fear you have died a failure. For one such as yourself, I'd call that a terrible shame."

Before he had a chance to even consider the truth in the words the blue man had spoken, Edgar Taft was effortlessly wiped from the Earth in a burst of fleeting-but-intense pain, followed by death's embrace.

Edgar Taft deserved much better.

Coming Soon

CATCHING HELL

Part 2:
Destination

Death Dresses Poorly

Ethan is a directionless twenty-something who has finally cast off the heartbreaking responsibilities of his broken boyhood home, but not without irreversible scars and sarcasm. After surviving a tragic accident, he begins to suspect he may actually have something to live for. Is it a hidden purpose? His new beginning? Finding a decent cup of coffee?

The answer is unclear, until one morning a familiar stranger appears. The poorly dressed man at Ethan's door seems to have all the answers. But with those answers comes a grave proposition.

Witty and realistically sarcastic; full of self-redemption and the dark, cosmic inner-workings of life and death. Comically sharp yet lighthearted, Death Dresses Poorly is the bittersweet tale of a young man's journey through the discarded baggage of his childhood.

Between Conversations

In the world of Ryuujin, heroes rise and fall, but there are always stories that slip through the cracks. The tales of the people who shape the years to come. Heroism and betrayal. Conversations between friends and enemies that will change the course of the world.

These are nine stories from a world that is historic, modern, and terrifyingly futuristic. A world where science and magic intertwine, and give birth to the unknown souls who become heroes, and the legends who fade away into history.

From the author of the renowned dark comedy Death Dresses Poorly, and from the world of his hit science-fantasy duology Catching Hell comes a collection of adventure, drama, joy, and terror as we look into the lives of the powerful, the meek, and the people who make the world turn over the course of centuries.

www.ingramcontent.com/pod-product-compliance
Lightning Source LLC
Chambersburg PA
CBHW030542260626
47157CB00006B/2158